If I Should Fall

HEATHER NADINE LENZ

Plum Tree Press

UNITED STATES

www.heathernadinelenz.com

Plum Tree Press
Published by Plum Tree Press
First Edition November 2017

Copyright © 2017 by Heather Nadine Lenz
Cover design © Lisa Book
Editor David Yost

If I Should Fall is a work of fiction. Names, characters and
incidents are either the product of the author's imagination or
are used fictitiously. Any resemblance to actual persons, living,
or dead, or events is entirely coincidental.

All bible versus within this novel are from the The World English
Bible, which is a Modern English translation of the Holy Bible
under public domain.

Book ISBN-13:   978-0-9980129-1-9

Printed in the United States of America

To my parents Marjorie and Richard Brown

If I Should

Fall

CHAPTER 1

Colossians 3:12-14
12 Put on therefore, as God's chosen ones, holy and beloved, a heart of compassion, kindness, lowliness, humility, and perseverance; 13 bearng with one another, and forgiving each other, if any man has a complaint against any; even as Christ forgave you, so you also do. 14 Above all these things, walk in love, which is the bond of perfection.

CHARLOTTE FLUNG OUT A HAND and turned off the alarm informing her it was five thirty. She rolled over and reached out a hand, searching for Adrien to cuddle up against for a few minutes before getting up. For a split second each morning, she still sometimes forgot. Her husband was gone.

Charlotte opened the back door and shivered as the icy cold bit into her bones and caused her fingers to tingle.

Snowflakes caught on her lashes and stung the tip of her nose. Shutting the porch door quietly behind her so as not to awaken her children, she drew in a deep breath of the fresh pine scented air. She clutched the railing, careful not to slip on the icy porch stairs. When her feet hit the ground, her boots made no sound as they sank into the freshly fallen snow. She paused, taking in the quiet.

The pain was throbbing in her back again. Her head was aching, and her body was heavy with fatigue. She rolled her shoulders in an attempt to twist away from the pain. Gazing out at the moon reflecting on the lake, her sense of disjoint-edness diminished.

The new soft layer of white snow created a hush, an echoing silence covering the earth, which stood in stark contrast with the inky black of Payette Lake.

The rhythmic splashing of the waves onto their small strip of snow covered sand and dock was the only sound in the early morning darkness. Charlotte yawned, wondering if the lake would freeze over this year.

She wished she hadn't tossed and turned all night, worry-ing. She wanted to look glowing and beautiful this evening, not haggard with rings under her eyes.

Charlotte shook her head, admiring the snowflakes being swallowed up by the black water of the lake.

Yesterday Adrien had said he was considering taking the new career transition to the California. Why would he want to leave the riveting beauty and fresh air of this small lake-side town in the mountains for a job in a smog-smothered, traffic-invested city?

He couldn't be serious. Could he? Would he move nine hundred and thirty-eight miles away from his children to California? No, she closed her eyes and turned her face up to the falling snow. It must be yet another false threat to manipulate her into letting him come home.

She would push it out of her mind. Early morning was her time rejuvenate. She had another hour and a half until the kids awoke, and she needed to use every minute of it.

Charlotte stepped into the glass pool room and set the baby-phone down on the table. Her kids weren't babies anymore, but she still wanted to hear them if they woke up and called for her.

As usual, the next step was to switch on the sauna before removing the cover from the thirteen and a half by twenty-seven-and-a-half-foot pool Adrien had made for her. Count-ing to three, she took a deep breath and pulled off her boots, ski jacket, and red fleece pajamas, and pulled on a speedo two piece. Her breath steamed in the frigid air. She pushed a button and the endless river flow system turned on. Shiver-ing in the cold, she took a deep breath and jumped into the stream of water, inadvertently giving a yell when the cold water knocked the air out of her lungs.

The pool was heated to seventy-seven degrees, but her skin was already tingling from standing outside in the icy cold admiring the lake.

Charlotte adjusted her goggles and pushed forward, taking her first smooth freestyle strokes into the river stream. As always, all her worries washed away within the first minute. She was in a moving meditation, flowing in time and space.

Thirty minutes later she stood up and checked her watch, and saw that she had swum just over one thousand five hundred meters. She usually could swim two hundred meters more in the same amount of time. Why was she so sluggish?

She swam six days a week and included sprints into her practice to improve her speed. Despite her discipline and effort, Charlotte's endurance and speed had not only stagnated but decreased in the past three months. As she jumped out of the water and carried her glass water bottle into the sauna with her, she analyzed what could be causing the chronic pain and fatigue in her body. It didn't shock her that she immediately lay the blame on Adrien's shoulders. Heartache is a debilitating force, she decided.

For months she had let herself drift in currents of anger, grief, and fear.

As she headed into the sauna, Charlotte pushed the door closed on her emotions.

Shedding her swimsuit, she pulled a fluffy orange towel around herself and poured some orange aromatherapy oil into the water bucket before ladling the water onto the hot stones. Orange scented steam billowed up, and she relaxed back onto the wood, breathing in deeply. The heat began permeating her muscles, and she let out a sigh as a sense of well-being seeped in with the heat.

Every muscle felt worked and relaxed except her solar plexuses, which were clenched in a tight ball. Some days, the thought of these fifteen minutes of bliss was what got her out of bed in the morning.

Breathing in the steam, Charlotte reflected that the most satisfying warmth always came after a chill and deep breaths of pure cold air. The most profound relaxation settled into her body after exercise or hard work.

Wouldn't Adrien miss how blissful it was to step into a hot shower after his daily cross-country ski session through the frigid beauty of Ponderosa Park? Or did he take this daily ritual for granted, unaware of how blessed they were to live here? Adrien knew that pleasure is amplified by the experience of extremes. What was so great about year round moderate to warm weather, anyway?

Who needed the ocean if you had a crystal clear lake?

Charlotte's head began spinning, and she laid down on the narrow wooden bench. What would they tell their kids if he was serious about the move? Aurélie was six and already in first grade. She would take the news hard. At three years old, Gabriel would do anything to spend as much time with his Dad as possible.

Gabriel considered Adrien his personal superhero.

Charlotte instinctively knew that it wouldn't matter how hard she worked to compensate for the absence of Adrien. Charlotte couldn't fill up the hole in Gabriel's world if Adrien moved away. She didn't want to admit it even to herself, but her heart ached for another reason. If Adrien took the job, it would be closing the door on ever repairing their marriage. It would mean divorce. Please God, help me keep Adrien close to his kids. She hesitated, before adding, keep him close to me. She hadn't given up hope.

Charlotte glanced at the clock. It was already time to head inside. Reluctantly Charlotte turned off the sauna and slipped into her boots. She ran through the snow covered yard to the tiny cabin, her skin steaming in the frigid darkness. Twenty minutes later she was showered and dressed in warm cotton tights, a textured mini skirt and a cashmere sweater that matched her pale blue eyes. After a quick application of makeup, she blew her long blond hair dry. She let out a deep sigh as she put on crystal earrings and a matching sparkling pendant necklace her mother had gifted her when she had finished her Ph.D. in psychology.

Charlotte placed a pot of water on the stove top and added essential cinnamon oil to scent her home. She pulled out a pitcher of berry and vegetable smoothie she had made the night before and downed a glass.

Charlotte walked through the open floor plan of her tiny cabin, quickly straightening, picking up and returning objects to their rightful homes before making coffee.

At six thirty she settled down with a cup of dark espresso coffee in her immaculate kitchen and took a moment to appreciate the beauty of the red roses and pine bough arraignment she had put together with her daughter the night before. Then Charlotte pulled out her bible and read for a few minutes before opening her journal and adding a few thoughts and prayers. Charlotte opened up to the latest song on which she was working in her music notebook. She read through the lyrics, a smile touching her lips as she realized how to finish the chorus.

"Mommy?"

Charlotte looked up from her notebook, suddenly panicked. Had she lost track of time? She checked her watch. It was ten minutes until seven. She let out her breath.

"You're up early Gabriel. I laid your outfit out on your bed last night. Go get dressed and then I'll make you some breakfast," she said, pulling her little boy up into her lap. She breathed in his sweet smell and enjoyed the warmth radiating from his body.

"I want to cuddle first," he murmured, holding his bunny tight in his small arms.

Charlotte carried him to the family room and grabbed a fleece blanket. She wrapped him up in it and returned to the kitchen. Charlotte pushed the button on her Jura espresso maker and carried her son and the steaming cup of coffee to the table. Settling her son on her lap, she took a sip of her coffee and worked a few more minutes in the morning calm, finishing her song. Charlotte noticed the smooth and even breathing of her son and looked down. He had fallen back asleep in her lap, cocooned in the warm blanket. She leaned back in her chair, looking out at the snow falling, and enjoyed the warm heaviness of her son in her lap.

"I'm awake Mommy."

Charlotte looked up as her daughter descended the stairs

in a pink wool sweater dress and geometric patterned tights. Her curls were pulled back in a lopsided ponytail, and eight different colored barrettes were clipped randomly all over her head.

Every fiber of Charlotte's body wanted to braid her daughter's hair in a waterfall, so it was smooth and perfect, with one tasteful barrette. Instead, she said, "Good for you getting dressed for school by yourself sweetheart."

Aurélie grinned, revealing two missing teeth. "I did my hair too, look," she declared while turning in a circle.

"Wow, Aurélie, all by yourself? But you know, I'm happy to do your hair for you," answered Charlotte. She took the last drink of her espresso.

Aurélie shook her head. "I'm not a baby anymore."

"But not too big for your morning snuggle I hope?" she asked, and opened one arm wide.

Her daughter hesitated for a moment and then broke into a grin. She ran across the room to the bookshelf, grabbed a book, and slid across the hardwood floor in her stocking feet to a stop next to the table. She climbed up on the breakfast nook bench next to Charlotte.

Charlotte lifted the blanket and Aurélie snuggled in next to her brother. Charlotte wrapped her arm around her daughter and joy vibrated in her chest, a song of serenity and unconditional love. She kissed the top of her daughter's head and breathed in the scent of her shampoo. Thank you for these beautiful children, she prayed silently.

"Read it, Mommy," said Aurélie impatiently and rubbed her brother's cheek. "Gabriel, it's story time. Wake up."

Charlotte loved mornings, and these few minutes of reading to her kids were the best of all. All too soon she reached the last page and reluctantly closed the book. She looked at her watch.

"Can you bring me down Gabriel's clothes honey? They're on his bed. We need to leave in thirty-two minutes."

"Do I have to?"

"Aurélie," said Charlotte in her warning voice.

Aurélie stomped back up the stairs and brought down her brother's clothes.

Charlotte quickly dressed Gabriel while he cried that he wanted to stay in his pajamas.

"I know you want to stay in your pajamas," she soothed him. "It is cold outside, and you are snuggled up with me so cozy warm. But you know what? Jenny will not be happy if you aren't at preschool today to play with her. And I need to go to work."

"I want to stay home with you," Gabriel insisted, tears slipping down his face.

"But tonight after Mom picks us up from Grandma's, we go to pizza with Daddy," Aurélie reminded her brother while slipping an arm around his shoulders and giving him a kiss on his tear stained cheek.

"Can we have ice cream too?" he asked.

"Yes," Charlotte replied, distracted by the clock on the stove. They were running a few minutes behind schedule. She hurried into the kitchen and defrosted three whole grain pumpkin spice muffins she had baked and frozen the past Sunday for the week.

She ignored her daughter's protests that she didn't want to eat the same thing as the day before. Aurélie insisted the cereal her Dad let her eat in the morning, with the sugar stars in it, was yummier than a stupid muffin.

Charlotte seethed inside for a moment and then let the emotion go. The kids ate healthy food all week with her. If they ate sugar every Saturday morning, it couldn't hurt. A wave of fatigue rolled through Charlotte; it made her ache for Adrien. He had always fed the kids breakfast, made their lunches, and delivered them to school.

Charlotte ate a bite of muffin while she packed their lunches with whole grain ham sandwiches, cucumber, carrot and pepper sticks, mandarin oranges, a container of plain yogurt, and a box of seven whole grain pretzels. As an after thought, she slipped in a bar of Swiss chocolate too.

She filled their thermoses with unsweetened cinnamon spiced tea and snapped the lids of their lunch boxes closed. She placed the same lunch into her brightly striped cloth lunch handbag but poured steamed milk and a double shot of espresso into her thermos.

She paused inwardly as the smell of espresso filled the kitchen, mixing with the smell of cinnamon. Good grief, she thought. How many cups of coffee have you started drinking every day? Why are you so tired? She had gone to bed at the same time as the kids the past four nights in a row. She just couldn't shake the fatigue. She shrugged. She worked hard. Weren't all Moms tired?

CHARLOTTE DROPPED OFF her daughter at school and then drove to her son's pre-school. She held Gabriel's hand, like a little bird fluttering in her own, as they climbed the steps.

"I miss Daddy," he said as she pulled off his scarf and jacket.

"I'm sure you do love," she answered as she pulled off his boots. "You go to his condo tonight and the whole weekend, okay? Then you two can have some guy time." She bent down to look for his school slippers under the bench.

"I want you to come too, Mom. Please?"

"It is your special time with your Daddy, Gabriel. I need to work and clean the house back up. I will meet you, as always, at the coffee shop for hot chocolate, and then we'll go to church like we do every Sunday, okay?"

"And tonight we go to Pizza with Dad at the Toll house. Because it's Free day."

"Well, usually it is Friday, but this week it is Wednesday because tomorrow is Thanksgiving."

"So we aren't going together for pizza?" Gabriel's eyes started to fill with tears.

"Yes, we are going for pizza, and then you go to sleep at Daddy's house," repeated Charlotte. Every time she had this conversation with Gabriel, shame and guilt flooded her nervous system, leaving her shaky and unbalanced.

She was a psychologist, and her marriage had fallen apart. She, of all people, knew how hard separation and divorce was on children, and how it could cause temporary if not permanent damage if you didn't handle it extremely well. She had been certain she would never have her children go through the experience of a broken home like she had. Yet here she was.

"Both your Daddy and I love you very much, Gabriel. We both feel so lucky to be your parents."

"Then why does Daddy live in town?" Gabriel asked, his eyes round, pleading. "Why doesn't he want to be with us all the time?"

"Your Daddy and I both need our own homes right now so we can be happy and be the best parents possible for you and your sister," she answered. Her abdomen was clenching again, a ball of pain radiating into her back.

Every other mother and father in the entry room had overheard their entire conversation. There were definite downsides to living in a small town, too, she decided: gossip being number one on the list.

Gossip was as hot here as the air was fresh.

"Charlotte, is that you? You look, um, different. Are you sure you don't want to cut your hair? It was so beautiful when you wore it short in high school."

Charlotte turned around and cursed internally. Jessica Higgins was standing in front of her in a red wool sweater dress that clung to her perfect figure. Her curly golden brown hair reached halfway down her back and was tied loosely back with a red ribbon. A few curls had escaped and framed her delicate features.

"Hi Jessica," said Charlotte, forcing a smile.

"I haven't seen you in, what, ten years? Are you here to celebrate Thanksgiving?"

"We've moved home from New York. This is Ocean's first morning at pre-school here," replied Jessica, while kneeling down and hugging her daughter.

Charlotte fought herself from rolling her eyes. Did she really name her child Ocean?

"David made the bestseller's list and could quit his government job to write full time. We have bought the prettiest house out on the lake. You'll have to come by for a cup of coffee and see it after we kiss the kids goodbye."

"Thank you for the invitation, but I need to go to work," called out Charlotte as she hurried toward the door.

"I heard about you and Adrien. Too bad you let him get away from you. It must be so hard on your kids."

"See you next week," called out Charlotte over her shoulder, and opened the door.

It was a short drive to her office. She dialed her Mom as she stepped out of the car and made her way up the sidewalk to her office. "Hi Mom, how are you? I just wanted to remind you that you need to pick up Gabriel early from preschool for his dentist appointment."

"I have it all printed out here on the calendar you gave me Charlotte. I'll pick up Aurélie and take her to ballet and then I will bring them both back here for cookies and milk."

"Fruit and nuts Mom. Not cookies, okay?" added Charlotte as she closed the car door.

"Will do. Fruit, nuts, cookies and milk," laughed her mother. "Don't worry sweetheart. I know what I'm doing. Now you have a good day. Don't get too emotionally drained."

"Thank you so much, Mom. I love you. Oh, Mom, I ran into Jessica this morning. She's moved home."

"Well isn't that nice."

"She is anything but," snapped Charlotte as she almost slipped on the icy pathway near the coffee shop.

"Oh dear. Well, people change. Maybe she regrets bullying you all those years."

"She invited me over for coffee, then rubbed my separation in my face." Charlotte sighed. Her breath came out as a white cloud in the cold of the morning.

"Shake it off beautiful. Happy people aren't mean."

"She looked damn near glowing with happiness to me."

"Do you want to stop by for lunch and talk?"

Charlotte tilted her head to one side, considering for a moment. No. It was best not to bring up past negative emotions. And her Mom had a lot to do to pack for her trip. "That's okay Mom. I have too much work today and you have a vacation to get ready for. I'll see you when I pick up the kids."

"You have yourself a good day then love."

Charlotte stepped into her cherry wood floored office and slipped out of her boots and into a pair of heels. She turned on the heat before opening the blinds to reveal a view of the lake and the snow covered mountains.

She told herself to shake Jessica off as her Mom had advised. Charlotte set an arrangement of roses and pine down on the coffee table and lit some candles. She poured some of the cappuccino into her mug and took out a flute and a bottle of sparkling apple cider as a knock came at the door. She smoothed her skirt and opened the door.

"Good morning Charlotte," said a deep baritone voice.

Charlotte smiled up at the broad-chested man with dark unruly hair who towered above her. He was a construction worker, and one saw his huge muscles and rounded belly even through his sweater.

"Good morning Dan." She knelt down and reached out a hand. "Good morning Arwen." The eight-year-old buried her face in her father's jacket. Charlotte waited patiently.

"Say good morning Arwen," insisted Dan, while patting his daughter's brown hair. "You liked the session last week. Remember? I'll be back in an hour to take you back to school."

Slowly, Arwen let go of her Dad and stepped forward. She placed her hand in Charlotte's and mumbled good morning. Charlotte gave a wave to Dan and motioned at a selection of warm slippers.

"It's good to see you Arwen. Would you like to change into some slippers, or keep your boots on?"

Wordlessly, Arwen slipped out of her boots and slipped into a soft pair of blue slippers. Charlotte beckoned Arwen towards the sofa. She poured her a glass of apple cider and placed a bowl of whole grain pretzels next to the flute.

"It's good to see you Arwen. Would you like to tell me more of what your mother was like?"

THREE HOURS LATER Charlotte stepped out of her office and took a deep breath of the pine scented air. She made her way down the street toward the lake, carrying a steaming cup of tea in her hands.

The first session of the morning with Arwen had taken a toll. She still had to fight back the tears when a child talked about the loss of a parent. She stood on the end of the dock, taking in the sound of the waves gently massaging the shore.

She closed her eyes, attempting to soak up the healing energy of the lake. She thanked God for her profession. As hard as the session had just been, she loved helping people.

One last deep breath and she walked back toward her office. In nine minutes she had an online session. There was a time when she wasn't sure she would be able to keep her business afloat.

That was before. Now she had clients from all over the world. McCall was a small town. Heaven knew she wouldn't be able to have a full practice if she couldn't offer online counseling. When Charlotte started her online therapy platform, she was confident it addressed a latent need. She hadn't, however, foreseen just how popular distance therapy would be, or how big her team of psychologist and psychiatrists would grow.

A huge advantage for her clients was the flexibility. Especially if they were depressed, it was immensely helpful that her clients didn't have to leave the house to come to therapy.

From the very beginning, Charlotte had invested her marketing activity into targeting men. In Charlotte's experience, women tended to prefer face to face contact; they found it consoling to sit across from a sympathetic counselor.

Charlotte had discovered that most men found the process of arranging a therapy session, traveling to the office, and sitting across from a therapist, as awkward and arduous. Quite a few men had a mental hang up when it came to pursuing a therapy session; it didn't matter how desperate they were, the negative association prevented them from seeking out the help they needed.

For this reason, Charlotte promoted her counseling sessions as therapy but also provided life coaching sessions. Was it the word 'coach' that made the difference for the men who signed up through her online therapy platform? Charlotte shrugged. She wasn't certain.

Increasing numbers of individuals were willing to pay a life coach to help them make their professional and personal dreams a reality. Charlotte had supported men and women in the transition to a new career, through the emotional rollercoaster of starting a new business, and through going from barely able to run to participating in a marathon.

What Charlotte did know, was that the boom in demand for the 'life coach' services via her website was also attributed to the increasing pressure on men and their shrinking supportive circle. More clients than she could count had told her that they had lost track of their friends. The pressure of juggling their desire to provide for their family, with the new effort to be involved in raising their children, left little time for friendships with other men.

When the pressures and stress of life or tragedy struck, many men didn't have anywhere to turn; they had neglected their friendships; there would be no meeting other men to watch a game, to hit the golf course, or undertake an activity together. Charlotte advised all of her male clients to walk in nature while they talked to her for the session, which she faithfully referred to as 'life coaching.'

For some reason, most men found it easier to talk about what was weighing on their hearts when they didn't have to look at her, and when they could engage in physical movement. If she discovered that one of her 'coaching' clients was suffering from mental illness, she advised the client try a few therapy sessions.

Charlotte took a breath and answered her phone. "Good morning Jackson, where are you walking today?"

"You're killing me with this walking requirement," replied a gruff voice.

"I thought you told me last week that you've dropped five pounds in the last month from these regular hour walks?"

"You're right Charlotte. I'm weary today is all."

"What if you head out for a ten-minute stroll and then the rest of the session you can spend relaxing," suggested Charlotte. "Tell me as soon as you step out the front door. I would like to hear about what is causing your weariness."

"I guess I can do ten minutes of walking."

An hour later Charlotte ended the call. In the end, Jackson had walked the entire session, and he had made progress on his goal to reduce his stress level and increase his patience and equanimity. They reviewed his weekly plans to increase his fitness level, reconnect with his friends, and develop a new relaxing hobby he could enjoy together with his children and wife.

Charlotte knew there were both benefits and disadvantages to providing her treatment online and she was always analyzing how she could best minimize the difficulties while increasing the advantages to her potential and existing clients.

Charlotte wanted to make sure that her clients understood that she was hanging on their every word, so at the end of each session she wrote her client an encrypted email and insisted her entire team do the same thing after each counseling session.

The email summarized what her client had discussed with her and offered them the conclusions they had come to, her insight, and proposal for next steps. She had received countless letters telling her how healing it was to receive the emails and be able to refer to them over time.

People had a tendency to focus on the negative instead of rejoicing in incremental victories.

Charlotte walked outside for some fresh air, thinking over the session and her business. She had been earning a sizeable income for the past nine years, but no one, not even her husband, knew how affluent she was. Charlotte liked it that way.

She drove a ten-year-old SUV, wore the handful of designer clothes to work she had purchased a decade ago and lived in the same tiny cabin on the lake she had inherited from her grandfather.

Charlotte loved her simple life, even now that Adrien was gone. She didn't need the luxury to be happy. Her wealth represented security and freedom and gave her a sense of confidence that she would always be able to care for her children and herself.

Charlotte let out a huge sigh as she opened the door to her office, the cold still hanging onto her coat as she hung it up next to the door.

She rubbed her upper abdomen as she walked to her desk and logged in to her online therapy platform to meet her next client. Her stomach was clenched tight again, radiating pain to her back. Charlotte took some deep slow breaths. Her client Jackson wasn't the only one who needed to de-stress.

Sure the past ten years in which Charlotte had built her practice and given birth to her two children had been intense. But even now that her business was thriving, she worried. Apparently, her stress was now appearing as a clenched ball of pain in her stomach.

She needed to unwind and have faith. Maybe I should join Elodie to try out an hour of yoga, thought Charlotte, like she keeps insisting.

After a few more sessions it was already two o'clock. Charlotte turned her attention to the administration work demanded by the online therapy portal business she had created. Every psychologist on her portal had a Ph.D. and had undergone a rigorous interview and background check.

They had even had to travel to McCall, Idaho or Boise, for a personal interview. Charlotte had wanted to take no chances.

She took a sip of her sparkling mineral water. She had exactly forty-two minutes to finish the article for Psychology Today magazine before she left to pick up her kids from her mother's house.

Her mother had the night shift at the hospital. Working in administration was a vast improvement from the early years her mom had spent in housekeeping at the Shore Lodge hotel. Charlotte was proud of her mom and resolved never to be the cause of her mother arriving late for work, even if it was a bit of a rush and stress to get out of her office on time.

As Charlotte hurried up the slippery path up to the parking lot, dizziness smashed into her like a tree collapsing onto the top of her head. One moment she was walking, her breath steaming in the cold, and the next she was looking up at concerned faces staring down at her.

Charlotte took a deep breath of cold air, willing her memories to slide into place. She remembered the dizziness slamming into her, but not the fall to the ground. How long had she been lying here?

"Are you okay there?" asked Mr. Davis. "Mauve, let's take her to the hospital. I'll go get our car."

"What time is it?" Charlotte asked, sitting up. "I have to go pick up my kids."

"Take is easy, Charlotte," answered Mrs. Davis while helping her to her feet. "We'll give your mom a call and tell her you fell and will be late."

"No, she has to go to work. I have to go and pick up the kids. I'm fine. I don't need to go to the hospital."

"But you're bleeding," said Mr. Davis.

"Let's go get you looked at, just to be sure; there's a Love. We wouldn't want anything happening to our best psychologist, now would we?"

"I must have slipped on the ice. Listen, I'll go pick up the kids and then stop by the hospital on my way home. Don't worry Mr. Davis."

"If you're sure..."

"I'm sure. I'm fine. Everything is under control," answered Charlotte. "Thank you for the help."

As Charlotte slid into the car, she realized she had forgotten it was the night to trade the kids off to their Dad. Their bags lay, already packed, by the front door at home. She had meant to take them with her in the morning, and now she would need to collect the kids from her Mom and drive all the way home on icy roads to pick up the overnight bags.

Should she call her sister and ask her to pick up the bags and bring them into town? Should she call Adrien and ask him to pick up the kids at the cabin instead of at the pizza parlor, as planned?

Her abdomen and back still hurt. She was dizzy. Charlotte took a deep breath. No. She hated accepting help. Everyone in town was already looking at her with pity in her eyes and she hated it.

Well, I'll show them all, thought Charlotte. I can do this. The words ran in a constant loop in Charlotte's mind on the drive to her mother's house. I am brave. I am self-sufficient. I am the artist of my life. I can do this.

"Mom?"

"Yes dear," answered Charlotte, gripping the wheel of the car tighter as it slid on a patch of ice.

Maybe you should have had Adrien pick the kids up at the house, Charlotte thought. Then instead of driving on these icy roads, you could be curled up in front of a crackling fire with a mug of hot chocolate. No, she shook her head. She always met Adrien for pizza before the trade off. The kids looked forward to pizza night all week.

"Mom, don't get mad, okay?"

"Why would I get mad Aurélie?" asked Charlotte, distracted by the pain. She chanced a glance in her review mirror at her daughter on the seat behind her. "Wait, did you find and eat the rest of my birthday chocolates?"

"Do you think I could have lots of presents for Christmas this year? Just this once? Please?"

Aurélie had spoken so quietly Charlotte could barely hear her. She took a deep breath and pulled the car into the parking lot of the pizzeria. Getting out, Charlotte walked over and opened her daughter's car door. Charlotte knelt down on eye level with her daughter, smoothing the blond curls away from Aurélie's cheeks as she smiled ruefully.

It wasn't easy to explain her conviction to her girl. She believed materialism hollowed out the soul and robbed people of wealth that could be spent on experiences and personal growth, rather than on belongings. She knew there were lots of ways to make Christmas special without piles of presents; Her mother had managed just that when her Dad had disappeared with all their savings.

"You'll only have one gift awaiting you on Christmas morning because we save our money to do fun things together, or to learn and grow as people," explained Charlotte. "Like receiving the ice-skating lessons you keep asking for honey." She kissed her daughter's forehead and smiled brightly, despite the ache beginning to throb in her muscles. Was she getting sick?

"Katie gets lots of presents for Christmas and she goes to ice-skating lessons. All the kids in my class get lots of toys," said Aurélie softly, a tear slipping down her cheek. "I want to know what that's like, opening up lots of presents. Just once Mommy. Just this year. I won't ever ask again, ever."

"Families have different values sweetheart. And some children don't get any presents. Anyway, did you think about where we would put those toys? There isn't enough space in our home."

Charlotte noticed the tears wetting her daughter's cheeks but was distracted by her vibrating iPhone. A patient was calling her emergency number.

"Then why does our home have to be so little?" asked Aurélie, huddling down in her seat.

"I love having our home right on the lake, don't you honey? Not everyone has a private beach and dock. I have to answer this, okay?"

Charlotte glanced over and noticed for the first time that her three-year-old son was fast asleep. She swore silently. Charlotte would never get Gabriel to sleep by eight now, she thought. But then she remembered she wouldn't be putting him to bed; Adrien would.

Luckily, her patient was only calling to cancel her appointment for the next day. Charlotte was off the phone in under two minutes.

"Mom?" whispered Aurélie. "What if I spent Christmas at Daddy's this year? Because he said…"

The fuzzy blue scarf wrapped around Aurélie's neck muffled her words. Aurélie gazed down at her blue boots.

The cold was creeping up the back of Charlotte's legs, and her fingers were going numb in the night air. Still no sign of Adrien's car.

The last thing Charlotte wanted was to fight with her daughter inside the pizzeria. She closed the car door and returned to the front seat, turning on the car and heater. She stared out of the windshield at the snow covered pine trees and the moon already coming up over the mountains.

She didn't trust herself to turn around and look at her daughter. Give me a hand here, God, she prayed. Help me to remain a calm and loving Mom, because I am on the verge of crying and snapping something I know I will regret. I feel so betrayed by Adrien and hurt that Aurélie wants to be with him, rather than with me for Christmas.

"So tell me now. What did your father say?"

Aurélie jumped up and down in her car seat, her enthusiasm only restrained by her seat belt.

"He said if we come to him for Christmas, he will have lots of presents for us on Christmas morning."

"But you are spending Thanksgiving with your Daddy. We agreed you would spend Christmas at home, with Grandma, Élodie, and me."

Aurélie didn't answer. A moment before the cold was tingling along Charlotte's spine, numbing her fingers and toes. Now her face was flushed with heat. She wanted to tell Aurélie she couldn't go. She wanted to call Adrien and tell him that he could go to hell, and take his presents with him. Instead, she turned around and looked at her daughter in the backseat and asked, "Is that what you want honey? Do you want to spend Christmas with your Daddy?"

"Yes," came a tiny voice from the backseat. "You're not mad, are you Mom?"

"What?" replied Charlotte, gripping the steering wheel harder. She cleared her throat. "No, I'm not angry Aurélie."

Thoughts galloped through Charlotte's head like wild mustangs chased by a cougar. She had tried so hard to make every Christmas with her children special. Had she failed? Had she gotten it wrong? Maybe if she had had lots of carefully selected presents awaiting her kids under the tree on Christmas morning, they wouldn't want to spend it with their Dad this year instead.

Charlotte thought back on her Christmases with her kids. On Christmas Eve she always made them homemade huckleberry pancakes with berries they had picked and frozen the past summer in the morning.

After breakfast, she helped them make wish boats out of twigs or popsicle sticks and decorated them with fir boughs, pine cones, and holly berries.

Adrien and she had taken them sledding or ice skating after a lunch of everything that was normally not allowed: hamburgers, French fries, and milkshakes in town. They returned in the evening and took their wish boats down to the dock.

Charlotte helped the kids place all natural beeswax candles on the wish boats. She held out a match so they could light the wicks, tiny pinpricks of light in the gathering darkness. They each made a wish before gently pushing their boats out onto the waves of the lake, unless it had frozen. Then they set it out on the ice instead.

They were all pink cheeked and chilled by the time they climbed the steps to their tiny cabin. Each year, Charlotte put her children into a festive pine scented bubble bath surrounded by candles and snuggled them into new pajamas by four thirty. After a dinner of sandwiches and homemade pumpkin soup, they all curled up in front of the fire to watch a Christmas movie with popcorn and Christmas cookies. Serene delight always settled deep into Charlotte's soul when her children were cuddled up in her lap under a quilt blanket, her cheek resting on the top of their curly heads.

Before bed, they drank whipped-cream-topped hot chocolate with multicolored sprinkles while roasting chestnuts and marshmallows over the open fire.

On Christmas morning she watched her children open a present. She served them her famous cinnamon rolls, eggs, maple syrup sausages and fresh squeezed orange juice at a table decorated with fresh pine boughs, red Holly berries, pine cones, and candles.

After breakfast, they defrosted the car and headed to church in McCall. After church they always baked at least six different kinds of Christmas cookies, her children scattering sprinkles and leaving chocolate icing fingerprints all over her usually pristine white Ikea kitchen cupboards.

In the early evening Charlotte bundled the kids up in their snowsuits and waited with a basket full of cookies for her sister to arrive and take them to her mother's for a turkey dinner with all the trimmings.

The children always shouted with delight when they heard the sleigh bells in the distance. Within minutes Élodie would turn the bend and come into sight, driving two white Arabian horses, their breath steaming in the winter air. Charlotte nestled her children under a blanket, before climbing into the sleigh with Adrien and handing out Christmas cookies.

Charlotte rubbed her forehead and down the bridge of her nose. When she was growing up money had always been too tight for more the one present. But her mom's waitressing paycheck hadn't kept them from enjoying a magical Christmas together every year. Christmas had always been her favorite two days of the entire year.

She had been so proud of their Christmas traditions and their focus on the real meaning of Christmas. Charlotte had thought she was doing everything right. She had thought their Christmases, and their life, was perfect. Until Adrien had cheated. And now her beloved daughter wanted to leave her on Christmas too. Charlotte wanted to place her face in her hands and cry. Not the pretty silent tears like you see in the movies, but the type of crying that left dark smudges under your eyes and snot dripping down. The sobbing that required tissues and a stiff drink. She would never advise her patients to drink a big glass of red wine in a situation like this, but that's what she felt like right now, more than anything. Or even some kind of shot, the kind they advised someone upset drink in the old fashioned movies she loved, and she hated hard liquor.

"Mommy? He said you should come too. To Christmas at his house."

Charlotte took a deep shuddering breath and turned to face her daughter. "I don't think that's a good idea honey. But listen, of course, I'm not mad you want to spend Christmas with your Dad. You live with me most of the time now. I'm sure you miss him. But next Christmas, even though there is only one present, you will spend it with me again, okay?"

"I want you to come to Daddy's with us for Christmas," declared Aurélie, "then you can meet Kathy."

Charlotte's eyes grew wide. It was as if she had stepped on an ant hill and they were swarming up her legs, biting their way along her calves and up her back.

"You'll love her Mom. Dad calls her his angel. Do you think she is? A real one I mean? Grandma told me we can't always see their wings."

So Adrien had a new girlfriend already? Charlotte's heart skipped a beat, and she realized she was holding her breath. Shake it off Charlotte, she warned herself. She had been the one to ask for a separation, so why was her mouth opening and closing like a fish pulled from the lake by a hook, frantically trying to breathe in a suddenly airless world?

You don't love him, she told herself. He is a selfish jerk, an idiot, a home-breaker. His cheating nearly shook you to pieces, like a gleaming cathedral obliterated by an eight magnitude earthquake.

One minute, everything was gleaming arches and perfect symmetry. The next moment, he hadn't come home all night, and dynamite exploded inside the gleaming glass building which had been her life. One explosion and everything crashed to dust and rubble.

She sat up ramrod straight in the front seat, squaring her shoulders and lifting her chin. I am successful; I am strong, I am self-sufficient, she told herself. A vision of her kids spending Thanksgiving with Adrien and his new angel girlfriend flashed in front of her eyes.

Hot tears escaped and burned down her cheeks, and she ground her fists into her eyes. You are not crying over this. You do not love Adrien anymore.

Ah hell, she thought, letting her head fall forward on the steering wheel. Who are you kidding? You still smell his favorite green sweater every night before falling asleep.

A fist pounded on the window, and she jumped.

Charlotte looked out at a tall, muscular man with penetrating pale blue eyes, dark brown hair and a two-day beard. He opened her car door and leaned into the car. Adrien was close enough for her to feel his minty breath on her cheek. She breathed in the scent of soap and mint mouthwash.

Damn him for smelling so good, she thought.

"What the hell are you doing out here? I've been waiting for you in the pizzeria for over half an hour," he grumbled. "Wait, are you crying? What happened? Is it the kids?"

Frantically Adrien opened the back card door. Gabriel was still peacefully sleeping like a chubby cherub, and Aurélie was curled up on the car seat next to him. Charlotte watched Adrien kiss their son on the forehead and smooth his curls away from his eyes.

"I didn't see your car," mumbled Charlotte.

"Daddy! I missed you! We're coming to you for Christmas," she shouted. Gabriel awoke in response to his sister's yelling and the cold air rushing into the car.

"I walked over from the condo," answered Adrien.

By the time Charlotte jumped out of the car and smashed

the car door shut behind her, Adrien was holding a child in each arm and grinning. His teeth flashed white under the streetlights as he kissed Gabriel, and then Aurélie on the cheek and whispered something to them. The cheers of her children echoed through the dark. They snuggled their heads into his green cashmere scarf and wrapped their tiny hands around his North Face jacket. Aurélie reached up and rubbed her hands on her father's cheeks.

"You need to shave Daddy; you're scratchy."

"Am I? Let's check," he answered with a grin and nuzzled his chin against her cheek.

"Stop Daddy, it's scratchy," giggled Aurélie as Adrien kissed her nose.

I used to be a piece of that joy, thought Charlotte. Now I'm a spectator.

She sighed, her fury seeping out through her skin, as if she had stepped naked from her sauna, and collapsed into a snow bank. She began to shiver, despite her knee-length black jacket, turquoise scarf, and knee-high boots. Her North Face would have been warmer, but she knew she looked elegant in this dress jacket, with its belt pulled tight around her waist, and she had wanted to look gorgeous.

Apparently, the effort she had put into her makeup and clothing choices had been ill spent. Adrien had someone new keeping him warm at night.

You have to get over him Charlotte; she told herself yet again. She almost convinced herself that she was healing, and then he would be standing in front of her, and she was lost at sea. He was such a great Dad, and he was the sexiest, most charming man she had ever met. Her whole body ached to wrap her arms around his waist and join in the family hug.

"Charlotte, I said, shall we go in?"

Charlotte blinked, turning her focus back to her husband. She hadn't been enough for him before, and he didn't want her now. She could go inside and sit across from him and put on a big smile for her children. The pizza would steam in front of them, and the children would chatter about their day and Christmas. A vision of Adrien with an arm around a raven beauty flashed in her head. Dizziness overwhelmed her, and she shot out a hand to brace herself on the car door handle, hunching over.

"Charlotte? Everything okay?"

"What?" Charlotte shook her head slightly in an attempt to refocus. The dizziness passed, and she straightened up. "Fine, I'm fine. I mean, I'm not feeling well. I'm going to head home. I'll pick up the kids on Sunday, at the coffee shop, okay?" Charlotte didn't wait for a response from Adrien. She stepped forward and kissed both of her kids on the cheek. "I love you both. I hope you have a beautiful Thanksgiving with Daddy. Don't eat too much of Gram's apple pie, okay?"

"But Mommy, Daddy is ordering banana split ice-cream sundaes for dessert, with sprinkles and whipped cream. You have to come to dinner," protested Aurélie as Adrien set her down next to her brother and grabbed their bags out of the car.

"Yes, please come to dinner Charlotte. I already ordered your favorite pizza," agreed Adrien.

"I want to discuss Christmas. And California."

Charlotte shook her head and opened her car door. "Sorry guys. Have fun okay? If you need anything, you can call me. If the kids get sick or they are homesick or..."

"They'll be happy Charlotte," interrupted Adrien, while shaking his head. "I hope you feel better soon. Try to enjoy the break. You always used to complain that you didn't get enough time. Wait, how did you use to put it? 'Me time,'" he said, snapping his fingers. "Now you have an extended weekend of 'me time.'"

Wordlessly, Charlotte slid into the car. She gave a wave through the window as tears slid out against her will. Charlotte began her drive home.

When she had said she needed some 'me time,' she had meant an hour to read a book or meet her sister for two hours of cross country skiing in Ponderosa Park. She hadn't meant an entire Thanksgiving away from her kids. Tears slipped silently down her cheeks. But it wasn't until she shut the front door of her tiny home behind her that she slipped down to the floor, rested her head on her knees, and sobbed. Her kids were gone. She had banished Adrien from their home.

Her mother was with her sister in Hawaii for Thanksgiving.

She was all alone.

She didn't know how long she sat on the floor in the dark. The phone began ringing. She didn't answer it. The caller hung up and redialed.

At last, Charlotte picked herself up off the floor and answered the phone.

"Charlotte, are you okay?"

"Adrien?"

"Are you feeling better?"

"Are the kids okay?"

"Sure, they're here in the bath. Listen, Aurélie told me your family is in Hawaii for Thanksgiving. Why don't you reconsider coming to Thanksgiving at Ma's house? You know the family would love to see you."

"No, it's okay. I'm still not feeling well." Charlotte fell onto the leather sofa in the living room. The cold of the smooth surface seeped through her clothing, causing her to shiver. She hated this damn couch. Sure, it was beautiful, but she had always hated the first-anniversary present she had received from Adrien. I mean, what was he thinking buying a sofa he wanted and offering it up as an anniversary present?

"Are you sure you want to spend Thanksgiving on your own? Can I bring you anything?"

Charlotte could hear splashing and the happy chatter of her children in the background.

"Stop being so nice Adrien, okay? It doesn't make it any easier," Charlotte answered while rubbing the bridge of her nose. Her head hurt like hell.

"Make what easier Char? Hello? Charlotte?"

"Make it easier to stop missing you," exploded Charlotte, instantly regretting her honesty. Great, she thought. Now he knows how pathetic I am. He knows I still miss him. Damn.

"Good," he answered. "I miss you too."

Charlotte sighed. Of course, Adrien wanted her to adore him, even now. He was accustomed to everyone adoring him, men and women alike.

"Let me move on Adrien, okay? Lord knows you have. Maybe it's better if we stop meeting for pizza and coffee. We can just hand over the kids like we did tonight," she said in a monotone voice while gazing out at the lake in the starlight. She shivered.

All of a sudden the only thing she wanted to do was slide into a hot bath and then climb under her mint blue flannel duvet and go to sleep.

"I still love you, Charlotte. Char, did you hear me?"

"Yes," she answered. She cleared her throat, forcing the hot tears behind her eyes to stay there. "Don't play games, Adrien. You've already hurt me enough."

"No, of course not. I," Adrien stuttered. Charlotte could picture him running his hands through his hair. He always did that when he was stressed. "I didn't think you would ever give me another chance. I mean I had hope, but then. I love you, Charlotte. I miss you and the kids. I want to come home. It was a mistake."

"And what, I'm supposed just to forgive that night and welcome you home with open arms?" asked Charlotte.

She grabbed the gray Ikea blanket and pulled it over her body, but the cold still seeped into her from the leather couch. She closed her eyes.

The pain in her abdomen hurt like hell.

"Do you still love me, Charlotte?"

Charlotte could hear her kids laughing in the background.

"Daddy, we are ready to get out now. Daddy! Daddy, are you crying?"

Charlotte froze in mid-step. Adrien was crying? The only time she had ever seen him cry was at the birth of their children and when his best friend died in a skiing accident.

"Listen," Adrien cleared his throat.

"I need to pull the kids out of the bath. I've got to go. Reconsider Thanksgiving okay?"

"I love you, Adrien."

There, she had said it. She thought she would feel fear and trepidation after letting the words escape. Instead, a peace settled down her spine, relaxing her shoulders, opening her chest, smoothing her breathing, and leaving only fatigue.

"I will always love you, Charlotte," he answered. Charlotte heard Gabriel burst into tears in the background.

"Uh, oh, Gabriel can't find his special bunny. I'll call tomorrow. Sleep tight."

It wasn't until Charlotte poured lavender vanilla scented bubble bath under the running water that the smile disappeared from her face.

Hope bubbled up within her like champagne bubbles in a crystal flute glass. Maybe they could put their family back together again before it was too late.

CHAPTER 2

Luke 17:3-4
3 Be careful. If your brother sins against you, rebuke him. If he repents, forgive him. 4 If he sins against you seven times in the day, and seven times returns, saying, 'I repent,' you shall forgive him."

CHARLOTTE STEPPED OUT onto her back porch for a breath of fresh air, taking a steaming mug of cinnamon spiced tea with her. Habit had propelled her through the first two hours of her day. She had swum one thousand eight hundred meters, but it had taken her twenty minutes longer than it should have. She enjoyed an extended session in the sauna in an attempt to restore a feeling of wellness to her body, showered, dressed, wrote in her faith journal, and finished writing a new song. She had organized every closet and cleaned her tiny home until it was sweet-smelling and clean. Now she was at a loss for what to do.

It was Thanksgiving, so she had the day off of work. There was such a multitude of choices that she couldn't settle on what to do next. Curl up in front of the fire with a new book? Go hiking in the woods? Drive down to Boise for Christmas shopping and go out to lunch? She could go into town and enjoy a day of pampering at the Shore Lodge spa for the first time in her life. Or she could go into the office and finish a few articles she had been postponing. Or, heaven forbid, she could do nothing more than watch movies all day. When was the last time she had let herself do that? Had she ever?

The truth was, she was having trouble enjoying the free time. She wasn't feeling her best, and more than anything, she missed her kids. It was one thing to escape for a day when you knew you could return and scoop your children into your arms whenever you wanted to. It was another to have no choice over their absence for a holiday.

She admonished herself that there were lots of tired moms out there who would love a day all to themselves.

Charlotte heard her phone ringing as she opened the back door to the cabin. The only person who would call her home phone at this time was Adrien.

"Adrien, what's wrong?"

"Nothing. We're going sledding and then to Ma's for dinner. Listen, I wanted to discuss this in person, but I couldn't wait. I haven't been this jacked up since you told me you were pregnant. They mailed me the work contract; it's a sure thing now, Char. I got the job down in California. Can you believe it?"

"Seriously? But you're not considering going, are you?" gasped Charlotte. "You wouldn't just leave the kids."

"Come with me."

Charlotte was too stunned to respond. Adrien was living in town. She climbed the stairs and sat on Gabriel's bed. Besides the separation, she had never wanted to live anywhere else in the world. Growing up, most of her friends had moved away to cities all over the Northwest and the country.

For a few months, she had wanted to remain in her university town, but Adrien had made her remember how much she loved the beauty of the lake, the fresh smell of pine, the charming little town, and the ski hill a few minutes drive away. It had been their dream to raise a family in McCall and for their children to experience the magic of growing up immersed in nature. She couldn't imagine Adrien could be happy in a big city, and certainly not in California; his nickname was "Mountain Man" for a reason. Adrien spent all his free time in the outdoors.

"McCall is our home, Adrien. It's our dream to raise our kids here," she answered.

"Well, life is change, and we need to be flexible, Charlotte.

It's my dream job."

"It's your dream job to work in human resources? Since when? How are you going to be happy sitting behind a desk all day?"

"It's at Apple. Seriously, I was competing with people with decades of experience and MBAs. They hired me instead because they said they like mavericks."

Charlotte picked up Gabriel's teddy bear and hugged it tightly. "I'm not moving the kids to California, Adrien. I'm not moving them away from my mom and sister and your family and all the kids' friends. My business is here."

"I'm sure you could find new clients. Just rent a new office, and set out your sign," he answered. "What's the problem?"

Charlotte's skin prickled with sweat as liquid heat poured through her. "It's not easy to build up a new practice, Adrien."

"Aren't most of your clients from your online platform anyway? That makes you extremely mobile, doesn't it?"

Charlotte's eyes widened. She hadn't told him about her online platform. How did he know? Did he know how much money she earned too? No. She collapsed back on the bed. She had always submitted their tax return. He didn't know how much she made.

"I am not belittling your business, Charlotte. Quite the contrary. I am extremely impressed to the point of awe. I mean, you have earned a fortune."

He knew.

"You looked at our tax return," Charlotte answered, and collapsed backward onto the bed.

"You got that right, gorgeous. You can imagine the emotions that arose when I saw it. The first word that comes to mind is betrayal."

Charlotte jumped up off the bed, the teddy bear falling to the floor. "How dare you. You betrayed me."

"Here I am, thinking we need the money I earn risking my life jumping from a plane into wild forest fires each summer, and it wasn't necessary anymore, was it?"

"I've hated your smoke jumping for years. It scares the hell out of me every time they call you in to fight a fire. But I couldn't tell you to stop. You insisted it is part of who you are," she shouted.

"And you said you were so proud of your sexy hero," he shouted back. Adrien breathed out in exasperation. "Talk about pressure. What was I supposed to do, quit smoke jumping and work at the gas station instead? There aren't exactly a lot of jobs in this little town in the middle of nowhere."

Charlotte went to the window and rested her face against the cold glass. "I should have told you."

"You think? It's not just the money, Charlotte. It's that you built up a whole business by yourself and didn't tell me."

"I knew you already were insecure and resented my Ph.D. I didn't know how you would handle me earning so much more than you too," she explained.

"Didn't you have any faith in me at all? I'm proud as hell, Char. I'm part of that success, don't you understand? You didn't do it alone. I was the one supporting you through that Ph.D. I was the one up most nights with sick babies so that you could get your sleep. Or don't you remember any of that? Why couldn't you let me share in the success?"

"I didn't think of it like that. I just don't know why." Charlotte began to cry.

"Aren't you the psychologist here? I'm pretty sure it all goes back to your Dad waking up one day and disappearing from your life with all his and your mom's savings, leaving you all with nothing."

Charlotte didn't answer. She just watched her breath steam against the window pane. He was right, but she couldn't bring those words to her lips.

"The night I discovered that you had been lying to me, I went to the bar, and that's when... everything fell apart."

Charlotte stood up and slowly walked toward the stairs.

"You can't blame me for cheating on me, Adrien. You could have come to me, instead of going to a bar."

"It was one night, Char. One night. I can't even remember it."

Charlotte pressed the button of the espresso maker, soothed by the smell of the aroma filling the room.

"Like hell, it was one night."

"We were happy, Charlotte. We could be happy again. Your secret threw me for a loop when I was at an all-time low anyway, wanting to get out of smoke jumping and ski patrolling and move on to a job fit for a father of two small children. But do you know what? I couldn't find one. Do you know how many job interviews I went to in town? I felt like a joke; I failed every job interview I went to here."

"Why didn't you tell me?" asked Charlotte, her body trembling. It was all too much to take in. She needed a brandy. Where was that bottle a client had given her last Christmas?

"I was ashamed, Char. I wanted to show up at home one day and say, I found a great job. A job that you can be proud of me having. So you can be proud of having me as your husband."

"That's stupid. You're an idiot."

"Nice. Real nice."

"But it is. I don't love you for what job you have. You ruined everything. Or I, I mean we..."

"Shouldn't have kept secrets from one another? Yeah. I think so too."

Charlotte found the bottle and poured herself a shot. She threw it back, choking a bit as the liquor burned the back of her throat.

"What I want to say is, now I've found a great job, and I'm asking you to support me and to give putting our family back together again a chance. Please, Charlotte."

"And if I say no?"

The line went silent.

"Hello?"

"I've been the primary caregiver, Char. I'm confident I could win custody."

"Yeah right. I'm the Mom. What judge is going to agree to you winning full custody? Don't turn me into the bad guy because you want to run away from us down to California." Charlotte slammed the shot glass down on the counter.

"It's not running away if I want you to come with me," shouted Adrien into the phone.

Charlotte heard him inhale deeply and exhale slowly, trying to calm himself down. "Come to Thanksgiving, Char, and we can go for a walk afterward and talk it all over in person."

Charlotte stepped outside and started gathering some firewood to calm herself down. If they went for a walk, at some point, the bastard would pull her into his jacket and wrap her up in a hug.

She would breathe in his clean smell and feel his muscles rippling under his shirt and look up into his smile and be lost to all reason. Adrien was accustomed to leveraging his charisma to get what he wanted. He could charm a baby out of its pacifier or an ego-inflated policeman into ripping up a speeding ticket.

What would happen if she got back together with her kids' beloved Dad, only to insist he move out a second time if he cheated again?

She was bitter enough; moving far from her family and friends and opening a new office in California was a huge ask. If she did it, and he cheated, what then? Who would she be beneath that resentment?

She couldn't face Adrien, or his ultimatum until she fortified herself mentally. She longed to be a family again, to curl up in front of a crackling fire, to swim together in the lake, to watch the sun splash its colors across the sky at sunset from the summit of a mountain. But protecting her kids was pivotal for Charlotte. She wouldn't chance asking Adrien to come home, only to watch her children suffer when he moved out again.

"I need time to think. I'll see you Sunday. Kiss my kids from their Mom."

She hung up the phone before he could respond.

CHAPTER 3

Jeremiah 17:7-8
7 "Blessed is the man who trusts in Yahweh,
and whose confidence is in Yahweh.
8 For he will be as a tree planted by the waters, who
spreads out its roots by the river,
and will not fear when heat comes,
but its leaf will be green,
and will not be concerned in the year of drought. It won't
cease from yielding fruit.

ON FRIDAY CHARLOTTE LET her regular morning routine
carry her to the pool room. Her mind worked the entire
swim over her dilemma. Should she try to put her marriage, and her family, back together again and move to
LA? Or should she proceed with a divorce and watch her
children suffer as their Dad transferred to another state?

Charlotte shivered, cold causing her teeth to chatter as she
made her way to the sauna, poured lavender oil into the
water bucket and poured the mixture onto the hot stones. The
scent and the steam did nothing to reduce the anxiety coiling
in her stomach, like a nest of baby snakes squirming in a knot.
There wasn't a real risk that the court would award him full
custody of her children if he moved to California, was there?

As Charlotte stood up to grab her cucumber-infused water,
nausea hit her hard. She ran naked from the sauna out into
the snow and threw up behind a tree.

A few minutes later, Charlotte stood up, white-faced. She was trembling from cold, and her feet had gone numb from standing barefoot in the powdery white. Charlotte headed back into the glass pool room and jumped in the pool. Her nausea had diminished. Her feet tingled as she fell onto the wooden bench in the sauna. A few minutes later, her stomach began rolling again, and she closed up the sauna and pool before running up the snowy steps towards her empty cabin.

After a quick shower, Charlotte opened up the medicine cabinet to take out the mouthwash, and there stood an unopened package of tampons. She couldn't remember when she had bought the box. She counted back, astounded at how fast the time had flown while being a single mom. There had been that night two months back when Adrien had dropped the kids home and stayed for dinner.

As if her situation wasn't complicated enough, now she would need to add in the possibility of being pregnant. It had been hard enough with a baby with Adrien's help.

How could she possibly balance two kids, a new baby, and her business? She would have to hire a nanny, she decided, as she juiced spinach, blueberries, raspberries, Swiss chard, and carrots together.

Or she could ask her Mom to give up her job and pay her to be the nanny instead. She was only a few years from retirement anyway. That would work, wouldn't it? Charlotte shook her head as if she could fling the unwelcome thoughts from her head. Her Mom loved her job.

Don't get ahead of yourself, Charlotte. There are plenty of reasons why you missed a few periods, like stress, over-exercising, or weight loss. Yes, she nodded her head. She had lost a bunch of weight recently, which confused her.

She hadn't changed anything in her disciplined schedule, but her waistbands were loose. The stress of being a single mom was obviously getting to her. Her reflection in the mirror even looked more haggard, with an off color.

Sighing, Charlotte promised herself that she wouldn't worry about babies, or Adrien and his ultimatum, until tomorrow. Today she would enjoy a break from worrying. Charlotte drove into town to her office. She only had two sessions this morning. The first hour went smoothly. At eight-thirty, Charlotte tried to connect with her new client Kayla, who was suffering from postpartum depression, to no avail. She called her mobile phone and house number. No one answered. Charlotte waited ten minutes and tried again. A disquiet was building within Charlotte. Her clients all prepaid for their sessions. If they didn't call twenty-four hours in advance to cancel the meeting, she didn't refund the money. Missing their counseling slot was like throwing money out the window, and from what Kayla had told her, money was very tight in their household. Charlotte dialed the emergency contact number.

Kayla's husband answered on the first ring.

"You've got Jefferson."

"Hello, I'm Charlotte Lynn. Your wife is missing a pre-paid therapy session with me. I'm worried. Could you drive home and check on your wife?"

"I'm a long-haul truck driver. I'm clear out in Nebraska, and Kayla's at home with the kids in Cali."

"Well, is there a neighbor or friend you can call to go over to check on your wife?"

"Sure, I can do that."

"Great. Could you or Kayla call me back to let me know she is okay? She can re-schedule her session with me free of charge."

"You don't think I need to call the police?"

Charlotte hesitated, reviewing the session she'd had with Kayla. Did her husband know something Charlotte didn't? Kayla hadn't once said anything that would red flag she was a danger to herself or others. In fact, Charlotte had complimented her on how well put together she looked for a woman with triplets. Kayla had smooth, shiny hair, pink cheeks and wore a beautiful shade of pink lipstick that matched her sweater during their Skype session.

Kayla had told her she was feeling depressed and it was difficult for her to feel connected to her three babies. She was just bone-crushingly tired. Charlotte had watched Kayla kiss and snuggle a triplet in each arm as she talked, which had been reassuring. Charlotte had told Kayla that she might be suffering from postpartum depression and recommended referring her to a psychiatrist who could prescribe anti-depressants. Kayla had insisted she didn't want the drugs going through her breast milk, and would prefer another session with Charlotte instead.

"Well," Charlotte said, a bit uncertain. "First you could try calling your wife again and sending the neighbors over to check on her. But if you don't hear from her within a few hours, then I would call the police. I always think it is wise to err on the side of caution."

"Sure thing, Charlotte. Thanks for the call."

By late morning Charlotte was feeling better, but she was missing her kids like a toothache that radiated through her whole body. If she couldn't be with them, then she would do something she couldn't easily do with them here: get in the car and just drive away.

Charlotte redialed Jefferson's number as she walked outside. It clicked to voicemail. Charlotte sighed. She couldn't count how many times clients had stopped therapy without explanation. It was hard not to take it hard. She always wondered what she could have done to get clients who still needed help to return to counseling.

She climbed into her eleven-year-old SUV, placed a hot coffee into the cup holder and put on Tchaikovsky's Violin Concerto in D Major. The roads were snow-covered until she hit the main road. Thirty minutes later Charlotte was passing Cascade Lake, having finished her coffee in time for the twisty road ahead. Driving the winding curves through the forest canyon required two hands on the wheel, but she had traveled the road enough times to be able to glance out the window.

The road ran parallel to the white water rapids of the Payette River. It was such a beautiful drive that Charlotte wondered why she didn't make the two-hour trip down to Boise more often. Then again, she didn't usually have a day all to herself. The drive would be a different experience with a six-year-old and a three-year-old in the backseat.

Charlotte smiled as the classical music rolled through the car. She clicked on her seat heater and opened the window, letting in a blast of icy, pine-scented air. Charlotte took a deep breath and a sense of well-being settled over her body at last, like a blanket warm from the dryer tucked in around a drowsy baby. If only she could shake the fatigue that had been plaguing her lately and the stabbing knife in her belly and back, she would feel vibrant.

Whenever she left the forests of Idaho, she missed the fresh air. It was deliciously addictive. Stepping out into a new morning and breathing in the delicious air was a reason she didn't want to move to LA. She wanted her children to have a childhood in the mountain air, hiking through pine trees and splashing in crystal clear lakes, not growing up in smog and sitting in traffic. Her mom would tell her to stop worrying and have faith. Charlotte could hear her mom's voice in her head, "It's never what you worry about, love. Don't worry over it, pray about it."

Yeah, well, what do you think about Adrien threatening to take the kids with him to LA half the year, God, huh? Charlotte tried to imagine living without her children half the year as she drove through Horseshoe Bend and began to ascend the steep grade up the hill.

To her surprise, Charlotte could. If she knew it would be the very best for them, she could let them go. If it would make them happy, enable them to thrive, develop resilience, and give them the ability to unfold into the most beautiful version of themselves, then she could live with the sorrow of separation.

But would living half the year in LA be the best for her kids? Should she consider moving with Adrien down to LA, to keep the family together? Should she file for divorce and the right to full custody?

As Charlotte drove on Highway 55 into Eagle, her anger flared. Well, at least two could play at the bribing kids game. She wasn't going to break her commitment to the one-present-on-Christmas rule. However, she was going to have that one present be huge. For Gabriel, she would buy the Playmobil knight castle with an entire army of knights with their weapons and horses for which he had been begging her for months.

She had said no because it would take up too much space in his tiny room. However, the truth was that she had read product reviews and was scared she wouldn't be able to put the thing together on her own. But maybe if she found a toy store in Boise, she could offer to pay someone there to put it together for her.

For her daughter, Charlotte would buy the piano Aurélie had been asking for ever since she started lessons. She had been uncertain where she could fit such a large piece of furniture. But they didn't need an entryway coat closet, did they? They could hang their jackets above the washing machine instead. Then there would be space in the tiny home for the piano in the front entry.

Usually, she turned left and headed into downtown Boise. But today she needed to find a piano store and a toy store. She needed to sit down and plan, and she needed another coffee. She turned right into Eagle and looked for a coffee shop or restaurant so she could strategize. As she took a left onto Eagle Road, she spied Joe Mama's Breakfast Eatery and pulled in.

A few minutes later she was relaxing in front of a steaming cup of coffee and had just ordered a ham and cheese omelet with avocado and red peppers when she heard a voice calling her name.

"Charlotte, you gorgeous thing, I thought that was you." Her heart began pumping, and her entire body went rigid as Elizabeth slid her arms around her and kissed her cheek before sitting down in the opposite chair.

Elizabeth slipped out of her black wool dress coat to reveal a royal blue silk dress tied with a red belt. Charlotte noticed the men around the restaurant glancing over. Charlotte wasn't surprised. Elizabeth had always invoked the same reaction in people as her brother did in women. Eyes gravitated to them in any crowd.

"Elizabeth, what are the chances of running into you?" she asked, forcing a smile.

Elizabeth's laughter bubbled over.

"I know, life is so strange," she said as she pushed her bouncy long blond hair over her shoulder and leaned forward, her blue eyes twinkling. "George is just running to the bakery to pick up some pies. I was going to bake them homemade. You know what terrific pies I make. But honestly, I am exhausted. It just wasn't possible. Do you want to know why? Are you ready?" Elizabeth paused for dramatic effect, then waved her hands out like the diva she was, and practically sang,

"I'm pregnant."

"Congratulations. I'm sure you will have a beautiful baby," said Charlotte. Her sister-in-law could drive her crazy, but her dramatics were entertaining.

"I know, right? I told George, 'honey, with your brains and my beauty, we should have, like ten kids. It's time to get started. We would be doing a disservice to the world otherwise.' I mean, hello? Our children will be amazing."

Charlotte winced. The pain in her back was acting up again. Her mouth had gone dry while Elizabeth talked a million miles an hour, per usual. She took a sip of her coffee and took a deep breath. But before she could answer, Elizabeth placed both arms on the table and lowered her voice. "Now I heard Adrien wants you back again. Hooray! You will be a family again. I am just giddy with the joy of it, honestly," gushed Elizabeth. "We all know kids from broken families grow up weird. Wait, why are you down here again?"

Charlotte didn't know where to start. Did Elizabeth know how offensive she was being and didn't care, or was she that stupid? Elizabeth knew Charlotte's Dad had walked out on them and they had never heard from him again. Charlotte was from a broken family.

Elizabeth also knew Charlotte had thrown Adrien out of the house after that night. It wasn't a matter of him wanting her back. It was the other way around, she seethed. And her kids were not going to grow up weird. After all, she wasn't weird. She was polished and educated and had her entire life running beautifully. Everything was fully under control.

Elizabeth hadn't noticed Charlotte's hurt silence.

"Were you down for some shopping then? I love the red trench coat by the way. Très chic darling. Although, how you can stand wearing the same clothes over and over for ten years, I don't know," exclaimed Elizabeth. Her laughter rang out, revealing her perfect white teeth. "Now what did you say you are doing in Boise?"

"I just drove down this morning for a day of shopping," commented Charlotte

"I just adore what a bright little morning bird you are," exclaimed Elizabeth, while reaching out and shaking Charlotte's shoulder. "Adrien always said you are up before the sun. Ah, here comes George. We better leave soon, or we'll miss Dad's stuffed mushrooms. We missed Thanksgiving, so we are going up today."

Elizabeth turned to see a tall man with wood glasses, curly brown hair, black jeans and a red V-neck sweater enter the restaurant. She smiled when she noticed his red sneakers. Charlotte liked Elizabeth much more for the fact that she was in love with a man like George. It wasn't that he was unattractive. He just wasn't particularly good-looking, either. Instead, George was intelligent with a kind heart and a wonderful sense of humor.

"What is my favorite sister-in-law doing here?" he asked, grinning from ear to ear. He pushed his glasses back up on his nose, his face clouding over. "You are still my sister-in-law, right?"

"Of course she is, George. They're getting back together again. I told you in the car. Honestly, don't you listen to anything I say?" asked Elizabeth, a pout forming on her red lips.

George gathered her into his arms. "Perhaps I just get distracted by your beauty, love," he said and gave a wink over Elizabeth's shoulder at Charlotte while swallowing a grin.

"Or perhaps you haven't stopped talked since you opened your eyes this morning."

"Adrien and I are not getting back together. Or, I don't know. Maybe. Probably not, though. Did you know Adrien says he is moving to LA? Would you want your new baby to grow up in LA instead of McCall? Well, would you?"

George released his wife and gently smoothed his hans down Charlotte's shoulders. He held onto her upper arms. He looked into her eyes.

"It sounds like you are going through a tough time. What

about coming down for a weekend with the kids? You could have a shopping day with Charlotte and leave the kids with me. What do you say?"

"I'm all right," answered Charlotte reactively, trying to shrug George away. He gripped her arms tighter.

"You can divorce Adrien, but please don't cut us out of your life. We love you. You're going through a tough time. Let us help."

All of a sudden tears started slipping down her cheeks. She was horrified. Everyone was staring at them. In the next instant, Elizabeth threw her arms around Charlotte, and she was engulfed in the citrus scent of her Chanel perfume. "You are falling apart, Charlotte. Of course you are. You must miss Adrien so much. Why didn't you call me?"

"I'm not having a breakdown," murmured Charlotte into a cloud of blonde hair in her face.

"He wants you back, Charlotte. Just call him, and he'll come home," whispered Elizabeth. "Everything will be as it was before."

"Eliza," reprimanded George. "You know it isn't a matter of Adrien wanting Charlotte back. How could you say something like that?"

Elizabeth took a step back, smoothing the hair out of her face. She looked down at her designer dress boots. "I know." Just then the waiter appeared with her omelet and a blueberry muffin. Charlotte wanted nothing more than to get away from all the eyes and ears taking in the scene.

"He cheated on her, not the other way around," said George to Elizabeth.

"It was just one night," insisted Elizabeth. "One mistake in fifteen years of marriage. Why throw away all those good years because of one mistake? And it didn't mean anything. It's not easy, you know," She tossed her hair and lifted her perfectly upturned nose. "He has women throwing themselves at him all the time."

"So what are you saying, that if you had a one-night stand, it wouldn't be a big deal?" asked George.

"Don't be ridiculous, George. I wouldn't ever do that. I know you would, like, never be able to get over it." "Exactly.

Then why should Charlotte?" he asked.

"We promised each other we wouldn't fight over this again," complained Elizabeth.

"You're stressing me. Stress is not good for the baby. I read it in an interview with Angelina Jolie."

"Yeah well, then try thinking before you open your mouth for a change," retorted George.

Both Elizabeth and Charlotte's mouths fell open. Charlotte had never heard George say anything other than supportive and loving words to Elizabeth in all the eleven years she had known them.

Elizabeth broke into tears. Charlotte froze in shock for a moment. She wanted to shove her sister-in-law and shout, 'yeah, why don't you think before you talk?' Instead, she opened her arms wide, and Elizabeth stood up from her chair and stepped into her embrace. Charlotte patted her on the back. You are a therapist, she told herself. Empathy flows up in you for patients who make far worse mistakes than snarky comments. You can handle this. She sighed, burying her face into Elizabeth's velvety coat and squeezing her tight.

What was it about a family that made you want to hug them and shake them all at the same time?

George waved a waiter over to the table. He asked for the bill and for Charlotte's breakfast to be boxed to go. "I'll pay the bill. You two can go to the car," George said with a wry smile. He kissed his wife on the cheek and patted her back.

Charlotte let out an inward sigh of relief. George was intuitive; he had probably caught her staring at the door.

"He's wrong you know. I think before I talk," admitted Elizabeth as they walked out the front door. "Which makes it worse."

"I know," replied Charlotte evenly.

"No," sobbed Elizabeth on her shoulder. "I can be a real you-know-what."

"No argument here," laughed Charlotte. "And I'm still waiting for an apology, you know." Charlotte pulled back and looked at Elizabeth with a smile. "Or you could just give me your designer purse, and we call it even."

Elizabeth opened the back door to her brand-new BMW

SUV and dumped the contents of her purse onto the seat. She held the bag out to Charlotte. "I'm sorry about what I said. I just want you to feel a part of our family again. And when he did what he did, he didn't just lose you; I lost you too. You haven't talked to us since you threw him out."

"I was kidding about the purse, Eliza."

"Lord, please help me," grumbled George as he approached them. He took off his glasses and rubbed a hand over his face.

"It isn't even lunchtime, and today has more drama than a high school before the prom. Here's your breakfast, Char."

"Well, take a break then, honey. Change of plans. You go and hit a round of golf before we drive up to McCall like you wanted to. I'm going to shop with Charlotte, and we'll drive up to my parents at two this afternoon."

George looked at his wife, to Charlotte, and back again. "Well, Charlotte?"

Charlotte shrugged. "Great."

"It's settled then," exclaimed Elizabeth. She threw her arms around her husband and gave him a hug. He smiled and lifted her chin to give her a kiss.

"Call me later," said George. He smiled at his wife before turning to Charlotte and giving her a hug goodbye.

Elizabeth took the Car keys out of Charlotte's hand the minute they stepped in front of the car. She insisted on driving. Charlotte was surprised at how happy she felt climbing into the car next to Elizabeth. She would appreciate Elizabeth's company. Her entire life she had never lived alone, and she wasn't accustomed to living a solitary life. Ever since Adrien moved out, loneliness had been slowly slithering its way up her spine.

Her sister was her best friend, but Élodie had been busy lately. Her mother would drop everything to spend time with her if Charlotte asked, but she had a full work schedule, and the remaining energy she had she poured into Gabriel and Aurélie. In the evening or on the weekends, her Mom was happy to curl up with a good book, hit the gym, and catch up with her church volunteer work.

Charlotte hadn't known how helpful Elizabeth would be on the shopping trip. Charlotte didn't need to worry about directions to the piano store or look up reviews. Elizabeth knew the best music store in town, and they found the perfect piano in under an hour. Her sister-in-law even negotiated a small price reduction on the piano, free transport to McCall, and a complimentary tuning session upon delivery.

Three toy stores later, they found the knight castle Charlotte wanted. The sales clerk insisted they didn't put toys together when Charlotte asked. But it only took Elizabeth a few minutes of flirting to convince the teenage clerk.

He agreed to put the castle together for them on his lunch break in exchange for bringing him back a free lunch from his favorite restaurant.

By noon Charlotte had the fully constructed knight castle in the trunk. Charlotte hated shopping and was ready to call it a day. Dizziness and fatigue were plaguing her, and the pain in her back had returned. There was no stopping Elizabeth, though. She dragged Charlotte into the discount clothing shop next to the toy store, and they went through the racks until they found Gabriel and Aurélie some adorable new school clothes. On the way out of town, Elizabeth drove them to a sushi restaurant.

"This place has the best sushi in the city," insisted Elizabeth as she stepped out of the SUV.

Charlotte stepped out of the car, but before she could take another step, the aching pain in her abdomen intensified, wrapping its way around to her back. The last thing she remembered was calling out to Elizabeth as she fell.

CHAPTER 4

Revelation 2:10
Don't be afraid of the things which you are about to suffer.
Behold, the devil is about to throw some of you into prison,
that you may be tested; and you will have oppression for
ten days. Be faithful to death, and I will give you the crown
of life.

*T*HE NEXT THING CHARLOTTE KNEW, she was staring up at a
bright blue sky with Elizabeth hovering over her face.

"Are you okay, Charlotte? What happened?"

Charlotte tried to move her head and cringed. Dizziness
crashed through her, making her nauseous. She rolled over
on the black pavement and threw up into a bush.

"I'm calling an ambulance," said Elizabeth. "Hold on, sweetheart. Everything is going to be okay."

"No ambulance. Eliza, just help me up."

Elizabeth helped Charlotte struggle to her feet. "I'm fine,
Eliza. I'm probably just coming down with the flu. I'm sorry
you are around me pregnant. I don't want you getting it too."

"Never mind that, Char. I'm taking you straight to the hospital. You should see yourself. You look like hell. Here. I'll
help you into the car."

Once they were in the car, Charlotte tried to talk Elizabeth
into driving straight home to McCall, but Elizabeth wouldn't
be swayed until Charlotte explained that her general practi-
tioner was a family friend.

She called and asked if he could see her as soon as they drove into town.

"I'll just call George and tell him I'm driving you up to McCall and taking you to the doctor's office. He can drive up behind us."

CHARLOTTE OPENED HER EYES two hours later when Elizabeth's car door crashed shut. She eyed the front of her doctor's office. Charlotte climbed out of the car and stretched.

"I feel much better, Eliza. You can go to your mama's for dinner," she said. She glanced at her watch. "It is only a quarter past three. You still have time to get there before they eat all the stuffed mushrooms." She smiled over at her sister-in-law.

George pulled into the parking lot and jumped out of the car. "Everything okay there, Charlotte?"

"I'll be fine. Just a bout of the flu. Thank you for driving me up, Elizabeth. I can drive myself home though."

"I don't know," began Elizabeth. "I can come back and drive you out to your place. Just call me."

"I'll be all right," smiled Charlotte. "Thank you for the help shopping. Hug my kids for me, okay?"

AFTER A SHORT WAIT in the front room, Charlotte sat on a paper-covered table, awaiting the arrival of Dr. Johnson. The paper rustled as Charlotte fidgeted. Could she be pregnant? Each pregnancy had caused nausea, weight loss, and fatigue.

"Hey there, Charlotte. How's my favorite therapist?"

"Hi, Dr. Johnson," she smiled at the short sixty-year-old man with thick black hair and kind brown eyes. "Thank you for coming in for me. Are you sleeping better?"

"You're the patient this time, Charlotte," he chuckled. "But yes, I fall asleep faster thanks to your sleep hypnosis download you gave me. I have to admit that I was skeptical at first. But I can't argue with the results. So, tell me why you're here instead of enjoying leftovers with your family."

"I was walking in the parking lot of a sushi restaurant in Boise, and dizziness hit me. I fainted. Once I regained consciousness, I threw up. I've had some pain in my abdomen and been feeling nauseous all day. It's probably just the flu. Unless I'm pregnant."

"Really? I'll send a nurse in, and we'll check your urine to see if a baby is causing your symptoms. He'll do a blood test too. I'll be back in a few minutes for your exam, okay?"

Charlotte nodded, and a few minutes later a nurse appeared with a cup and sent her to the bathroom. Charlotte handed her cup to the nurse and returned to the examination room. All of a sudden, the dizziness, fatigue, nausea, and loss of appetite gave her hope.

Charlotte closed her eyes, remembering the silky smooth feel of newborn Gabriel's skin as she snuggled him in her arms. Aurélie's feet pattered across the floor. She pulled herself up onto the couch, running a hand gently over her brother's back, kissing his cheek, cooing in his ear. Adrien threw the last branch on the fire and looked over his shoulder, a smile spreading across his face at the sight of his family nestled together. I want that, decided Charlotte. I want it all over again.

Dr. Johnson entered the room and shook his head. "You're not pregnant, Charlotte."

"Are you sure? I was almost certain I must be," said Charlotte while shaking her head. She began massaging her lower back as she talked. "Why else would I have those symptoms?"

"Does your back hurt you?" observed Dr. Johnson.

"Yeah, it's been bothering me for a long time now. I must have hurt it while carrying Gabriel around, or while swimming. I can't seem to shake it."

"Are you still swimming thirty minutes a day?"

"Yes," nodded Charlotte, placing her hand back in her lap and letting out a sigh, releasing the disappointment with a gush of air. A baby wouldn't fix her marriage, she told herself. It wouldn't put their family back together again.

Dr. Johnson stepped forward and proceeded to check her pulse rate, respiration, and blood pressure.

He pressed his fingers gently to her throat and above her

collarbone, checking her lymph nodes.

"Have you been trying to lose weight? I noticed from your chart that you've lost twelve pounds since the last time you were here three months back for strep throat."

"I've been eating the same as usual. I guess I've lost my appetite, though. Food hasn't been agreeing with me lately. I do make a vegetable and berry smoothie every morning, and that goes down well."

Dr. Johnson examined her eyes and ran his hands down her arms, turning her palms upward and looking at them as well. "How have you been feeling otherwise?"

"Extremely fatigued, even though I sleep eight hours a night. Stressed too, I guess. My abdomen balls up in pain quite often due to worry and anxiety. You know Adrien moved out."

"Can you lay down and reveal your abdomen please?"

Charlotte lay back, and Dr. Johnson began to palpate her stomach. "How intense is the pain on a range from one to ten?" he asked.

"I don't know. Five?"

"Says the woman who found childbirth fun," said Dr. Johnson, while taking out his stethoscope and applying it to Charlotte's abdomen.

At last, he straightened up and motioned for Charlotte to do the same. "I'd like to run some tests, Charlotte. I don't think you have the flu. You look as fit as ever. Your loss of appetite, nausea, fatigue, and the pain in your abdomen and back could all be related to the stress and heartache of being a single mom since Adrien left.

Then again, they could be symptoms of something more serious. I love you like family, Charlotte, and I don't want that to cloud my judgment. I'd like you to go to the hospital tomorrow morning for a CT scan just to be sure. I'll call over to the hospital and set up the appointment, okay?"

"Are you sure that's necessary? I don't want to pay for unnecessary tests."

"Do you want me to face your Mom if I don't go the extra mile for her little girl?"

"No," laughed Charlotte.

"Good. Now go home and eat some delicious food, if you

can, and curl up with a movie that makes you laugh. Don't eat anything in the morning to prepare for the CT scan. I'll talk to you tomorrow."

"Thanks, Dr. J," smiled Charlotte.

"You're welcome. Hug the kids for me."

ELIZABETH WAS WAITING in her car with George when Charlotte walked into the parking lot. They wanted to drive her home, but she insisted that she was fine; it had been a combination of low blood sugar and exhaustion that had caused her to faint and throw up.

"Then you will need some of Ma's home-cooked goodness," replied Elizabeth, while proudly pulling out a made-up plate of food for Charlotte to take back with her. She replaced the food on the front seat of Charlotte's car and took both of Charlotte's hands in her own. "Now, you go warm dinner up and eat every bite. You are getting too thin; you have to remember to eat, Char. And whatever happens between you and Adrien, promise me you will come down with the kids for a visit. Or we'll have another girl's day out."

Charlotte nodded, and Elizabeth threw her arms around her sister-in-law and gave her a hug.

"Drive safe now, Charlotte," said George as he opened the car door for his wife to climb in.

Charlotte got in her car and noticed that George was still standing beside his SUV, waiting to make sure she drove off safely. He gave a wave as she pulled out of the parking lot.

When Charlotte arrived home, she warmed up and ate her dinner while watching a comedy, as Dr. Johnson had instructed her.

But as soon as she spooned up the last bite of fluffy mashed potatoes, she pushed the pumpkin and apple pie away and climbed into the shower to warm up. Charlotte was shivering, despite the warm cabin. Seconds after her head hit the pillow, she was asleep.

She awoke at her usual time and immediately headed outside for her swim, like always, despite the fatigue weighing on her shoulders like a hundred-pound hiking pack. When she jumped into the pool the cold water gave her a temporary adrenaline kick, and she swam with her usual steady stroke for a little over ten minutes before she stood up again. She was too tired to do more. She did some easy breaststroke for ten more minutes, willing her body to cooperate.

After twenty minutes she gave up and climbed slowly out of the pool. When she stepped out of the sauna, she was dismayed when the usual inner wellness didn't flow through her like a serene river of crystal clear water.

She dressed in cozy black cotton tights, and a cream wool knit sweater dress. She tied a bright red and black geometric scarf around her neck in an intricate knot. A swipe of bright red lipstick to match her scarf and another coat of mascara, and she was ready for the day.

Yesterday had been an abnormality, she decided. A bit of indigestion, dizziness, and stomach pain were common afflictions. She was an athlete, she reasoned. Which of the triathletes she trained with in her summer club didn't have pain in their back like she did, or knee or hip problems? Dr. J was just overly cautious, and this morning would be a massive waste of time.

She sat down on the bench at the kitchen table as always. But instead of reaching for her Bible or song lyrics book, she pulled out her phone and entered her symptoms into WebMD. After a few minutes, she pushed her phone away and rested her head on the table. Self-diagnosis, she decided, was a dreadful idea. There was an entire list of different reasons suggested on WebMD as to why she had her combination of symptoms.

At eight Dr. Johnson called her and told her she had an appointment at nine. Charlotte prepared her fresh veggie and berry smoothie to drink after the CT scan and a chai tea latte and headed into town. The last way she wanted to spend her morning was in the hospital waiting room.

The minute after she signed in, she was led back for the CT scan. But she spent a long time after her scan waiting for Dr.

Johnson to call her back to review the results of the scan with her. She was thankful she had brought a travel mug with a hot chai tea latte inside and an engrossing book.

Charlotte was halfway through her new book by the time Dr. Johnson appeared. His smile didn't reach his eyes. Charlotte had spent innumerable hours watching patients over the years. Despite his light-hearted greeting and invitation to follow him back to a conference room, she wasn't fooled. She knew sadness when she saw it. Sometimes it was a curse to be intuitive to body language and emotional resonance.

As soon as the door shut behind him, she said, "It's bad news, isn't it, Dr. J?"

"Take a seat, Charlotte. Why don't we call someone to be here with you? I know your Mom and sister are on holiday in Hawaii for Thanksgiving, but what about your Elizabeth, or your mother-in-law?"

Charlotte fell back into her chair. There would only be one reason why Dr. Johnson would want someone to be here with her. "So it's that bad?"

"I would like you to have someone here," pleaded Dr. Johnson. "You will need the support." He settled into the chair next to her, leaning forward and resting his arms on the table.

"No. Just tell me. I want to process it on my own. Whatever it is."

Dr. Johnson abruptly stood up and hurried out of the room as he called, "Right, well then, actually, I just need to grab your chart."

He didn't walk out fast enough. Charlotte saw the tears threatening to escape. She burst into tears the minute the door whispered shut. Dr. Johnson was extremely professional. If he couldn't control his emotions, it meant something serious.

Charlotte didn't know how much time passed before the broad-shouldered doctor returned to the room. By the time he sat down next to her, she had stopped crying.

"Charlotte, the CT scan revealed a growth on your pancreas and liver that need to be checked out. It could be cancer. I've made some calls and arranged an appointment for this afternoon with the best oncologist in Boise. I've also called in a colleague to cover my practice for the day. With your permission, I'd like to drive you down to Boise and accompany you to your appointment."

"But I am fit. I eat super healthy. I don't smoke and rarely drink. Are you sure? I mean, sure, I have some pain, and I haven't been feeling well. But, you know, not terrible. Not like I have cancer," she said.

"To see you sitting there, perfectly put together with pink cheeks and your veggie smoothie," he paused, to motion at the green glass bottle of juice she had yet to drink on the table in front of her, "those are my thoughts exactly. That is what I thought last night, and I ordered the CT scan because your eyes are ever-so-slightly tinged yellow with jaundice. Then your blood test came back this morning showing a raised level of the pancreatic enzyme amylase. And the CT scan clearly shows masses growing on your pancreas and liver. That's why I want to head down immediately to a specialist. He was planning on spending the day on the golf course, but we are childhood friends, and he agreed to come in this afternoon. I know what a shock this must be, how terrifying."

That was exactly it, thought Charlotte. She was terrified. She wanted to throw herself into his arms and cry. "I have two questions," she said in a smooth voice.

"Go ahead," nodded Dr. Johnson.

"When do we leave? And can we pick up some fancy coffees before we go?"

Dr. Johnson laughed, then rubbed his forehead with one hand. He took a deep breath and looked up at her again.

"I'll buy you the fanciest coffee they have in that coffee shop, Charlotte."

ON THE DRIVE DOWN to Boise, Charlotte quizzed Dr. Johnson about his wife, four children, and seven grandchildren. They discussed politics, the new skiing season, and complained together about the increasing number of ill-mannered tourists to their resort town. As Dr. Johnson drove toward downtown Boise and St. Luke's Hospital, he asked, "how long have you been suffering from the pain, fatigue, and nausea?"

Charlotte let out a sigh and looked out the window at the

foothills and mountains rising above downtown Boise. How long had it been? She thought back.

"A few months? I swim six days a week, but I've been swimming slower and slower. The fatigue has been impacting my endurance. I've had an irritable stomach for months now too, but I attributed it to stress. It's only lately that the pain in my abdomen and back have plagued me. And this relentless sense of unease in my body. I'm used to settling down at my kitchen table with a coffee each morning, after a swim and a sauna session, and experiencing a sense of wellness radiating throughout my entire body. Lately, I've sat there trying to ignore the pain from my clenched abdomen and in my back. I attributed it all to stress, took some pain reliever, and tried to forget about it. I thought, if I gave it time, it would just go away."

A MUSCULAR, FIT MAN with shaggy brown hair and laugh lines around his eyes entered the room. He wore a white doctor's coat over a gold shirt. He shook Charlotte's hand before clapping a hand on Dr. Johnson's back.

"Hello, Ms. Lynn. My name is Dr. Brenson," he said in a soft, deliberate voice. He pulled a chair over to sit in front of Charlotte. "I have reviewed your results. It grieves me to tell you that Dr. Johnson was correct. You have stage four pancreatic cancer with liver metastasis. I'm sorry to say it isn't operable. Apart from chemotherapy, there is nothing else we can do."

Charlotte let out an uncontrollable cry and quickly covered her mouth with her hand, her breath caught in her throat. Dr. Johnson patted her back as silence descended, cold and quiet, over the room. Charlotte rounded forward, staring down at her empty palms in her lap. She took a shuddering breath. And then another. After a few moments, she straightened up and brought a shaky hand to her forehead.

"The cancer isn't operable? So how long will I live?" she asked in a voice so quiet that both doctors instinctively leaned forward to hear her.

"The average is not the point here. You are not a statistic,

Ms. Lynn. What I want to focus on now is beginning the optimal treatment plan for you to achieve the best quantity and quality of life possible."

Charlotte looked into the hazel eyes of Dr. Benson. There was compassion in his eyes. It helped smooth her ragged breathing that Dr. Benson wasn't placing a barrier between them with statistics, but she needed to know.

"Please tell me what the average for my case is. You know I will look it up afterward on the internet anyway. It is best if I hear it from a specialist who knows my case."

"The median length is between two and six months," answered Dr. Benson. "The five-year survival rate of stage four pancreatic cancer is about one percent. There is a significant difference between two months and five years though."

Yeah, thought Charlotte. The difference between Gabriel being eight instead of three and Aurélie being eleven instead of six. Five years was all the difference in the world.

"I want you to accept the possibility of leaving us in two months, but retain the hope that you could be here in five years," continued Dr. Benson. "If you want to fight this cancer, I am going to do everything possible to extend your life as long as possible."

"I can't believe this," she stammered. "How could this happen?"

"Would you like to hear your options now in an information session, or would you like to make another appointment when you can have a family member with you?" asked Dr. Benson in a gentle tone.

Charlotte stared unblinkingly at Dr. Benson for a moment before answering. She looked over at Dr. Johnson, and he reached over and held her hand. Dr. Benson patiently endured the silence cloaking the room, maintaining eye contact with her.

"I'd like to bring my Mom with me, next time. I'd, I'd like to wait," stammered Charlotte.

AS THEY WALKED BACK OUT into the sunlight, Charlotte was praying. She gazed at the leaves in hues of red, orange, and yellow on the trees along the street, at the dusting of snow on the mountains rising above Boise, like powdered sugar on a cake.

"What did you think of Dr. Benson? It won't hurt my feelings if you want to meet with another doctor and get a second opinion, or if you just weren't comfortable with this oncologist."

"What?" Charlotte looked over at Dr. Johnson as they approached his car, pulling her focus back to the man beside her. "I liked him. What are his experience and reputation?"

"He has thirty-two years of experience in oncology."

Charlotte was quiet in the car on the drive back up to McCall, retreating inward. She slipped out of her boots and pulled her knees to her chest, wrapping her arms around them. Dr. Johnson turned on some jazz music and drove in silence, frequently glancing over at her, as if to be sure she was still breathing as they turned yet another bend next to the crashing white of the river next to the road. Charlotte startled when her phone rang. It was Adrien.

"Where are you?"

"Why?" Charlotte's thoughts and pulse began to race. Was she supposed to pick up the kids today? Were they waiting for her?

"We are at the cabin, and you're not here. The kids and I wanted to bring you a surprise."

Charlotte's spirits lifted. She wanted nothing more at that moment than to curl up with her children under a blanket by a roaring fire. She had an urge to tell Adrien about her diagnosis, to rest her head against his broad chest as he wrapped his arms around her, and to have his strength and love melt through the fear that had locked her inside a solid wall of ice. She was freezing.

"Why would you assume I would be at home today?"

"Who would you be with, Char?" laughed Adrien. "We went to your office, and you weren't there, and your Ma and sister are still in Hawaii."

Charlotte rubbed her forehead.

He made her sound unsocial or something. She had plenty of friends and colleagues in town and all over the country with whom she kept in contact.

"Listen, we're in the cabin. I used the hidden key. What time will you be here?"

Charlotte sighed and dropped her head down onto her knees. Should she ask them to go back to the condo? She didn't know. Part of her wanted to process the news she had received today alone. Another slice of her wanted to cocoon herself in the warmth of her family. If only her mother and sister were in town, then she would have somewhere to run.

"Charlotte? Are you still there?" asked Adrien, his voice betraying his nervousness.

"No. Tell the kids I will be home in about half an hour," she answered and hung up before he could respond.

Charlotte stared out the window. Should she tell Adrien about her diagnosis? Was it fair to ask Adrien to come home, now that she would need his help? A grimace came to her face, and she shook her head. She had made up her mind.

"Dr. J? Could you do something for me?"

"What is it, Charlotte?"

"Please keep my cancer diagnosis a secret. I don't want anyone to find out. Not even Mom and Élodie, okay?"

Dr. Johnson didn't answer immediately.

He let out a huge sigh and continued in a soothing voice, "I will respect your wishes, of course. I want you to know, though, how important social support is when facing a cancer diagnosis. Numerous studies have revealed how essential emotional support is in facilitating the psychological adjustment to cancer. Telling the people who love you will provide love, support, and higher well-being, not to mention the practical help you will need with the kids when you aren't feeling well."

Charlotte didn't answer him. After a moment he cleared his throat and began tapping his fingers on the steering wheel in agitation. "Look, don't you think they will notice the change in you, especially after the chemotherapy? I thought you wanted to bring your Mom to the next appointment."

Charlotte still didn't say anything, but she reached out a hand and rubbed Dr. Johnson's shoulder. "I know this must be hard for you, to diagnose the little girl who grew up next to you with cancer, Dr. J. Your wife and my Mom have been best friends since kindergarten. I know you must be in shock too. I am so unbelievably grateful you drove me down to Boise today."

She took a deep breath, and let it out, willing the tears brimming behind her eyes not to slip down her cheeks. "The kids have had a hard enough time adjusting to our separation. The last thing they need is more upsetting news and change. I just want Christmas to be as normal and happy for them as possible. It's only four weeks away."

She paused, searching her heart. There was something more. She was fumbling around in the dark, trying to make sense of her feelings in the fog of her worry and fear.

"You don't need to be stoic, Charlotte. You can lean on the people who love you at a time like this. They would want to be there for you."

"Yes. That's it, Dr. J. I want to be stoic. Don't we all, when put in a terrible situation, want to be the one described as stoic and uncomplaining? Only I hold no illusions about myself. If everyone knows, I don't think I will be able to be strong. I think I'll fall apart and give up trying to live as normally as possible. Telling my family won't provide me with the strength I need to be the best Mom, under the circumstances, that I can.

If no one knows, then I have to pretend everything is close to how it was before, when I was healthy. As I said, I don't want the kids to worry about their Mom being ill, at least until we share a magical Christmas together."

"You don't want to push your body too hard, either, Charlotte. You can't pretend this away," warned Dr. Johnson as they pulled into the parking lot of his doctor's office. "I know it's normal not to be able to accept the truth of a stage four cancer diagnosis."

"I'm not in denial. I am going to go through all the information that Dr. Benson sent home with me and start on his recommended chemotherapy as soon as possible. I'm going to fight this, Dr. J. I have two little kids at home who need their mama. But I want to make sure that it is balanced with quality of life, too: for my children and me. Just in case I have two months and not five years, then I don't want to spend that time in a hospital away from them."

"Oh, God, please help me. Your mother will never forgive me when she finds out I kept it from her."

"Well then, she won't ever find out. I'll tell her I was diagnosed in Boise, by Dr. Benson, which is true. Now, don't let today interfere with your sleep, Doc," she said and managed a wan smile. "We just got you sleeping better for the first time in months." She kissed his cheek and jumped out of his car, and didn't look back as she drove away in her SUV toward home.

CHARLOTTE TURNED THE LAST BEND in the road and pulled into her driveway. She took a deep breath and checked her reflection in the mirror. Charlotte took out a lipstick and rubbed a bit of it on both of her cheeks before adding moisturizer to give her a more vibrant glow. Once her lips were a matching shade of pink, she stepped out of the car and made her way to the front door. Charlotte paused before opening the front door. All she wanted to do was to take a quick hot shower and crawl into bed.

The door sprang open, and her kids stood jumping up and down before her with huge grins on their faces. She couldn't help but smile back, despite how her heart ached in her chest.

"Mommy, come and see! What took you so long?" yelled Aurélie.

"I helped too, Mommy," insisted Gabriel, while lifting his arms up to be picked up. Charlotte swept him up in her arms and hugged him tightly. Tears threatened to spill over as soon as his soft cheek pressed to hers.

Aurélie tugged at her jacket. "What took you so long Mom? We've been waiting for ages. Come on, come look."

Charlotte kicked off her boots, hung up her jacket, and followed her daughter through the immaculate white kitchen into the living room. When she entered the room a grin lit up Adrien's entire face, and he threw out his arms, "Well, what do you think?"

Adrien was relaxing by the window in one of two modern

eggshell-shaped chairs the blue of a robin's egg, his legs crossed on a matching footstool.

Gabriel squiggled in her embrace to be put down as Aurélie jumped up and down, yelling, "Do you love it, Mom? Well? Do you?"

Charlotte's eyes traveled the room. She gasped, taking in the new light, soft gray modern sofa with throw pillows the same shade of robin eggshell blue as the two new chairs directly opposite of it. A new circular table in bright white stood in the center of the furniture grouping, with a pale green vase filled haphazardly with pink and red roses. Charlotte slowly sat down on the sofa, rubbing her hand along the seat cushion. She picked up one of the cushions and hugged it to her chest, resting her cheek against the fabric. It was as soft as a newborn baby's cheek.

"Look at these, Mommy," announced Aurélie. She unrolled a blanket with a pale blue and gray herringbone design and jumped up on the sofa to place it around her mom. "Isn't it soft, Mommy? Feel," she insisted while jumping up and down next to her on the sofa.

"The throw pillows and two blankets are made of cashmere," announced Adrien proudly. "Cindy at Mountain House assured me that it is the softest, warmest material there is. Do you love it?"

Charlotte leaned back, strangely empty of emotion. You are in shock, she realized. It's just too much to be surprised with in one day. She closed her eyes and took a deep breath.

"What's wrong, Char?" asked Adrien. "If you hate it, I can return it tomorrow. It's all worked out with Cindy. She can come and pick it up first thing in the morning for a full refund, and you can go through her catalog and pick out your favorite design yourself. It was the window display."

A smile came to Charlotte's lips, and she opened her eyes, taking in her remodeled living room. A warmth expanded across her chest; an inner glow was emanating from her heart and dispersing through her body. "No, I love it all. I was just overwhelmed. It is the living room I have always wanted."

Adrien high-fived the children, "We did great work, team," he said and threw them over his shoulder. Their squeals of joy filled the room. He set the children down on the couch and walked to the kitchen. "I've been working a second job as a bartender during the week at the Shore Lodge, and my parents helped me out too," he answered as he stood up and crossed the small space to the kitchen, where he opened the fridge. He smoothed his shirt down and pushed his hair out of his eyes. He took out a bottle of champagne as he smiled at her from across the room.

"How did you know this is what I wanted?" asked Charlotte, still a bit breathless.

"I picked it out, Mommy," declared Aurélie, while standing up to her full height and then doing a twirl.

She ran to her school bag, pulled out a crumpled paper, and held it out to Charlotte.

Charlotte smoothed the paper out on her knees. It was a photo she had pulled out of an Architectural Design magazine with the furniture grouping, only in a cavernous white floored modern house in Switzerland with views of rolling vineyards, Lake Geneva, and the Alps sparkling white in the distance. She had used it as her bookmark for more than a year. Adrien popped the champagne bottle and filled two flutes. He took out a second bottle of sparkling apple cider and filled two plastic wine glasses for the kids. He brought the drinks to the coffee table, handed Charlotte one, and sat down next to her on the sofa.

"I know you hated that cold leather sofa. So I decided to surprise you with one that you would love instead," said Adrien.

"Watch Mommy," called Gabriel, who was being turned in one of the blue chairs around and around in circles by his sister. "It's like a merry-go-round. Cool huh?"

"They swivel so you can curl up in the sunshine with your book and look out at the lake," clarified Adrien. "When company comes over, you can turn them back forward to face the sofa and fire."

"Thank you. I love it," said Charlotte. She took a sip of champagne, letting the bubbles dance in her mouth.

"Okay kids, time to go home," announced Adrien. "It's time to go get ready for bed."

"But Daddy, we are home," insisted Aurélie. "I'm tired. I don't want to get in the cold car."

"I want to stay with Mommy," announced Gabriel.

He ran across the room and flung himself in Charlotte's lap, almost causing her to spill her champagne on the new couch.

Charlotte drank down the rest of her glass and handed it to Adrien. She wrapped Gabriel up in the blanket with her, resting her cheek on the top of his head. She didn't want the kids leaving either.

"You can leave them here with me," she said.

"I want to be with them Char. It's my day," answered Adrien in a soft voice. "I know you hate being away from them. But I need my time with them too."

"Then stay too," she answered. The words were out of her mouth before she realized what she was saying. Perhaps it was due to the champagne on an empty stomach, or the extravagant surprise present he had just given her that caused her to ask him to stay the night. Or it could be that the word cancer was reverberating through her head. More than anything, she wanted to fall asleep tonight knowing her kids were sleeping peacefully upstairs, with strong arms wrapped around her.

"What does that mean, Char?" Adrien wrapped an arm around her.

Aurélie placed her glass down on the coffee table before climbing onto Adrien's lap.

Charlotte didn't answer him. She rested her head on his shoulder and watched the flames flickering the fireplace. Snuggled up together on the couch, she listened to Aurélie chatter about her day. Within minutes the warmth of the blanket and the fire permeated her weary body. Her eyes slid closed, and she felt herself slipping away into the sweet oblivion of slumber.

She only half awoke when Adrien's strong arms slipped beneath her and picked her up. He carried her to bed and tucked her in under the duvet in her sweater dress, but carefully pulled off her geometric scarf.

Charlotte wondered in half-sleep if she should shift out of her tights and pull off her dress, but she before she could summon the willpower, she was pulled back down into a deep sleep.

CHARLOTTE AWOKE NOT TO the usual ringing of the alarm on her phone, but to the smell of cinnamon and cardamom spiced tea and Adrien's voice calling her name softly in the dark. Adrien clicked on the lamp on the nightstand and sat down next to her, holding out a cup of her favorite tea. He was wearing only his red boxer shorts, and Charlotte drank in the sight of his defined stomach and muscular shoulders as if he were a glass of frosty lemonade and she had spent the entire day walking through hundred-degree heat.

"Good morning, beautiful," he said. "You slept ten hours. You fell asleep even before the kids went into the bath last night."

She sat up abruptly, the events of the previous day crashing into her consciousness like a mallet hitting a bell. Her ears were ringing and her head reverberating with the reality that one, she had stage four cancer, and two, Adrien had arranged the most thoughtful present of their entire relationship yesterday.

"Relax, Charlotte. I woke you up a half hour earlier than you usually wake up, so we can talk before the kids run down the stairs. I know better than to come between you and your morning routine," he chuckled.

"I can't believe you are up this early," she managed to say. She pulled up her pillow, relaxed back into the cozy warmth of her bed, and took a sip of tea.

"I can't believe I am up this early, but it is amazing what one will do to win back the woman he loves," he said and climbed into the bed next to her. He pulled the flannel duvet up to his chin. "I love you and the kids," he stated while staring up at the ceiling. "I want to come home. I want to be a family again."

"I want that too."

Her gaze met his, and something inside her shifted. He could be as stubborn as she was. She hadn't married a pushover, that was for certain. The problem was, her will and determination were an even match for his. It had led to more than one fight in their relationship. She had wanted to stay in Michigan and take on an assistant professorship while working on her Ph.D. It was Adrien who had insisted she marry him and move back home. He had argued that she would be happiest the sooner she was close to her family. Now she couldn't imagine her kids not growing up in McCall, surrounded by the love of her Mom, her sister, her in-laws.

During the Christmas trip home for the holidays, they had driven out to the tiny cabin on the lake she had inherited. Hand in hand they wandered down to look at its private beach and dock.

"It's a once in a lifetime chance," Adrien had said. "We can raise our family here, where they can swim, hike, ski, skate, and be close to our families." She had still hesitated, thinking of how much she would enjoy being a professor when her Ph.D. was complete, and the rewards of working in research and teaching, instead of in counseling.

She couldn't do research and be a professor of psychology in little McCall, Idaho. To tilt the scale in his favor, Adrien piled on one more incentive: he promised to build her an endless river indoor swimming pool and sauna in their yard overlooking the lake.

It was ironic that the positions had changed one hundred and eighty degrees, and now she was trying to impress upon him how wonderful it was to live close to supportive family, in a safe, charming resort town where the kids were constantly out in the beauty of nature. He was the one insisting on moving to a city for his career. She hadn't seen this one coming. Then again, she decided, she hadn't seen the infidelity or the cancer coming either. She had repressed all warning signs.

"I have to take this chance, Charlotte. There isn't anything here for me," he argued. He sat up and rested his back against the bed board, his bare arm touching hers.

"Your family is here," she retorted, her pulse rate beating a staccato in her chest. She turned to look him in the eye. "Why aren't we enough for you?"

"Come on, Char, you know that's not fair," he answered. He reached out and traced her cheek with his rough fingers. "You wouldn't want to give up your job, would you? You don't have to. You have both a profession and a family."

He buried his unshaven face into her neck and kissed her. "Let's wait a year, and then you can go anywhere you want," she offered. "Just not now. It is too soon, too sudden. I can't just pack up so many things and take off for California."

"They insist I need to be at work by January 5th, Charlotte. I already think that is considerate. I mean, it is more than a month from now."

"I can't go, Adrien. I can't go for at least six months, even if I wanted to," she responded. Weariness flooded her system.

"Why?" asked Adrien, slumping back onto the bed and staring up at the ceiling.

Charlotte considered telling Adrien about her diagnosis. She looked down at his unshaven face and placed the empty cup of tea on the nightstand table and couldn't bear to tell him. Charlotte didn't want him coming home again because she was sick, but because he loved her and would do anything to make their family whole again.

She snuggled down and placed her head on his chest, breathing in his clean scent and said, "You could start your own business."

"Start my own business?"

"Just think about it," pleaded Charlotte before leaving the room. She slipped into her boots at the back door and ran through the snow to the pool room. By the time Charlotte returned with steaming skin to the tiny cabin, Adrien was on his way out the door, to go cross-country skiing in Ponderosa Park.

"Hey there honey," he whispered and gave a wave. "I'll be back in an hour to cook us up a big breakfast."

"Oh, so not cereal with sugar stars?" she asked with raised eyebrows. "Do you know how much sugar is in cereal like that? Better you just feed them a piece of cake. At least they will understand that you are giving them dessert for breakfast," she lectured.

"I won't buy the star cereal," he replied, with a grin. "I'll purchase the one with rainbow marshmallows in it instead."

"Adrien," she growled.

"Come on, lady, you know I'm playing with you. No more sugar cereal, General," he said, as he saluted her on his way out the door.

After he had left, Charlotte took extra care with her makeup and hair before settling down with a cup of coffee at the kitchen nook. She opened her Bible and journal and took up her pen. Five minutes later she gave up. Who could concentrate when they just found out they had stage four cancer? She grabbed her Mac laptop and began searching the internet to find out as much as she could about stage four pancreatic cancer. It couldn't be as bad as the statistics made out. There had to be hope. Perhaps somewhere in the country, they had a new effective treatment?

After reading an enormous amount of general information, she stumbled onto a section of a website with the personal stories of patients. She became quickly addicted to the pancreatic cancer survivor stories, which gave her something she needed more than anything else this morning. Hope. The cancer survivor stories all included the therapy process through which the patient had gone. Charlotte tore out a piece of her notebook and began to take notes. If these treatments worked for Roger, Cassandra, and Peter, why couldn't they heal her too?

Charlotte scoured the internet for more patient stories and found another site about pancreatic cancer. Only this website included the stories of people who had fallen prey to the ravages of the disease and died. Tears slid down her cheeks as she read the accounts by husbands and wives, daughters and sons. Each detailed the fight their love ones waged against cancer to survive, and how they died despite their best efforts.

More than anything, Charlotte wanted to close out the page and find another website filled with stories of pancreatic cancer survivors, but she couldn't will herself to click away from the site, like spectators at the scene of a gruesome car wreck. On Monday I'll face this head-on in the first meeting, she thought. Do I want to drive down to Boise and discuss treatment options alone?

"Mommy, why are you crying?" asked Gabriel.

Charlotte jumped. She hadn't heard her son descend the

stairs and walk up to her. He climbed up next to her on the bench and put a small hand on her cheek. Charlotte took his hand in hers and then swooped him up. She carried him to one of the new chairs and wrapped him up in the soft cashmere blanket. "I was just reading a sad story, honey, that's all."

Gabriel's eyes were already closing again. Charlotte enjoyed the comforting weight of him in her arms and swiveled the chair around to watch the sun coming up over the lake. She swallowed back tears and forced herself to take deep, slow breaths and exhale twice as slowly as her inhalations. She took a shuddering breath and closed her eyes. Tears burned the backs of her eyes, slipping silently down her cheeks despite her best efforts to hold them in.

What was she going to do?

Why Lord? Why me? Can't you send this affliction onto some evil man somewhere who is rotting in jail for being a serial killer, instead of to me? Charlotte opened her eyes and paused internally. She knew life didn't work like that.

I'm scared, God. Help me through this okay? Help me fight this with every ounce of strength, so Aurélie and Gabriel don't grow up without their Mom. Or at least give me the five years.

An inner serenity washed through her. Her soul was at peace since the first time she heard the words stage four pancreatic cancer. If she had learned anything from the cancer survivor stories, it was that you needed to have hope and faith that healing was possible. And, she decided grimly, she would rather die with faith and hope than in despair and terror.

A grim smile came to her lips. Easier said than done. It sure would be nice about now to be one of those people with unwavering faith in God and his plan, she thought. She'd gone to church every Sunday her entire life, she prayed every day, and yet still she was far from being one of those people other would call 'religious.'

She could get behind the repercussions of free-will and its potentially evil consequences. But what about natural disasters, disease, and famine? Sometimes Charlotte could sense the throbbing suffering of millions of people spread out across the world. She shook her head and leaned it back on the chair. Careful not to wake her son as she stood up, Charlotte grabbed her Kindle and settled back down again, tucking the blue blanket around her son's feet. She searched the store for grief and came across Man's Search for Meaning, by Viktor Frankl, and began re-reading the book.

When Aurélie bounded down the stairs and threw herself into the chair next to her, it was if she had taken a sip of champagne and bubbles of hope were lifting her spirits. It could be worse, she thought to herself. You have these gorgeous children, and they're healthy. She sent up a prayer of thanks. Better me than them God. Thank you.

"Would you like to watch cartoons?" asked Charlotte.

"Really? Before breakfast?" asked Aurélie, bouncing on the chair.

"Sure. Daddy will be back soon. He's making breakfast," she smiled.

"Okay, but I want my story still," insisted Aurélie, holding out Miss Rumphius.

"That's one of my favorites," said Charlotte, as Aurélie squeezed onto the chair next to her. I am going to savor every moment of today with these beautiful children, she promised herself. She opened the book and began to read.

A FEW HOURS LATER, Charlotte lay curled up on the sofa with a cup of hot tea, reading Man's Search for Meaning while her children played. Adrien sat across from her drinking coffee and reading the newspaper.

"Daddy, I want something new to play. I want the marble tracks," declared Aurélie.

"Then clean up your fairy Lego castle first," he muttered, distracted by his paper.

"I don't want to put it away. I just built it. I want to play with it again afterward," insisted Aurélie, stamping her foot.

"You know the rules, Aurélie. One thing down at a time. You can put the castle away carefully in the box, and it won't break. We can take it back down again after you are bored building with the marble tracks," replied Adrien.

Aurélie began to whine, and Charlotte put down her book. Her head was pounding. "Come on Adrien, is it going to kill you to have the cabin be a bit of a mess for just one afternoon? Let her keep her castle down."

Adrien glared at Charlotte. "It is not about making a mess. I was inspired to do it this way after reading about the Montessori method.

The kids are happier if they are guided to choose one thing to play at a time and only have that one toy set out. I have a multitude of carefully selected Montessori learning toys and tools."

"Well, she doesn't look happy to me," argued Charlotte.

"She is a child. They don't always know what will make them happy," Adrien insisted. "Look," he opened the closets of the shelf and waved his hand as if he were showcasing a Ferrari. "So many educational options from which to choose. The kids never complain about being bored, but if they do, we do something outside, and they happily return and settle down playing again. How have you not noticed since I've been gone?"

Charlotte shrugged. She had just taken down whatever the kids wanted and cleaned it all up again after dinner every night. Adrien helped Aurélie put away her Lego castle into a box, placed the lid on top, and lifted it back up onto the top of the shelf.

"It's a good idea," announced Adrien.

"What?" Charlotte could feel her stomach rolling like she had swallowed a large glass of slimy slugs. She had battled nausea all morning. Charlotte decided the big breakfast was a bad idea. She did much better when she stuck to espresso and her veggie berry smoothies.

"Opening a business. I'm considering it, Char. I've had an idea rattling around in my head for awhile now. I guess I was just too afraid to go for it, let alone say it out loud."

"Mom, I'm waiting," yelled Aurélie.

"Well you have to tell me now," insisted Charlotte.

"A survival trip agency."

"A what?"

"So, people would pay me to take them into the wilderness, and I would teach them how to survive without anything but a few tools and the clothes on their backs," answered Adrien, beginning to pace and gesture. "You have no idea how many people out there want to unplug from the modern world. They want a David Thoreau experience. To know that they can survive with the bare minimum. I was talking about the idea in the bar the other night with the guys, and they all agreed it was a genius idea."

Charlotte walked back into the living room. She took a few deep breaths, and then reached up and took down the marble track box and placed it on the floor.

"I think it's a brilliant concept too," said Charlotte. "We should start by doing some research."

"No," answered Adrien. He ran his hand through his hair and shook his head. "Listen, no offense Char, but I want to do this on my own. You need to let me build this without your help. Can you do that?"

Aurélie threw one of the ramps across the room when the marble didn't roll down the ramps and into the cup as she had planned. The wooden block smashed into her teacup, knocking the contents onto the floor.

"Aurélie!" yelled Charlotte. "What are you doing? What's wrong with you?"

Adrien and the kids stared at her in surprise. Charlotte took a deep breath. Nausea and pain were fraying her nerves.

"Sorry, sweetheart," Charlotte said while settling down onto the floor next to her daughter and wrapping her arms around her daughter, kissing her tear-stained face.

Adrien joined them on the floor. "Are you frustrated it doesn't work?" he asked. "It is a challenging game. I'm proud of you that you could concentrate on it for over twenty minutes. We can figure out together what went wrong here, and then if you want, I can help you build it again? It's a hard game love, don't feel bad."

"Go on Aurélie, give it a try," added Charlotte.

"Me too," insisted Gabriel, who jumped up from playing with his cars to join Aurélie.

Twenty minutes later Adrien had rebuilt the tower with the

kids. Aurélie took a marble and placed it on the track and Gabriel did as well. The marbles rolled down two wooden ramps, through a tunnel of chimes, and back and forth along various ramps. All of a sudden the marbles shot off the track and went rolling across the room, instead of going into the turn and falling into the end basket. Adrien cursed and ran his hands through his hair.

"No! What did I do wrong here? We need to build it again so that it works this time," insisted Adrien.

"I don't want to," insisted Aurélie.

"I want to paint, Mom, can I?"

Charlotte nodded, and Aurélie went to the shelf, opened the doors and took out a box of painting supplies and carried it to the kitchen table.

Adrien turned to Gabriel. "Knock it all down, buddy, so that we can start all over. You can be my assistant builder."

"Oh no," Adrien snapped his fingers. "I forgot about Aurélie's ice-skating lesson. It starts in thirty minutes."

"What ice-skating lesson?"

"I signed her up for ice-skating lessons. Everyone into the car. Let's go. I have her bag already packed in the trunk. We need to shake a leg if we want to get her to the rink in time for her lesson," he said.

Charlotte pulled Adrien into their bedroom. "I've reconsidered," she whispered. "I'm not ready for you to move back home," said Charlotte. "Not quite yet. Just give me three weeks."

"Wait, what?" exclaimed Adrien. "Is this about not wanting your help with the new business?"

"It's just a lot to take in. Just three more weeks, Adrien, and then you can come home for Christmas if you still want to. I'll meet you for pizza like usual Friday night to trade off the kids," Charlotte added and left the room.

She knew the real reason she was pushing Adrien away. She wasn't ready to tell him about the cancer. The question was: how long could she keep it a secret?

CHAPTER 5

CHARLOTTE WATCHED HER DAUGHTER glide over the ice. The teacher showed Aurélie how to complete a turn, and Aurélie gave it a try. Seemingly effortlessly, she completed her first three-hundred-and-sixty-degree turn. Her smile spread from ear to ear, and her eyes traveled the stands, searching for her Mom. She waved at Charlotte, and Charlotte waved back, her face lit up with shared joy. It was so exhilarating to watch your child master something for the first time.

Adrien had taken Gabriel sledding when Charlotte had insisted she was fine watching Aurélie's lesson alone. She needed the time to think and plan anyway. Charlotte took out her phone and began dialing colleagues to find out who could take over her online clients on Monday when she needed to drive back down to Boise. Luckily, she didn't have any customers coming into her office on Mondays, so that made things less complicated.

How was she going to drive down to Boise for chemo-therapy treatments and make it home in one day? She assumed she wouldn't feel good after the treatment. It was a windy two-hour drive in the best of weather. Four hours on snow-covered roads sounded miserable. And how was she going to balance it with work?

Charlotte shook her head. She couldn't just disappear from her client's lives one day to the next. She needed to at least have a colleague to whom she could refer them. Charlotte's head began to spin. It would be easier to plan, she thought, if they could tell me definitively if for sure, and on what day, I am going to die. She laughed out loud at herself. Why did she keep thinking that?

When her father walked out, he had shattered her sense of security. She had fought to feel safe again every way she could figure out, which meant Charlotte had a proclivity to want to plan and control as much as she could. Sure, it drove her family crazy sometimes, but she had a clean home and a successful business and was always perfectly put together. The only problem was that even those you loved the most could be so unpredictable.

It was a smart decision not to tell anyone about her cancer, she reflected. Charlotte could organize and plan, and there would be no one to get in her way. She would manage the disease like anything else. But what in the world should she make a plan for?

Should she assume she was going to live and make a plan to overcome the logistics of getting down to Boise for treatment, or should she believe she could die in two months?

THE NEXT DAY CHARLOTTE wasn't prepared for all of the ill-looking people in Dr. Benson's waiting room. After checking in at the receptionist's desk, she fled to the restroom. She stood in front of the mirror, assessing her reflection until someone came running into the stall behind her and started throwing up. Charlotte fled the restroom and settled into a seat in the waiting area, thinking, there must be a mistake. I don't look like these unfortunate souls. I look healthy. Maybe Dr. Benson false diagnosed me. Perhaps I should get a second opinion.

"Charlotte, we're ready to take you back," said a cute nurse with bright blue eyes, red hair, and a sprinkling of freckles across her nose. She smiled warmly at Charlotte.

Charlotte couldn't manage to smile back. Wordlessly, she stood up and followed the nurse down the hall, the only sound the squeaking of the nurse's shoes against the shiny floor. Each minute slowed while Charlotte waited in the patient examining room for Dr. Benson to appear.

After all the hours Charlotte had spent counseling individuals suffering from panic attacks and post-traumatic stress anxiety, here Charlotte was, breathing as if a bear was chasing her through the woods with no help for miles, failing to even try to use the tactics to calm her system. All she could think of was: I can't leave my kids. They need their mama. This can't be real; I don't have cancer. Those three sentences repeated on an auto loop in her mind. She couldn't find the stop button.

"Charlotte, how are you today?" asked Dr. Benson. He crossed the room while holding out a hand. She instinctively shook his hand, and he placed his other hand over hers, giving it a pat.

"I don't have anyone with me," she said so quietly, that he leaned in so he could hear her words. She looked down at her knee-high leather boots. "I don't understand how I can have cancer. Are you sure? I mean, I eat lots of fruits and vegetables, I don't smoke, I don't drink more than a glass of wine. I take my multi-vitamin; I swim thirty minutes a day. I even floss every day."

"I'm sorry, Charlotte, but you do have cancer. Now, the first thing I am going to do is to show you your CT scans so you can visualize for yourself what we are going to battle," he continued while placing a film on the wall and turning on the light behind it, so it was illuminated. "Do you see the mass here on your pancreas? And here on your liver?"

Charlotte tried to swallow. Her mouth had gone dry. She nodded at the doctor.

"Those growths on your pancreas and liver are malignant."

Dr. Benson flipped off the light and sat down in the chair beside her while referencing his chart. "The bad news is that the tumors are not operable. The good news is that your immune system is strong enough to handle chemotherapy immediately and we don't need to put in a stent. Your bilirubin levels are not too high. Personally, I don't know how your bloodwork can be looking this great with the size of cancerous growths we see. All that health-conscious living must be helping you, Charlotte."

"Obviously not," replied Charlotte, "or I wouldn't have cancer now."

"Or," countered the doctor, "the cancer could have grown even faster if you hadn't taken such good care of your body. Let's talk about treatment. Do you want to fight this as aggressively as possible, or are you more worried about preserving quality of life?"

"I'm a fighter. I can take it," answered Charlotte with clenched fists.

"Then I recommend that we pursue six rounds of chemotherapy with Folfirinox, followed by radiation, and then another six rounds of chemotherapy.

Folfirinox is a combination of five chemotherapy agents. You will receive a couple of infusions. First, you will receive eighty-five milligrams over two hours of oxaliplatin, four hundred milligrams of leucovorin over two hours and one hundred and eighty milligrams of irinotecan over ninety minutes. Four hundred milligrams of 5-FU will be given as an injection into your cannula or central line. After this, you will be given an infusion of fluorouracil through a drip or pump – over 22 hours.

"This means that you will need to stay in hospital unless you have a central or PICC line, in which case the 5-FU infusion can be given to you through a small, portable pump. This regimen will be repeated every two weeks for the first six cycles. If all goes well, the chemotherapy will extend the length of your life. It is important to keep up with your healthy lifestyle as best as you still can, Charlotte."

"Are there other options?" managed Charlotte.

"Another possibility would be to treat you with gemcitabine. Then one thousand milligrams would be given to you over thirty minutes once a week for seven of eight weeks with a week of rest, then again every week for four more weeks.

Folfirinox can be very toxic, and it results in greater side effects than the gemcitabine regimen.

However, a study completed in 2010 proved that Folfirinox is more effective at prolonging life. Within the study, forty-eight percent of patients pursuing the Folfirinox regimen were alive a year later, as opposed to just twenty percent of those receiving gemcitabine.

Additionally, nearly one-third of patients following the Folfirinox regimen in the trial had some tumor shrinkage, compared with only nine percent of patients receiving gemcitabine." Dr. Benson paused. "Do you have any questions yet?" Charlotte shook her head no, and the doctor continued.

"I tend to prescribe gemcitabine to patients unsuitable for a Folfirinox regimen. These individuals are too weak to be suitable for Folfirinox, or they prefer to extend the quality of their life for as long as possible. I highly recommend we start off with Folfirinox, which will give you the best chance of extending your life."

"What about clinical trials?" asked Charlotte. "I read about plenty of stage four cancer survivors who decided to try something new."

"Most of my patients spend plenty of time researching their disease and treatments on the internet. I agree, however, that clinical trials are something we could look into if you do not respond to the Folfirinox.

I would like to remind you that you are more than welcome to visit another oncologist and receive a second opinion on your case.

It is essential to me that my patients feel that they have a good relationship with me and trust my treatment plan."

Charlotte sat, considering for a moment.

After a pause, she looked into Dr. Benson's eyes and shook her head, "No. I'll stay with you."

Kind, direct and soft-spoken, Dr. Benson was someone Charlotte had felt instantly comfortable with, but that hadn't stopped her from researching his career. Dr. Benson was the best oncologist in the state of Idaho, and if she wanted to stay close to home for treatment, at least for now, he was her best choice.

"What are the side effects?" asked Charlotte. "You mentioned that Folfirinox is high in toxicity, which makes me nervous. What if I get severely sick due to the chemotherapy? Will you switch me to gemcitabine?"

"Not to begin with, no. I am going to start you out on the full regimen. If the complications are too severe, then the first step will be to pursue a dose reduction. We can seek to alleviate or mitigate some of the regimen's more serious side effects by adjusting the dosages."

"When does treatment start?" she asked.

"I don't want to waste any time. Luckily, we had a spot open up, so how does today sound? Could you stay the night? In the future, we will be able to give you the infusion of 5FU through a small portable pump carried on a belt or in a holster that you can wear home with you once the pump is connected to your line and the infusion has started.

But you would need to come back to the hospital to have the pump disconnected, and I know you live up in McCall. For the first two rounds I want you here, then I will find a district nurse who can go to your home in McCall to disconnect the pump. The chemotherapy nurse will explain how to look after the pump and what to do if there's a problem."

Charlotte's mouth went dry, and she gasped, "Today? I didn't bring a bag with me."

"We have everything here you need," said Dr. Benson while standing up. "The sooner we start fighting this cancer, the better."

"I guess now is as good a time as any," she answered.

"Good. I will be checking in on you, but you will also have a specialist nurse and a chemotherapy nurse taking care of you today."

FORTUNATELY, HER MOTHER had been happy to take the kids for the night. Charlotte didn't know she was capable of lying so well. She had cheerfully told her mom that the colleague she was meeting in Boise had been delayed and his plane wouldn't get in until the next day. Would she be willing to take the kids for two nights?

Charlotte leaned back in the chair and watched the colorless liquid dripping into her IV line. She closed her eyes and tried to pretend that she was in a spa, then gave up. It wasn't working.

The room didn't smell of citrus or lavender, and there was no soothing music. Next time she came in here for a round of this in fourteen days, she was going to be better prepared. On the bright side, she decided, she had a perpetually well-packed purse with her at all times. She took out her Kindle and began to read. She had a feeling it was going to be a long night in the hospital.

As soon as Charlotte was out of the hospital the next afternoon, she rushed to her car. She drove like a wild woman back up to McCall, expecting at any moment to have to pull over to throw up, but it didn't happen.

The anti-sickness tablets they gave her appeared to be kicking in. She returned to town in record time and realized she hadn't had any lunch. It was just past four in the afternoon. They had had food available at the clinic, but she had been too terrified to eat.

Why the hell are you doing this to me? Charlotte was seething. She went to church every Sunday and donated money and time to charitable causes. She tried to live with faith and be a good mother, daughter, sister, wife, friend, and person.

Making a snap decision, she drove to the Shore Lodge hotel and walked into the restaurant. She had transferred all her clients to another colleague for the week. Her kids were in school. All her life she had played by the rules and lived a healthy life.

If she was going to be throwing up soon, well, she wanted to feel like she had earned her head hanging over the toilet. Healthy living be damned, Dr. Benson, she thought.

"Hi Zack," she smiled and slipped onto a bar stool. "I'd like a martini and keep them coming."

"Charlotte? I've never seen you here before," laughed Zack, while running his hands through his shoulder-length hair and pulling it back in a ponytail. "This is a surprise."

"Yeah, well, sometimes a woman needs a drink and to get away from it all," answered Charlotte and winked at him. She turned and looked out through the two-story windows overlooking the lake and the mountains. "Now don't you go telling on me, Zack. I don't need to be yet more fodder for the gossip mill in this town."

Zack laughed and leaned forward across the bar. "Well, that all depends, beautiful. Are you a good tipper?"

"You're blackmailing me?" gasped Charlotte. "I thought we are friends."

"We were best friends." Zack shrugs. The smile had disappeared from his face.

"Why did we drift apart?" "Adrien held me up against a locker and threatened to 'beat the living daylights' out of me if I didn't keep a distance."

"He didn't," breathed out Charlotte, her thoughts spinning. "I'll beat the living hell out of him myself."

"High school was a long time ago, sweetheart. I'm over you," he answered while wiping a wine glass dry, replacing it, and taking another.

"You mean over it," she corrected.

He met her eye, pausing in drying the glass in his hands. A tense pause fell over them.

"You know I was in love with you."

Heat flashed through her body, from her face all the way to her toes. Zack had been a cute kid, but no one would have thought he would end up as a dancer on Broadway in New York to pay his bills while he pursued becoming a published novelist. It wasn't so much his physique that made him so attractive. His green eyes radiated an intelligence and warmth, and a smile was always playing at his lips as if he knew a joke he might be willing to share with you.

"Well, you can have any woman on the planet now, Zack."

"Well that's true," he smiled, and she couldn't help but smile back. "I've had three of them today already."

Charlotte knew her eyes were widening, and she forced herself to swallow. "That's, you know, I don't judge."

"I'm just messing with you. So what kind of martini would you like?"

"I don't know. I haven't ever tried a martini before," Charlotte admitted. "I just think the glass it is served in is pretty. Is that dumb?"

Zack smoothed his fingers over his beard and then snapped his fingers. "One huckleberry martini is coming up for my future triathlon training partner," he said. "Would you like any appetizers from the kitchen?"

"Yeah," answered Charlotte. Inwardly she sighed. It wasn't likely she would be competing in any more triathlons. "I'd like French fries and a hamburger. And afterward the velvet cake and fresh strawberries with homemade ice-cream."

"I'm already in training. Sugar and fried food are a no-go for me."

"Eat a hamburger with me, Zack, I'm buying," she answered with a smile. "I'm the only guest in the place right now."

Zack shrugged, his eyes sparkling. "I never say no to a hamburger. You can eat my fries."

Charlotte tipped back the last of her martini and motioned at the glass. "Fill her up, Zack."

"How are you getting home, Charlotte?"

Charlotte tilted her head to the side. That was a question she had never had to answer before, as she had never drunk more than one glass of wine her entire life. She made a snap decision and took out her phone.

"Hi Mom, it's Charlotte. Listen, you don't work tonight, right? Could the kids stay the night with you and you take them to school tomorrow? I need to meet a work colleague this evening. Can you? Thanks, Mom. Listen, do you want to have a spa morning with me tomorrow, my treat? Yeah? Perfect. I'll meet you at Mountain Cove at ten. I'll set up an appointment. Thanks so much, Mom. Love you."

She placed the phone down after she had convinced her sister to take a day off work and join them at the spa the next day. Then, martini glass in hand, she wandered over to the front desk and asked if they had any rooms overlooking the lake they were willing to give her for half price.

At first, they resisted, but Charlotte knew at least half the rooms in the place were empty on that night thanks to Zack.

By the time she returned to the bar, the waiter was just

setting down two plates filled with gourmet hamburgers and French fries. Charlotte motioned at her glass, but Zack set three bottles of Perrier sparkling mineral water on the bar and a Coke before he came around the bar and settled on the bar stool next to her.

"You don't get another drink until you've drunk all three bottles of water," he said and took a big bite of his hamburger. "Believe me; you'll thank me later."

"Hey Zack," called Harry, the manager of the hotel. Charlotte wondered if he shaved his head because he liked the look, or if he began to bald at a young age. Either way, it suited him, and he had plenty of sex appeal with his six-foot-two height and soft brown eyes. He approached the bar and held out a hand. "Charlotte, I thought that was you. Always nice to have a pretty face around the place. Taking your break already, Zack?"

"It's my fault," spoke up Charlotte. "I didn't want to eat alone. I don't want him in any trouble because of me."

"Relax, beautiful, the bar is empty," replied Harry. "I'm happy he is sitting down with food in his hands. He isn't going to like what I have to tell him."

"Hit me with it, Harry," said Zack and took another bite of his hamburger.

"Elaine just called in. She has food poisoning, so we have no one to help you bartend the wedding this evening. I tried calling Joe, but he isn't answering. Any other ideas?"

"I'll do it," spoke up Charlotte, raising a hand as if she were a student.

Zack and Harry looked at her for a moment, then looked at one another and started laughing.

"You don't even know how to order a drink, much less make one," answered Zack with a grin. His face sobered as he turned his attention back to Harry.

"There is no way one bartender is going to cut it for a wedding of over two hundred and fifty people with an open bar, Harry. You know that. Why don't you work it with me tonight, just like old times before you put on the fancy suit and started running this place?"

"Come on Zack," answered Harry as he stepped around

the bar and poured himself an orange juice with a dash of sparkling water, lime, and mint. "You know the last time I bartended was in college. Besides, if you had a pregnant wife nearing nine months along and two little ones at home, you would know how important it is I get home tonight."

"Does the wedding have a signature cocktail?" asked Charlotte. "Then I could just learn that and be responsible for making just that one drink and pouring beer and wine."

"No such luck kid," answered Harry. "We don't do signature cocktails."

"Well, tonight you sure do," answered Charlotte. She finished her water and waved a hand at Harry. "Make me a drink, will you handsome?"

"Why do you want to bartend?" asked Zack as Harry grabbed a shaker and poured a shot of vodka, some freshly squeezed lemon and a dash of raspberry syrup inside before giving it a shake.

"I need one night to change things up. Maybe I'm tired of sitting behind a desk and listening to people's problems," answered Charlotte.

"Yeah, well, being a bartender isn't much different," laughed Zack.

Charlotte watched as Harry placed a spiral of orange rind in the martini and placed the frosty glass in front of her. Zack and Harry were both looking at her, waiting. "Is that all?" ventured Harry.

Charlotte threw her hands up in the air. "Oh hell, you both know about Adrien cheating on me. The whole town does by now."

"The dumb bastard," muttered Zack.

"I'm sorry Charlotte," said Harry.

"So, let's return to the signature drink," answered Charlotte. "You could offer them at a discounted price so that plenty of people will be lining up in front of me instead of Zack here."

"There is one problem," interjected Harry. "We can't just choose the signature drink without consulting with the bride."

"Then bring her on down here," said Zack and finished Charlotte's last French fry. He smiled and winked at Harry.

"Go personally offer the bridal party a free drink tasting

at the bar," suggested Charlotte. "And explain you want to offer her a signature drink for her guests at a reduced price. She'll come."

TWENTY MINUTES LATER Charlotte was talking and laughing with Katie the bride from Boise and her bridal party as they tasted four different drinks. Katie finally settled on the evening glory, which consisted of pomegranate juice, orange juice, citrus vodka, and a dash of champagne.

A few minutes later Harry came up and touched Charlotte's elbow, making her jump.

"I still have no idea why you're doing this, but thank you. You'll need to change into this," he said, holding up a neatly folded uniform that matched Zack's. "You didn't ask me how much it pays."

"Why don't you just give me my room here for free and we call it even?" suggested Charlotte. "I need to get away from my life for a night."

"A night away sounds mighty good to me about now too," answered Harry, grinning. Suddenly the smile vanished from his face, and his eyes widened. "Don't tell my wife I said that. Well, I'm on my way out. Good luck tonight, Charlotte. Zack, make sure everything runs smoothly. Call me at the first touch of trouble. We need these weddings, especially in the offseason."

Charlotte entered the event room with its panorama windows overlooking the lake. On each table, gigantic vases were brimming with pine boughs. Hanging from the pine branches were tiny red vases, some holding battery-operated candles, and others holding white roses, greenery, and bright red holly berries. For a second Charlotte saw herself gliding across the floor in Adrien's arms during their wedding reception in the same room.

A flash of anger set her teeth on edge. It was one thing for your husband to cheat. It was another to have the entire town know your picture-perfect family wasn't one anymore. Charlotte didn't know what hurt her pride more, Adrien's infidelity, or everyone knowing about it and giving her sad looks since it happened.

Charlotte had never been on the receiving end of pity, and she detested it, which came as a shock.

How often had she pitied others and felt she was exuding good will in the process?

The room would be empty for over an hour, but she and Zack were already preparing the ingredients and bar for the party. At each place setting lay a bright red gift box. Charlotte couldn't resist herself. She undid the ribbon on the gift box to see what was inside. Nestled inside the box were personalized mint boxes, two chocolate truffles, and a bottle of liquor. The note said: So your evening starts as sweet as ours has. Thank you for sharing your love, friendship and best wishes with us. Love, Katie & Bryant.

Charlotte was carefully retying the ribbon when a voice said, "You can have one if you want. I have extra."

Charlotte jumped in surprise and turned around with a guilty look on her face. Katie was standing in front of her in an elegant lace gown with red holly berries woven into her pinned up long raven hair. "No, of course not. My curiosity just got the best of me. I was dying to see what was inside such a shiny red box."

"What do you think?" asked Katie.

"You look gorgeous. Elegant," said Charlotte while carefully replacing the box on the table.

"I have a few extra. Here," said the bride, handing Charlotte a red box from a table by the dance floor.

"Thanks," beamed Charlotte. "I hope the entire evening is magical for you Katie."

Charlotte returned to Zack behind the bar and helped him cut up fresh limes, pomegranates, lemons, oranges, and star fruit for the cocktails.

ll of a sudden a wave of nausea rolled through her. She ran out the banquet room, down the stairs and outside. Charlotte cursed herself for her whimsical idea to become a bartender for a night and for the martinis and fried food she had eaten. She hadn't rebelled her entire life.

She had always chosen moderation and acted responsibly, reasonably. You can't rebel against cancer, love, she told herself.She drank in huge draughts of the icy cold air. Her heart was pounding harder than it did during a mile-long swim at high altitude. Her breath was coming in ragged gasps. Impending doom flooded her thoughts. Dear God, I'm dying, she thought. Not yet. I'm not ready yet.

She started trembling, the cold seeping through her white blouse. She didn't know how long she stood there shivering before she straightened up and looked up at the stars sparkling overhead. She let out a ragged sigh before her breathing began to smooth. It had passed. Her nausea and the pain in her chest and lungs were gone.

Charlotte looked at her watch. Eleven minutes until the start of the cocktail hour. She walked back inside and into the ladies' room on trembling legs. She splashed her face with water, powdered her face and added some eyeshadow, mascara, and bright red lipstick.

She took a deep breath. She stared at her reflection in the mirror. Come on Charlotte; you're a psychologist. You are not dying. You know that was a panic attack with a side dish of cocktails and fried food.

Now she needed to go up and bartend for the evening. She thought longingly of her cozy bed and what it would feel like to slip into it with a hot tea and a good book.

What have I gotten myself into this time? Please help me get through this, she prayed, so I don't collapse in on myself like a dying star. Harry and Zack are counting on me.

When she walked into the ballroom, she saw that a few guests had already filtered in and made their way to the bar. She joined Zack and smiled brightly. "Any orders for signature drinks?"

By eleven the last wedding guests were leaving. The younger guests were heading onward to a bar down the street to continue the gaiety of the evening. Charlotte was surprised at her disappointment that the evening was at an end. She had expected, after the panic attack and the intense day, to be dead on her feet. Instead, electrical energy coursed through her veins. Every time Zack had moved behind her to reach for a bottle he had pressed his hand on her lower back to warn her not to collide with him. His hand was like a brand, searing its way through her blouse.

Every time he came near, her body ached with the desire to feel his fingers caress her bare skin, and her cheeks burned with embarrassment. Charlotte reprimanded herself that a married Christian woman should not have scandalous images running through her head about a man other than her husband. But no matter how hard she tried to banish visions of Zack and herself, the harder they dug into her mind, refusing to let her go.

"Well, it looks like we can call it a night. That's the first time I have earned fewer tips than a co-worker. I have to admit my ego is a bit bruised."

"You can keep all the tips. I have a free room with a view out of this arrangement."

"Thanks, Charlotte. Until I begin selling more books, I can use the extra cash."

"I loved your last book, Zack, even more than the first one," she said. "You just need to find your target readership, and once they get ahold of your books, they will love them as much as I do. Hey," she snapped her fingers, "You know who I ran into in town? Jessica. She and David have moved back home. She said David is writing full-time now. Maybe you could meet to discuss marketing strategies."

"I don't know," Zack answered, smoothing his fingers over his beard. "I don't know if my pride could take going to David for advice."

Charlotte laughed. "Go on, Zack. David is such a shy, quiet guy. I'm sure he will love having someone call him up and invite him out for drinks. I still don't understand how Jessica snagged such a kind man. She's something else." She hoisted herself up on the bar and started swinging her legs back and forth.

"She's not that bad. You make her nervous, Charlotte, and she ends up saying something stupid," he answered.

"She ends up saying something mean," insisted Charlotte. She pushed Zack's shoulder.

"Whose side are you on, anyway?"

"What are we, ten again?" laughed Zack. "There are no sides, Charlotte. Jessica and I are friends. I know Jessica idolizes you because we had dinner together two weeks ago. She wanted to know all about you, and she was infuriated when she heard Adrien did what he did."

"She knows about the affair because of you? Thanks a lot, Zack. Perfect."

"Come on. The last guests just left." Zack placed his hands around her waist and lifted her up off the bar. "Give me a dance before we call it a night."

"There isn't any music anymore," protested Charlotte.

Zack took out his iPhone, grabbed an empty cardboard paper towel roll, and snapped open his Swiss Army knife. He carefully cut out a rectangle in the paper towel roll and placed his iPhone inside. Country music filled the room. Zack held out a hand, and Charlotte still hesitated.

"Don't tell me you've forgotten how to two-step," he said and grinned at her.

"It's been at least ten years since I last danced," admitted Charlotte. "I may well have."

"What the hell have you been doing with your time?" he asked as she placed her hand in his, and he drew her in, putting his other hand on her lower back.

"Studying, building a business, creating a cozy home, enjoying my two beautiful children." He smelled so good that she had an urge to place her cheek against his neck and drink in the smell of him.

"You never did know how to let loose."

"I guess I can be intense," admitted Charlotte.

Zack spun her and pulled her in close. "You were fun tonight. I've never seen you laugh and enjoy yourself the way you did behind the bar. It almost didn't feel like work, having you at my side."

"How come you never married, Zack?" Charlotte couldn't help but ask. She looked up, and he caught her gaze.

"Maybe I never found the right lady," he answered, looking into her eyes. "Or maybe I found the right girl, and then she married someone else."

Zack paused, holding her gaze, searching her eyes.

Her heart was pounding in her chest as she said, "I'm sure you've met hundreds of women far prettier and more fun than I am. Perhaps even as smart as I am too."

"Well, that's true," admitted Zack and Charlotte pushed him away in mock protest.

Zack opened his arms, and she stepped back into his embrace. They picked back up the two-step as his expression grew serious. "They were a lot of things, but they still weren't you, Charlotte."

Charlotte threw her arms around his neck and gave him a hug. She buried her face in his neck and inhaled the scent of his spicy cologne. His arms tightened around her, and he gathered her up, picking her up off the floor. When he set her down his mouth hovered within inches of hers, his breath warm on her lips.

"I'd give anything to kiss you right now," Zack whispered, then took a step back. "It wouldn't make you mine, though." He leaned in and kissed her cheek. "Good night."

Charlotte closed her eyes as he walked away. By the time she stepped into her suite and went to the window, exhaustion had hit her at last. She looked out at the moon reflecting on the dark surface of the lake, hating herself for what had almost happened, and thanking God that it hadn't.

Charlotte stripped off her clothes, for once throwing them on the floor on her way to a hot shower instead of carefully hanging them up in the closet. Ten minutes later she was curled up on the king-size bed. Charlotte filled her glass with sparkling water, snuggled even deeper under the feather duvet, and gave a sigh.

As a counselor, she would never recommend denial and running away from your life as a coping strategy. But hell, she thought, where has healthy and responsible gotten me? The night had veered dangerously close to the edge of indiscretion, but it had been the most fun she had had in a long time.

CHAPTER 6

James 1:12-14

12 Blessed is a person who endures temptation, for when he has been approved, he will receive the crown of life, which the Lord promised to those who love him.

13 Let no man say when he is tempted, "I am tempted by God," for God can't be tempted by evil, and he himself tempts no one. 14 But each one is tempted when he is drawn away by his own lust and enticed.

*T*HE MINUTE SHE STEPPEd into the suite, she turned around to face him. The door swung slowly shut, and she closed the distance between them, placing her arms up and around Zack's neck. He reached up and traced his fingers down her cheeks, cupping her face in his hands.

He gazed into her eyes, not moving. She lifted up onto her tiptoes and pressed her lips to his.

He pulled back, slowly unbuttoning her blouse.

He pulled her shirt down, kissing her bare shoulder as the fabric fell to the floor. His hands were in her hair, and then he swept her up in his arms.

Just as his lips were about to caress hers, bile rose in the back of her throat.

"I'm going to be sick," she said.

When she opened her eyes, her stomach was rolling. She couldn't place for a moment where she was or any of the events of the previous day. Then it hit her like a bird hitting a windowpane. She had stage four cancer, she had had her first chemo treatment, and she had spent the previous evening eating French fries and multiple pieces of cake and drinking martinis.

At the thought of food, Charlotte threw aside the duvet, sprang out of bed, and hurled herself to the toilet. A few minutes later, she eased herself down on the marble floor and closed her eyes.

What would Adrien think if he knew she had spent the evening flirting with Zack and the entire night dreaming about him?

She threw up again, thinking of the all the drinks she had consumed the night before. Serves you right, Charlotte, she said to herself. She waited for regret to come to the surface. It was a surprise to meet grim satisfaction in place of shame. Her entire life she had done the right thing: always moderate, responsible, disciplined. Now she had cancer.

For some reason, overeating, drinking, and flirting last night had buoyed her spirits. Not that she had any intention of repeating the previous night's shenanigans.

Aurélie and Gabriel deserved to have every minute of whatever time she had left, and she wanted to give it to them. The kiss would have been a terrible mistake. Her cheeks burned at the thought of what had almost happened.

Charlotte boiled water in the coffee maker and opened her purse. Her purse, like her life, was well-organized. She had hand sanitizer, a zipped bag with extra underwear and tampons, a complete makeup kit, a mini deodorant, hand lotion, and a mini perfume inside. H
er purse also contained a first aid kit, emergency snacks in a zipped bag, a small sewing kit, wet wipes, a Swiss Army knife and her Kindle loaded with books.

She even carried around a mini entertainment package containing crayons, mini coloring books, stickers, a mini puzzle, bubbles, a Matchbox car and two army parachute men. At the bottom of her purse, she found her snack box and clicked it open. She searched through the various tea types until she found ginger orange. The ginger would help with the remnants of her nausea.

She curled up in her robe next to the window and looked out at the sun coming up over the lake. It was only six in the morning. She climbed back into bed and closed her eyes, but sleep eluded her, so she got dressed and headed downstairs for some breakfast, hoping some toast would soothe her stomach.

Over an English muffin and a steaming cup of tea, Charlotte ruminated over how she should best organize the next few weeks of her life. Planning was one of the things she was best at, and she was going to leverage it to make her fight against cancer as smooth as possible.

She wasn't a fool.

It didn't matter how good she was feeling now, sitting here eating breakfast. How would she feel after the next couple rounds of chemotherapy? Worse. As a psychologist she knew, better than the majority, how emotions could drain a person of energy and joie de vivre. You could repress them, reject them, or run from them, but they'd come back around if you didn't deal with emotions.

She knew she had been running from the anger, fear, and sadness invoked by her diagnosis. At some point she would most likely fall apart, she thought. Until that point, she wanted to get as much done in whatever time she had left.

Wait, what do I want to get done?

Dr. Benson said she could have two months or a few years left. How does someone live with that information? Damn him. He should have given me a definite date when I will die, and then it would make this a hell of a lot easier to plan, she thought. She shook her head.

It was a ridiculous thing to want. Life just didn't work that way.

Charlotte took a sip of her coffee and wondered what her Mama would advise her to do. She smiled, her shoulders relaxing down her back. Charlotte rubbed the back of her neck and down between her shoulder blades.

Her Mama always said, "plan for the worst and hope for

the best," so that was just what she was going to do. If she were to die in two months, what did she want to have accomplished before then? Her mind was a complete blank. Maybe you should be asking what God wants you to get done in the next few months, thought Charlotte.

Like hell, said a voice in her head. Her fists tightened instinctively, and she ground her teeth. Why had God let this damn cancer grow in her body? For the hundredth time, she agonized over why he had afflicted her with terminal cancer.

"Well, that's a beautiful angel. I have one almost just like it dear."

Charlotte looked up. A lovely woman in her eighties with white curly hair and twinkly blue eyes motioned at Charlotte.

"Excuse me, what?"

"Your necklace," pointed the woman while approaching the table.

Charlotte fingered the rose gold necklace and smiled as the woman held out her similar chain for Charlotte to see.

"I got it from my Mom for my fifth birthday, and I have worn it every day since," replied Charlotte.

"You don't say. Mine was also a present from my mother. Now, have you seen your angel lately dear?"

Charlotte's smile fell from her face as the woman pulled out a chair and sat down next to Charlotte uninvited.

"Excuse me?"

"Your angel. I saw mine just this morning. She always appears as a deer. I went to the window when I woke up, and she was standing right down there near the water."

Charlotte didn't know what to say. She examined the women's starched blue blouse, black twill slacks, and carefully applied makeup. The women didn't look mentally unhinged. She seemed like the kind of Grandma you'd want to curl up next to with a cup of hot chocolate.

"Perhaps you are one of the lucky few who can see their angel," Charlotte decided to say.

"Well, that's because most people fail to look," insisted the woman. "Do you have a particular favorite animal you see quite frequently?"

Charlotte tilted her head, considering both the woman

and her question. She decided to play along. "Well, there is a mourning dove that sings near our cabin sometimes. Once in a while, I see one in town, near my office, or in the woods."

"And does it show up just when you are feeling particularly at a loss, in trouble, or when you are praying to God for help?"

Charlotte took a sip of her coffee, buying time. "Maybe," she admitted.

"I'm Charlotte by the way." She held out her hand.

"Mary Corkrin," answered the woman. "I remember you. That's why I came over. You were working the bar at my youngest grandson's wedding last night. I love weddings. It reminds me of my own sixty-four years ago. Do you enjoy working here?"

"Oh, I was just filling in to help some friends. I'm a psychologist."

"Mary," called a handsome man with silver hair from the door. "We'll be late."

"We're on our way to a family gathering at a friend's cabin. Pleased to meet you, Charlotte. Remember, you have more help available than you acknowledge." Mary patted her lovingly on the arm and walked toward her waiting husband, who took her hand in his. Hand in hand, the couple walked out of the restaurant.

Once her nausea had passed, Charlotte grabbed her new swimsuit, pulled it on, and threw the robe around her. Drinking and eating fatty food was one thing, but she wasn't going to miss her thirty-minute swim.

Charlotte stepped outside onto the snow and ran to the heated outdoor pool and dove into the water. After half an hour of laps, she pulled herself out and settled down into the Jacuzzi, resting her face on her hands and looking out at the lake through the steam billowing up around her.

Why is this happening to me? Charlotte closed her eyes. Are you even listening?

The only sound was the waves of the lake lapping against the beach. Then a dove began cooing in the pine tree above her. Charlotte twisted up to look at the dove, and the conversation with Mary resurfaced.

Staring at the dove, listening to its soft song, her soul found rest for the first time since her diagnosis, and one thing became crystal clear. Adrien deserved to know about the cancer. The question was, what would he say? Would he secretly resent her for being ill? The last thing Charlotte wanted was for Adrien to come home, to take care of her, out of a sense of obligation.

CHAPTER 7

Exodus 23:20-22

20 "Behold, I send an angel before you, to keep you by the way, and to bring you into the place which I have prepared. 21 Pay attention to him, and listen to his voice. Don't provoke him, for he will not pardon your disobedience, for my name is in him. 22 But if you indeed listen to his voice, and do all that I speak, then I will be an enemy to your enemies, and an adversary to your adversaries.

CHARLOTTE WAITED FOR HER MAMA and sister in front of the Cove Spa. She was feeling fatigued, but thankfully her nausea had diminished. Charlotte wanted this day with her Mama and sister to be perfect just in case. Just in case she deteriorated during the chemotherapy. Just in case she was taken from them in two months instead of five years. At last, she saw her sister and mom pulling into the parking lot. Why did they always have to be ten minutes late?

"Hi Mama, are you excited to be pampered today?" asked Charlotte as her mom pulled her in for a hug.

"What's this spa day all about, Charlotte?" asked Élodie while giving her sister a kiss on the cheek.

"You know how expensive spa treatments are? You know we think it's a waste of money."

Charlotte let out a huge sigh.

"Well, as I said, it's my treat, so do me a favor and try to enjoy it, yeah?"

"But honey, you told me to free the whole day. It's only ten in the morning. What are we going to go and do in an hour or so when are we are done here? You don't need to pick up the kids until three."

"I've signed us all up for a massage, facial, and body wrap this morning. In between treatments, we can relax in the Jacuzzi, steam room, and sauna, and then take the plunge into the ice water. I'm taking you all out for lunch at the hotel. In the afternoon we'll come back here for pedicures and manicures."

"Charlotte, what are you thinking? What is all of that going to cost?" asked Élodie.

"I had a good year at the practice, Élodie. I've got this. Just do me a favor and try to enjoy it?"

Élodie laughed. "Okay, okay. Although, we could have just waited and gone skiing together when the hill opens up."

During the massage, Charlotte tried to enter a state of relaxed bliss but found her thoughts turning in circles like a caged animal. Around and around spun her first goal of organizing at least fifteen years' worth of birthday presents for her children. The problem was, fifteen years ago they hadn't even launched the iPhone or iPad. She wouldn't be able to buy Aurélie's most coveted present for her sixteenth birthday. It certainly hadn't been invented yet. Who even knew what Gabriel would wish for when he turned sixteen. Perhaps by then, they would have light-regulating glasses that enabled the wearer to access all the knowledge and entertainment of the world in new three-dimensional worlds.

Charlotte tried to refocus on the feel of the hands gliding over her legs. She wouldn't admit it to Élodie, but she wasn't getting much out of this massage. She was too preoccupied with wondering what she could buy her teenage children.

The important thing is that they have a present from their mother, Charlotte told herself. You do not have the luxury of being perfectionistic this time.

Charlotte thanked the masseuse and entered the steam room. Settling back into the citrus-scented warmth on her towel, she wrapped her arms around her belly. It was as if there was a ticking bomb inside her stomach, but no one knew when it was set to go off. No. That night after her kids went to bed, she was going to curl up on her new sofa and plan out every present.

Tomorrow she was going to start acquiring all of them. But where in the world was she going to store fifteen years of gifts? She hadn't thought of that. Nor whom she was going to entrust with giving them to her children each year on their birthday. Adrien? No, she shook her head. She didn't completely trust him with this. Her mama? Élodie?

Élodie opened the door to the steam room and beckoned to Charlotte. "Come outside into the Jacuzzi with us."

Charlotte followed her sister. On the way outside, a young woman handed each of them a glass of champagne. Élodie accidentally dropped her towel, and Charlotte snatched it up and wrapped it around her sister's hourglass figure, "Élodie, you have to put on your swimsuit to go into the Jacuzzi."

"No complaints here," called a voice from the Jacuzzi. Charlotte and Élodie turned to see a muscular, tattooed man in his early twenties.

Élodie returned inside to change, and Charlotte followed her. On their way out, Élodie almost fell face first into the water, but Charlotte grabbed her elbow and steadied her.

Charlotte waved her champagne glass in front of her sister. "How many of these have you already had Élodie?"

Giggling like school girls, they slipped into the outdoor Jacuzzi and toasted one another and their Mom, who already had drunk half her flute.

"We've always had to keep an eye on you," said Charlotte to Élodie.

"How many nights did I stay up late pacing in front of the door, waiting for you to come home?" asked Anna.

"When she did come back," snorted Charlotte.

Élodie splashed Charlotte. "Well, not everyone can be perfectly grave and responsible all the time. It's annoying."

"Are you calling me boring?"

"Girls, don't fight. We're in a spa," whispered Anna.

"People are trying to relax." She nodded her head toward the young man sitting across from them with his head leaned back on the edge of the pool.

"Hey don't mind me. I'm enjoying the show. And the view," he spoke up and winked at Élodie.

"My name's Jake. I'm new in town. I'm opening a new travel business here."

"Where are you from?"

"Switzerland."

"You don't have an accent," commented Charlotte.

Anna smiled at Jake. "Well isn't that lovely. Why did you choose McCall?"

"It's the perfect little town close to deep wilderness. I'm just finalizing the permits and roll-out details now. You would be amazed how many men want to spend their holiday learning to survive alone in the wilderness with no electricity or modern tools. I'm looking for a business partner who knows the forests fifty miles in like the back of his hand. Any ideas?"

Charlotte was speechless. What were the chances that this man showed up out of the blue and wanted to open the exact same business her husband had in mind?

Charlotte closed her eyes briefly in an attempt to refocus. She decided it was likely this foreigner was nothing more than a tourist with a big mouth passing through town. They had met enough of them over the years.

"Sorry, we can't help you," Charlotte answered.

"That's not true," Élodie protested. "What about Adrien? Or Zack?"

Charlotte elbowed her sister in the ribs while glaring at her.

"No, they wouldn't be interested," insisted Charlotte. "But good luck."

"Well, I'll leave you my card at the front desk. If someone comes to mind, give me a call," Jake said as he climbed out of the pool.

Élodie's eyes traveled over his body and fixed on the barb wire tattoo around his bicep. She whistled at him, and he turned around.

"I'll give you a call regardless," Élodie called out, just as he lost his balance and fell into the Jacuzzi with a splash.

Élodie rushed forward as Jake came up spluttering.

"Are you okay?"

"Can't say I've ever been whistled at before." Jake wiped

the water from his eyes and grinned at her.

"Now that I find hard to believe," said Élodie while looking up at him from under her long lashes. She reached out and traced a finger along his tattoo. "Where did you get this?"

"In Switzerland after a few too many drinks," answered Jake. "So, how would you feel about going out to dinner with me tonight?"

"I have horses to ride this evening. How about tomorrow?"

"Sure. Like I said, I'll leave my card at the desk. Give me a call later, and we'll decide on details."

"Careful on the way out this time," grinned Élodie.

Charlotte's stomach was twisting, which had always been a warning signal. Now she couldn't be sure if it was her body reacting to the chemo or her cancer.

They watched the Swiss man walk inside, and then Élodie and Anna burst out laughing.

"Leave it to you, Élodie, to find a date even at a ladies' day at the spa," laughed Anna.

"Finding men isn't her problem; it's keeping them around that's the trouble," spoke up Charlotte.

"Charlotte," exclaimed Anna. "What's gotten into you? That was mean."

Charlotte sighed. "You're right. It was mean." Charlotte turned to her sister. "Do you forgive me, Élodie? I don't know what came over me. You're lovely. It's just that you've gone after the wrong type of guy over and over again, and I hate seeing you get hurt. Perhaps you shouldn't just choose guys because they're handsome and ride a motorcycle."

"Well this time will be different," insisted Élodie. "You laugh all you want to, but that there was love at first sight. You will all be swallowing those smirks when you are sitting in the first row at my wedding."

"Sitting? Won't I be the maid of honor?" asked Charlotte in mock outrage.

"Right. You'll be standing by me at my wedding as my maid," laughed Élodie. "What language do people speak in Switzerland anyway? Swissness?"

Charlotte's face fell into her hands. "Tell me you know that isn't a language."

"You're just jealous your kids won't grow up bilateral," retorted Élodie with her hands on her hips.

"You mean bilingual, Élodie," replied Anna. "Can you get me a refill of champagne, love?"

"Sure thing, Mama."

As soon as Élodie was out of earshot, she whispered to Charlotte. "She is a gorgeous little thing, but it sure isn't fair how you got all the smarts in the family, now is it? I'm glad she has you around to look out for her. She needs you. Be kind, Charlotte."

"She has you, Mama," replied Charlotte, her heart in her mouth.

"Yeah, but you're the one she listens to, even if she doesn't act like she values your insight."

Élodie returned to the Jacuzzi and announced their facials were in ten minutes. As Élodie started telling stories, Charlotte's mind wandered. It warmed Charlotte's heart to hear her sister and mother laughing together. They had both lived their entire lives in McCall but had never afforded the luxury of a day at a spa together before. The day was turning out to be a massive success.

"MOMMY," CALLED OUT AURÉLIE, throwing herself into her mother's arms.

Joy radiated out of Charlotte's heart center, and she kissed her daughter's pink cheek. Then she snuggled Gabriel's cheek as she strapped him into his car seat.

"You are very lovable, my little bunny," she told her son. "And so are you," she added, kissing her daughter on the top of her head.

Charlotte had never been so happy to head home with her kids before. As soon as Aurélie was buckled in and she was driving down the road, she announced that they were going to have lasagna, vegetables, and dip, with banana split sundaes for dessert.

"Our favorite," yelled Aurélie.

"With sprinkles?" asked Gabriel.

"With sprinkles," Charlotte agreed.

She pulled the car into the driveway. Charlotte unloaded the kids and carried the groceries into the house. Hopefully, the kids wouldn't notice the lasagna was frozen and not homemade. The day of indulgence and laughter at the spa with her mom and sister had increased her sense of well-being, but fatigue was weighing heavily on her shoulders. She placed the lasagna in the oven and prepared the vegetable sticks and dip while her kids settled down at the table with apple and kiwi slices.

"How about you two take your bath now? Then after dinner, we can curl up in front of the fire for an extra-long story time. Look what I bought at the store." She held up a new bottle of organic lavender bubble bath and a package of new bath toys.

Charlotte checked her reflection in the mirror for the fifth time that day. Generally, she didn't take much time in front of a looking glass, but she couldn't stop glancing at her reflection. Every time Charlotte looked at her glowing cheeks, it reassured her that she was still healthy and vibrant.

Or at the very least, under the professional makeup, she looked that way, and that was how she wanted her kids to remember her. As her children pulled on their pajamas, Charlotte went out into the living room and arranged the camera next to the vase of roses and holly on the coffee table.

She selected all of Aurélie's and Gabriel's favorite books and placed them ready on the table as well. When her kids came bounding out of the bathroom in their fleece pajamas, she wrapped them up in a soft cashmere blanket and pressed the button on the camera before settling back down to read.

Of all the activities she did with her children, reading to them was her favorite. It was her opportunity to create a cozy cocoon for them in which they experienced a sense of safety, comfort, and love. It was a few minutes a day in which she conveyed her love of reading.

She hoped it would awaken their awareness of all the new worlds and perspectives they could acquire by opening a book one day when they learned to read.

More than anything else, Charlotte wanted her kids to remember these moments they spent curled up next to her listening to her read to them. So she was recording the hour-long story time. She had hired a freelancer through UpWork who would perfect the video. As soon as he finished, he would send her copies of the video on both a USB stick and on three DVDs. A

lthough she was a very private person, she planned on placing the video on YouTube and linking it to a new website she had created just for her kids. No one ever knew, perhaps YouTube could someday cease to exist, but somehow the odds of that seemed smaller than DVDs and a USB stick becoming broken or misplaced.

By the time Charlotte finished Miss Rumphius, her children had both fallen asleep. She leaned forward, whispered, "my beautiful children, you are such lovable people. I am so lucky to be your Mama. Take good care of each other." She smiled and then turned the camera off.

Leaning back into the warmth of sleeping children, she paused, took a deep breath, and willed herself to get up. She should carry the kids upstairs and tuck them into their bed. Her body was weary with fatigue. A tear slipped down her cheek, followed by another.

All at once it was as clear as an alpine lake what she wanted to accomplish in the upcoming weeks.

Charlotte wanted her online therapy business to continue, no matter what happened to her. She believed in the importance of being able to reach people for therapy who couldn't make their way into an office. Adrien had never been good at remembering birthdays.

She wanted to ensure her kids would have a special birthday for the next fifteen years. She wanted her children to grow up in McCall, close to the extended network of their family and friends and for their educations' financing to be secured. Most of all, she wanted at least one more Christmas with her children.

She had her goals. It was time to plan. The first two goals she was certain she could attain, but the last two weren't under her control alone. Charlotte didn't know if she would be able to celebrate Christmas this year at home. A last tear slipped down her cheek, then she closed her eyes and surrendered to slumber.

SOMETIME IN THE NIGHT, Charlotte awoke with pain screaming in her upper back. She counted to three and willed herself up from the couch. First, Charlotte carried Aurélie up to bed, and then returned down the stairs to deliver Gabriel into his bed as well. As she took the last step up the stairs, she wondered how much longer she would be able to carry them up to bed.

Don't think like that, Charlotte.

Too tired to wash her face or brush her teeth, she pulled off her dress and slipped under her flannel duvet. Before she took a second breath, she was asleep.

"MOM, ARE YOU SICK?"

Charlotte sat straight up in bed. "What, why would you say that? Why are you up at this time? It's early, go back to sleep."

"But it's light outside," insisted Aurélie.

Charlotte snatched up her watch, and her heart stopped. It was ten past eight in the morning. Aurélie was already ten minutes late for school, and so was Gabriel. She had an online therapy session scheduled for twenty minutes from now. She would never get to her office on time. What was happening to her? It couldn't already be unraveling.

Why hadn't she set her alarm? She hadn't had her swim, nor her morning routine. The thought of getting herself and Gabriel dressed and the kids fed and lunches packed was too much. Instinctively she grabbed her phone. Two minutes later the preschool and school had been informed her children were both ill with the flu.

Charlotte threw a sweater, pearls, and jeans on and wandered bleary-eyed into the kitchen. Her clean kitchen was littered with dirty plates and glasses. The freezer was empty of muffins. She had forgotten to buy milk or bread at the store. What was she going to feed them?

She opened the fridge, then the freezer again as her children sat on the kitchen nook bench, proclaiming that they were hungry.

Charlotte placed her hands on either side of her head. The first day after chemo she hadn't had trouble. Why was she feeling so terrible two days later?

Did the side effects skip a day? Or was it a symptom of the cancer itself in her abdomen?

She cut up some apples and bananas and placed some whole grain crackers on the table. "Guess what, eat those, and I am putting some of my homemade cinnamon rolls into the oven, okay?"

Charlotte took a deep breath and turned on her Swiss Jura espresso and coffee machine, noticing the piles of books and toys scattered all over her living room. She made herself an espresso and drank it while surveying the mess. She looked at her watch. Nine more minutes until her appointment.

"Mama, is it Saturday?" asked Aurélie, confused. "Aren't we supposed to be at Daddy's on Saturday?"

"You know what, we are taking the day off from school, love. You and Gabriel get to take the rest of your apples and oranges and curl up in my bed and watch cartoons. Hurry you two, I am working from home today, and I have a session in five minutes."

Charlotte raced to her bedroom and set up Netflix on her laptop as the children cheered behind her and climbed into her bed. Charlotte ran to the bathroom and examined her reflection. She grabbed a makeup remover cloth and removed the black raccoon marks under her eyes. That's what you get from sleeping in your makeup, thought Charlotte.

Could this morning be any more hectic? She washed her face with cold water. Glancing at her watch, she saw that she only had time to dust some powder on her face and put on the brightest red lipstick she had before the session started. With one minute to go, she slid across the hardwood floor in her socks, sat down on one of the new chairs in the living room, and snapped open her laptop.

She signed into her account while swiveling in the chair to ensure her client wouldn't be able to see the mess of her once-immaculate home.

"Good morning, Mark. Tell me, how was your week?"

After a therapy session with Mark and another with Sasha, Charlotte brought her kids their cinnamon rolls.

"This is the best day ever," announced Aurélie.

"Best day," nodded Gabriel in agreement, his gaze glued

to the cartoons. Charlotte fell forward on the bed. Well, go figure, though Charlotte. The first day I fail at holding everything together, and it's their best day ever. Aurélie kissed her cheek before taking a big bite of the gooey cinnamon roll in her hand.

Charlotte told herself to get up and tackle the rest of the article that was due at the end of the week and the to-do list she had created regarding the kids' future birthday presents.

But before she knew it, her eyes were closing. Just ten minutes, she thought. I will get to that article, and the cleaning, and making some lunch, and run to the store.

CHARLOTTE OPENED HER EYES. She sprang up from the bed, and lights blinked in front of her eyes. Where were the kids? She looked at her watch. It was three in the afternoon. She had slept for hours, and the kids had gone without any lunch. Charlotte raced into the living room calling her children's names in a panic. She found them at the kitchen table coloring.

"Hi Mom," chirped Gabriel. "We're coloring."

"I can see that, honey. You must be famished. You should have woken me up," Charlotte said and sat down opposite her two bright-eyed children at the table.

"It's okay Mom, I made us peanut butter sandwiches," said Aurélie, while continuing to color in her jungle safari coloring book next to her brother.

Charlotte looked at the kitchen. Part of a leftover peanut butter and jelly sandwich lay on a plate on the kitchen counter along with all the other dishes. Charlotte also noticed the chocolate wrappers.

"Wow, Aurélie, I'm impressed," said Charlotte, considering if she should call her mother for help. It was just then that Charlotte realized she hadn't called her mom that the kids hadn't gone to school. Charlotte glanced at the clock. Her mother must already be waiting in front of Aurélie's school. She raced to her bedroom and picked up her phone.

"Oh Mom, I'm sorry. The kids are home with me today."

"Her teacher just told me, honey. Why didn't you call?"

"I forgot." Charlotte rubbed her forehead.

"That's not like you," responded her Mom. "Are you sick too, honey? I'll just drive right over."

Charlotte looked around the room in a panic. Her Mom couldn't see her home like this; she would immediately know something was seriously wrong. It hadn't ever looked like this, not even when she had pneumonia.

"Actually yes, I am. Could you stop at the store for me? We're out of milk, bread and, well everything," admitted Charlotte.

"Sure thing, love. I'll be there in about an hour," replied her mother. "See you soon."

Charlotte looked around the room and groaned.

AN HOUR LATER CHARLOTTE heard a knock at her front door. Charlotte looked around at the sparkling clean house and inhaled the scent of citrus simmering in the pot of water on the stove. She smoothed her hair back on the way to the door. That is one advantage of a small home, thought Charlotte. You can clean it up in an hour.

"I've told you, Mama. You don't have to knock."

"Of course I do. It's your home, baby. It's a sign of respect, that's all."

Charlotte tried to take the bag of groceries out of her mother's hands, but she said, "Go on now, I've got these. There are more bags in the trunk."

"Grandma," yelled Aurélie and Gabriel as they threw their arms around their Grandma.

"Mom let us stay in our pajamas and watch cartoons all morning because she was sick," announced Gabriel.

"Well what fun," answered Anna. "Now I am going to make you some sweet and sour chicken, pea pods, and rice. How does that sound?"

"My favorite," cried Aurélie, hugging her Grandma again. "Thanks, Grandma."

"Yuck," declared Gabriel.

Anna patted Gabriel on the top of the head and smiled.

"I'll just give you some plain rice and chicken. How's that sound honey?"

Anna turned to Charlotte, who was putting groceries away and shook a finger at her. "Now you go get into bed, baby."

"She's not a baby," laughed Gabriel. "She's a Mama."

"Well, she'll always be my baby," insisted Anna, and gave Charlotte a kiss on the cheek. "No matter how old she gets."

Charlotte shut the door behind her and climbed gratefully into her bed. She pulled her laptop onto her lap. She couldn't pretend any longer that she would be one of the people who sailed through chemotherapy without it severely impacting her life and energy level. One day like today was enough. She didn't want it to repeat itself. Charlotte closed her eyes and grimaced, gritting her teeth, and then let out a rush of air. It was time to call Adrien.

"Adrien?"

"Hey, Charlotte."

"Listen, I was wondering if we could switch our arrangement for the next two weeks? Could the kids spend Sunday night through Thursday with you and spend the weekend with me? We would switch only until Christmas. I have a lot on my plate right now."

"I don't know, Charlotte. You insisted the children stay with you during the week, remember? Now we have our flow."

"Well, things have changed. At least for now, it would help me if you could do this," Charlotte cleared her throat and pressed her fingers to her closed eyes. "I need your help."

"If you let me come home, you wouldn't have to be doing this alone."

Charlotte sighed. "I'm not ready for that, Adrien. Listen," she paused, willing herself to say the words, "I'm begging you to do this. Please."

"No, Charlotte. If you don't want me coming home, then I'm not having the kids live with me here the entire week in this condo. It's just too small."

"Fine," snapped Charlotte and almost hung up on him. "Wait. What if you moved home, and I moved into your condo for the next two or three weeks? Then would you switch with me?"

Charlotte heard only silence in response. "Adrien? Are you still there?"

"You must be pretty desperate to be willing to live here for a few weeks. You won't be able to do your morning swim and sauna. You haven't missed more than a handful of days of swimming since we moved into the cabin."

"Well, I'll have to do something else then," answered Charlotte, frowning. She would miss her swim, but to be honest, she wasn't sure she would be up to it during chemo anyway. "Maybe I'll do yoga instead," she answered.

"You hate yoga," laughed Adrien.

"Well, I've haven't tried it before. Maybe I'll love it. Élodie has been pestering me for years to try yoga. Apparently, there are full yoga classes online."

"Tell you what, Charlotte, I'll even go buy you a mat in your favorite color and deliver it to you. Do you want to tell me what is going on at work that we need to do this change?"

"It exhausts me just to think about it, let alone talk about it. Listen, I've got to go. Could you come tonight already?"

"Tonight? Are you serious?"

"My mom is making your favorite: sweet and sour chicken," offered Charlotte. "You could join us."

"I'll eat anything that woman puts in front of me. She is the best cook in McCall. Wait, don't tell my Mom I said that. See you in thirty minutes."

THIRTY MINUTES LATER CHARLOTTE'S eyes flew open when she heard Adrien call out from the front door. What was he doing here? The sound of her kids' little feet running to throw themselves into his arms reminded her of their agreement. She realized she must have fallen asleep.

Why was she so confused today? The door to her bedroom creaked open, and her Mom came and sat down on the king size bed. Anna smoothed the hair away from Charlotte's face just as she had when Charlotte was a little girl.

"Are you okay in here? Did you know Adrien was coming?"

"I'm sorry, Mom. I called and asked him if he could switch with me for the next two to three weeks and take care of the kids during the week. He's going to move back home, and I'm going to go into the condo," answered Charlotte. Even with all of the naps she had taken that day, her body was exhausted. She didn't feel up to going out and even sitting through dinner.

"But you love your home," answered Anna. "Don't let him talk you into giving it up. It's his fault that you are separated. I won't let you hand over your life to him, Charlotte."

Both of them jumped when Adrien spoke up behind them. "Don't worry, Anna. I'm not going to take the cabin from Charlotte. I wouldn't dream of it. It was her idea."

"It's true," said Charlotte while sitting up in bed. "It was my idea, Mom. It's just temporary. I have a huge workload for the next couple weeks before Christmas."

"You could have asked me, Charlotte. I would have helped out more," answered Anna.

"You have your job and your volunteer work, Mom. No, you are already helping us enough with picking up the kids and taking care of them Monday through Friday from three to six. We are indebted enough to you."

"That's true," agreed Adrien. "The kids love spending the afternoon at Grandma's house."

"Well, okay then. Dinner will be ready in ten minutes."

AFTER DINNER, CHARLOTTE took a small suitcase and packed for the upcoming two weeks. She hated the thought of leaving her kids, but she couldn't let today reoccur. Silent tears were staining her cheeks. The day had been a disaster. It had shown her that she wasn't up to taking care of them on her own during chemotherapy; they had spent hours completely unattended. She hadn't even fed them lunch.

Charlotte reminded herself that the weekend would come before she blinked twice, and then she could savor two days of time entirely devoted to enjoying being with Aurélie and Gabriel. And if she needed help, she would have to call and ask for it sooner next time.

"Hey Charlotte," Adrien stepped into the bedroom and set down his suitcase. "Your Mom said I could come into town with you tonight. She'll put the kids to bed. That way we can stop by the store and pick up anything you want, and I can help you settle into my place."

Charlotte turned to look at her husband. He looked sexy in his flannel shirt and worn jeans. She wanted to rest her head against his firm chest and have the weight of his arms wrap around her as she told him about her cancer diagnosis, of how scared she was, of how angry she was with God.

"Char? What's wrong, love?"

Without thinking, Charlotte took two steps closer to the embrace she longed for. Looking up into his eyes, she said, "Adrien, I."

Gabriel came running into the room and flung his tiny arms around her legs. "Don't go, Mommy," he cried. "Don't leave me alone."

Charlotte picked her son up and hugged him fiercely. She turned toward the window to recompose herself, overcome for a moment at how everything in her life was turning out wrong. She blinked back tears, taking a deep breath, and counted backward from ten. She didn't want her kids to see her cry.

Focus on the positive, she told herself, sucking in a deep breath. I'm grateful my children are healthy, they are safe, they are loved. I have a lovely mother and sister whom I love very much. We have enough money. I love where we live. Charlotte breathed out, closed her eyes. I am grateful my job imbues my life with meaning. My relationship with God will carry me through this. He will strengthen me. I can do this. I can.

Her Mom came into the room and scooped Gabriel out of her arms. "It's time for a bubble bath, sweetheart."

Charlotte kissed her son's cheek and whispered, "I love you," before Gabriel was carried off to the tub.

"Char?" asked Adrien.

Charlotte plastered a smile on her face and turned back around. She was a mannequin in a window, rigid on the outside and hollow on the inside.

"This is progress, Charlotte. I know it must have been hard."

"What?" Charlotte's thoughts raced.

How did he know about the cancer?

"Asking me for help. I know that must have been hard. You hate asking anyone for help, ever." Adrien spread out his arms. "You don't have to do this all on your own. You don't have to be perfect all the time for us to love you."

"Damn you, Adrien," said Charlotte. She had been able to hold it all in, and those few words melted her exterior. Tears stung the back of her eyes, then began slipping down her cheeks. Charlotte placed her face in her hands and cried. Adrien stepped forward and took her into his arms. He kissed her tear-stained cheek, and she let her head rest against his chest, just as she had been longing to do. Adrien rubbed her back and rested his chin on the top of her head. A few minutes later, Charlotte drew back.

"Adrien," began Charlotte, but he interrupted her.

"We should go. Just follow me, okay? I have a plan."

"WHAT ARE WE DOING HERE?" asked Charlotte, rolling down her window looking up at the Mexican restaurant.

"You go on inside and drink a strawberry margarita, and I'll be back in an hour with your groceries and the yoga mat," announced Adrien. He opened the car door and unbuckled Charlotte's seat belt. "Go on, get out."

"You don't have to do that. I can do it tomorrow," insisted Charlotte.

Adrien was already shaking his head. "I'm doing this for you whether you want it or not. Humor me."

"Then give me a second, let me write you a list," said Charlotte while taking out a pen from her purse.

Adrien held out a hand.

"Let's go."

He didn't let go of her hand when she had climbed out of her SUV but held it on the way into the restaurant.

"Hey, Sally, can you set up Charlotte with a virgin strawberry margarita and some chips and salsa? This should cover it." He placed a twenty on the bar. "Go ahead and order another one if I'm not back in time," he told Charlotte and tilted her chin up to look at him. He gave her a soft, brief kiss on the lips. "Whatever it is at work, you're going to get through it. You'll blink twice, and we will all be together under the Christmas tree." He smiled at her, turned on his heel, and left.

"Wow. Wish I had a guy like that," said Sally, leaning forward on the bar. "Here's your drink."

"Sally," ventured Charlotte. "You know we're separated."

"Sure, sure. I know the whole story. It's a small town, what do you want? He's still in love with you. And a hot ass like that? Honey, I would bring him back home to keep me warm at night."

Charlotte was speechless. She didn't know why she was surprised. It wasn't the first time someone had openly offered up advice on her private life. It wasn't exactly her favorite part of living in a small resort town in Idaho.

"He's not the only one with a 'hot ass' in town," smiled Charlotte.

Sally's eyes grew wide, and she leaned in even closer. "Who? Have you been carrying on with someone new?"

"No," yelled Charlotte. "No," she repeated, forcing herself to modulate her voice. "I don't need to start an affair to open my eyes and appreciate the view once in a while."

"Come on, dish it, girl. I may just go and snatch me some loving myself if you aren't looking for any."

Charlotte tilted her head in thought. Sally was a huge gossip and not brainy, but on the other hand, she was athletic and pretty, with long brown curly hair and bright blue eyes. Her best attribute, in Charlotte's opinion, was that she was the first to show up on someone's doorstep, offering help when someone was in trouble in town. Sally was on the same volunteer committee as her Mom.

"Here," offered Sally, placing a shot on the bar with a lime. "On the house. Now spill."

"I don't drink, Sally." Well hell, decided Charlotte. I have a stage four cancer diagnosis. What can a drink hurt? Charlotte looked at Sally for one more moment and then downed the shot in one go.

"Have you seen Zack since he moved back from New York?"

"Zack's back in town? Since when?"

"A while now, Sally. You better move fast. He is working

over at the Shore Lodge."

"Is that so? I don't know. Don't get me wrong, Charlotte. I know you all were best friends for many years, and he was cute in high school and all. But,"

"That was a long time ago," interrupted Charlotte. "Wait until you see him now."

Charlotte took out her phone and showed Sally a YouTube video of Zack dancing.

"Well pinch me," said Sally. "I must be dreaming. Zack can dance like that? Who would have thought?" Sally placed another shot on the counter, and Charlotte began to tell her about her night of bartending at the Shore Lodge.

"I'll tell you what," Sally said as she made a tray of drinks. "I'm going to ask Zack out first chance I get. Maybe I'll even head over to the Shore Lodge after my shift."

By the time Adrien returned to pick her up, Charlotte almost fell off her barstool when she tried to stand up. Apparently, two shots were enough to take the feet right out from under her. Adrien found it amusing. "Since when do you drink? It looks like I'm driving you home. You can pick up your SUV tomorrow."

Adrien opened the truck door for her and helped her up onto her seat. It was just a few blocks to his condo, which also had a view of the lake, even if it didn't have the shorefront property to go with it. Adrien led Charlotte up the stairs and unlocked the door. He kicked off his boots and stood in the middle of the living room, a big grin on his face.

"What?" asked Charlotte. She looked around, and only then did she notice the flowers on the kitchen counter. Adrien went to the fridge and waved inside.

"Look, I know what you like."

Charlotte examined the contents and smiled. She was shocked he would know what she loved to eat as she had always done the grocery shopping in their marriage, and he had always complained that there weren't enough tasty snacks in the house. Adrien grabbed her hand and led her into the bedroom. "I changed the sheets for you," he said.

On top of the bed were a stack of fresh towels and a box of chocolates. Adrien had stuffed another bouquet of flowers into a vase next to the bed beside a bottle of sparkling mineral water. Spread out on the floor next to the bed was a brand new, pale blue yoga mat.

"I can't believe you did all this for me," said Charlotte. "Thank you." She turned toward Adrien and reached out a hand to cup his cheek.

He moved his head and kissed the palm of her hand.

CHARLOTTE TOOK A DEEP BREATH and walked toward her office. She almost wished Adrien had been able to stay the night, instead of leaving to go back home to the kids. Maybe they really could be a family again. Maybe she could convince him to stay in Idaho.

Charlotte slipped off her boots in her office and slipped into heels. She walked over to her desk and sat down, staring into space for a few more minutes. Then she picked up the phone.

Two hours later she stood up and stretched. Melancholy rolled over her soul, and she walked over to her espresso coffee maker and pushed the button.

The delicious fragrance of espresso helped a little to soothe and uplift. She was thankful that three of her colleagues were willing to take over half of her clients until after Christmas; this meant she had more time in the next three weeks to focus on her health and strategize for the future.

Charlotte sat down on the couch and pulled her legs up beneath her. Her body was surprisingly limber and pleasantly fatigued from the hour of beginner-level yoga she had tried that morning for the first time. She had expected to be depressed after missing yet another session of swimming, but instead, she was relieved to find a new morning routine that worked in Adrien's flat.

After the short break, Charlotte pulled out her laptop and got to work. She needed at least fifteen presents times two, and she wanted to finish her list by that evening. Part of her thought what she was doing was crazy. Shouldn't she spend this time with her children, instead of sitting at a desk?

I'm not going to die within the next few months, like the scariest statistics forecast. I don't need to do this. Charlotte's mouth went dry, and she rested her forehead on her desk. Was she acting crazy? Should she call up her closest psychologist friend Sebastian and ask him? She tapped her pen on the side of the coffee table.

No. It was a good idea. It would be a permanent weight off Charlotte's mind to know she had prepared for all of her kid's birthdays. I mean, how hard could it be to figure out presents in advance?

Charlotte opened her Mac laptop and started researching. She was immediately overwhelmed. There were uncountable options. She couldn't know what her kids would be interested in a few years from now. Would Aurélie still love ice-skating? Would Gabriel still love music? What about when they became teenagers? What will you even give a teenager in a world a decade from now?

Charlotte slapped her hands to her cheeks and dragged them down to her neck. She had broken out into a sweat, despite the cold office. Perhaps this wasn't a feasible plan after all. Flushed with heat, Charlotte jumped out of her chair and threw on her jacket and boots.

Outside, she drank in the cold air and walked along the lake through town. Lost in her anguish, Charlotte didn't even realize her feet had carried her to the Shore Lodge. Hesitating just a moment, she pushed through the front doors and headed to the bar.

"Hey, Zack." Her eyes traveled over his shiny long hair and the two-day beard. She noticed his eyes lit up when they saw her.

"Hey, yourself. Can't keep yourself away huh?"

"They do make an amazing hamburger here. Can I buy you one?" Charlotte asked. She saw the hesitation in Zack's eyes as he leaned forward on the bar. "I need some advice on what to a buy a teenager for their birthday," she explained.

Zack laughed out loud. "Why would you come to me, of all people, for advice on something like that?"

"Because you have the best imagination of anyone I know. You are a writer, right?"

"Tell you what," answered Zack. He tapped his fingers against his lips. "My break is in half an hour. Think you can be patient until then to have lunch with me?"

"Sure thing. I'll have that huckleberry martini while I wait."

"It isn't even lunchtime," answered Zack. "Should I be worried?" Charlotte watched his eyebrows knit together in a frown.

"Make me the drink, Zack." She sat up straight on her bar stool and winked at him.

"Yes miss," he answered.

AN HOUR AND TWO MARTINIS later, Charlotte bit into her hamburger across from Zack.

"A teenage boy or a girl?" he asked before stealing a French fry from Charlotte's plate.

"Both," answered Charlotte.

"I have been thinking it over, and I think teenagers, even the boys, are romantics. They're idealists. You would do best giving them something with personal meaning. I'd advise jewelry for the girl and a watch for the boy. Both are timeless. In fact, they can both even accrue more prestige and meaning the older they are, unlike other gifts."

"You're brilliant, Zack. I wouldn't have thought of that. I don't wear much jewelry myself. Anyway, I don't have anything of any real value."

"Why's that? Hasn't Adrien gifted you any over the years?"

"It's not my thing."

"But surely your Mom…"

"He ran off with all her jewelry. You know that." She turned her focus out the window to the view of the lake. They sat in silence for a moment until Charlotte felt his hand reach out and pat hers.

"I'm sorry. I forgot. Anyway, it was a stupid idea and not at all original. I'll think of something else."

Charlotte smiled ruefully and shook her head. "No, I love the idea."

Zack snapped his fingers, "I've got it. We both know how much you love books. You could gift them your favorites."

"I don't know how excited they would be about that. Sure the kids love books now, but they are small. What if they don't read? And it isn't very personal."

"Who are these gifts for, anyway?"

"Aurélie and Gabriel," answered Charlotte. She instantly covered her hand with her mouth. Two martinis before lunch were too many.

Zack choked on his bite of hamburger. He took a large drink of water and croaked out. "What the hell? Why are you planning out these presents? They aren't teenagers from years. You're a bit crazy; you know that?"

Charlotte swore internally. How was she going to explain this? He was looking at her as if she had lost her mind.

"I know you like to be well-prepared and organized, but this is going a bit far, even for you. Don't you think?" asked Zack.

Charlotte didn't answer. She was a frozen statue. She held her hamburger halfway to her mouth as if she had been caught red-handed in the process of stealing a priceless work of art.

"Holy shit, you're not running away from your family, are you? You aren't going to disappear and just leave your kids behind with Adrien?"

Charlotte stared at Zack in disbelief. Hadn't she told him about her cancer? She thought she had let it slip the night she got drunk bartending. Charlotte swallowed loudly and set her hamburger back down.

"I might not be around for future birthdays," she answered at last. "I have cancer."

"Calm down," answered Zack.

"I'm not my father," hissed Charlotte. "Why would you think I'm capable of running out on my kids?"

Zack looked around at the other diners staring at them. "Of course you're not your... wait a second. Fucking hell, cancer? You're not dying are you? That's not funny, Charlotte."

"Who jokes about something like having cancer?" Charlotte jumped up from the table, spilling her water in the process. She ran out of the restaurant and down a long hallway of hotel room doors. She knew how bizarre her behavior looked, but she couldn't help it. The minute Zack had asked if she was dying, every fiber of her body hit the gas pedal and screamed go as if she could outrun the truth.

Charlotte heard steps gathering speed behind her, and a hand clasped her elbow, and still, she struggled forward. Zack yanked her arm, and she pulled hard. She lost her balance and tumbled forward on the floor. Zack landed with a thud on the floor beside her.

"Dear Lord, Charlotte, what the hell is going on with you?"

She burst into tears just as they heard a door opening down the hall and voices. Zack pulled her to her feet and hustled her down the stairs and into the empty banquet hall.

"You can't tell anyone, Zack. Promise me. I don't want anyone to know," said Charlotte. He was still holding her hand, his fingers entwined with hers.

"You have cancer."

"Pancreatic cancer," she murmured.

She burst into tears. Shame, hot and burning licked at her skin. Zack didn't deserve the burden of her secret. She would have to ask him to keep the truth from her family; it was the only way she knew how to keep living her life as normally as possible. If they didn't know, then she needed to put on a brave face. She had to be able to put on a brave face to get through this.

Zack pulled her to him and wiped the tears from her cheeks. He murmured how sorry he was and protested she had to inform her mom and Élodie. Zack only relented when she promised to tell them the day after Christmas. It was then that he pulled her to him, and even through her grief and confusion, desire, warm and aching, flashed through her. She lifted her eyes to look up at him.

"I'm so damn sorry, Charlotte. I wanted to believe it was some sort of sick joke or something; I don't know. Of all the people." He kissed her tear-stained cheeks and rested his forehead against hers, closing his eyes. "I've always loved you," he murmured. "I'll do anything for you. You call me day or night."

He took a deep breath, then hesitated, his lips a centimeter from her own. Every particle of Charlotte's vibrated. She ached to melt into his kiss, just like she had wished all those years ago in the woods when they'd lain together on a blanket under an ocean of stars. But he hadn't kissed her, and the next day Adrien had asked her to the dance. Summoning all her willpower, she pulled backward.

"I'm sorry I've unloaded this onto you."

"Shh," he answered, wrapping his arms around her. "You had to tell somebody. I'm glad I'm the one you trusted."

Charlotte threw her arms around his neck and gave him a fierce hug before turning on her heel and rushing out of the hotel.

THAT NIGHT CHARLOTTE CURLED up in bed and listened to the waves washing against the shore through the cracked window. Her mind kept flashing through the events of the afternoon. She had come very close to kissing Zack. As if her life wasn't a seething mess right now, she had thrown in Zack into the mix. Perfect, Charlotte.

What the hell were you thinking? You love Adrien. Stop being selfish. Your kids need you. You can't be wasting time adding drama to your life; pancreatic cancer is enough drama all on its own. Why did you go to the hotel to see him in the first place?

She considered the rest of the day. She had stayed up until three in the morning working on the birthday present project. Just when exhaustion threatened to take over at about ten at night, she was overcome by a frantic energy electrifying her body at the thought of a future in which her kids celebrated a birthday, and she didn't exist.

She had finished the list of fifteen presents for each child. Now it was just a matter of purchasing, wrapping, and storing them. Groaning, she rolled over in bed, clutching a pillow to her chest.

Who could she entrust with saving and giving her children their birthday presents? There was only one answer: her Mama. But could her Mom store all those gifts for so many years? What if someone broke in and robbed her and stole all the presents? What if something happened to her?

Charlotte shook her head. Too bad, she thought for the thousandth time, that there isn't a gift and card service that will do the storing and sending for me.

Who should she trust to store and send her kids their cards in the mail?

Her sister was a clear choice. You should have a backup too, thought Charlotte. It can't hurt, and it certainly can save the day. If one person forgot to send off the card in time, then the other person most likely would remember. At least they would receive one card.

It was a bit unorthodox, what she was doing. She knew some people would think it creepy to receive cards from a dead person, let alone gifts. Help me, Lord, is what I'm doing crazy? She paused inwardly, waiting for an answer. Nothing came.

All she experienced was the aching pain in her abdomen and a rolling of her stomach. Charlotte reasoned that even if the presents and cards didn't spark joy in Aurélie and Gabriel, they would have a sign that their mother loved them very much once a year until they were grown.

Charlotte decided then and there to write two cards per birthday for each child first thing in the morning and give one of the sets of cards to Élodie, and the other to Zack. She knew why she had settled on Zack. She just instinctively knew that he was a man of his word. If he agreed to the task, she could trust that he would make sure the birthday cards were sent to her kids each year.

Deep down she feared that Adrien would react to her death by finding someone new to wake up to each morning. There was no doubt in her heart that he would grieve her. It was rather that she suspected he would deal with her death the way he had when his best friend had died: just move forward. Charlotte was almost positive Adrien would not be an enthusiast of her sending presents and cards to her children from the grave.

Trust has never been your strong suit, thought Charlotte as she climbed out of bed and went into the kitchen to make a tea. Charlotte shivered in the bare feet and ran on tiptoes back into the bedroom. She climbed back under the duvet with the hot cup of orange vanilla spice tea and leaned back against the pillow. As she took a sip of tea, she wondered what she would write on each card. With a start, she realized that she would have thirty cards to write the next day. Where would she purchase thirty perfect birthday cards in the morning?

She shook her head. No, the content of the card was the important thing. She had beautiful stationery. It would be possible to make the cards herself. The first step would be writing the cards. If she found the time, she could always decorate them in a second phase. The question was, what should she write?

THE NEXT MORNING CHARLOTTE woke at five-thirty, despite the minimal number of hours she had slept the night before. It was as if her body was once again recalibrating to her usual wake-up time. Bleary-eyed and in pain, she tried to close her eyes and descend back into sleep. She tossed and turned.

Giving up, she tumbled out of bed onto her yoga mat and turned on yoga today. By the end of the hour, she experienced a slight increase in well-being. At least her muscles were warm and pliant, even if it had done nothing to alleviate the pain in her abdomen radiating to her back.

The minute Charlotte entered her office she sat down at her desk with an armful of colorful paper. She began the card for Aurélie's seventh birthday.

Happy Birthday, Aurélie!

I love you so much Aurélie! You are a smart, beautiful, and creative little girl with a kind and generous heart. I pray that you feel truly loved and cherished today and know how wonderful you are! I would give anything to be with you today, but I want you to know that a part of me is with you always. Nothing in my life brought me more joy and wonder than you and your brother Gabriel. I wish you a magical birthday.

I'm sending you a kiss on the wind. - Love, your Mom

Happy Birthday, Gabriel!!!

You are four years old, and I wish you lots of fun and joy on your birthday. I love what a brave, courageous, empathetic, and adventurous person you are. I would give anything to be with you today, but I have faith that your Dad and family will make your birthday special. Please never forget how lovable you are, and all the people in your life who appreciate you. I love you so much little bunny! - Love, your Mom

Charlotte wiped the tears from her cheeks and placed her head down on her desk. Writing these cards was harder than she had thought it would be and on more than one level. Charlotte sat back up and picked up her pen. She stared at the paper for ten minutes and set down her pen again. A flood of negative emotions was giving her writer's block. She went to the coffee machine.

How was she going to write fifteen cards per child without repeating herself over and over again? She sighed as she sat back down at her desk and looked at the clock. It was ten past nine. She had plenty of time. She picked up the pen and sat poised. Nope, nothing new was coming. She was stuck. After finishing her coffee, Charlotte put on her boots, mittens, jacket, and scarf and headed outside for a walk to the lake. Before she knew it, her feet were carrying her into town, and she was stepping through the door of the Rocky Mountain Chocolate shop.

"Charlotte, what a treat to see you. Adrien said you are staying in town at the condo because you are overwhelmed with work." Charlotte's mother-in-law didn't even pause to give Charlotte a chance to answer. She just kept right on talking.

"You feeling alright? I have to be honest. You look like hell. Have you still been eating all that green crap? I'm telling you, it's the vegans who are the weak ones. There is nothing healthier than a big piece of lean beefsteak every couple of days or so. Especially for us women. It gets your iron levels back up. Vegans, like you, well they just compensate for the lack of animal protein with lots of sugar. And don't fool yourself, honey, grape sugar, raw cane sugar: it doesn't matter,

Charlotte. It's still sugar. And sugar just is not healthy darling. It's a fact. You can google it. Or look it up on YouTube. Hold on; I'll look it up on my smartphone here."

Charlotte's head began to pound. She wasn't a vegan. Why did Tracy keep insisting she was just because she didn't want to eat a steak the size of a dinner plate? What was she thinking, coming in here? Was she that lonely, or desperate? It didn't matter that it was the best chocolate available in the state. A few minutes with her mother-in-law was not enough to compensate. Forgive me, Lord, but Tracy is difficult to stomach. Want to help me out here?

"Do you know what, Tracy? You have me convinced," spoke up Charlotte.

"What?" Tracy looked up from her phone in evident surprise. "Really?"

"Sure. I'm sure it would help to eat some more protein. The problem is, I just can't stomach cooking it. But I would eat it if you put it in front of me."

"Well but that is no problem at all. You come over, and I'll make you dinner anytime you want. Or better yet, I can even come to you. When should I come? Those kids need to eat more protein."

Charlotte took a deep breath and let it out. "Well, I'm working evenings these days. But I suspect Adrien would appreciate the help with dinner. Like he told you, he has the kids during the week until Christmas."

"But what about you, honey? What are you eating for dinner? You have to take care of yourself." Tracy looked at Charlotte over the top of her eyeglasses as she held out a piece of chocolate on a tray. "Try this."

"I'll figure something out. Don't worry about me." Charlotte took the truffle and let the velvet feel of the chocolate melt in her mouth.

"Of course I will. Like I told you on your wedding day. 'Now you have two Mamas.' That was heartfelt you know. I don't just go saying things I don't mean. I'll drop off a plate to your office on the way home from your cabin, honey. No, no, don't try to contradict me. Now, what would you like?" She gestured at the glass display of chocolates, and before

Charlotte could reply, Tracy was filling a small box with an assortment. "Here. On the house, love. Good luck with the work," said Tracy as she came around the counter, handed Charlotte the chocolates, and gathered her into a bear hug.

Charlotte thanked her mother-in-law and strode out of the office. She was surprised to find a smile on her face and a lighter step than when she had walked in.

She was so preoccupied that she collided right into the man walking in the opposite direction. She slipped on the icy curb and almost fell flat on her face. A strong arm leaped out and grabbed her, pulling her back to her feet.

"You idiot, watch where you are going," breathed out Charlotte in a rush of rage. It was arduous to be understanding with the pain pulsing through her abdomen.

"Watch out now, you could be talking to your future brother-in-law," answered the man still holding her in his arms.

"Jake?"

"None other," answered Jake, throwing his arms out wide. "Hey, did Élodie tell you we talked about Adrien? She said your husband would be the perfect business partner for me for my new business venture."

"What?" asked Charlotte, dazed. She took a step back and shook her head. "What are you talking about?"

"I told you in the spa, remember? I'm starting a new extreme wilderness adventure business. Élodie said there isn't anyone in town who has better wilderness survival skills than Adrien."

"Well, that's true," admitted Charlotte.

"He's been a smoke jumper and ski paramedic for years, right? And he has spent weeks at a time adventuring out into the wild without taking a bunch of modern equipment with him."

What the heck, she thought. I'll tell Adrien about Jake. He can decide for himself. Just then Charlotte watched a dove fly down and poop on Jake's head. He swore, took out a package of tissues, and tried to clean the mess out of his hair.

All of a sudden Charlotte's eyes widened, as she recalled the conversation with Mary at breakfast at the Shore Lodge. Was that a sign to get away from this guy?

Her stomach was a tight coil of pain.

"Good luck with your business, Jake. I've got to get back to work."

"Isn't your office just a few blocks away? Listen, let me clean up, won't you? Then give me just ten minutes to listen to my proposal? Élodie told me Adrien is interested in opening his own survival business. We could join forces, as equal partners. This thing is going to be big."

If Adrien gets fired up about starting a new business venture as an entrepreneur, then he will want to stay in McCall, thought Charlotte.

Then if I don't beat this plague or my body, I can die knowing the kids will be surrounded by the love and support of their extended family and all their friends. Besides, it wouldn't be polite not to let him get cleaned up.

"You know what, Jake? You've piqued my interest. I'll hear you out. Let's go to my office."

CHAPTER 8

Proverbs 3:5-6
5 Trust in Yahweh with all your heart,
and don't lean on your own understanding.
6 In all your ways acknowledge him,
and he will make your paths straight.

"*P*LEASE MAKE YOURSELF comfortable," said Charlotte as she handed Jake a cup of coffee and sat down in her chair diagonal from her therapy coach.

"You have a real cushy life here, don't you? Sit back, gaze out at the lake and drink coffee while pretending to give a damn about what your clients are telling you.

" A bitter edge had crept into the normally light-hearted baritone of Jake's voice.

"Excuse me?"

Charlotte's heart jumped into her throat. Had she just seen a glimmer of hatred flash over Jake's features? Adrenaline shot through her veins. Her pulse raced.

"I want nothing more than improved mental health, well-being, and success for each of my clients," insisted Charlotte.

"Easy, Charlotte," Jake laughed. "I was trying to make a joke because," he paused, running his hands through his hair before intertwining them and placing them behind his head. He leaned back and placed his feet up on the coffee table. "Look, I'm jealous. I mean, you have your little business, a great husband from what Élodie had to say, two cute kids, and a sweet sister and a devoted mom. And you live in this charming little town. It's everything I want."

Charlotte examined Jake as he leaned forward and picked up his coffee cup. Had Charlotte been mistaken? There was no trace of anger or bitterness in his face or body language. It was if Charlotte had imagined it.

"Thanks."

Jake took a sip of the hot coffee and smiled at her.

"Great coffee, by the way. I didn't expect to get a decent cup in a small little town in the middle of nowhere USA."

"It is my favorite simple pleasure," admitted Charlotte.

"Mine too. Listen, you should buy your sister this coffee machine. Her coffee is like drinking mud." Jake's laughter rang out in the office.

"Wait, what?"

"Didn't Élodie tell you I'm staying with her now?" Jake leaned back and placed his feet up on the coffee table.

"You're what?" Charlotte leaned back in her chair. What the hell was Élodie thinking, having a strange man staying with her? She shook her head. "No, she didn't mention it."

"From the look on your face," laughed Jake. "I think I know why she didn't want to speak up."

She couldn't say she was surprised by the latest of Élodie's selections. The man was gorgeous, and Élodie tended to throw care and reason to the wind. Like the time she had sold all of her possessions before setting out on the Pacific Coast Trail with a best friend, followed by three months traveling through the country in a trailer. But something wasn't right about this guy. Charlotte had spent enough time watching and listening to people talk to get a sense of the dark waters running just under the surface of a very convincing façade.

"Please tell me you are just renting a room from her," Charlotte said. She cleared her throat and looked down at her feet before looking him in the eye.

"I am here to tell you that you have nothing to worry about," said Jake with a hand over his heart. "It was love at first sight. I won't mistreat your sister, Charlotte. It would be a foolish thing to do seeing as I want her brother-in-law as my new partner." He looked at Charlotte, waiting for a response.

She just stared back, examining his demeanor.

Élodie was already sleeping with him. Mama is going to kill her, thought Charlotte.

"Élodie told me you and your mom don't believe in living together before marriage and everything. Most of us have a different outlook on that these days."

Charlotte's nails bit into her palms. She sensed her pulse speeding up and ground her teeth.

The last thing she needed right now was to deal with Élodie throwing herself dramatically on her therapy sofa and crying about another broken heart. There just wasn't the time or energy within her body to give.

"This has disaster written all over it." Charlotte tensed. She hadn't meant to say that out loud.

"Easy now; have some faith, Charlotte," answered Jake, while leaning forward and patting her on the upper arm.

Charlotte retracted as if she had been hit in the face. What did this guy know about having faith? She had more faith in her little finger than he did in his whole being. Charlotte sighed. Or did she? When was the last time she had prayed? She had missed her daily bible reading and journaling for days now. She had prayed less since the diagnosis.

"Hello Charlottte, you still with me?"

Charlotte blinked her eyes, returning her focus to the man lounging in front of her, and nodded.

"Not all men are scoundrels, you know. But Élodie has told me about the handful of jerks that she has encountered so far. So I won't hold it against you that you are worried. You love your little sister. I'm protective of my little sister Samira too."

This guy is trouble, thought Charlotte. Hopefully, this handsome foreigner doesn't up and disappear and take Élodie's heart with him. Or at the very least, please hinder him from taking all her valuables with him when he walks out the door as the last boyfriend did.

"You mentioned faith," said Charlotte. "Does that mean you are a church-going man?"

"Can't say I'm opposed to the idea. We tend to think most super-religious are either delusional or closet hypocrites."

Jake narrowed his eyes for a fraction of a second while regarding Charlotte. Charlotte tensed. Was he insulting her?

"But after spending time with your Mama," Jake continued, "Well, she's changing my mind. She had Élodie and me out with her delivering meals to the sick and old people around town yesterday. That woman does not preach, she acts. I can respect that. So I'm even going to church with Élodie and your Mama this Sunday."

Charlotte relaxed back into the chair with a sigh. Fatigue pulled at every inch of her body. Maybe she was wrong about this man; her intuition on people had been faulty a few times in the past. Perhaps he was kind and loyal, and would make her sister happy. They could live together in sin in a state of peaceful domestic bliss; it wasn't her place to judge. She threw up her hands.

"Go on then. Tell me about your business idea, and let me see that business plan of yours."

Jake scooted to the edge of his seat and laid out his notes for the firm on the coffee table; he began to explain his idea. His eyes lighted up, and he took on an intensity that didn't match his usual laid back and charming attitude. Jake talked to her about the rising demand for learning wilderness skills due to television survival shows, and movies such as Into the Wild. He discussed the current competition in the market in the United States. He took out his iPad to show her the websites of two of the best wilderness survival adventure businesses in the country.

Charlotte reviewed Jake's different value offerings, ranging from a weekend to the three week-long trips into the wilderness at various levels of intensity. The most extreme trip lasted between one to three weeks and entailed traveling out into the woods with nothing but a knife, flint, canteen, and the clothes on the participant's back.

"Why in the world would anyone pay money to do this? Are you sure there are people out there who will want to do this on their holiday?" she asked and set a trip description back down onto the coffee table.

"I'm telling you, demand for these adventures is only increasing. Doctors, firemen, engineers, businessmen, teachers, heck, even stars want to go on these kinds of trips," answered Jake, leaning forward and looking Charlotte in the eye.

"But why?" asked Charlotte.

"People want to be more self-reliant and find a deeper connection with nature. There is a growing risk of burnout among professionals that are continually connected and overwhelmed by the flood of information that crashes down on them every waking moment. They want to disengage from the modern world and discover the joy found in simplicity and nature. They want to rediscover or cultivate more patience. It also creates an inner sense of stability and confidence to know you can venture out into the wilderness with little more than the shirt on your back and be able to survive."

Charlotte picked up another paper. It explained the survival training in detail. Jake leaned back on the sofa, letting her read in silence. The training included learning how to locate water in the wild and apply the solar treatment and filtration systems. It taught how to build a fire with natural friction and how to create survival shelters. A section of the training taught how to pad clothing with natural insulation for warmth.

The development of hunting skills was an extensive part of the training. Included in the course would be learning how to safely use and sharpen a safety knife, how to use primitive hunting tools, how to track and observe animals, how to develop controlled stillness and movement in the hunt, how to stalk, and how to apply camouflage, as well as trapping methods. A study of wild plants for food and medicinal use rounded out the course.

The ultimate extreme wilderness trip would prepare someone to stay alive in ten-foot-deep snow. Charlotte had read enough. She knew Élodie was right. Adrien would be perfect for this. The man spent as much time outside every day in nature as he could.

How many times had they fought about him heading out into the woods to hike for a week with minimal gear, often all alone? She had filled the basement with modern camping equipment Adrien refused to take with him, which Charlotte had always considered both stupid and dangerous.

If I can convince Adrien to join Jake in this, then he could give up his job opportunity in California and stay in McCall, she thought. There was a hitch, though. If Adrien was off for weeks or weekends at a time, then who would be taking care of her kids if she died? Would it be better for the kids to live in California and have their Dad coming home every night and spending all weekend with them? Or was it better to stay in McCall near their extended family and have their Dad away for days or weeks at a time?

"I don't know, Jake. It looks like if Adrien joined you, he wouldn't see much of the kids."

Charlotte looked at the notes again and pursed her lips. Jake and Adrien would need investment capital for the business; they would need a professional business and marketing plan to secure financing.

"Look here, Charlotte," said Jake, picking up a printed sheet in a bright folder. "You'll see on the next page that I want to open an office in town and hire a starting team of at least two more people, who Adrien and I would train so they could join us out working the trips.

We would switch off every other week being out in the wild, except for a few weeks in the summer, when we would offer the longer survival week courses. The rest of the year, one of us would be at the office in town, and the other out on a trek with clients.

The partner in McCall would man the storefront, do the administration and digital marketing work, and take out those who sign up for two hours in the afternoon on a guided cross-country skiing or hiking tour teaching basic animal and plant knowledge or basic survival skills."

"Okay, but you need to work everything out to a level of fine detail," answered Charlotte. "You need a solid business plan."

"We Swiss are known for our precision," answered Jake. "Of course I have a business plan." He took out another folder and held it out to her.

"Right. It's just that the numbers aren't correct, in fact, this won't work." Charlotte sighed. It looked like Jake had just printed a business plan template off the internet and inserted some random information and numbers.

"Maybe you could help me with the business plan?" he asked with a big smile.

"You sound like you know what you are talking about."

"It would take me hours to write a business plan," she protested, looking up from the documents in her hand. Her mind was already racing forward to implications of Adrien joining the business.

If Adrien was gone only every other week, she knew her Mom, Élodie, and her mother-in-law could take over when he left. They would prefer it to him moving away with the kids. And anyway, she reasoned, Mom is close to retirement. She always declared she wanted to help out with the kids even more once she stopped her work at the hospital. There was no doubt in her mind that her Mom would swoop in and do anything possible to support her grandchildren if Charlotte died.

She slammed the file in her hand on the table and bounced to her feet.

"I could help you out. Adrien would be a perfect business partner for you. How do you see the partnership working?"

"Fifty-one and forty-nine. I know from my Dad's experience that it is important to make clear from the beginning which partner has the authority to decide if there is dissension on a business choice." Jake watched Charlotte raise her eyebrows and waved his hands at her. "Don't misunderstand me. We would try to decide everything together. I want it to be an equal partnership as much as possible. But if there were to be a fight, then I want it clear that I have the final say."

"I can't say Adrien will like that. He has a massive ego and a stubborn streak."

"Well, he'll like the fact that he only has to put up a third of the first investment capital. In exchange, he has to find the two new employees, and fire them if they don't work out. When should we call Adrien and spring this on him? I can't wait to get the ball rolling forward on all of this. We could open this summer."

"Easy there, tiger," answered Charlotte with a gleam in her eye. "That's in six months. Before we launch, you'll need to finish the business plan, meet with the bank, rent your new office, develop a marketing plan, build your website, hire employees and develop business processes and more. But first things first; we need the business and marketing plans ironed out. Then you and Adrien can work on all the other elements."

"You said 'we.' Why would you invest all that time into helping me if you don't even know if your husband wants to join me in this new business?"

"I want him to agree to this as much as you do," answered Charlotte. She held out her hands, stopping him before he could ask why. "I have my reasons. Now I have some work of my own to get back to finishing. Do you have time tomorrow at three to work on the business plan?"

Jake agreed and thanked her. She walked him to the door, and he went to leave, but turned on his toe and kissed her on the cheek. "Your sister is right about you. You are one smart woman."

The hairs on the back of Charlotte's neck stood on end. For the first time in weeks, she knew she should feel buoyant with unbridled hope. Instead, there was an unease tingling down her spine. Why? She had walked right into a viable opportunity to entice Adrien to stay in McCall. All she had to do was make the proposition as appetizing as possible. She could do that, couldn't she? Why wasn't she happy?

Charlotte's stomach twisted all the way back to her desk until she saw the cards. She glanced at her watch. It was eleven-thirty. Her shoulders slumped, and the pain flared up in her back. She needed a walk to clear her head and something to eat. She had forgotten to pack her lunch like usual that morning. The birthday card goal had distracted her.

Once outside, she walked to her favorite dock and looked out over the water at the snow-covered pine trees along the shore. Please help me with these cards, she prayed. I don't want every card just to say how much I love them. I want to give them more than that. Snowflakes began to float down, catching on her eyelashes and the tip of her nose.

A memory of Aurélie building her first snowman on the ice of the lake, when it froze completely a few years back came to her. A gentle smile came to her lips. She straightened up. That was it. She would write a favorite memory into each birthday card. She hurried back to her office. She sat down at her desk, and this time, her pen could hardly keep up with the words tumbling forth from her onto the page.

A knock came at the door, and Charlotte jumped. She looked out the window and noticed it was dark outside. What time was it? She had been so deeply engrossed in her work that she had lost all sense of time and space. Charlotte went to her office door and opened it. Tracy stood on the doorstep with a picnic basket. She held it up. "I bet you my chocolate shop you haven't eaten anything since that chocolate this afternoon. Am I right or am I right?"

"You know me pretty well."

"Look, I found the most fabulous container. It keeps food warm for a long time. I wish I could stay to give you some company while you eat, but I better scoot home to John. He'll be missing me about now. We have our favorite show to curl up and watch at nine, and I want to take a hot bath first. I made a new batch of almond-covered truffles today, and I'm plum tuckered out."

All at once Charlotte realized how hungry and weary she was. When inspiration had struck, she had forgotten all about going to get some lunch.

"Thank you so much, Tracy. I appreciate it." A tear slipped down her cheek. She wiped it away, embarrassed.

"To hell with the show," answered Tracy. "I'll stay here with you. Obviously, something is wrong. I have a very keen intuition. Always have had a sense of knowing what's going on with people." Tracy put an arm around Charlotte and pressed her head to her ample chest. She rubbed Charlotte's back. Charlotte wrapped her arms around Tracy and gave her a hug and then pulled back.

"I'm just famished and tired is all. I'll feel better after I eat."

Tracy narrowed her eyes at Charlotte.

"Really," insisted Charlotte with a bright smile. "Why don't you come out to the cabin after church on Sunday? We could cook brunch together."

"Now I know something is wrong. You like to curl up with a book after church in front of the fire at home. I know you get worn out on socializing after listening to people talk about their problems all week."

"Family is important," answered Charlotte. She took a deep breath. "It will be fun. You could call Elizabeth. Maybe she wants to drive up this weekend too. If you don't mind, I'll ask my mom and Élodie, too."

"It sounds fun; we've never cooked together. But no offense, sweetheart, but we may as well have it at my place instead. You don't have enough chairs for everyone at yours."

"You don't mind?"

"I'd be delighted. Now eat that before it gets cold. See you at church."

Charlotte raced back to her desk as soon as Tracy left. She only had three more of the thirty birthday cards to write, and she wanted to finish them before exhaustion and pain prevented her from doing so. Charlotte took up the pen and continued. At last, she went over and opened the basket and took out the plate of food. Scalloped potatoes and ham, green beans, steak and a homemade roll steamed in front of her. Nothing had ever tasted this good to her in her life.

After she was done eating the home cooked dinner, she noticed the second container and opened it up. Homemade chocolate chip cookies were stacked with a note. "Take care of yourself. Love, Tracy"

Charlotte glanced at the cards on her desk. She wanted to decorate them, but she didn't have the energy. Instead, Charlotte grabbed the cookies and headed home. For once she was too tired to read before bed. Instead, she was going to curl up on the sofa with a hot cup of tea, eat the entire stack of cookies, and watch something on Adrien's Netflix.

PURE HABIT WOKE CHARLOTTE at the crack of dawn. She moaned and rolled out of bed onto the yoga mat and loaded the yogatoday.com website. A prayer was sent up to heaven that she wasn't at home. It had been hard enough to fall out of bed onto the yoga mat in her pajamas. There wasn't an angel in hell's way she could have jumped into a cold swimming pool this morning. Rolling over, Charlotte grabbed her water bottle and drained half a liter of water. She fumbled for the ancient grain cracker box next to the bed and stuffed some in her mouth. Taking a deep breath, she took another sip of water, urging her stomach to settle as she pushed back into downward dog.

Two hours later Charlotte entered her office at a quarter to eight. It was beyond her why it had taken her so long to get going this morning. After the yoga, she had taken a long shower in the hopes that the hot water would revive her.

But as soon as she had dried off, she found herself climbing back into bed and falling asleep for another hour. The good news was that when she awoke, her body had lost the tension and pain that had been plaguing her for longer than she could remember.

Charlotte made herself a cup of coffee and sat down at her desk. She checked her calendar. It was Tuesday, so she had until Thursday night to make as much progress as possible before then. The best would be to finish the presents and cards in one go. Charlotte took the pile of cards to her copy machine and began to copy all thirty cards. On second thought, she scanned every card and saved all of the images as pdfs in a compressed file. Charlotte labeled each card with the date it should be mailed.

She decided then and there to send a third copy of the cards to her closest psychologist friend, Sebastian. It couldn't hurt to ask him if he was willing to send the cards out to her kids on their birthdays. She had already told him all about her cancer. He wouldn't mind, she knew he wouldn't. He had already told her he would do anything and everything to help her when she had called him.

The downside of having a doctorate in psychology, she decided, is she knew what coping mechanism she was using: control. The cancer was uncontrollable, but this was something she could do, and it gave her a small dose of calm.

Just as Charlotte was finishing writing the email to Sebastian requesting his help, there was a knock at the door. Jake was already at the door. Time seemed to be seeping through her fingers like water, no matter how tightly she clenched them together. She went to answer the door.

"Good morning, Jake."

"You look like you slept well. You look better than yesterday," Jake said while slipping out of his boots and into the slippers Charlotte held out to him.

"I do?"

Jake nodded. He followed her to the coffee machine and watched her pull out two white porcelain cups with matching saucers.

Charlotte smiled, offering a quick prayer of gratitude up to God for a day of reprieve from the pain. She turned around to hand Jake his cup of coffee with a smile.

"Let's get to work, Jake, and pound this out as fast as possible. I have a busy day. I want to drive down to Boise for some shopping once we're done working here." She settled down in her therapy chair, and Jake leaned back on the sofa diagonally to her.

"You don't say," he answered and rubbed his chin. "I was thinking of traveling down to Boise myself sometime in the next week for some shopping myself. Would you like some company? I could drive us. Then we could discuss business on the trip down and back. If you don't get carsick, then you could work in the car. We could head out now."

Charlotte blinked her eyes rapidly while processing the unexpected proposal. "You don't even know how that would save me," she answered. "I can use every extra second I can find today. My only question is: does your vehicle have a big trunk?"

"Sure does. So finish that coffee, lady, and let's go," answered Jake as he gathered his leather messenger bag that served as his briefcase.

Charlotte scanned the office, trying to assess what she should bring. She grabbed her purse and her laptop.

"Let's go."

BY THE END OF THE TWO-HOUR DRIVE, Charlotte had finished reviewing the business plan and had managed to crunch the numbers. The papers had scribbled notes all over them that would be incomprehensible to anyone but her. Charlotte knew she had almost finished. With her notes, she would only need a half an hour to modify the document on a laptop.

There was a light bounce in her step when Jake dropped her off in the front of the mall. He arranged to pick her back up at the same spot in two hours at one, and they would go out for some lunch.

Charlotte took out her gift list from her purse and looked down at it. She decided to start with the toys and work upward in age. The first stop was the toy store.

An hour and a half later, she was finished with the first six years' worth of presents. She requested they keep the mountain of purchases at customer service for her while she did some more shopping for other gifts.

The last stop was at the gift card store. Charlotte was just itching to pull a couple of all-nighters to be able to complete the cards like the vision of perfection in her head. That morning she had to reject her perfectionistic neuroticism and face the facts. Charlotte had cancer and severe fatigue. She realized that time was simply not available to decorate thirty cards, much less five of them. Creating beautiful cards was time-intensive, and she wanted, she needed, to spend her energy on her clients and playing with her children instead.

So she had resolved to glue her birthday letters into beautiful pre-made cards. Now, standing in the store under the fluorescent lights, the decision was eating at her like a swarm of mosquitos. She purchased fifty cards in under twenty-five minutes. She cringed at how quickly she had to throw the cards into her basket.

Charlotte had always had a love of cards and could have spent the entire morning meandering down the aisles and examining the messages and design of the different options. If she couldn't make the cards herself, she at least wanted to select the best ones possible, and with great care.

Time just wasn't on her side.

Jake picked her up as arranged. He didn't even blink twice when she asked him if he would be willing to carry the bags from the toy store to the trunk. When they had finished loading all her presents away in the car, they went out to lunch at the Cheesecake Factory. It was the first day in ages that Charlotte's stomach didn't hurt her, and she was going to enjoy it as much as possible. The salmon, alfredo pasta, and asparagus had been delicious, and Charlotte still was hungry. Charlotte ordered the strawberry shortcake, the fudge cake, and the caramel cheesecake for dessert. Jake watched her sample each dessert in amusement.

She finished half of each dessert, and Jake ate the rest. By the time they walked out, they both were ready for some fresh air, and Jake wanted a chance to walk around downtown Boise for the first time.

Charlotte promised Jake they could drive to downtown, but first, she begged him to drive her to Costco. A client of hers had told her that they had some of the best deals on jewelry in Boise, and Charlotte was just a few presents shy of being done with her list.

Charlotte flashed her card to the greeter at the door of the cavernous warehouse and practically ran to the display cases housing jewelry. Her eyes immediately gravitated to a pair of sparkling diamond earrings and below to a stunning diamond pendant necklace.

The set even had a matching bracelet. She also selected a pearl necklace with matching earrings. It took her a bit longer to decide on an expensive watch. She tracked down an employee to open the case so she could look at the watches on Jake's wrist. At last, she had found one.

On a final whim, she chose a diamond sapphire ring for her daughter and a ring encrusted with rubies and diamonds for Gabriel as well for his future wife. She wasn't sure if he would even ever want to get married.

Then again, as Zack had said, it was a gift with meaning and high worth. He could always sell it if he hated it. Charlotte paid for and collected the boxes. Jake whistled as they walked out the door.

"Your family will have one merry Christmas to look forward to," he commented.

Charlotte looked back at him, stunned. He thought all these presents were for one Christmas? She opened her mouth to explain, and then closed it again. The last person she was going to tell her secret to was this guy.

CHARLOTTE AND JAKE SPENT the afternoon strolling through the downtown Boise together. They stopped for coffee at the Flying M café and settled down with her laptop. Charlotte took out her notes scribbled all over her printed copy of the business plan and quickly modified the document on her Mac notebook.

Jake bought her another chai tea latte and a pumpkin scone, and they started a new marketing plan document to hash out the exact details of promoting the new business.

Charlotte decided it was as if she were a rechargeable battery and someone had plugged her into an electrical station overnight. Her body hummed with energy. There was an excitement traveling up and down her spine. The afternoon reminded her of the time when she had worked out her first business plan for her online therapy business. The hope, the expectation, the creative juices, the high risk: all of it left her with a happy buzz.

By the time they left the Flying M, Jake had a complete business plan and a quarter of a marketing plan started, and each of them was grinning from ear to ear. Charlotte emailed the business plan to Jake. S

he saved the documents on her laptop and USB stick. On the drive back to McCall, Charlotte closed her eyes and offered up a prayer of thanks for sending Jake into her life. Now it was up to her to try to deliver this opportunity in a way so that Adrien would not only say yes but be as proud and excited about the partnership as the job offer in LA.

As Charlotte watched the river crashing along the winding road back up the mountain to McCall, her spirits suddenly sank into her boots. Adrien was an incredibly proud man. All at once she realized that if she pitched this partnership and business opportunity to Adrien, or if he had any idea of her involvement in it, he would reject it out of hand.

He wanted to prove to himself and the world that he could stand on his own two feet and build something from the ground up on his own. He wouldn't want her to have a significant involvement. He needed this to be his source of independence and pride. She turned to Jake and turned down the rock music.

"Adrien can't know that I have had anything to do with helping you with any of this. He can't know I even know about it."

"That's crazy. Why?"

"He already resents me making more money than he does. The last thing he needs is to find out that I went behind his back and helped with his business."

"Perhaps you're not giving him enough credit. I for one would be touched to have a wife who cared enough about me to invest time and effort into helping me build a business."

"Adrien wants to prove he can achieve success on his terms and without my involvement. It is so ingrained in men that to be a 'real man' you need to be the head of the household by breadwinner. It is hard to change the unconscious beliefs about who we are and what it means to be a husband and father."

"It sounds like a familiar story," replied Jake, shaking his head. "My Dad earned all the money and made all the important decisions for the family. He wouldn't think of doing a load of laundry or changing a diaper."

"Yeah well, that sounds like my father-in-law. I think Adrien has a sense of being 'less than' his Dad because he was the one home raising our kids when they were babies and toddlers, instead of earning the income like his father. I have so much gratitude and pride in who Adrien is as a father. But it messes with your head. I think that is why he has always had the need to go off into the wild on camping trips and work as a smoke jumper."

"Well, he sounds like a hell of a guy, and that's why I am so interested in being his partner. This business could be just what he needs to get his feet back under him. I mean," Jake shook his head, "what is more 'classically' male than going out into the wilderness to teach survival courses?"

"You're right. That's why I want Adrien to know he has achieved this all on his own," insisted Charlotte. "I don't want him to know I am involved in any way."

"If you say so. I just can't help but wonder if it will come back to hit us in the face. Secrets don't stay secrets in a small town long."

"We'll just tell everyone you came to me for therapy," suggested Charlotte.

"Hell no. I'm not crazy," answered Jake, shaking his head. "No way are we saying that."

Charlotte sighed. "Normal people come to me too, Jake. Listen, you can tell them it is part of your job training that you're in life coaching. You know, so you can also teach your clients mental resilience tricks they will need when they are out with only the shirts on their backs in the wild."

"I like that. That's a damn good idea. We should do that for real," answered Jake as he slammed the gas pedal to the floor to overtake a truck hauling a trailer of fresh-cut pine logs.

"I don't know if I'll have time for that. But I have some amazing books I can gift you."

BY THE TIME THEY ENTERED McCall, it was past dinnertime. Jake dropped Charlotte off at her office and carried all of the presents in for her. Charlotte spent the next hour trying to figure out where to put all the gifts. She couldn't bring them to her mother's house or Élodie's because the truth about her cancer would need to come out.

Adrien was staying at their cabin. She certainly didn't want to store them at his condo, and there was no space in her office. Taking a deep breath, she pulled out her phone and dialed Zack.

"Zack, can we talk?"

"I've meant to call you. I apologize for the other day. The shock of the news about your cancer and my feelings for you were overwhelming. I shouldn't have tried to kiss you."

Charlotte swallowed. Why was it her mouth always went dry when tears slid down her cheeks? "I don't know what to say."

"Don't say anything. We're friends. I'm going to be a good friend to you if you need me to be. Where are you?"

"I'm in the office."

"Great. I'll swing by there when my shift ends in half an hour so we can talk. I have a customer to serve."

Fatigue washed over Charlotte the instant the call ended.

She had had every intention of sitting down at her desk and working on pasting her letters into the birthday cards for Aurélie and Gabriel this evening. The pain was pulsating between her shoulder blades, like the screech of a bow pulling against a violin, emitting a teeth-grinding cringe. She lowered herself onto the sofa. First, she would need to take a little break. There was no way she could even tackle the easy task of cutting, pasting, and adding stickers to her cards.

Pain seared through her solar plexus, which was clenched in a tight ball of pulsating agony. Charlotte lay down and pulled her knees up to her chest.

Phone still in hand, she did a Google search for solar plexus pain, and a YouTube meditation appeared in the listing. She pressed play and rummaged through her purse on the coffee table for pain medication as a calm voice filled the room in accompaniment with ocean waves. Charlotte swallowed some medicine and collapsed back down on the sofa. Within minutes she was sound asleep.

When Charlotte opened her eyes, Zack was gently shaking her awake.

"Charlotte? Are you okay?"

"Dear God, I feel like I'm dying," she moaned and pulled her knees up tighter to her chest. The medication had only dampened the pain. Her entire body was throbbing with the torment emitting from her abdomen and back. She took a shuddering breath.

"I'll call an ambulance."

Charlotte sprang to sitting, wincing in the process. "No. I'm all right."

Zack eyed her warily, his phone still poised in his hand to dial for help.

"Really," she insisted while placing a hand on his arm. "This is just one of the delightful experiences of cancer."

She managed a weak smile.

Zack sat down slowly on the sofa next to her as if she were made of priceless crystal and a wrong move could send her shattering to the floor. "So. How did your family take the news?"

"I," she cleared her throat and turned her eyes from him

to the view out the window. The lake was inky black in the darkness. The veracity of her cancer diagnosis was radiating through her body. Was this just the beginning? What would it feel like toward the end?

She pictured herself beaten hollow and ghostly by pain with her children sitting on the bed beside her. I don't want them to remember me like that.

Please, God. I want them to remember me vibrant and laughing while swimming with them, skiing with them, hiking with them in the woods, and reading to them in front of a crackling fire.

I won't ask you to reprieve me of cancer, but I pray with every fiber of my being that you deliver my children from seeing me wither away in front of their eyes.

Please keep them here, where there are so many people who can step in to love and support them. Don't let him take them away to California.

All at once she was tempted by a vision of jumping into the icy dark water, drinking it in as the liquid swallowed her up beneath its weight. How long did it take to drown? The terror and pain couldn't last long. And then, there would be no more pain, nor struggle. The fear would diffuse away as she lost consciousness.

"Charlotte?"

She blinked her eyes, shook her head slightly, and brought her awareness back to the room. No. She wouldn't ever do that to her children. No matter how horrifying it gets, Charlotte, you can't ever leave your kids with the slightest doubt that you fought with everything you have to stay with them as long as possible.

"Could you help me? It is an enormous favor. I will understand if you say no," she said, her voice quiet from the pain and fatigue.

A tsunami of emotion hurled itself at Charlotte as she explained how important birthdays were to her. Memories spilled out of her of how her mother had managed to make every one of Élodie's and her birthdays special, no matter how tight money was, or how battered her mother was with fatigue and worry. If she could make one wish, it would be that her children would have magical birthdays for the rest of their childhood.

"No one is going to stop me from giving my kids beautiful birthdays, Zack. No one," she yelled, throwing up her arms, her anger lending her a flicker of energy. "Whether I am here to see them or not."

Zack held up his hands in surrender. "I can't understand why anyone wouldn't want to give Aurélie and Gabriel magical birthdays, Charlotte. I don't know why you are so worked up about this."

Charlotte sighed. "Adrien doesn't think birthdays are important. In fact, he berates me every year for making such a big deal about them. It's crazy because he's the one who is aggrieved at Christmas that I only want the children to receive one special present and not more. Sometimes no matter how hard I try, I can't understand the man."

"Yeah, but if he knows that this is your wish, I mean, certainly he will ensure it comes true."

Charlotte just looked at him, and then shrugged.

"You haven't told him yet."

It wasn't a question. The statement echoed in Charlotte's head. She hadn't ever wanted to say it out loud. It was a rotten smell of aging fish and days-old refuse. Her marriage was a hollow shell of a house without trust. Without a foundation of trust on which to build its walls, was there ever a chance for it to withstand the slightest storm? Could you love someone without trusting them?

"It's time to tell him the truth," agreed Charlotte.

CHAPTER 9

Matthew 17:18-20
18 Jesus rebuked him, the demon went out of him, and the boy was cured from that hour.
19 Then the disciples came to Jesus privately, and said, "Why weren't we able to cast it out?"
20 He said to them, "Because of your unbelief. For most certainly I tell you, if you have faith as a grain of mustard seed, you will tell this mountain, 'Move from here to there,' and it will move; and nothing will be impossible for you. 21 But this kind doesn't go out except by prayer and fasting."

ZACK MADE THEM CUPS of tea and tucked a blanket around Charlotte. He agreed to store all the presents for her for as long as she needed. She gave him a USB stick with a copy of all the birthday cards and told him that when she found the time, she was going to print them all out and make them into proper cards that could be mailed, but until then, the USB stick would be insurance.

If anything prevented her from finishing the cards, would he print them out and send them for her every year, on Gabriel and Aurélie's birthdays?

He nodded, and she also entrusted him with a copy of the video of her reading to the children.

Charlotte kept waiting for Zack to argue with her that all her efforts were unnecessary because she was going to fight cancer and win. He didn't.

Instead, he took her hand before he left and said, "This is a beautiful thing to do for your kids. I am honored you trust me with this. But why me? Why don't you entrust the presents and cards to Adrien or your Mom? Hell, I know Élodie would love to do this for you."

Charlotte's gaze shifted to her shoes. A silence fell over the room.

"Charlotte?"

"They might think it's creepy. You know, the kids getting cards and presents from their dead Mom every year." She twisted the edge of the blanket around and around her hand.

"Since when did you start caring what other people think? Think over Galatians 1:10: 'For am I now seeking the approval of man, or of God? Or am I trying to please man? If I were still trying to please man, I would not be a servant of Christ.'"

"Thank you. You're right. I thought you didn't go to church anymore Zack."

"I don't. But that doesn't mean I don't still read the Bible."

Zack removed all the presents from the office and stored them in his car, and then he walked Charlotte to Adrien's condo. He gave her a hug on the front walk and kissed her cheek before turning on his heel and disappearing into the swirl of snowflakes falling soundlessly around them.

Charlotte turned the key in the lock of Adrien's front door. She entered Adrien's condo and fell onto the couch. Charlotte was so thankful for everything that she had been able to accomplish that day. Now she was too tired to put on her pajamas. Counting to three, Charlotte dragged herself off the couch and to the bedroom.

She slipped out of her black-and-white printed wool A-line skirt and black wool tights and pulled the red sweater off. She tossed the fake double strand of pearls on the floor and slipped into bed. Her eyes were closed an instant later.

THE NEXT DAY CHARLOTTE began to ache from missing her kids so much. It was almost noon, and her stomach was growling. More than that, Charlotte realized she was lonely, and there was only one person she wanted to see. She took out her phone. Ten minutes later her mother placed steaming bowls of homemade pumpkin soup down on the table. Charlotte smiled at her mother in thanks as she brought back a plate stacked with slices of homemade seven-grain bread and a stick of butter.

"Well, this is a delightful surprise. When was the last time you came for lunch?"

"Do you cook like this for yourself every day?"

Anna gave a chuckle as she shook her head. "I have two little angels with me after school every day. They are mighty hungry by the time they settle in at the table. I make an extra portion of whatever I prepare for myself for lunch and give it to them at four-thirty. And yes, before you ask, they get my homemade chocolate chip cookies."

Charlotte ate a spoonful of the spicy pumpkin cream soup and savored the warmth spreading through her body. She hadn't known her mother was going to such an effort for her kids. Here she had been lecturing her now and again about feeding Gabriel and Aurélie too much sugar, and she had been feeding them a nutritious homemade meal every late afternoon.

"Well, now I know why they don't fall to pieces when they get home and declare they are hungry," she commented. "But they always eat the dinner I make too."

"That doesn't surprise me. Those two have metabolisms like a hummingbird. Now, what brings you home for lunch?"

Charlotte fought an overwhelming urge to unload the news of her diagnosis onto her mother.

She wanted to bury her face into her mother's shoulder and let the tears flow, to breathe in her clean citrus scent, and to have her mother's arms wrapped around her. Tears burned in her eyes, and she brushed them away. It was time to tell her Mom.

"You don't have to keep it a secret, you know," said Anna. She placed her soup spoon down on the table and reached out for Charlotte's hand. "I know."

Anna came around the table and opened her arms. Charlotte stood up and walked into her embrace. "I don't know what he can be thinking, wanting to take a job in LA. He doesn't belong there any more than you and the kids do. Still, if you decide to move with him, I won't try to talk you out of it, Charlotte. You don't have to fear me falling apart. It will kill me to have my grandkids so far away, but what is important is that they, and you, are happy."

Charlotte blinked the tears away, her arms still wrapped tight around her mother. She gazed at the wooden kitchen cabinet and oak kitchen table lit up with sunlight in bewilderment. A sigh escaped her lips, and she hugged her mother tighter, taking her mother's misperception as a sign that her real secret should remain one, at least for a little longer.

"Thanks, Mom," she cleared her throat. "But I am going to do everything I can to encourage him to find a new job here at home."

"That's my girl. I have to admit I am happy to hear that answer. Now," exclaimed Anna, while giving Charlotte a tighter squeeze and letting go. "Let's eat our soup while it's still hot."

As Charlotte savored the comfort food and chatted with her mother about her work at the hospital, her eyes roamed the room. Even grown with two kids and a house of her own, it unlocked something tight inside her chest to walk through the front door and smell the familiar combination of citrus, bleach, and homemade bread.

It didn't matter that the kitchen table was scarred and beaten and the sofa in the living room was over twenty years old. Charlotte would prefer to be sitting here with her mother over relaxing by an infinity pool behind a multimillion-dollar home. Sitting at this table, with the sun shining in the windows, Charlotte experienced what she always did when she came home. She closed her eyes, submerging herself in the feelings of comfort, warmth, and contentment. Home would always be her safe place to fall.

"You okay, honey?"

Charlotte blinked her eyes open and smiled. "Thank you, Mama, for giving us such a beautiful childhood. It couldn't have been easy, you know, all on your own."

"I wasn't alone," answered Anna and nodded her head upward. "He sent me help when I needed it in the most unexpected ways. Say, speaking of unexpected, we have a visitor in McCall I've meant to talk to you about."

"Oh?" Charlotte raised her eyebrows as she buttered another slice of homemade bread.

"Your Daddy came around last week, asking about you. He wants to see you, Charlotte."

Charlotte inhaled the bite of bread in her mouth and began choking. Tears streamed in her eyes as she struggled for breath while trying to cough it up. Anna rushed around the table and pounded her on the back. The bread dislodged from her throat, and Charlotte collapsed back onto her chair.

"He just appears out of nowhere wanting to see me? Why? I don't ever want to see that man again."

Anna sat back down across from Charlotte and pushed her soup bowl out of the way. She leaned forward across the table. "I respect that, Charlotte. I know he hurt you when he walked out on us. But you go on and remember Luke seventeen verse four. Even if they sin against you..."

Charlotte held up her hands, interrupting her mother. "'If they sin against you seven times in a day and seven times come back to you saying 'I repent,' you must forgive them.' I know, Mom. It's one of your favorites. I know. But how the hell is that fair? Why don't I just go on and lie and cheat and walk out on people? Then I could just turn around and repent and ask to be forgiven?"

"Oh beautiful," her mother answered as she rose and walked behind Charlotte's chair. She encircled her arms around Charlotte and pressed her cheek to her daughter's. "Don't start judging people like that. There are people out there who have gone through a world of hurt; it blinds them, causes them to turn too fast and send everything around them crashing to the floor. Then there they are, examining the damage, and they don't have the means to make things right."

"Mom, what the hell are you trying to say?"

"Hey, don't you talk like that in this house."

"Mom."

"I'm saying," began Anna with a sigh and then kneeled down in front of her daughter, taking her hands and giving them a squeeze. "Your father was abused by his parents, honey. The night before your Dad left, he lost his job. He hit the bars in town and came in rolling. When he came in the door, you asked him if you could have a new pair of ice-skating lessons, and he told you no. You started to whine, and he lifted his hand. I saw what was coming and jumped in between you. He collapsed against me. He was even more petrified by what had almost happened then I was. More than anything else, he never wanted to end up like his father."

"I don't remember any of that."

"Of course you don't. You were little. I told you your Daddy was sick, and he went to bed. I fed you dinner and tucked you and Élodie into bed. I marched into the bedroom once you two were fast asleep and gave your Dad an ultimatum. Until he promised to go to therapy and permanently quit drinking, he was no longer living under the same roof as us. The next morning, when I woke up, there was a letter on his pillow."

Charlotte watched her Mom take a deep breath and blink back tears. "He wrote that he didn't trust himself to stay sober. Your father didn't trust himself around you two girls. He wrote that he loved us all too much to stay with us. We deserved a better man in our lives. Six months later I received the divorce papers."

Charlotte watched her Mom cry and felt heat stinging the back of her eyes. She swallowed, took a deep breath, and counted to ten.

"Yes, but he never sent so much as a card Mom. He just disappeared from our lives altogether."

"Well, that's just the thing, honey. Your father showed up two days ago wanting to know why we've never touched the money he's sent. I said we never received any checks. He sent a letter that got lost in the mail, telling me he was opening bank accounts in our names: one for you, one for Élodie, and one for me. He's put money in our accounts for the past thirty-one years, and we didn't know about it."

Charlotte's buried her face in her hands. All these years she had assumed her Dad had walked away and never looked back. A great void had opened up under her feet, and she hung suspended.

"There's more you need to know, but I'll let him tell you,"

concluded Anna. "I explained where your office is. I suspect he'll drop by sometime this afternoon."

"Mom, you didn't," exclaimed Charlotte, her heart beating like a herd of antelope escaping a ravenous lion.

Dear God, she prayed silently. After everything you've thrown at me this year, you need to load on more suffering and heartache? In response she sensed nothing. There was no reply. Charlotte had never experienced such a crisis of faith as she did as she hugged her mother goodbye and gave a tight-lipped smile on her way out the door. For the first time in her life, she doubted if there was anyone up there looking over her at all.

CHARLOTTE SAT AT HER DESK, waiting for a knock to come at the door. Would her father show up? Would she even recognize him? It was as if she had fallen into a pool teeming with slimy eels writhing all around her and she was quivering with terror. Any moment an electric eel would slide over her skin, blasting her with its five hundred volts of electricity.

She went to the window and opened it, hoping the rush of frigid fresh air would blow away some of the creepy adrenaline slipping over her. She returned to her desk ten minutes later, a little calmer, and examined the list on her desk.

She stared at the phone. She picked it up, and then replaced it. Three more times she repeated the action. "Come on Charlotte, this is for the best," she said aloud. Taking a deep breath, she picked up her phone and dialed the number of her favorite colleague, Dr. Sebastian Treubach.

"Hi Sebastian, this is Charlotte."

"Charlotte, this is a surprise. It's good to hear your voice. How are you feeling?"

"Surprisingly reasonable, considering the cancer. Listen, I am just going to come out with it. Would you be interested in buying the therapy platform? If you check your email, you will see that I just sent you the financials of the business for the past five years so that you can gauge the profitability. The second document contains my asking price for the practice."

Charlotte's question was met with silence on the other end of the line.

"This is the wrong decision, Charlotte. I would be interested in buying the practice. But I think you need to give yourself some time. It is never wise to make life-altering decisions in the middle of a crisis."

"No. I've considered this carefully."

"But you were just diagnosed. Things could improve. Or you could outsource some of the work and retain the business for at least a few more months. I can take on more of your clients to ease your load."

Charlotte's eyes burned. "I don't know what to do."

"Then wait," answered Sebastian. "I'll take half your clients. Reduce down by fifty percent. See how that feels."

Charlotte stared out the window at the lake. She didn't answer. She was so proud of being a businesswoman. Her platform was the first to offer qualified therapy online. In the meantime, quite a few competitors were competing for clients with online and distance therapy sessions. However, her platform had the best reputation. She didn't want to see the quality of the business suffer if she couldn't invest the necessary time required to vet new therapists and ensure high customer satisfaction via regular online and telephone customer surveys.

"Are you really capable of taking on half my clients?"

"Yes."

"Then I will send you a list by the end of the day with the contact details of my clients. I will inform them myself of the transfer to your care and why I need to step aside. I will go talk to my lawyer and ensure that if I should die, then you will receive first opportunity to purchase my business for the equivalent of one year's revenue."

"Have you assiduously considered this decision Charlotte? Perhaps you should sleep on it and let me know tomorrow. You're undervaluing the business price."

"No. Your concern and help have made up my mind. I'll continue running the business as long as I am capable. If that changes, I will sell it to you and have you take over."

"It is a brilliant business you have built up. We reach people who wouldn't make it into one of our offices. I will be proud to take stewardship in addition to my physical practice."

"That's good news. Thank you."

"I'm honored I'm the one you thought of selling to first," he answered. "Wait, I am the first, right?"

"Yes," smiled Charlotte. "You're the first."

"Take care of yourself, Charlotte. We'll talk soon."

"Goodbye."

Charlotte hung up the phone. She had expected weariness to wash over her like a thick fog blocking out all sunlight. Instead, a weight was lifted from her shoulders. Retaining the business was the right choice, at least for now. She was light and effervescent until she heard the knock on her office door.

TWO DARK, SOULFUL EYES drank her in. A handsome man stood silently in front of Charlotte. His dark hair and beard were dusted with a few gray hairs. He wore a starched blue button-up shirt, black worn jeans and a North Face jacket. He was holding a bouquet of three dozen tulips in shades of pink, purple, and red.

"You look even prettier in person than in the photos your Mama showed me." He held out the flowers. "I hope these are still your favorite."

Charlotte stood rigid. It was too much to take in. After her father had left, her mother had thrown away every photograph with him in it. She had hazy recollections of her father, but she was astounded to discover he was so good-looking. Then there were the flowers. She would never have thought he would notice, nor remember something so trivial as a little girl's favorite flower.

"Dad?"

"Well, I don't know if I deserve to be called that, but yeah. It's me. Can I come in?"

Charlotte stepped back, and her Dad stepped past her into the office. Charlotte took the bouquet of flowers and went to the kitchen nook to put them in a vase.

"How did you get tulips in December?"

"I ordered them from Holland."

Charlotte turned back around to face her father with the vase of tulips in her hand. "What are you doing here, Dad? Why now?"

"You deserved to have a good Dad, a source of love and support. I'm sorry I wasn't that man for you, Charlotte. I wanted to tell you that in person."

"Oh, Dad. I don't know what I can say." Emotions swirled her insides; it was as if a tornado had swept her up and was turning her round and round so fast that the world was a blur beyond the whirlwind of dust and debris. So she stood frozen to the spot, clutching the vase of flowers like it was a cliff ledge and she was hanging over a five-hundred-yard gorge.

"You don't have to say anything at all. I just knew you deserved a heartfelt apology and I wanted to encourage you to spend the money in your account. I just found out from your Mama that you didn't know I've sent you money every month since I could get myself a good job. But hopefully, you can use that money now to bring yourself and your kids some joy or security."

"You know about my kids?"

For the first time, Charlotte watched a smile spread across her father's face. "Your Mama showed me some pictures. They're beautiful, Charlotte. Just like you."

"Thank you."

"Listen," he replied while digging his trembling hands into his jean pockets. "I know this is all a lot to take in. So I'm going to say goodbye for now. I'll be staying at the Shore Lodge hotel. If you would like to talk more, then you meet me at the hotel at noon for lunch tomorrow. If you don't come, I'll understand."

He didn't wait for an answer. He turned on his heel and left the office before Charlotte even had time to set down the vase of flowers.

IT HAD BEEN AN INCREDIBLY long day. Charlotte could think of only one place she wanted to be, and she didn't want to waste a single moment more. Her children were still in school, but just this once, she was going to lie and say she needed to take

Aurélie out early for a dentist appointment.

Charlotte's smile glowed on her face as she waved at Aurélie through her classroom window. Aurélie smiled and waved at her, and then carefully placed her pencils in their case and stacked her books into a neat pile in the center of her desk. At last, she walked to the door.

"Mommy, what are you doing here?"

Aurélie's teacher, Mrs. Symms, walked over to the door behind Aurélie.

"I need to take Aurélie out early for a dentist appointment," explained Charlotte.

"No problem, Aurélie has finished her work for the day anyway. She is a talent in math," smiled her teacher.

A few minutes later, Charlotte and Aurélie arrived at Gabriel's preschool. When Gabriel saw Charlotte at the door, he yelled, "Mommy!"

He ran across the room and flung himself into her outstretched arms. Charlotte buried her face in his hair, and joy exploded in her chest, seeping out to warm her continually cold fingertips and toes.

Once she buckled the kids into the car and climbed into the driver's seat, she turned around and said, "I missed you so much this week; it made my whole heart hurt. So I picked you up early from school so we can go have some fun. We are going night skiing and then out for nachos and hot chocolate."

"What? You told my teacher I have a dentist appointment," exclaimed Aurélie.

"Well, yeah, but you don't. I just wanted to get you out of school," smiled Charlotte.

"But that's lying, Mom. You never lie. You said that telling the truth is important," insisted Aurélie. "Like in the Berenstain Bear book. Like in the Bible."

Charlotte paused, the smile frozen on her face. Her daughter had a point. She sighed and rubbed her forehead. "You're right," she sighed. "I shouldn't have lied. Next time I will tell the teacher I need you to get out early and leave it at that."

"What are nachos?" asked Gabriel. "Are they a cookie?"

"You'll like them. And if you don't, I'll buy you some French fries instead. Okay?"

By the time Charlotte drove back to the cabin, threw the ski equipment and clothes into the car, and drove the winding road up the mountain, she was wondering if she had been too ambitious. Her stomach was rolling, and her abdomen was squeezed up like a rock. The pain was radiating through her back, making her clench her jaw.

The moment she clicked into her skis and looked over at her children's beaming faces, she changed her mind. How many more afternoons like this did she have left?

They took the chairlift up the hill. Aurélie was like a wind-up toy. A continual stream of chatter issued from her lips, and Charlotte listened, bemused. Their first morning, Aurélie had been a half hour late for school because Adrien hadn't woken up early enough to figure in cuddle time. Gabriel had thrown himself to the floor and refused to leave without 'his' story wrapped up in a blanket at the kitchen table.

Charlotte smiled. Children loved structure and routine, and she was proud of Gabriel for demanding what he needed. She respected Adrien all the more that he had decided that providing comfort to Gabriel was more important than the kids being late for school.

When the chairlift reached the top of the hill, Aurélie was in the midst of explaining the fight two of her friends were having. Charlotte held tight to Gabriel as she helped him off the chairlift and they headed for the easy blue square run. Gabriel followed his sister down the hill, doing smooth turns, his skis pointing in toward each other in a pie shape. By the time they made it down the hill, both children were red-cheeked from the cold and smiling. They were also ready to go in for something to eat.

"But we've only done one run," protested Charlotte. "Let's do one more."

"Please, Mom. I want to try the nachos. Please," begged Gabriel. "My legs are tired."

My everything is tired, kid, thought Charlotte. However, she insisted they do one more run down the mountain before going into the lodge. She didn't know about the kids, but she was certain that once she was in the warm lodge with food high in fat and sugar in front of her, she wouldn't want to return afterward to the slopes. The kids followed her, complaining, to the ski lift, and they rose into the air on the chair in silence. Charlotte gazed down at the pine trees beneath her skis, which made her remember a scientific study she had recently read while researching her diagnosis.

It revealed that breathing in forest air for an entire day in summer increased the strength of one's immune system to fight off pathogens and abnormal cell growth. She made a mental note to spend as many days in the spring and summer in the woods as possible as the chairlift approached the top of the mountain.

Their second run down the hill, the clouds shifted, and the setting sun pierced the darkness and lit the clouds with shades of pink, orange, and purple. By the time Charlotte deposited the skis in the trunk and climbed the stairs with the children to the lodge, her body was weary and hurting, but her spirits high. Both kids were still grinning from ear to ear.

In the end, Charlotte ordered them all hamburgers and French fries instead of nachos. She bought three mugs of hot chocolate with whipped cream and huge brownies for dessert. Gabriel's and Aurélie's eyes grew large when Charlotte set the platter down onto the table.

"Is that all for us?" asked Gabriel.

"Even the brownies?" asked Aurélie.

Charlotte nodded and took a big bite of her hamburger. Within moments of silence, the children's boisterous chatter returned. It began to snow outside, and Charlotte smiled as she finished her last bite of brownie. Her phone rang just as Charlotte was wiping the whipped cream and chocolate off of Gabriel's face.

"Charlotte? Where the hell are you?"

Charlotte's hands flew to her cheeks. How had she forgotten to call Adrien?

"Adrien! I forgot to call you. I don't know where my head was." Charlotte winced.

"You forgot? You can imagine how worried I have been, not to mention your mother. You failed to inform her she didn't need to pick up the kids. She called me in tears, asking where you were."

Charlotte's heart sank to the floor. She pulled the phone away from her ear and checked. Her mother had called and texted over ten times looking for her.

"I forgot."

"You never forget. You're the most organized, punctual person I have ever met. I can imagine you exacting revenge on me or something by doing this, but you didn't even call your mother. What is going on? Where are you anyway? I'm at the condo, and I called the cabin. I know you're not there either."

"I took the kids night skiing."

"You did what?"

"I'm up on the mountain. We just finished dinner in the lodge," Charlotte stammered. "I'm on my way out the door, though. You can go ahead to the condo."

"No."

"What?" Charlotte was distracted by Gabriel's heavy eyelids. He was falling asleep in his chair. She needed to get him into the car. She wasn't sure she could carry him down the stairs in her ski boots. She berated herself for not changing into her boots when she had stowed the skis and poles in the car.

"I'm not moving back to the condo. I gave up the lease. Tomorrow I put my things in storage. I decided I am moving home."

"You can't decide that on your own."

"I'll be there when you get home," he answered, and hung up the phone.

Charlotte rolled through anger, resentment, and weariness. If Adrien moved home, she couldn't keep her cancer a secret. She had to tell him.

By the time she opened her car door, and the icy wind slapped her in the face, she was in pain and exhausted. The sight of Adrien stepping out onto the front step made her close her eyes in relief. She wouldn't have to put the kids to bed. Gratitude poured into her soul that Adrien was home to help. Wordlessly, Adrien opened the car door and gathered up the sleeping Gabriel into his arms.

CHARLOTTE BLINKED HER EYES open to the sunlight flooding her room. She groaned and reached for her phone to check the time. Charlotte sprung out of bed when she saw that it was eight-twenty-two in the morning. So much for decades of waking up at five-thirty, she thought as she rushed into the living room in search for her kids. She found them sitting in the kitchen nook, each eating huckleberry pancakes and maple syrup sausages.

"Mommy," yelled Gabriel and scooted down from the table. He ran across the room and lifted his arms out. Charlotte scooped him up into her arms into a hug and held him, his sticky cheek pressed to hers, drinking in the warm smell of his shampoo scent mixing with that of the maple syrup. "I missed you. You slept a long time."

"Daddy's pancakes taste better than yours," declared Aurélie with a grin.

"That's because I don't try to make them healthy," chuckled Adrien from the kitchen. He flipped three pancakes on the griddle and walked over to Charlotte with the spatula still in his hand. "You look like hell froze over and then melted into a hot mess. Go climb back into bed, and I'll bring you some breakfast." Adrien collected Gabriel from Charlotte and carried him back to the table to finish his meal.

Charlotte began to protest that she was fine until a sharp blade of pain tore into her abdomen. She stumbled back into her bedroom and bed. A few minutes later, Gabriel climbed into her bed, and Aurélie followed with a pile of books. Adrien appeared by her bedside and held out the steaming cup of coffee. Just the smell of it cheered Charlotte. She pulled herself up and sipped the coffee gratefully. A delicious cup of coffee was her most treasured daily pleasure. She opened Iggy Peck, Architect and began to read to her children.

Adrien returned ten minutes later with a stack of huckleberry pancakes, sausages, and scrambled eggs. He set the plate down on her bedside table. Charlotte ate while listening to her children talk about helping their dad make pancakes that morning using some of the huckleberries they had picked in the woods the previous summer and frozen.

She glanced out the window at the sun sparkling on

snow-covered pine trees. Her eye caught sight of a gleaming red BMW SUV parked in their driveway. Was someone about to ring the doorbell? Charlotte began to panic. She wasn't up to seeing anyone today, let anyone see her. Her recent trip to the bathroom had revealed a bird's nest of hair piled on top of her head, dark circles under her eyes, and splotchy skin. She hadn't had the energy to do anything but wipe the smeared mascara off and splash cold water on her face. It wasn't much of an improvement.

"Hey Adrien," she called out from the bed. "I am not up to a visitor, Adrien. Do you think you could handle it?"

Adrien entered the room with a dish towel in his hands. "Who would come by on a Saturday morning, anyway?" Charlotte motioned out their bedroom window toward their driveway. "A car has pulled up into our driveway."

"Oh," he answered and turned back to her with a big grin revealing the dimples in each cheek. His eyes sparkled as he turned back to her. "It sure is a thing of beauty, isn't it? I was going to get it in midnight blue, but then I spotted that gorgeous candy apple red. Do you love it?"

"A new car?"

Adrien's grin disappeared from his face at the tone of Charlotte's voice. He crossed his arms over his chest and leaned back against the wall. "I went to the bank. I was going to pay for the car outright, but apparently, some of your accounts don't have my name on them."

Charlotte stared back at Adrien with huge eyes and a pounding heart. Everything that she had worried would happen was already starting. Now that he had found out about the money, he was going to try and spend it just as quickly as he could. How much did that new car cost? She hardly noticed when the kids bounded out of the room to go and play.

Charlotte pulled her phone to her and did a quick search. She closed her eyes in pain at the ticket price; this was just the start. What would be next? A new boat she would guess, or a new snowmobile to drive into the backcountry, or both. She was sure expensive holidays would follow, which would be better than the thought of him paying for round after round of drinks for all his friends at their favorite bar in town.

Charlotte saw a movie of her life spin out in front of her eyes. She saw the countless days she had spent holed up in the library instead of out partying and playing. She saw herself as she toiled over new client acquisition and building up her business in her office in town.

The heavy weight of risk and fear of failure descended once again onto her shoulders. All those years of anguish, she had fought through them to create freedom from financial instability for herself and her family. In a short time, he would spend all the hard-won security on shiny playthings and fleeting pleasures.

"I can't believe you bought yourself a new car without talking to me," she said, opening her eyes.

"I bought it for you," exclaimed Adrien. "You can't go on driving my kids around in that old junk of a car. Why should you? The trouble with you, Charlotte, is that you don't know how to enjoy life."

"I think I'm going to be sick," said Charlotte and sprung from the bed to the bathroom, slamming the door behind her. A few minutes later, she rested her head back on the wall of the bathroom.

It was her fault. Her kids were still young. Charlotte had thought she had a few years before she needed to place a large chunk of her money into education trusts for Aurélie and Gabriel.

Sure, she had money invested in stocks, but she had far too much cash just sitting in the bank. It had made her feel safe as if she was prepared for any misfortune life could throw at her. How wrong she had been, and stupid.

She had always remonstrated with herself that her misgivings about Adrien were wrong. As much as her worries about Adrien had nibbled at her nerve endings like little piranha fish, she had always swum away from her worries.

She had always told herself she was wrong: Adrien wasn't foolish and selfish. Adrien was sweet, thoughtful and loving.

But if Charlotte didn't survive this cancer, what kind of life would Aurélie and Gabriel have with such a financially reckless father?

"CHARLOTTE, ARE YOU OKAY? Let me in," called Adrien.

"It's not locked," called Charlotte.

Adrien opened the door and came in, shutting it behind him. He slumped to the floor next to her and stared blankly at the wall in front of them. "I'll return the car this afternoon and stop the order for my dream SUV."

Charlotte spied the time on Adrien's watch and noted that it was already almost eleven. How had the morning gotten away from her? Before her diagnosis, she had swum, had a sauna, wrote song lyrics, gave her kids breakfast, made all their lunches, and worked three hours by this time. Here she was, a big mess, still sitting in her pajamas. All of a sudden Charlotte remembered her father's offer to meet him for lunch at the Shore Lodge.

"Adrien, could you watch the kids while I run into town? You'll never believe this. My father is in town and wants to meet me."

"Wait, what?" He stood up, shifting from foot to foot. "The thing is, I already made plans for lunch myself. Could you switch lunch to dinner?"

Charlotte considered, tilting her head to the side in thought. "I just want to get it over with, love. Could you switch your lunch to a dinner instead? Who are you meeting, anyway?"

"This is what I'll do. I'll just find a sitter for the kids, and once I do, I will run over to my lunch appointment. We'll meet back here later this afternoon. How does that sound?"

"Who will come over so short notice? My Mom is working today, and so is your Mom. Maybe you could call Élodie; I'm not sure if she is on shift…"

"Charlotte," spoke up Adrien. "You need to go jump in that pool of yours for ten minutes and then hit the shower. That will brighten you up and work out your jitters. I know you must be wound up at the thought of seeing your Dad. I've got this. Go. You can trust me."

CHARLOTTE TUGGED AT THE red scarf around her neck and smoothed down her geometric patterned wool black-and-white skirt. She scanned the lobby and restaurant in the Shore

Lodge once again, searching for her father. Zack spied her at the bar and waved her over. Charlotte walked over, a smile bubbling up and crowding out some of her nervous anxiety.

Just as she approached the bar, a man dressed in wool gray dress slacks and a bright blue buttoned-down shirt turned on his barstool. "There you are, Charlotte. I was beginning to worry you wouldn't show up."

"Hi Dad," she answered. She stepped up, and uncertain of whether to hug him or kiss him or shake his hand, she patted his shoulder instead. "Hungry?"

"I sure am. Zack here tells me your favorite thing on this fancy menu is the cheeseburger and fries. That doesn't sound like you. You always liked fish, even as a child. But what should I know? I've been away a long time."

"No, you are right. I'm still that way. My taste has just changed recently."

Charlotte watched her father lay a twenty on the bar. "Keep the change, Zack. It was good to see you again."

"You recognized Zack?" asked Charlotte as they settled down at a table.

"He recognized me. The last time I saw him, he was a scrawny kid chasing you down our street. He tells me he is working on his third novel and bartends to pay the rent. Have you read his books?"

"Of course."

The waitress came, and Charlotte and her father ordered salmon with a side of quinoa rice and sautéed vegetables with hollandaise sauce. Charlotte took a sip of her lemonade while her father sipped his Manhattan. She began to twist her plain gold wedding band around and around her finger.

"So is he any good? What does he write?"

"He writes mysteries. He is very talented. It is a hard business. Perhaps it would help him to make some connections to get more exposure."

"Speaking of relationships, that's what I wanted to talk to you about today. I'm thrilled that Adrien contacted me and asked me for that recommendation."

"Excuse me, what?"

"You knew of course," began her father and then studied

her face, falling silent. "Well, you clearly didn't know." His shoulders slumped, and the faint smile on her father's lips vanished. "I hoped it was your indirect way of reaching out to me. I leaped at the chance."

"Why did Adrien ask you for a recommendation?"

"He wanted a job at Apple in human resources. I happily wrote a recommendation for him. I could think of nothing better than having you in California near me. I was hoping we could forge a new relationship, on whatever terms you would accept me back into your life."

Charlotte couldn't believe what she was hearing. How could Adrien contact her father behind her back? She had confided in him all of her dark and deepest resentments and insecurities regarding her father's departure. How had Adrien even found him? Charlotte wouldn't have known where to look. She took a deep breath and let it out slowly. It didn't help much.

"Can you rescind your recommendation?"

"Why would I do that? I don't understand. He's already been offered the job."

"Is that a no then?"

"Yes, I mean yes that's a no. What is going on, Charlotte?"

"I don't want my children moving. All of their family and friends are here."

Charlotte saw a hurt expression flash across her father's face and modified her statement. "Most of their family is here, Dad. Aurélie, Gabriel, and I are happy here. We are not moving."

"It is a great job they offered Adrien. He said you would be happy to stop working and devote all your time to enjoy the kids."

"Oh, he said that, did he?" Her hand shot out and grabbed her father's drink, and she downed the remaining contents. The liquid was tasty, but it didn't burn pleasantly on its way down.

"I'm surmising that also isn't true? Can I ask why you just downed my Coke instead of your lemonade?"

Charlotte looked into the soulful dark eyes of her father and smiled. "I thought it was a bourbon or whiskey in the glass."

Her dad shrugged his shoulders and looked out the windows at the lake.

"I haven't had a drink in twenty-eight years. I, more than anyone, can tell you it isn't wise to reach for a drink when dark emotions are threatening to overwhelm you."

Charlotte clenched her fists in her lap, staring at her untouched hamburger. "I have a doctorate in psychology, Dad, thanks. I think I know all about healthy and unhealthy coping mechanisms."

"I am extremely impressed what you have accomplished, Charlotte. How is Élodie? I was hoping to meet her here yesterday for lunch, but she sent a message that she would only meet me if you did first. Some things don't change, even after all these years," he laughed softly to himself. "She always did have you do everything first. Any new food, jumping off the dock into the lake, trying out water skiing, or ice skating."

"I'm her big sister. That's normal." Guilt flooded through Charlotte at the mention of Élodie. She had been so wrapped up in her cancer diagnosis and bucket list that she hadn't talked to her sister all week; usually, they had a quick chat every day.

Guilt was quickly replaced with a growing sense of unease. Why hadn't Élodie called her? Was there something terribly wrong and Charlotte hadn't even noticed? What kind of sister was she?

"Excuse me a moment Dad. I'm just going to run to the ladies' room."

The minute Charlotte entered the hotel lobby she dialed her sister. Élodie picked up on the first ring.

"Charlotte," Élodie exclaimed, "I'm so sorry I haven't called this week. You must think I'm a horrible sister."

"Not at all, that was how I was feeling for not calling you." Charlotte paused in mid-step as she walked in front of the crackling fire. She eased down onto the sofa and basked in the warmth radiating from the fireplace. Élodie sounded strange, different.

"Are you okay, Élodie?"

"Yes, oh Charlotte, this one is the one."

Charlotte noted the euphoria in her sister's voice and

smiled. She hadn't ever heard her sister so happy, but she was wary. There had been too many times in the past when she had held her sobbing sister in her arms. Élodie had always been very quick to fall head over heels in love. It made for a blissfully happy Élodie one moment, and the next, Charlotte was holding her sobbing sister in her arms after the relationship all too quickly fell apart. Please God, she prayed, if this man isn't the man Élodie is going to marry, let him disappear before Élodie invests even more of herself into him.

Just as quickly as Charlotte offered up that prayer, she called it back from floating up to heaven. If Jake disappeared, it would mean that he wouldn't be opening the new extreme survival holiday business. Adrien wouldn't have a new job offer in McCall to entice him to stay. Charlotte glanced at her watch. Her Dad would be wondering where she was.

"I'm here with Dad at the Shore Lodge having lunch; we just ordered. Is there any chance you want to come down and join us?"

"I can't believe you agreed to meet him."

"Why would you say that? Am I so unforgiving?"

"I'll be there in fifteen minutes. Order me a hamburger and fries, okay?"

Charlotte stared at the phone and then stormed back toward the restaurant. So her sister, like Adrien, and even her mother, considered her unforgiving. Well, I'll show them, she thought.

CHAPTER 10

Matthew 6:9-15
9 Pray like this: 'Our Father in heaven, hallowed be your name. 10 your kingdom come, your will be done, on earth as it is in heaven. 11 Give us today our daily bread. 12 And forgive us our trespasses as we also forgive those who have trespassed against us. 13 And lead us not into temptation, but deliver us from the evil one.' 14 "For if you forgive men their trespasses, your heavenly Father will also forgive you. 15 But if you don't forgive men their trespasses, neither will your Father forgive your trespasses.

CHARLOTTE FELL ONTO HER CHAIR across from her father and offered up a bright smile. "So, where were we?"

"I wish I had known you didn't want to move away. I would never have leveraged my good connections in my company to put in a good word for him. I don't even know him, Char. I only did it with your happiness in mind."

"I understand that, Dad, and I appreciate the gesture too. Listen," began Charlotte, and paused to reach out and grab her father's hand across the table. Give me the strength to say those three words, she prayed. Memories of hurt and anger at growing up without a father were clinging to her like tree sap. She looked her father directly in the eyes and took a deep breath. "I forgive you for leaving. If you want to be a part of my life now, well, I'm open."

Her father didn't smile. He sat frozen, the color seeping

out of his cheeks. "You mean that?"

Charlotte nodded. It was as if she was the first one out of the water in a triathlon. She was both shaky and victorious. "You have to promise me you aren't going to walk out on me all over again."

"I am a different man than I was, Charlotte. I won't disappear from your life this time."

No, thought Charlotte, I will most likely disappear from yours. She wished she believed, deep down, that she could recover from the pancreatic cancer wreaking havoc on her body. It was hard to have faith that she could heal. Her stomach was rolling; she was in too much discomfort to eat the food sitting in front of her. She fought against the constant impulse to round forward around her pain and forced herself to sit up straight and examine her father. Did she trust this handsome man, who had walked out of her life and only now, decades later, reappeared? The answer was, yes.

She gave her father's hand a squeeze and smiled. What did she have to lose now?

"I trust you." The words seemed to float right out of her mouth. For the first time, she saw that her father's walking away had nothing to do with not wanting her. Something in her chest loosened, and her shoulders slid down her back. Her breathing softened, and something like hope emanated from her heart center.

Élodie entered the restaurant and spied Charlotte and her father. As Élodie approached the table, Charlotte rose out of her chair to embrace her sister in greeting. No sooner was she on her feet than the world begins to spin into a blinding blur. Élodie screamed when Charlotte pitched forward. She heard the crash of glasses and plates smashing to the floor around her, and then darkness enveloped her.

CHARLOTTE BLINKED OPEN her eyes and stared up into worried dark eyes. It took her a moment to recognize the man as her father. Élodie was on the floor beside Charlotte, whispering reassurances in her ear that the ambulance was on its way.

Charlotte sat up abruptly, shouting out, "No. I don't need an ambulance."

Collapsing in the restaurant and ending up in the hospital would be a disaster, she decided. Now, more than ever, she didn't want her family to find out about her cancer diagnosis.

She wanted to place the majority of her savings into educational trusts for the children before Adrien discovered she was battling stage four cancer. The past week had proven to Charlotte that it was the only way to take her last breath in peace. Otherwise, she would worry that Adrien would sprint through the money and leave nothing for Aurélie and Gabriel's education. How could she organize that from a hospital room?

There was also the new appearance of her father. Charlotte wasn't sure if he would want to stick around once he found out she ill.

Last of all, more than anything else, she wanted to entice Adrien into abandoning his plans of taking the job in favor for partnering with Jake in the new business. Charlotte had promised Jake she would dream up a great name for the extreme wilderness survival business, as well as an entire branding concept and marketing plan, before he pitched his offer to Adrien.

Élodie stood poised with her phone in her hand, protesting they should call for help. Wincing, Charlotte stood up on shaky legs. She forced a smile on her face. The pain in her abdomen was radiating all the way around into her back.

"I'm fine, Élodie. I'll just head home."

"I'll drive you," insisted Élodie. Élodie snatched up Charlotte's purse before placing her arm around Charlotte's waist as they walked out of the restaurant and to the parking lot. Their father followed them to the parking lot, clearly at a loss for what to do or how to act. At the car, he awkwardly patted Charlotte's head, as if she were six again. Élodie stood up on tiptoe and kissed him on the cheek, which apparently surprised him.

"I'm in town for the rest of the week. Just in case you want to see me. Only if you are feeling better..." he rambled, looking from Charlotte, to Élodie, and back again.

"Sure, Dad," answered Charlotte. "We'll call you."

"If there is anything I can do, anything at all, just call."

As Élodie pulled out of the parking lot onto the main road, she muttered, "What a weird day." She paused and glanced at Charlotte before returning her gaze to the road. "What are you not telling me?"

"What?"

"You're keeping something from me."

"You're one to talk," snapped back Charlotte. "I heard about your relationship with Jake from him. Why didn't you call and tell me about your first date?"

Silence fell over the car. Charlotte knew Élodie always considered carefully before speaking. Her buoyant and flirty behavior masked her sensitive and thoughtful nature. Charlotte watched the row of picturesque storefronts in the tiny town go by outside her window. It was only a few minutes later, when they had driven out of town and toward Ponderosa State Park, that she said, "I didn't want to look like a fool."

"You were waiting to see if this new relationship had a real chance before you were going to tell me. I hate that, Élodie. I love that I'm the one you turn to when your heart breaks."

"Yet you don't trust me, with anything," countered Élodie softly, her eyes still glued to the road.

"That's not true," began Charlotte, and then it was her turn to fall silent.

"You didn't tell me about Adrien cheating on you, and you didn't tell me that you were working so hard that you were close to suffering a severe burnout. You could ask me for help with the kids."

Charlotte spied a deer bounding through the woods to her right. The gossip in town was unbelievable. Not only did they all know about Adrien's affair, but they already knew she was staying in town at the condo, 'because of too much work.' Charlotte was relieved they didn't know the real reason, namely that she had stage four pancreatic cancer and was frantically preparing for the worst case scenario.

Perhaps she should tell Élodie she was terminally ill.

"It's not that I don't trust you…"

"It's that you don't trust anyone."

Élodie shrugged. "I know. Adrien and I have commiserated over this fact more than once, let me tell you."

Hurt hit Charlotte in the stomach and knocked the air out of her. She couldn't believe Élodie had talked about her with her husband behind her back. Well, she resolved, I'm not about to tell her about the cancer now.

Charlotte had never been so relieved to get away from her sister before. She had to insist three times that Élodie didn't need to come in with her; Adrien was at home and would take care of the kids, and she would climb into bed.

The minute she entered the front door the kids came running toward her, flinging themselves into her arms. Adrien came to the door and helped her out of her jacket.

"You look like you're dying a slow death," greeted Adrien.

Charlotte's mouth fell open. How had he found out? While Charlotte stood grappling with what to say, Adrien swept her easily up into his arms and carried her down the hall.

"All that work has hit you hard. Come. I'll tuck you up on the couch with the kids and make you a roaring fire. You three can watch a movie, and I'll make a roast and potatoes for dinner."

Charlotte began to answer that she would be okay, but he kissed her cheek and insisted, "Doctor's orders."

Charlotte let out a sigh as Adrien tucked the cashmere blanket in around her and the kids on the sofa. Adrien had always taken such good care of her when she was ill, and all through both pregnancies. She couldn't count how many times he had had her curl up on the sofa or in bed while he brought her delicious homemade dinners and steaming cups of tea.

Charlotte ran her hands through her daughter's soft curls and sighed. Adrien hadn't only taken care of her. Each time the children had fallen ill, it had been Adrien pacing the floor with the baby in his arms in the dead of night.

He had always taken the night shifts, ensuring she could get the sleep she needed to perform at work the next day. Charlotte closed her eyes and enjoyed the comforting weight of her children curled up on either side of her.

Adrien sure doesn't make it easy to love him, she thought.

And he makes it impossible not to, all at the same time. She opened her eyes and watched Adrien push the final handful of kindling under the logs and light the fire. He straightened up, met her gaze, and smiled, causing the laugh lines around his eyes to appear. "I love you, Charlotte."

It was as if someone had poured a cup of icy cold water down her spine. Suddenly, she knew how wrong it would be to place the majority of the savings in the bank into educational trusts without telling Adrien her plans first. He deserved to know the truth about her cancer diagnosis, too. She should tell him everything, and trust. Trust that he would continue to be a wonderful father to their kids, even if it meant he had to move away.

"I love you too," answered Charlotte, and Adrien planted a kiss on the top of her head before going into the gleaming white kitchen.

Trust for Charlotte was a gorgeous, recalcitrant horse. If she pulled herself up into the saddle, she could have one of the most blissful rides of her life. Then again, she could be thrown straight into a fence and break her neck. It was a risk Charlotte wasn't yet ready to take.

ON SUNDAY EVENING Charlotte turned the lock and stepped into the condo in town. She had read her kids their goodnight stories and tucked them into bed before heading into town to live in Adrien's place for the week again.

Charlotte had pleaded a mountain of work as her grounds for moving out. Adrien had believed her when she had said she would much prefer to stay in the cabin, living as a family again. It was the truth. The day had played out like something from a feel-good movie, and she didn't want it to end.

Charlotte had woken up after twelve hours of sleep with less pain than she had experienced in weeks. She had managed a slow ten-minute swim and a quick sauna before a breakfast of toast, coffee, and green berry smoothies with her kids. After getting dressed up and intricately braiding Aurélie's hair, she and Adrien had gone to church with the kids. Charlotte had had a moment of panic after the service when she realized she had forgotten the brunch.

Her mother-in-law had insisted on Elizabeth driving up from Boise with George for the day. She had also invited not only Charlotte's mom and sister, but Jake and even her father were present. Charlotte was still horrified that she had completely forgotten about the brunch at her mother-in-law's after church.

Fortunately, her mother-in-law had done all the shopping and cooking. There wasn't much for Charlotte to do except make her famous ham and cheese scones, while Élodie put together a fruit salad. Tracy poured each woman a glass of champagne before starting to work on baking an apple strudel for dessert. Charlotte's mother pitched in with making the vanilla sauce to accompany the strudel.

Tracy pushed Elizabeth into a chair, where she sat with a hand resting on her rounded belly, chatting with the women as they prepared lunch. Charlotte had worried that the day would be strange and awkward with her father there, but it was the opposite. Laughter and conversation flowed smoothly throughout the lunch and followed the group on their walk through the woods together after lunch, like helium balloons waving in the wind.

It was exactly the festive day of perfection one wished for on Thanksgiving or Christmas. Charlotte had made this comment to her mother while they walked hand in hand through the woods, behind the crowd.

"That's the thing about perfect days," laughed her Mom. "They tend to happen when everyone is relaxed and happy. Holidays raise expectations; expectations can cause stress, which brings out the worst in most of us. We end up lashing out or feeling resentful, and the day is tainted."

Charlotte had thought this over, breathing in deep breaths of pine-scented air, savoring the sound of her children laughing as they tumbled through the snow ahead of her. She noticed her Dad, who was walking with Jake and her kids up ahead, kept glancing back at her mom. Or was it just her imagination? Charlotte glanced at her Mom. Had she just smiled and winked at her Dad?

"Well, what would you say about celebrating Christmas

next weekend, Mom? We wouldn't tell anyone that's what we were doing. It would just be like today. A stress-free, perfect Christmas before the real run happens." Charlotte didn't add that she was worried she wouldn't make it to Christmas.

"Is this because Adrien wants to have the kids for Christmas this year? I thought you two were working things out. You two looked happy today."

Charlotte shrugged. "That's true."

"You're worried."

Charlotte smiled. Her mother had always been too intuitive for her own good. Charlotte began to open her mouth to defend her idea, but her mother pulled her in for a hug. "You don't have to explain, honey. It's a bit unorthodox, but I don't see why we can't be creative. Would you like to do it like we always have, and you come with the kids for lunch?"

"No, actually, I was wondering if you and Élodie would come over and do everything I usually do with the kids, with us. Then Élodie and I could help you cook the dinner at your house. What do you say?"

"A weekend with my two beautiful girls and grandkids? I'd say that sounds like heaven. What time should we come?"

"What about eight am on Saturday?"

"Tell you what, let's make it nine-thirty. You may be an early bird, Char, but your Mama is a night owl."

"I have the best coffee in town," enticed Charlotte. "And I know you love a hot sauna in the wintertime."

"Nine. And that's my final offer," laughed Anna.

CHARLOTTE SMILED AS SHE pulled back the covers and climbed into bed. She was going to save up this day like hot embers kept glowing overnight to fan into a fire again. Charlotte would remember this day the next time pain rolled through her body. Charlotte's phone rang, and she frowned. Who would be calling at ten at night? She hoped one of the children hadn't fallen ill. She didn't recognize the number.

"Hello?"

"Charlotte, it's your Dad."

"Dad, what is it?"

"Well, I was talking to Élodie's boyfriend today on the hike, and he told me all about his new business he is launching."

Charlotte punched the pillow next to her in a flash of anger. She had warned Jake not to talk about his business today, in front of Adrien. He was starting to irritate her every day with texts and calls pushing her to let him contact Adrien. If there was one thing that Charlotte despised, it was someone pushing her to do something. Now Jake had gone mouthing off on the hike. Had Adrien heard? Had Jake disregarded her warnings and pitched the ideas to Adrien?

"Charlotte, are you there?"

"What does that have to do with me?" She crossed her fingers that Jake had kept her help a secret. It was essential that Adrien knew nothing of her involvement; a partnership in the company needed to be his victory, without her help.

"Well, nothing and everything," answered her father. Charlotte grimaced. What did that mean?

"I am going to invest in his start-up and move back to McCall to run the business side of things. From my perspective, the start-up is fascinating, and I know the types I work with would love such a holiday. The demand is there, Charlotte. But the reason I would invest, and then move, would be to be close to you and Élodie, and my grandkids."

Charlotte fell back onto the bed. "I don't know what to say."

"I already talked to Élodie, and she is thrilled with the idea. But if you aren't ready to have me back in this small town, I would understand, Charlotte. I never expected you to forgive me, let alone let me back into your life. We can slow things down if you want. I'll keep my job in California and fly in once or twice a year."

"You're assuming that Adrien doesn't take the job."

"Yeah, well, Jake may have let slip you have plans for Adrien to join us in the business."

"He didn't," fumed Charlotte. "Did Adrien hear you two talking?"

"He was too busy catching up with Elizabeth and George and planning Christmas with them. I heard them behind us. So, what do you say?"

"You've never told me about your life. I mean, do you have

a wife or a girlfriend? You could even have more kids. I could have half-siblings out there, for all I know."

"There has only ever been one great love in my life, and I lost her. No, I've been alone all these years, working twelve- and fourteen-hour days. I lived for my job. It turns out it was worth it. I have invested well and lived frugally. I have more than enough to retire early, so to say. Investing in this business won't be a risk."

Charlotte's heart was pounding in her chest. She wasn't sure she wanted to hear the answer to the question she was going to ask. She had to ask it anyway. "Are you still in love with Mom?"

"I always will be, sweetheart. I always will."

THE NEXT MORNING Charlotte rolled out of bed and onto her yoga mat. Sixty minutes later she was warm and pliant, with a lump in her throat she couldn't dislodge. Was meeting Ben behind Adrien's back the right thing to do? The question plagued her in the shower, as she got dressed, and as she walked into town. She stood in front of the attorney's office, hesitating.

You should have done this years ago, she told herself. You haven't wanted to face the truth. It has sat on your mental to-do list; it is something you have wanted to get done for years. It has kept your mind spinning into the early morning with worry since the kids were babies. Now they are three and six. This is the right step, especially now. You don't have time to spare; you can't complicate or delay the decisions by including Adrien in this.

Shame, hot and prickling, flared in her cheeks, down her neck, and along the collar of her sky blue blouse. Well, at least you are doing it now, she told herself and pulled open the door.

"Charlotte," exclaimed Ben. "It is a pleasure to see you. I've been meaning to thank you for the homemade lasagna, vegetable platter, and homemade bread you dropped by to Sara and me when she came home with Adam."

"How is your new baby?" asked Charlotte, a grin coming to

her face at the image of Sara holding the dark-haired infant. It seemed like not so long ago that she had held newborn Gabriel in her arms.

"Driving us to delight and despair every day. He wants to party all night. I'm telling you, the sleep deprivation is torture, but holding him in my arms is pure joy. Now, let's get down to work," said Ben, while picking up a pen and leaning forward. "I have wanted to get you in here for estate planning for years. It's important. I didn't expect you to arrange a meeting before Christmas, though. I heard around town that you have been swamped with work."

"As you said, it's important," smiled Charlotte.

"So, what shall we start with first? We should create the last will, the health care power of attorney, your living will, your financial power of attorney, or the education plans you said you want for your kids?"

Charlotte was overwhelmed. She was embarrassed to admit she didn't even know what some of the items he listed meant. Well, it would be stupid to feign understanding when she had none.

"I'm afraid I don't know what a living will, or health care of attorney, mean."

"Well," answered Ben, leaning back in his chair and steepling his hands. "Imagine you get in a car accident, which causes you to fall into a coma. You can't speak for yourself. In this situation, the living will clarifies decisions regarding your healthcare. Tube feeding or mechanical respiration can prolong your life even in a persistent vegetative state with no hope of recovery. The question is, do you want to be kept alive by artificial means in this situation?

"A living will provides advance directive and makes your wishes clear about end-of-life care. If you become terminally ill and will die without life support, do you want artificial support? If you fall into an irreversible coma or persistent vegetative state, do you want artificial support? Do you want to receive pain medication or artificial nutrition? A healthcare power of attorney gives someone you name the authority to make health care decisions for you, if you no longer can, and to honor the wishes stated in your living will."

Charlotte rubbed her forehead.

"This is incredibly depressing."

"Charlotte, don't worry. We're young. What are the chances of you needing your health care agent and living will now?"

"I'd like to give my mother medical power of attorney for me," answered Charlotte.

Ben leaned forward across the table. "You most likely won't need your living will and health care agent until you are a little old lady. By then your mother may no longer be with us. Isn't there someone younger you can name? What about your husband, or Élodie?"

Charlotte shook her head. Her stomach was churning. There was a high chance her mother would need to step into her role as the agent of Charlotte's health care shortly. She had spent her entire career working at the hospital. It didn't matter that she worked in administration. Of anyone Charlotte was close to, her mother was the most comfortable in a hospital environment talking with doctors and nurses.

"No, I want my mom."

"Well, if I can't change your mind," sighed Ben. "Then let's fill these documents out."

Once the living will and healthcare power of attorney were complete, Ben disappeared to bring them back coffee. Charlotte used the respite to think about what she was planning to do.

"Well, what should we tackle next?" he asked with a grin.

"The education trust," answered Charlotte. "It's the most important to me to get done."

"Great. I suggest you open a 529 plan. We can review the options," answered Ben and held out a stack of papers to Charlotte.

Charlotte held up her hands, pushing the papers back across the desk. "I don't want a 529 plan. I want a trust."

"Charlotte, listen. I advise against creating a trust. Your contributions to a 529 plan will grow free of federal income tax burden for the benefit of Aurélie and Gabriel. The funds in a trust do not increase federal income tax-free; the trust must pay income tax on its earnings."

"I've scrutinized the choices. With a 529 plan, the account

owner has control of the assets. I know the contributions are treated as a completed gift to the child from a tax perspective, but the account owner can technically revoke the gift. They can close out the account, and eat the taxes and penalties to pull the money out. I find it imperative to set up an untouchable education fund, and a trust is the best way, from what I researched."

"You're not worried that Adrien would touch the children's college savings?" asked Ben while placing his hands behind his head and leaning back in his chair.

Charlotte set her coffee cup down on his desk and smiled at him. "Do I need to find a new lawyer to arrange the education trusts for me?"

Ben cleared his throat and sat up straight again in his chair. They regarded one another in silence for a moment. Recognition flashed in Ben's eyes. He shuffled through the papers on his desk. "So, an education trust it is. And Charlotte," he added in a quieter voice. "I'm sorry."

"I want separate educational trusts for Aurélie and Gabriel, and Mom to be the trustee of the trust. I want the stipulation that the money can only be used for tuition for either college or a trade school," explained Charlotte, while massaging her abdomen lightly with both hands.

"What is the amount you will want to invest in each trust?"

"Two hundred and fifty-three thousand dollars," answered Charlotte. "Each."

Ben's silver pen fell with a thud onto his desk, and he looked up at her. "How much?"

"You heard me," answered Charlotte. "Be sure to include a spendthrift clause into each trust, so the assets are protected from potential creditors."

Ben shook his head. "Do you mind me asking if you inherited money?"

"I inherited our cabin. The money I earned."

Ben leaned forward once again. "Do you mind me asking how? I mean, I can see the entrance to your office from my office window," he explained and nodded to the window behind Charlotte. "I don't see that many people are going in and out."

"Are you watching me, Ben?"

Ben's face flushed red. "No. I'll need time to draw up the paperwork and create the trust. It is more complicated than the other documents."

"I'm just teasing you, Ben. Listen, no one knew this, but I created an online therapy service with certified psychologists and psychiatrists all over the world. I was the first business online to provide remote treatment services. Now there are quite a few competitors out there, but we still have the largest market share."

"Remote therapy. You mean from home?"

Charlotte nodded.

"Used to be from home. Now with the latest digital devices, such as iPhone, we can schedule therapy anywhere, anytime, day or night. I have therapists all over the world. You could have a therapy session right now, at your desk, or on a hike."

"Why haven't you told anyone?" asked Ben.

Charlotte cringed as a wave of pain hit her. "I had my reasons."

Ben stood up and began pacing around the room. "You were afraid Adrien would run through the money, weren't you? You still are. That's why you want trust funds created for your kids' education."

Charlotte covered her face with her hands. Shame roared in her ears. Ben had known her and Adrien his entire life, but she hadn't realized how transparent it was that Adrien liked to spend money recklessly. "Is it that obvious?"

"No," Ben answered and stopped in the middle of the room to look at her. "I ran into him at the bar the other night when he was buying rounds for everyone, and he was talking about the new SUV he had special ordered. He was also talking about the purchase of a new boat."

Charlotte sighed.

"Please, Ben, get it done as fast as you can."

"Yes, of course."

"Promise me, Ben."

"You've been there for us whenever life has hit us hard, Charlotte. You don't need to ask me twice. I'll get this done as fast as I can and call you to sign the final paperwork. Now, let's move on to your last will. First, we need a break. In fact, you're looking extremely pale. We can continue this in a few days if you are wavering on your decisions. You seem downright panicked."

Charlotte's mouth went dry, and she took a sip of water. Panicked. Yes, that was the word that matched her inner landscape perfectly. Her entire body was on an adrenaline kick. She was on the high of fight-or-flight response yoga could only slightly diminish.

Ever since sitting in the oncologist's office in Boise and hearing that little six-letter word, it was as if she had been pitched into a pitch dark chamber. Instinctively, she knew there was a limited amount of oxygen. Her fingers were searching every inch of the walls, the floor, the ceiling. If only she could find a window, a door, a crack in the wall to pry open the tiniest bit to let in a fraction of more life-extending air. Charlotte sensed her time was running out.

Charlotte forced a smile on her face. "I'm fine. I want to finish this today, Ben."

"Well then, at least let me invite you to the coffee shop next door for a cappuccino and a slice of chocolate cake before we continue? My treat."

The minute Charlotte stepped into the aroma of dark-roasted coffee in the café, her shoulders settled downward and her breathing smoothed out. A few moments later, with a hot cappuccino in one hand and a plate of decadent raspberry chocolate truffle cake in front of her, she relaxed for the first time that day. After a half-hour of light conversation about their children, town news, and politics, they were fortified to continue. They returned to Ben's office.

Charlotte bestowed her mother with the financial power of attorney and proceeded to work out the details of her last will with Ben. At last, she said goodbye to Ben and walked slowly through the falling snow to her office. One thing was certain. Adrien was not going to be happy about what she had decided.

An enormous weight had been lifted from her shoulders with the knowledge that Aurélie and Gabriel's education financing would be secure. Charlotte fell back onto her office couch and pulled a throw blanket over herself.

Charlotte pictured herself waking up next spring to the smell of new grass, completely free of cancer.

Charlotte would give every cent to her name, her home, everything, to be cancer-free and able to be there to raise her kids. She went to the bookshelf and returned with her gold-edged Bible. Charlotte turned to Matthew 26:36–46. She read the verse aloud: "My Father, if it is possible, may this cup be taken from me. Yet not as I will, but as you will."

Charlotte threw the Bible across the room with such force, it hit the bookshelf and sent books falling to the floor. To hell with your will, she thought. I want to stay here with my kids. Tears slid down her cheeks as she fell in a heap on the floor.

Anger writhed within her like venomous baby rattlesnakes. They were kicking up such a racket; it was hard to hear anything over their hissing and rattling. Charlotte took up the Bible and re-read aloud: "My Father, if it is possible, may this cup be taken from me. Not as I will, but as you will." One deep breath sucked into her belly. One long smooth exhaled out as the words vibrated, a chord echoing. She waited for some profound sense that God was in the room, or sending her a message.

There was nothing but silence, an emptying out.

The alarm on her phone pierced the silence. She frowned, sliding up from the floor. It was time for her therapy session. As Charlotte was logging into her account to connect with her client, it hit her. True, she hadn't heard a message sent to answer her prayer. It was something far more valuable.

If God's son experienced fear and prayed to have the cup be taken from him, did she need to be plagued with guilt at her terror and wavering faith?

Two therapy sessions later, Charlotte was exhausted, but it was soothing to immerse herself in her work again. She was grateful that she could still work, even if it was in a reduced capacity. How long would she feel good enough to continue?

She knew the reprieve from suffering couldn't last long since she had another round of chemotherapy scheduled for the next day. Just as Charlotte was gathering her things and trying to decide if she should call her mother and tell her she would pick up the kids from school, Adrien burst into the office. He walked across her cherry wood hardwood floors, leaving puddles of dirty slush in his wake. Charlotte cringed. How many times had she asked him to remove his boots at the door?

"You have to take the kids this week. I need to go down to California."

Charlotte's head fell back on the edge of the sofa, and she closed her eyes. She had a doctor's appointment in Boise the next day and a round of chemo to go through. She couldn't tuck her kids into bed for the next two nights; she would be down in Boise. Perhaps two weeks later at the next round of chemo, it would be possible to be home with her kids in the evening. She hoped so.

Dr. Benson had discussed the possibility of giving her a small portable pump for future rounds of treatment. She would carry the pump on a belt so she would be able to go home once the pump was connected to the line and the infusion started. He had said he would contact the McCall hospital about having a nurse disconnect the pump when it was done. This second time, however, he wanted her in the hospital to monitor her reaction to the treatment.

"You can't go. I can't take care of the kids. I'm going out of town."

"Are you kidding? You didn't say anything about that last weekend."

"I can't change my plans."

Adrien placed his hands on his hips. "Well, you'll have to. I need to prepare for our move. Wait for it," he said and held out his hands as if warding her off. "I bought us a house." He lifted his arms up in triumph.

Charlotte opened her mouth and shut it again. Her thoughts were scrambling to understand, her stomach clenching as she stared at Adrien's smiling face. She had never agreed to move, on the contrary. They had left things at a stalemate. "You can't buy a house."

"And why can't I?" Adrien's hands had crossed over his chest, and his chin lifted.

"You would need a down payment."

"Don't treat me like an idiot. Of course one requires a down payment to purchase a house."

Her thoughts twisted. She had dropped by the bank just today after her appointment with Ben to prepare for the creation of the trusts. The bank manager hadn't said anything about Adrien. She knew there was no way he could withdraw money from her account; it didn't have his name on it. Where would he get enough money for a deposit on a house in California if not from one of her 'hidden' accounts?

"How much does a house down there even cost? Where would you get that kind of money?"

"Well that sure does beat all," replied Adrien through gritted teeth. "First you hide our money, then you ensure my name is not on any of the accounts. Now you downright sit there and act like we honest to God don't have the money for a down payment on our new home."

"Wait, what? It won't be my new home. I'm not moving."

"You sure as hell are, because one, I'm not living without my kids," he answered, then paused. He rubbed his five o'clock shadow and grinned at her, his eyes flashing. "And two, you won't have anywhere here to live in two weeks' time."

It's not true, she thought. Her hands balled into fists as the pain in her abdomen ate at her from the inside. "You didn't," she breathed out.

"Figured it out already? I always said I have the cleverest wife in town."

"You sold the cabin."

Adrien clapped his hands together and rubbed them. "I got myself a real boat full of cash for that cabin. You wouldn't believe how much people were willing to shell out for our little place right on the lake. That indoor endless river pool of yours and sauna were a real value-add. I give you full credit on adding that to the property. You were right about the all-white kitchen with granite countertops and new bathrooms we installed too. The real estate agent said it added a hundred thousand to the asking price."

Charlotte held up a hand to ward off the truth.

"You wouldn't sell the cabin. I inherited it. It's our home. You couldn't sell it without my signature."

"Tell yourself that all you want, honey, but I sold our cabin, and I bought a gorgeous new place down in sunny California. I'm flying out of Boise tonight to go sign the final papers and shop for some new furniture."

"We have furniture."

Adrien snapped his fingers. "Forgot to add that bit. I sold the cabin as is: furniture and all. The buyers loved it exactly as it is, so they threw in money for the furniture too. Isn't that great? Now I can go buy furniture to match the new house."

"You can't go. You can't leave me with the kids this week."

"Why the hell not? I had them all last week and did a right good job of it too, I might add. It's your turn. Ask Ma or your Mom and Élodie to help out."

"You can't leave me. Not this week. I have to travel out of town. I have important plans."

"Oh yeah? Give me one good reason why you can't cancel those plans." Adrien folded his arms over his chest. "Or are you having an affair?" he smirked at her. "Wouldn't that be rich? The perfect little Miss Church-Goer committing adultery?"

Silence, thick with tension, choked the room as Charlotte's brain clicked through choices. She could tell him. Right here and now she could tell him he couldn't leave town because she was going to Boise for chemotherapy.

Charlotte looked at Adrien's wide stance, jutting chin and thrust out chest and wanted nothing more than to wipe the smirk off his face.

"You know what they say," she answered. "The longer you're married to someone, the more similar to them you become. Maybe you've worn off on me, Adrien."

The smile on Adrien faltered as he searched her face. "You didn't," he said, uncertainty flashing in his eyes.

Charlotte had expected to experience satisfaction. Instead, she rubbed the heel of her palm over her heart. The pain was radiating into her chest now. She pulled her feet up onto the sofa and hugged her knees, resting her head on her knees and looked out the window at the still falling snow.

Her thoughts drifted to Saturday and Sunday. They had been such a happy family. That is what she wanted back:

the Adrien who tucked her up onto the sofa and made her dinner when she was ill. The man who held her hand in church and came up to hug her from behind as she cooked in his mother's kitchen. The man who played board games with her with the kids last Sunday night after dinner.

No, she couldn't tell him. She hadn't wanted to acknowledge it, but there was part of her that believed he would leave and go down to California whether she had cancer or not. That he wouldn't want to take care of a terminally ill woman, hollowed out by pain and suffering.

She wasn't even sure she wanted him to.

"It's Zack, isn't it? He's been waiting a long time for his chance. I guess you finally gave it to him."

Charlotte didn't answer. There was no energy remaining in her body. Only pain.

"Well to hell if I'm going to stay and take care of our kids while you make a cuckold of me."

The door to her office slammed. Charlotte grabbed her knees tighter and stared at the puddles of dirty water he had left behind. What was she going to do?

CHAPTER 11

Romans 8:18-22

18 For I consider that the sufferings of this present time are not worthy to be compared with the glory which will be revealed toward us. 19 For the creation waits with eager expectation for the children of God to be revealed. 20 For the creation was subjected to vanity, not of its own will, but because of him who subjected it, in hope 21 that the creation itself also will be delivered from the bondage of decay into the liberty of the glory of the children of God. 22 For we know that the whole creation groans and travails in pain together until now.

ÉLODIE WAS PERPETUALLY offering to come and take care of the kids to give her some breathing room. As yet, Charlotte hadn't taken her up on offer since Adrien had moved out. She had been too proud, wanting to prove that she could handle things all by herself. She took a deep breath as Élodie answered the phone.

"Guess where I am?" asked Élodie, not even answering her phone with a hello.

"At work?"

"Vegas," yelled Élodie. "Can you believe it?"

"You're not serious. You didn't say anything on Sunday."

"Jake surprised me with my plane ticket Monday morning."

"Don't go," answered Charlotte. "I have a bad feeling."

"Of course I'm going. Stop being such a worry mouse. I

can't wait to tell you all about it over a mug of spiced wine. Listen, I'm sorry I can't celebrate the Christmas day with you. We won't be back."

"Be careful, Élodie."

"I've got to go. Kiss the kids for me."

Charlotte stared at her phone. She hated to make this call. Her mother picked up her children from preschool and school five afternoons a week. She didn't want to ask her Mom to do even more, no matter what. Charlotte knew how much the volunteer work and her circle of friends meant to her. She was proud her Mom had built up such a full and meaningful life of service. Charlotte didn't want to burden her mother, but Adrien had left her no other choice. She could wait and ask her, in person, when she went to pick them up from her house.

No, she decided. It will be easier over the phone.

"Hi, Mom."

"Hey, honey. How's it going? Are you working yourself out from under that mountain?"

"What? Hey, I hate to ask you this, but could you take care of the kids for the next three days? I have to travel out of town, and Adrien just left to go down to LA."

"I work the next three night shifts at the hospital. If you had asked me sooner, I could have asked Karen to switch the weekend with me. But she's not here. She went to Spokane to visit family for the week. I have no one to call to fill in for me."

Charlotte pressed her face into her hands. What was she going to do?

"Honey? Are you there? Why don't you give Élodie a ring and ask her?"

"She's in the city of sin."

"She's where? Good lord, that girl. She didn't say a word about it on Sunday."

"Yes, well, I'll be over to pick up the kids soon, Mom."

"I'm so sorry I can't help you out, Charlotte. Is it an emergency? Because I could ask..."

"I'll figure it out. See you soon."

Charlotte closed her eyes and huffed out a large breath of frustration. What had she been thinking, not telling her family about the cancer? This was a nightmare. If they had known, then Élodie wouldn't have flown off to Las Vegas, and her Mom would have arranged time off from work to go down with her to the appointment and watch the kids. Now, what was she going to do? Was it even possible to cancel a chemotherapy treatment? She tugged her hair back, attempting to pull it into a ponytail despite its short length. It was the worst possible timing. Karen was visiting family in Lewiston with her kids, or otherwise, she could have brought the girls to spend two days with Karen and Ben.

Then Charlotte's gaze fell onto the bouquet of tulips her father had brought her.

"Desperate times call for desperate measures," she said aloud.

Without allowing time to second-guess herself, she dialed her father's number.

"Charlotte?"

"Hi, Dad. I don't know how to ask this, so I'm just going to come out with it. Could you drive the kids and I down to Boise tomorrow and stay two nights down there with the kids in a hotel? You can say no."

"That sounds like a grand idea. Do you need a holiday, honey? I heard from your Mom how many hours you've been clocking."

"No, I need chemotherapy."

She covered her mouth with her hand. The words had just popped out. Why in the world, of all people, did she just tell her father about the cancer? What would her mother think when she found out, that she had told her father first? With a groan, she fell onto her stomach on the sofa.

"You have cancer? Why didn't you tell me?"

"I haven't told anyone, Dad, and you can't tell them either."

There was silence on the line for a moment. "You haven't told your Mom? Élodie? Surely Adrien knows…"

"No one knows," interrupted Charlotte. She waited for her Dad to respond, but he didn't answer. After a moment she said, "This was a stupid idea. I'm sorry I asked, Dad. I'll talk to you later."

"Wait," yelled her Dad. "Of course I'll drive you down."

"You'll need to take care of the kids then, while I'm in the hospital getting the chemotherapy. It takes over forty-six hours. I don't want them to know about the cancer, at least not yet. You'd have to take care of them for two days without me around. Shoot, this is a stupid idea."

"Let me do this for you, Charlotte," he said and cleared his voice. "I want to do this. I'll deliver you to the hospital. I will take the kids to the zoo and out for pizza. I'll show them a good time. Please trust me."

"Okay." The word popped out of her mouth. To her surprise, she didn't want to reach out and retract it.

"But doesn't Aurélie have school?"

"I'll call her in sick."

"Are you sure you feel comfortable with this, Charlotte? You could always call your Mom and tell her about the cancer. I know she would want to know. She'd quit her job rather than forsake being there for you."

"It's about time they get to know their Grandpa."

"Well. What time should I pick you up?"

CHARLOTTE PACED BACK and forth in her kitchen. She had called her mother and told her she had asked her Dad to drive the kids and her down to Boise for a two-day overnight trip. Her mother had registered surprise but had reassured Charlotte that her father seemed like a new man. If her appointments were essential, then she would have to trust her Dad that he could watch the kids.

She ran her hand along the cold granite countertop and gazed out the window at the lake glittering in the first sunshine they had had in days. The snow was knee-deep out in the yard. No tracks were leading out to the glass-enclosed pool room. Once again she hadn't summoned the willpower to swim. Even five minutes sounded like too much when her alarm went off at five-thirty that morning.

She had hit the stop button, rolled over, and drifted immediately back into sleep. It was the children who had woken her up at six-thirty. They had come bounding onto the bed. Gabriel was clutching a storybook. Charlotte had pulled them in under the warm flannel duvet and read not only the one but a pile of children's books. At last, she had dragged herself out of bed and informed both children they were going swimming: together.

Now, dressed in a cozy cranberry colored sweater dress, wool tights, and soft leather boots she was happy she had hauled the kids through the snow to the pool room. They had both splashed and played in the river current for half an hour. Gabriel might now sleep the two-hour drive in the car down to Boise. She wandered to the front door and looked out the side window at the drive. Her Dad was ten minutes late. Was he coming? What if he didn't?

Just then she spotted his red rental car pull up into the drive. She opened the front door before he even stepped out of the car, waving, and called her kids to come put on their boots and jackets. She grabbed the bags and her purse and clicked her SUV open as she waved at her father. The kids tromped through the snow to the car behind her.

Her Dad stood by her SUV and waited. He bent down and offered his hand for a handshake to each child as if they were mini adults. Then he turned to her and hesitated, uncertainty clouding his handsome features. He held out his hand to her too. She took it in her own, shook it, and planted a kiss on his cheek.

"Thanks for doing this," she said.

Her heart hammered in her chest as she buckled her kids into their car seats. Thoughts screamed in her head. She asked herself what she was doing, entrusting her children to a man who had walked out on her decades ago.

There has to be another way, she thought. It wasn't too late to send her father packing and cancel her appointment. She shut the back car door and stood, hesitating, by the side of the car. Her father had already slid into the driver's seat and seemed to read her thoughts. He beckoned her to get in. She opened the car door but made no move to get into the vehicle.

"You have every reason to worry."

"Excuse me?" she asked.

"I ran out on you and your sister, and you haven't seen me since you were a little girl. If I were you, I would be hesitant to entrust the children to me too."

"That isn't exactly reassuring Dad," she said, and yet, it was somehow. She looked over at her Dad, at the melancholy in his eyes, and slid into her seat.

"I'm a different man than I was then, Charlotte. This is the perfect opportunity to let me prove it."

Charlotte just nodded and turned on the music she had downloaded for the trip.

They drove out of McCall in silence. Thirty minutes later both children were asleep from the early morning swim and the Dramamine she had given them in anticipation of the winding drive.

"Tell me about the cancer," said her Dad, his eyes fixed on the road.

"I'd rather not," retorted Charlotte. Her father didn't respond. After a few minutes of silent internal struggle, Charlotte decided it would be a relief to tell someone everything.

So she did. She explained her stage four pancreatic cancer diagnosis and her quest to secure personally written birthday cards and carefully selected presents for her children, in case she didn't beat the cancer to see them.

The entire convoluted relationship with Adrien came rolling out of her too. She told him about Adrien's devotion to her and the children. He had been the kid's primary caregiver when they were babies, and she was growing her business. She explained his rage and resentment when he discovered the wealth she had hidden from him, and her horror when it came to light that Adrien had betrayed her the night he didn't come home.

"And you know about Adrien going behind my back to apply for the job in California and that I refuse to go," she concluded. "Yesterday he showed up and told me he sold our cabin behind my back and purchased a new house in Cali without my agreement, let alone knowledge. What can I do, Dad? Is it even legal for him to sell our home and purchase another without telling me?"

Her Dad remained silent during the entire unraveling of her story. At last, she relaxed back into her car seat. Her questions hung in the air between them.

Her father didn't answer right away. Then he sighed.

"Idaho is a communal property state."

"Which means he shares equally in all my financial gains during our marriage and gives him an equal ownership interest in our property," sighed Charlotte.

"Did you sign the mortgage together?"

"We didn't need a mortgage. I inherited the cabin and the land as well."

"Well, that changes everything."

Charlotte waited for more, but her Dad just furrowed his brow and slowed to take the bend off the road. "Dad?"

"Real estate you acquire before marriage, or by inheritance or gift during the marriage, is considered separate property. Unless you signed a quit deed to add Adrien to the title as a joint owner?"

"No. I didn't add Adrien because I assumed it belonged to him equally in a communal property state."

"No. He can't sell real estate that doesn't belong to him."

"And the new house he bought in California? Am I liable for the mortgage he took out to buy that home? What a mess."

"What time do you need to be at the hospital again?"

"Not until two-thirty. I wanted to get down there early so we can go to lunch together first."

"Great, then we have some time," he answered and pulled the car over into a small pullout next to the whitewater rapids of the river. He glanced in the rearview mirror. "The kids are still asleep. Let's take a break, and I'll give an attorney friend of mine a call."

Charlotte checked her kids and then climbed out of the car and wandered over to gaze at the crashing water. She heard her Dad talking on his phone behind her, the individual words drowned out by the roar of the river. After a few minutes, he walked up next to her and stared at the deer drinking on the other side.

"Well, I have bad news for you. Mike said that if you live in a community property state, and Idaho is, and the house was purchased with money either you or Adrien earned during the marriage, then the law considers the new place community property that you and Adrien own equally. Which means that you are responsible for part of the debts he acquires during your marriage. The only way out of it is if you and Adrien sign a written agreement that makes the home he bought in California Adrien's separate property."

"Well hell," answered Charlotte and rubbed her forehead. "Could it get worse?" Her head was throbbing as if she had spent the last hour sitting millimeters away from a tuba trumpeting off-key in her ear.

"What I want to know, with all the bastards out there, why are you the one who has to deal with all this shit?" asked her Dad.

"It could be worse," shrugged Charlotte. "My kids are healthy."

Her Dad laughed and shook his head, "True. But this is a terrible deal you have to endure here, honey. I'm sorry. You just forget about this for now and focus on getting through the chemo. I'll try to figure something out to help."

"Okay," agreed Charlotte. "Let's hit the road again, yeah?"

"Sure thing, beautiful. I want to get some lunch in you before delivering you to your appointment," he answered and turned around.

Charlotte got in the car. By the time they were pulling into Boise, the kids had both woken up. Charlotte directed her Dad to the playground at Camel's Back where they would let the kids out to play for a half-hour before lunch.

"Where are we?" asked Aurélie

"Are we there yet?" chirped Gabriel.

"We're going to the Camel's Back playground," announced her father.

Both kids cheered. Charlotte scrutinized her father's interaction with the children for signs he would take good care of them the next two days without her. He pushed Gabriel and Aurélie on the swings and held Gabriel's hand as he balanced along a bridge. He gave every impression of being an attentive grandfather.

At noon they decided to eat at a bistro in Hyde Park. Charlotte barely tasted the food she put in her mouth; her thoughts were spinning too fast for her to appreciate the honey-glazed duck and spinach, pomegranate and blueberry salad. After lunch, they walked up the street to Goodies and bought the kids ice cream cones and lattes for themselves. It was only when Gabriel's ice cream fell onto the floor that Charlotte let out an inward sigh of relief. Her Dad immediately scooped Gabriel up and carried him to the counter, where he ordered him a new ice cream cone.

On the way to the hospital, Charlotte sent up a prayer that he would take good care of her kids. She had already asked her Dad to drop her off two blocks from the hospital. She didn't want to scare them by getting out right in front of St. Luke's Hospital. Charlotte climbed out of the SUV and opened the back door. She leaned in and hugged Gabriel.

"So, I love you both very much," she murmured and kissed Gabriel's soft, round cheek.

She reached over and hugged Aurélie and kissed her good-bye. "I hope you have a fun time with your Grandfather. Call me in a few hours to tell me what you've been up to, okay?"

"I have your phone number, and you have mine. We're staying at the Grove Hotel. Good luck, Charlotte."

Charlotte took a deep breath as she entered the hospital. She hoped the doctor would have good news for her today.

CHAPTER 12

Romans 5: 1-4
1 Being therefore justified by faith, we have peace with God through our Lord Jesus Christ; 2 through whom we also have our access by faith into this grace in which we stand. We rejoice in hope of the glory of God. 3 Not only this, but we also rejoice in our sufferings, knowing that suffering produces perseverance; 4 and perseverance, proven character; and proven character, hope:

A NURSE WITH STRAWBERRY blond hair and blue eyes smiled at Charlotte as she led her out of the waiting area and to an examination room. What was her name again? Her mind was a blank. She was practically shaking from nerves.

Charlotte didn't wait long before Dr. Benson entered the room. He shook Charlotte's hand and looked into her eyes. "Good morning, Charlotte. How are you feeling?"

Charlotte shrugged, glancing down at the floor. "Better than I expected?" She glanced back up at the doctor and tried to smile. "I hope you have good news for me."

"Well," Dr. Benson answered, crossing his arms over his chest, and then giving himself an internal shake, lowering them back down to his sides. "I'm sorry Charlotte. The tumor on your pancreas has grown significantly despite the last round of aggressive chemotherapy."

"Which means what?"

Charlotte examined Dr. Benson's face. She read reluctance

in the way he kept looking down at the chart in his hands and back up at her. Charlotte squared her shoulders and lifted her chin. "Tell me how long I have. Statistically."

"I do not like to give predictions. There is always a chance..."

"Just tell me."

Dr. Benson let out a deep sigh and ran a hand over his forehead. "The chances of you still being with us two months from now is low. The question is: do you want to continue with this aggressive round of chemotherapy? Or would you prefer to stop treatment and focus on palliative care?"

"I don't know." Charlotte's heart clutched in her chest. Would it be best to fight for every extra day she could spend with her kids? Or would fighting mean that the time she had left with them would be spent desperately ill and lying in a hospital bed? She didn't know what choice to make.

"Tell you what, let's review how the chemotherapy is affecting you, and then we will have a better picture. Did you experience any side effects due to the treatment? Afterward, did you develop a rash, feel short of breath, experience swelling of your face or lips, feel dizzy, unwell, or have pain in your abdomen, back, or chest?"

Charlotte tilted her head to the side in thought. "Yes, yes, and yes? I did feel dizzy and nauseated afterward. And I did have insane pain in my abdomen and back, but I'm not sure if that was due to the chemo or the cancer; I had that pain preceding the treatment."

Dr. Benson consulted his chart and looked back up at her. "Like I told you last time, your pancreas's ability to make the enzymes that aid in digestion is reduced by cancer. How is your digestion? Besides the nausea, are you experiencing any vomiting, diarrhea, loss of appetite?"

Charlotte furrowed her brow in thought. "I have had some nausea and diarrhea, but I don't know if that was due to the chemotherapy or the cancer."

"Well, you've lost weight in the past two weeks. I will send you home with some pancreatic enzyme supplements to aid your digestion and set up an appointment for you with our dietician who is a specialist in pancreatic oncology to help manage your symptoms.

"You told me last time that you swim every morning. Is that still possible at all?"

"I haven't felt well enough the past two weeks. I've tried some yoga a few times."

"That's good to hear. Unfortunately, people with pancreatic cancer often lose muscle mass. Keeping up with some gentle exercise will prevent the muscle loss, which will enable you to have more energy and better cope with treatment."

"I want you to be honest with me, doctor; I'm tough. Do you think I should stop the chemotherapy?"

Dr. Benson paused, studying Charlotte's face.

"What's most important to you, Charlotte?"

Charlotte didn't need to reflect; she answered immediately, "Spending quality time with my children is what I want the most. I don't want them to watch me suffering in a hospital if we can prevent it."

Dr. Benson took a deep breath and answered, "I would like to try one more round of chemotherapy since your side effects are not debilitating; if the round has no effect, then we could discuss with the palliative care team to whom I'll refer you. Do you agree?"

Charlotte nodded. "Yes, I'll try one more round. I'm not sure what palliative care entails, exactly."

"I'll see if I can arrange a meeting with our palliative care team tomorrow; they'll work with you to optimize your quality of life by addressing your wishes, any symptoms, and keeping you as comfortable as possible in regards to pain. How does that sound?"

Charlotte forced a smile on her face and nodded. Words failed her.

"The news you received from me today is tough to hear. We have some outstanding counselors. Like I said before, it would be a good idea to meet with one of them. Especially because you have been arriving at your appointments alone."

"Believe you me; I have an entire network of counselors with whom I can set up an appointment. I'll think about contacting one of my counselors from my online therapy platform," she answered.

"Do you love your work?"

Charlotte nodded, tears flooding her eyes. She swallowed the lump in her throat and bent her head to look at the hands in her lap. The last thing she wanted was to cry in Dr. Benson's office.

"Then keep working." Charlotte sent a prayer up to heaven to have such a perceptive and empathetic doctor. She knew the time constraints put on physicians and the pressure he must be under to treat as many patients in as little time as possible. Yet he never appeared rushed or stressed during her appointments.

"Everyone needs a healthy activity they can lose themselves in. Do you lose all sense of time and space while working? End most workdays with an inner sense of satisfaction?"

"Yes."

"Cancer patients benefit from a state of flow. I'm not saying you need to keep working. What I am saying is, if you quit, you need to find an activity you enjoy so much, that you forget your worries and everything around you. Otherwise, your thoughts will invariably shift to cancer, and the pain will feel even more intense."

Charlotte smiled. "That's good advice. I'm grateful you are my doctor. I'm going to pray for you. You have a tough job, and you do it well; I appreciate your empathy, your honesty."

Dr. Benson looked taken aback. "Thanks, Charlotte. Now I'll check in with you later today after your round of chemo."

"Wait, Doctor?"

"Yes?"

"Will I be able to spend Christmas at home with my family?"

"I can't answer that, Charlotte. I just don't know."

Charlotte wondered what it must be like to be Dr. Benson and to watch so many people lose the fight against cancer. She admired him for his strength; she wasn't sure if she could step into his shoes.

CHARLOTTE FOLLOWED THE NURSE down the hall and into a patient care room. The nurse hooked Charlotte up to the IV. As the liquid flowed into her arm, she arranged herself more comfortably. She took out hand warmers and tore the packages open. She usually used these in ski gloves, but today she placed them on her abdomen. The heat relaxed the muscles in her solar plexus. Next, she removed a citrus oil hand lotion and rubbed some onto her cheeks and her hands. The scent had always lifted her spirits. She took out a citrus spiced tea she had brought with her in a travel mug. She sipped her tea as she thought about what Dr. Benson had advised her.

Next, she took out her phone and opened her Audible app, flipping through the book she had already downloaded. She closed her eyes and let the narrator's voice carry her into the story. Her phone began vibrating, and she snatched it up. But it wasn't her Dad. Adrien was calling. She ignored it. If she answered the phone now, the anger would roar in her ears, and within minutes she would be a sweaty, shaking mess. It was the last thing she needed to deal with while drugs were being pumped into her body.

She had done everything she could to be strong and independent, and build security into her life. Now the cancer was threatening to turn the solid ground beneath her feet into a quicksand of vulnerability and weakness.

Well, she would hold on to every illusion of strength and normality for as long as she possibly could.

She had told her Dad, but she wasn't going to tell anyone else until she had to. She knew from her studies and continuing education as a psychologist that most people didn't know how to react when they found out that someone had been diagnosed with a terminal illness.

Even the most compassionate person often didn't know what to say or how to act and unconsciously avoided a terminally ill person. If Charlotte was going to deal with cancer alone, then she wanted to know it was her choice.

She couldn't bear the thought of those she loved leaving her in isolation because they didn't know how to relate. While it increased her resilience in the face of the illness to focus on the positive, she knew she couldn't hear someone telling her, 'it could be worse.'

Charlotte didn't see at the moment how it could be unless one of her kids was the one receiving the chemotherapy.

Her phone vibrated; her sister was calling her.

"Hi, Élodie. How's Vegas?"

"He asked me to marry him," shouted Élodie into the phone. "He proposed at the Venetian in a gondola as the words 'Will you marry me?' were projected into the sky above St. Mark's Square. Can you believe it? Just wait until you see my ring."

"You just met him a few weeks ago," sputtered Charlotte. "Isn't it a bit fast?"

"Jake said you would say that. We know most people won't understand; they've never experienced love at first sight."

Charlotte heard Jake in the background asking for the phone again. "Hey there, Charlotte, it's me again. Listen," he lowered his voice, and Charlotte heard him shut a door.

"About the extreme survival holiday business. I have talked to some investors here and some marketing people who have put together a great pitch for a website and a digital marketing plan for us, including search engine optimization.

I need the final business plan and that marketing plan you promised me. They're interested in investing. Also, I'm ready to pitch to Adrien. He'll need to invest some money in the business like I'm going to. I need his fifty thousand from his end wired to the business account I opened in Switzerland by the end of the week, so I can get the ball rolling on our new business."

"Come again?"

"I quit my job to go into business for myself, Charlotte. My savings are running down. I need to get this business rolling, with or without Adrien. A couple of colleagues of mine are very interested in partnering with me and have the money to commit ready to go."

The hairs on the back of Charlotte's neck stood on end. First the snap engagement, and now Jake was demanding fifty thousand dollars wired outside of the country.

"Why are you opening a business account in Switzerland? The plan was to open an account in McCall as we discussed."

"We'll open an account there too, of course. We just need one in my target market. I want to pay for the website and marketing campaign to reach my target audience over there. The Swiss work incredibly long hours and love the outdoors.

A holiday like we offer will be extremely attractive to them."

"I thought we were targeting key cities in the United States, like Los Angeles and New York."

"Adrien and I can sit down together with your Dad and go through all the business plans in fine detail when I get back to McCall. Unless you don't want to join in the venture and pass up this perfect opportunity to secure your husband his dream job?"

"Adrien's out of town. I can't talk to him for a few days about this. Can I talk to Élodie?" asked Charlotte, her voice a rasp.

Her mouth had gone dry. She took a sip of her tea, her jaw clenching as she ground her teeth. This handsome, smooth talker didn't know who he was dealing with, did he? Charlotte smiled. Like hell she was going to trust someone she had met a few weeks ago enough to wire him a large sum of money overseas. She didn't care if he was engaged to her sister. Élodie didn't exactly have a stellar track record of character judgment. Her naïveté was as endearing as it was aggravating. Charlotte needed to tell Élodie to get away from Jake and on a plane home as soon as possible. What could she say to convince her?

"Élodie can't come to the phone. She's changing into her wedding dress."

"Wait, what?"

"Wish us luck."

Charlotte stared at the phone. He had hung up on her. She instantly called Élodie's phone, but it flipped immediately to voice mail. Charlotte pounded her fists down on the chair, and a nurse rushed over.

"Everything okay?"

Charlotte shook her head, still in disbelief. "Have you ever been fooled into thinking someone was a great guy?"

"I hear you," replied the nurse. "When they develop a jerk radar, I'll be the first customer in line."

Charlotte glanced down at her phone. She had been itching to call her father twenty minutes after he dropped her off. Now it had been over two hours. She dialed his number. The phone rang, and rang, and rang. It clicked to voice mail.

Charlotte left a message for her father to call her as soon as he got the message. She turned her audiobook back on, extracted a lavender-scented eye pillow from her purse, and tried to pretend she was at a spa instead of at a hospital. It didn't work. Less than five minutes later, she checked her phone. Had her Dad texted her?

She redialed his number. Once again it clicked to voicemail. Don't worry, she told herself. Maybe he took them to a movie. They could be in the swimming pool at the hotel. Perhaps he hadn't heard it ring.

Forty minutes of anguish later, Charlotte's phone rang. "Everything okay, Charlotte?"

"Where were you? Why didn't you pick up?"

"It started to rain, so we skipped the zoo today in favor of going to a movie in the Egyptian Theatre."

Charlotte immediately looked out the window. It was raining. Her shoulders relaxed away from her ears. Everything was okay.

"Here, I'll put them on the phone."

"Hi, Mommy! Grandpa let us have popcorn, and candy, and soda and told us we could go swimming after he has a rest," said Aurélie.

"So are you having a fun time?"

"The best time. Mom, we have our own room. Can you believe it? Just Gabriel and I."

Charlotte heard her Dad shout from the background, "Tell her there is a connecting door open to my room."

"There's a connecting door to Grandpa's room. I'm going to put on my suit now, Mom. Bye."

"Hi Mommy, I miss you."

Charlotte smiled at how small her son's voice sounded on the phone to her. "Hey, there sweetheart. What movie did you go and see?"

"We're going swimming now. Bye."

"Charlotte? You still there?"

"Gabriel isn't a good swimmer yet, Dad. You need to be careful. I packed his water wings, but you need to watch him every second."

"I will. How is your appointment going?"

"So far, so good."

"Great, well I'll have the kids call you when I tuck them into their beds for the night."

Charlotte leaned back and closed her eyes. Aurélie and Gabriel had sounded happy. She focused on her breath, willing herself to relax. Her phone buzzed next to her, and she looked at the screen. Adrien was calling again. She ignored it, and it stopped. Thirty seconds later it began vibrating again.

She couldn't stand it anymore and answered the call.

"What the hell are you thinking, having your drunk of a Dad take care of our kids?"

"You didn't leave me much choice."

"Well, thank you for opening my eyes to the kind of person you are. Your new love affair is more important to you than the welfare of your children. You're out of your mind, you know that?"

"What?"

"Did you think I wouldn't find out? It's all over town you know. Everyone knows you're cheating on me with Zack."

"You have this wrong."

"Do I? I don't think so. Rhonda told me you bartended a wedding with him, and afterward, she saw you two dancing. She said you spent the night at the hotel. Are you doing this to get back at me? Is that it?"

Charlotte rubbed her temples with her hands. A pounding headache was returning. "It was one dance, Adrien. That's all that happened. That one dance."

"You expect me to believe he's not laying in bed with you right now?"

Heat flushed through Charlotte's body, and the room swam in front of her eyes. "You know, after this phone call, I wish he were."

Charlotte could hear Adrien's labored breathing on the other end of the line.

"I don't believe you."

"What exactly? That I want Zack lying here next to me, or that he isn't?"

Then Charlotte heard something that caused what color was left in her face to drain completely. A sob. Was Adrien crying? He never cried. Charlotte shook her head, battling mixed emotions. He had lied to her, cheated on her, accepted a job in another state without asking her, and sold her home behind her back. She had every reason to hate him. She sighed; she was hopeless. Despite everything, she still loved him.

"I didn't sell the cabin. I didn't buy a house in LA. When I found out about you and Zack, well, I wanted to hurt you, so I lied."

"So you're not in LA?"

"I'm standing in our living room."

"Then I suggest you drive on over to the Shore Lodge and have a chat with Zack yourself. If he isn't bartending, then they will know where you can find him. He'll tell you there is no affair."

"But if he's here, then what the hell are you doing in Boise?"

Charlotte hung up the phone without making a response. The flush had disappeared, and she was left feeling sticky and shivering. She called the nurse and asked for a blanket.

An hour later her kids called to say goodnight. After a moment's reflection, she turned off her phone when she hung up. The roller coaster of emotions of the day had taken a toll on her psyche. The oblivion of slumber was dragging her under and after the drama of the day and the liquid flowing into her arm; she didn't want anyone, or anything, pulling her back up for the night.

THE NEXT MORNING CHARLOTTE awoke to pain. It was as if she were a small goat who had spent the entire previous day trying to outrun a ravenous wolf. Her whole body ached, her head felt too small for her throbbing brain, and nausea simmered in her belly.

"You're awake. You don't look like you are feeling too great this morning. Let's feed you some breakfast and see how you are after that," chirped a tall, dark-haired nurse with laugh lines around her eyes and bright blue eyes. Charlotte guessed she was in her fifties, but these days, it was hard to know. Was she a young-looking woman in her sixties, or a woman in her late forties? In any case, the distraction from the sensations screaming in her body was welcome.

The nurse pulled the tray of food over to Charlotte's bed, and Charlotte's spirits rose a fraction of an inch when she spied the cup of coffee. She immediately grabbed the coffee and took a sip. She grimaced and set the cup back down. It was cold, metallic, and bitter.

"Yeah, they brought in your breakfast a while back. You've had yourself a real lie-in this morning, which is great. Sleep is very restorative. Do you know what? I am just about to go on break. Would you like me to bring you back a latte from the coffee cart in the lobby?"

Charlotte was horrified when tears sprung to her eyes. She had just been thinking she would give anything for a good cup of coffee this morning, but the IV was still attached to her arm, and she was too exhausted even to go and brush her teeth.

"Are you sure?"

"Of course," the nurse winked at her. "I know a coffee lover when I see one."

Charlotte took out a twenty from her purse and held it out to the nurse. "Keep the change, okay?"

The nurse waved the money away. "It's my treat. What kind of coffee would you like?"

"An extra-hot vanilla latte please," answered Charlotte while holding the money out still. "Take the money. Buy yourself and one of the other nurses a coffee too."

The nurse hesitated and then took the money from Charlotte with a smile. "Only if you let me bring you a blueberry muffin too."

"Deal."

Charlotte leaned back on her pillow and reflected on the power of little kindnesses. That was when a light bulb went off. What did other cancer patients with the terminal diagnosis do when they found out that their time was limited? Did they leave behind cards for their children and loved ones? Of course, they did. But what if they didn't have someone to whom they could entrust their cards?

Her mind these days couldn't focus enough to read or

listen to a book on tape. Dr. Benson was right. She needed something new to take her mind off of everything in her life. Now she had an idea of just what she could do with the hours she would be spending lying in bed or curled up on the sofa.

The nurse returned with a piping hot coffee and a freshly baked blueberry muffin. Charlotte savored the velvety taste of the coffee and every crumb of her treat; then she took out her phone. She had research to do if she wanted to start turning her idea into a reality. It was only when she had her cell in her hand that she remembered that she had turned it off the night before.

When the phone's screen lit up, she saw she had over ten messages and twenty missed calls. She didn't even stop to read them. She immediately dialed her father's number.

"Hey Char, how are you feeling this morning?"

"Is everything okay, Dad? Where are the kids?"

"We are just finishing brunch at the hotel. It's cold, but sunny today, so we are going to visit the zoo and then go out to lunch. If they have the energy, I'm going to take them for another swim and then let them watch a Disney movie."

"Hi, Mommy. Grandpa says I can sit in a wagon at the zoo. Bye," said Gabriel.

"He's three, Mom," protested Aurélie. "Don't you think he's a little old to sit in a wagon? You have to meet us at the hotel, Mom; you'd love it. We have a Jacuzzi in our room. If you put bubble bath in and turn it on, then, the bubbles go high. It's amazing. Love you. Bye."

"They are pulling at the bit to get to the zoo. I'll call you after lunch?"

"Great. Thanks, Dad."

"I'm having the time of my life. I might need to sleep a week after these two days, though."

Charlotte smiled and said goodbye. She checked her messages. Twenty messages had been sent from Élodie. Charlotte swore when she opened the first text and saw the first photograph. Élodie was posing in an extravagant A-line wedding dress with a crystal belt, deep sweetheart neckline, and swirls of organic edge lace decorating the overlay of the floor-length tulle skirt. The rest of the photographs showcased the wedding at the Bellagio Hotel, Élodie and Jake dancing, cutting a wedding cake, and drinking a glass of champagne together in front of the fountain.

Charlotte took the last sip of her coffee and dialed Élodie's number, but she didn't answer.

Charlotte jumped when her phone rang.

"Charlotte? Oh, thank God. Thank you for calling me back."

"What is it, Adrien?"

"I went skiing with Zack yesterday. I need to speak with you in person."

Charlotte panicked. Had Zack told Adrien about the pancreatic cancer?

"Are you still in Boise?"

"Yes."

"Well, please cancel the rest of your meetings and come home. Please."

Charlotte realized she had been holding her breath. She let it out and inhaled deeply. If Zack had told Adrien about her cancer, then Adrien would know she wasn't in Boise for business meetings.

"I can't do that. We will be home tomorrow."

"I'll be here."

"I've got to go. I'll see you tomorrow."

Charlotte needed a distraction, or she would drive herself crazy agonizing over her marriage. So she began researching. Charlotte took out her beautiful bound journal. The entire day fell away as she wrote out a detailed plan for www.onwingsofanangel.com in her journal. The nonprofit would enable anyone afflicted by a terminal disease to send in addressed cards for safe keeping. The cards would be mailed on the requested date in the future. Charlotte's mind was soaring like an eagle on wind currents. Her soul was serene, and her mind energized.

This service wouldn't just appeal to those dying of terminal cancer. There would be plenty of people out there who would want to pre-write all their cards for the year and hand them over to someone else to mail out on time. The nonprofit could earn money from paying clients to finance offering the service free to the terminally ill. The more she worked on the idea, the more certain she was, intuitively, that this all was going to work. She couldn't wait to fire up her Mac at home and start the business plan, marketing plan, and ideas for a website into a portfolio of documents. There would be the website to build and connections to make with oncologists and hospitals.

Maybe, Charlotte thought as she lay falling asleep that night, some good can come out of this cancer diagnosis, after all.

THE NEXT DAY CHARLOTTE called her Dad and told him to pick her up at the back of the hospital. Charlotte hoped her children wouldn't notice where they were. There was no choice either way, as she was too weak to walk a couple of blocks that morning.

The first thing Charlotte wanted to do when she saw her father waiting in the car was to pull open the back door and hug her kids. Unfortunately, the world was tilting dangerously to one side. Her father jumped out of the car when he saw her approaching and put an arm around her, supporting her to the car. "Hey, you two. I missed you so much," said Charlotte as her Dad eased her into the car.

"Are you sick?" asked Gabriel.

"You don't look good, Mom," added Aurélie.

"Well, maybe your Grandpa here will stop and buy me some sparkling water and a hot cup of good coffee, and I will feel much better than I am right now. Maybe he'll even buy you two some brownies. What do you say?"

"I say I could use three coffees myself. We had such a good time I wore myself out," answered her father with a wink.

AFTER STOPPING AT A DUTCH BROTHERS drive-through, her father began the drive back to McCall. Her children happily chirped like two little canaries about their holiday with Grandpa until the Dramamine kicked in and they fell silent. Charlotte looked over her shoulder at how angelic her two kids looked asleep, chocolate smudges on their cheeks.

When she had nowhere else to turn, her Dad had come through for her in a big way. Forgiving him was one thing. Seeing him taking steps to make amends was another.

Having her Dad here, sitting next to her, driving her home from her chemotherapy, healed the fissures in her heart in a way nothing else ever could.

Her Dad reached over, his eyes still fixed on the road, and patted her hand. "I'm sorry I ran out on you. I never stopped loving you, though. I just couldn't be that man, the good Dad. Not for a long time."

"But you're here now, Dad," she answered, and grabbed his hand, looping her fingers into his and squeezing. "You're that man now."

Charlotte heard her Dad swallow, and she knew he was choked up. She didn't look over. Her Dad came from a time and place where strong men didn't show their emotions. She let him have his moment, still holding his hand, pretending as if she hadn't noticed.

"So," he said, at last, clearing his throat. "I called around. I don't know what I can do to help you out of the raw deal Adrien is giving you."

"Well," sighed Charlotte. "He didn't sell the cabin or buy a new place in California. He just told me those lies to hurt me." Charlotte sighed again. It was as if she were continually sighing, letting out great gusts of worry, disbelief, and anguish.

"That's plum crazy."

"I know. He did it in revenge. Adrien accused me of having an affair with Zack."

Her Dad took a swift look at her. "He's a good-looking fella, that's for sure. I like him."

"I'm not having an affair, Dad."

"I'm not one to judge, Charlotte."

"Does that mean you cheated on Mom?"

"What? No, I mean, I've made my mistakes, too. Are you going to tell Adrien about the chemotherapy?"

That was the pivotal question, to which Charlotte still didn't have an answer.

She looked out the window at the pine-covered mountains

and spied a deer bounding away. Charlotte longed to run away, like the deer. The only problem was she would be taking cancer with her.

Her entire life Charlotte had found it impossible to trust anyone but her mother. It was the source of her ambition in school and the reason she had opened her own business.

It was what had impelled her to save every dime she could, and hide it from everyone, including her husband. Every friend that she made she held at arm's length, every new work colleague received an in-depth background check before they could join her business. Charlotte looked over at her Dad.

When she had summoned the strength to forgive and trust her father, he had helped her when she was in desperate need. Her Dad had proven himself worthy of her confidence in the past few days; perhaps this knowledge would enable her to summon the courage to trust Adrien with her secret.

"Well, sooner or later, I'll have to."

"I'm not telling you what to do, Charlotte. I just want to say that if he doesn't find out until you land in the hospital, and you give him no opportunity to be there for you, it could destroy him. If he loves you, then you not trusting him enough to tell him about your cancer will hurt him something awful."

Fatigue overcame Charlotte; her eyes were closing. Her father squeezed her hand, and she slipped away into sleep.

DISORIENTATION SWARMED CHARLOTTE when her father shook her awake, the buzzing in her head made it difficult for her to concentrate on his words. She was dead weary. Her eyes closed again, and in the twilight of slumber, she felt hands slip beneath her and strong arms gather her up.

Her eyes briefly blinked open. Her father was carrying her through her front door; he was laying her down on her bed. Adrien was at her side, slipping her boots and tights off; he was tucking her under her soft flannel duvet.

A smile floated to her lips when Adrien kissed her forehead. He opened the window, the crisp, pine-scented air flowing down on her face. A bird twittered its song in the tree outside her window as she drifted again into deep sleep.

When Charlotte opened her eyes the next morning, the room was dark. She reached for her phone to check the time, but it wasn't on her bedside table. She slipped out of bed and into the bathroom. The clock on the cabinet glowed five-twenty-eight in the morning.

Charlotte realized she must have slept the entire day and night without waking. She stretched her arms to the ceiling and smiled. The pain in her abdomen and back had abated, though a wave of nausea was rolling through her stomach. She saw her suit hanging on the hook on the back of the bathroom door and all at once, knew she wanted nothing more than to return to her regular morning routine. Dr. Benson had told her to try to exercise.

Minutes later she waded through the snow, turned on her sauna, and turned on the endless river. Without giving her willpower a chance to lessen, she jumped into the pool and pulled her goggles down over her eyes. She had no idea where her watch had gotten to, but it didn't matter. She would just swim as long as her body would allow.

After a few slow, smooth strokes of freestyle, she noticed the nausea was abating. Two minutes later she switched to a painfully slow breaststroke. She willed herself to keep up the effort of the gentle swimming for twenty more minutes. It felt like an eternity. At last, she climbed out of the water, slightly dizzy and breathless, and stepped into the heat of the sauna.

Charlotte poured drops of lavender-scented oil into the bucket of water and ladled the water over the hot stones. Relaxing back onto the bench in the steam, Charlotte worried about Élodie until forcing her sister from her mind. Instead, she considered how to spend the day. After bringing the kids to school, she had two counseling sessions in the morning.

Hopefully, she would have the energy to take the kids ice-skating and out for pizza afterward. She would call her mom and tell her she would pick the kids up from school.

Flushed with heat, Charlotte turned off the sauna and headed back through the dark to the cabin. After a shower, she put on a bright red dress and wool tights and applied some makeup. It made her feel better. It was only when she sat down at the kitchen table with her journal, Bible, and song notebook with a cup of steaming coffee that Charlotte noticed the large fir tree in the living room and the vases filled with red and white long-stemmed roses in the living room and on the kitchen table.

Fresh fir and pine boughs pinned with holly berries were attached the staircase banister. Charlotte rubbed her temples and dragged her fingers through her hair. Adrien always had been good at dramatic apologies. She wasn't sure the festive decorations and smell of fresh pine could fix things this time. She savored her first sip of coffee and looked out the window at the lake set aglow by the rising sun.

It was the first morning since the cancer diagnosis that Charlotte was experiencing a sense of normality. If someone had told her a month ago she would trade any five-star holiday in the world to be able to hold on to the serene calm of her usual routine, she would have laughed at them; now it was her truth.

Charlotte's focus shifted to her songbook. She picked up her pen and delved into creating new lyrics for a song for her kids. Her iPhone started vibrating on the counter. She flipped open the leather case to check who was calling so early in the morning. It was Jake. She seethed inwardly and turned off her phone.

She checked her text messages and saw that Jake had left nine texts yesterday. She tossed the phone back down on the counter. He wasn't ever hearing from her again.

She just hoped Élodie could get an annulment as soon as she got home.

Half an hour later, the bathroom door opening made her look up. Adrien walked in his boxers into the living room; his hair was ruffled from sleep. His face broke into a grin when he spotted her at the table.

"You were sleeping so deeply yesterday I checked that you were still breathing when I went to bed. Why were you so exhausted?"

"Chemo exhaust," answered Charlotte as she stood up and pushed the button on the Jura machine to grind and pour her a new cup of coffee. "I have stage four cancer, Adrien."

She couldn't meet his look. Adrien walked up behind her and looped his arms around her waist.

"I know."

"What? Zack told you."

"No, I ran into Dr. Johnson. Why didn't you say anything?" he murmured, and took her hand in his, tugging her into his embrace.

"I just really don't want to talk about it, Adrien. Is that okay? Can we have an entirely normal, peaceful day? Can you do that for me?

"You should have told me. Of course, I'm not going to take the job in California now. I called them yesterday and informed them of my decision."

"Thank you," she answered. Hot tears slipped down her cheeks.

"I've outgrown jumping into forest fires and spending the winter skiing the slopes as a ski paramedic. I'm ready for a career, and I'll find one. What I'm not ready for is living without you. I've already almost lost you once. I'm not doing it again. And we'll get you through this cancer together."

"I hope so," she whispered as she held out a cup of coffee to Adrien.

He was taking the news about the cancer so well; Charlotte was certain he was in denial. Or did he not know that her cancer was stage four?

Charlotte lifted herself up onto the counter, her feet dangling in midair. Dr. Benson had been direct about her chances of survival. She didn't think she was ready to explain in detail to Adrien about the severity of the cancer diagnosis.

Adrien took a sip of his coffee and looked down at his feet. "I called and told my parents about the cancer."

"But I haven't told my Mom. Or Élodie," protested Charlotte. "You should have asked me first, before telling them."

Adrien rubbed the back of his neck and looked at his feet.

"You better call them right now, Charlotte. Word spreads fast in this town. You don't want your Mama to find out from someone at the post office."

"Hardly," answered Charlotte.

Adrien deepened his voice in an impersonation of his

father. "My Dad said, 'you take care of our Charlotte, you hear? Anything we can do, you tell us straight off.' Ma said she could move in with us if we want the help."

"No," exclaimed Charlotte. "I mean, that's sweet, but…"

"Well, we agree on that," interrupted Adrien. His erect posture was gone. He slumped forward; his head hung as he continued to rub the back of his neck.

"About that night," he muttered. "I know you won't believe me, but it is eating me up inside not to tell you."

"I know what happened. You cheated on me."

"That's just it, Char. I don't know. I don't remember anything from that night. One minute, I'm taking the last sip of my second beer of the night, and the next I'm waking up on the beach alone."

"You expect me to believe that?" asked Charlotte, placing her face in her hands.

"No," answered Adrien, his voice almost a whisper. "But it's the truth, Char. I swear."

Charlotte dropped her hands from her face and looked into Adrien's eyes. He grimaced. "I can't promise I didn't cheat on you. I don't remember anything from that night but getting roaring drunk at the bar. The next thing I know for sure is waking up on the beach the next morning."

"What angel are the kids talking about if it's not your girlfriend?"

"You mean Kathy? She has been babysitting for me and helping me out with the kids for years. I didn't want to tell you. I wanted you to think I was handling everything here all alone."

"Your Mom's best friend? Are you kidding? All this time, whenever the kids mentioned Kathy, I thought they were talking about your girlfriend."

He rubbed his hand on the back of his neck, staring at his feet. "I don't expect you to forgive me for that night I didn't come home, or for threatening to sell our home, but I do promise to try to make it up to you. If you'll let me." He glanced up at her, his eyes searching.

Gabriel came sleepy-eyed into the kitchen, dragging his blanket behind him in one hand, and clutching a book in the other. "Story time," he announced. He walked pointedly to the kitchen nook. Charlotte followed. Apparently, she wasn't the only one who had missed their normal daily routine.

Charlotte closed the space between herself and Adrien and threw her arms around his neck.

"I forgive you. But I can't trust you," whispered Charlotte. "Not yet."

Adrien looked into her eyes. "Then I'll earn it."

Gabriel tugged at her arm, and she picked him up. She closed her eyes and pressed her cheek to the top of Gabriel's hair. He smelled like his coconut shampoo. She inhaled deeply. Adrien wrapped his arms around both of them.

"I'm sorry I didn't tell you about the money," whispered Charlotte. "It belongs to you too. We're a team."

"Me too," called a voice from the staircase. Aurélie came bounding down the last few steps. Adrien opened up an arm to let her in, as did Charlotte. Charlotte soaked in the warmth of her children and the strong arms of her husband around all of them. Charlotte wanted this warmth and security, for as long as she could hold onto it, for as long as she had left.

"I need to inform the landlord that I won't need the condo rental longer than the end of the month. It's time for me to come home and take care of my family."

"Mommy," complained Gabriel, squirming in her lap. "Read the story."

Charlotte looked at Adrien over the top of Gabriel's head, and he held her gaze.

Adrien snapped his fingers. "Sorry, Char, I almost forgot. Your Dad said to tell you he has to go back down home to LA, but he'll be back in a few days. He's planning on spending Christmas with us. We have it all planned out."

"Who's we? What have you planned out?"

"Mom," interjected Gabriel. "Read it," he insisted, holding the book in front of Charlotte's nose.

"It's going to be a surprise. I'm in charge of Christmas this year, remember?" Adrien winked at her and turned to make another cup of coffee.

Charlotte took a deep breath and blinked the tears from her eyes. Dr. Benson had explained that there was a hospice in McCall. He had instructed her that if her condition deteriorated and care became too much for her family at home, then she could talk with her palliative care nurse about arranging a transfer. She just hoped that transfer wouldn't happen before Christmas.

THE NEXT MORNING CHARLOTTE trudged through the snow for her slow swim and sauna. Afterward, she was drinking coffee at the kitchen nook when Adrien appeared in his long underwear.

"I propose I take the kids skiing and give you some peace. It snowed a couple of inches last night. The conditions are perfect for a ski day."

Charlotte stood up and stretched. Nausea had returned when she had stepped out of the pool today. Her abdomen was clenched into a ball of pain. She didn't want them to go skiing. Instead, there was a morning curled up next to the fire with a hot chocolate and a bowl of popcorn that she had planned for them. They could put on Christmas music and watch the kids decorate the tree.

"I'm coming too," she heard herself answer. It could be the last time she could glide down a ski hill, she realized.

"Are you sure that's a good idea?"

"I want to try."

On the ride up the mountain, Charlotte agreed that they should arrange for the kids to join the ski school. When she opened the door and stepped out into a flurry of snowflakes, Charlotte began shivering. She wasn't sure if it was from the cold or her nerves. Her worst fears could come true once the cancer started to win. Would Adrien stand by her in sickness, or would he run? Did she even want him to watch her fade each day, fighting a battle with the pain as she slipped into the dying process?

Charlotte shook her head. No, she would transfer to hospice. She didn't want her kids to see what would come, at least not in their home.

Adrien took one look at her shivering as she helped the kids out of the car and suggested she go into the lodge and drink a cup of coffee while he signed the kids up for ski school.

"I'll bring them to their ski teachers and then be up to get you from the lodge."

She kissed Gabriel and Aurélie and was just stepping into the welcome warmth of the restaurant when her phone rang.

By the time she had a steaming cup of coffee in her hands, she had found out that all the details regarding the educational trusts had been finished. Charlotte's shoulders released down her back, and she rolled her head side to side. Now whatever happened to her, the children would have their education financed and Adrien would have a specific amount of money he was allocated yearly. He couldn't blow through all the money within a short time.

"Hey there, beautiful, ready to hit the slopes?"

"Sit down for a minute," requested Charlotte. "I don't want to keep secrets anymore."

"Can you tell me on the chairlift, honey? I want to get in as many runs as we can before we pick the kids up in two and a half hours."

Charlotte suppressed her impatience and followed Adrien out. She reasoned the chairlift would be the best possible place to share bad news. Adrien would, in fact, be trapped next to her. There would be no way for him to storm away in anger, at least for the fifteen-minute ride. Charlotte rehearsed what she was going to say as she clicked into her skis and glided down to the chairlift.

The minute the chair rose into the air and they had pulled the bar down, settling their skis on the bar rest, she turned to her husband.

"I placed two hundred and fifty-three thousand dollars each into educational trusts for Aurélie and Adrien. I made a trust for you too, with a hundred thousand dollars in it. Ten thousand dollars will be released to you each year for the next decade."

Adrien banged his ski poles against the ski bar rest with a loud clang.

"We should have made that decision together, Charlotte."

The top of the mountain was fast approaching. Adrien was pushing up the safety bar and gliding away from her to the top of the run. Charlotte followed, her heart compressing in her chest and her vision was blurring. A bout of dizziness hit her, and she sat down on the side of the run. Adrien was already halfway down the hill. She watched as he attacked the powder snow with sharp turns. Ten minutes later the dizzy spell passed. Her phone rang, and she answered instantly, picturing Gabriel with a broken leg.

"Charlotte, it's your Dad. You have a minute?"

"I'm on the ski hill, Dad. Can it wait until tonight?" She still sat in the powdery snow, shivering, the cold seeping into her bones with every breath. They had been crazy to come skiing, she decided. It was far too cold. She worried that the children were suffering, and pictured their little bodies shivering from the subzero temperature.

"Well, no" her Dad paused, "Jake called me about wiring him the investment in the new business. He told me to call you right away and impart the urgency of informing Adrien about the business opportunity so he can wire his investment money over as well. Apparently Jake is meeting with some marketing and banking people in the next few days, and he needs the funds to build the website and promotional materials. It's exhilarating. He sent me the business plan and the beginning of a marketing plan he made, and they look great, really professional."

Those are my business and marketing plans, she thought. I'm sure Jake neglected to tell her Dad that, though. She shook her head. It was irrelevant.

"You didn't do it, did you, Dad? Tell me you didn't wire the money."

"What do you mean? Why not? Charlotte?"

"You wired the money already."

Charlotte buried her face in her hands. It was clear to her that her father may have just lost a significant portion of his retirement savings.

"Of course I did; I just called my banker and asked him to make the wire transfer. I think it's a brilliant idea for a new venture. I can't wait to go into business with my two son-in-laws. Are you worried that one shouldn't mix family and business? There won't be conflict, Charlotte. It is clear Jake, and then Adrien, get the final say on all decisions. I just offer my business insight and advice for them to take, or not. If they make a decision I don't agree with, well I will be able to swallow my pride. Though I won't be able to say I told you so," he laughed, "when I am proven right."

"Dad, it's not that, it's," Charlotte swallowed. "I think Jake might be a fraudster. He doesn't plan on opening the business; he only plans on taking the investment money, and running."

"Oh Charlotte, he just married Élodie. They sent me the pictures. Why would Jake run? I'm sorry, child. I've messed up," he stumbled over his words. "I appreciate why you find it so arduous to trust. But Jake is Élodie's new husband. It wouldn't be in his best interest to perpetuate fraud against his new family members, now would it?"

"He proposed to Élodie just as part his plan to secure our trust, Dad, in a final play to reap thousands of dollars. As soon as he has the cash, he will disappear, and neither Élodie nor we will ever hear of him again. Unless he thinks up a way to swindle more money out of us."

"It could be that working with emotionally and psychologically unbalanced clients has distorted your worldview, Charlotte. What you are describing is something that happens in a movie, not in real life. Here, I'll put your mind at rest. Jake has put my name, and Adrien's, on the Swiss bank account. I will call my banker and request he stop the wire transfer until he can ascertain whether my name is really on the account, or not. See? That way I will reassure you that everything is fine."

"I hope so, Dad," she responded. "Call me when you find out what id going on."

God help me, prayed Charlotte. Give me a sign if I need to tell Adrien everything. The call of a dove broke the silence and Charlotte searched the sky. The dove flew through the trees on her left and disappeared.

CHARLOTTE GLIDED SLOWLY THROUGH the powder down the hill. She had always loved the cold air rushing into her face, the sense of speed as she swooped through the snow, the thrill of knowing she could go sprawling if she hit an edge wrong. Today she enjoyed the pace of a beginner. Her body didn't have any power to go any faster.

It was as if she had turned in a Ferrari for a riding lawn-mower. She searched everywhere at the bottom of the hill for Adrien, hating being out in the bitter cold. Surmising that he had already taken the chairlift up, Charlotte did the same. The warmth of the restaurant and a cup of hot chocolate were beckoning her like sirens.

She wasn't sure if her body could make it down another run. The pain was a constant companion now. The second slow run down the hill through the powder Adrien called out to her. He must have lapped me, she thought.

"Are you okay Charlotte?" he called out as he slid to a stop next to her, a third of the way down the hill. "I've never seen you ski as slow as today."

"Are you still mad?"

"I'm hurt, Charlotte. After all our years of marriage, you don't trust me," he sighed. "But let's get you home. I know you Char; you're not feeling well. You're skiing like a little old lady. We'll go have some hot chocolate until the kids are out of their lesson, and I'll take you home and make you a fire and some lunch," he said while pulling up his goggles. He leaned forward and kissed her on the cheek. "I'm going to take good care of you, love."

Adrien smiled and then insisted that he follow Charlotte down the hill, just in case. He wrapped an arm around her as they climbed the stairs into the lodge and pulled out her chair at the table. Adrien returned to her with two steaming mugs and chocolate chip cookies. He sat down next to her, wrapped an arm around her shoulders and leaned in close, brushing his lips against her forehead.

"You have to tell me everything, Charlotte. Start with the cancer diagnosis. Don't leave anything out. I need to under-stand what happened."

Charlotte looked up into Adrien's face, searching. Finding only concern and compassion in his eyes, she began to tell her story of the past few weeks.

By the time Adrien had collected the kids from ski school

and pulled the car around to pick her up, Charlotte was trembling from exhaustion and the pain, but filled with gratitude. Adrien was going to give her the best gift anyone could ever give her. He was going to stand by her, move home and care for her, and they would be a family again.

Just one more Christmas with my family, Lord, she begged as Adrien helped her into the car and pulled the boots off her feet. Please. Just one last Christmas.

CHAPTER 13

Luke 2:9-14
9 Behold, an angel of the Lord stood by them, and the
glory of the Lord shone around them, and they were terrified. 10 The angel said to them, "Don't be afraid, for behold, I bring you good news of great joy which will be to
all the people. 11 For there is born to you today, in David's
city, a Savior, who is Christ the Lord.

12 This is the sign to you: you will find a baby wrapped
in strips of cloth, lying in a feeding trough." 13 Suddenly,
there was with the angel a multitude of the heavenly army
praising God, and saying, 14 "Glory to God in the highest,on earth peace, good will toward men."

*I*T WAS TIME. CHARLOTTE CALLED her Mom and asked her to
come for a visit when the kids were in school. The minute
her Mom stepped into the house, Charlotte broke into tears.
"I have cancer Mom."
"Oh honey," she cried and burst into tears too.
She threw her arms around Charlotte, and they stood in
the kitchen together like that until pain and fatigue forced
Charlotte to pull away and curl up on the sofa.
Charlotte listened to her mother making a pot of tea in the
kitchen. She closed her eyes.
Within moments she was fast asleep.

CHARLOTTE DIDN'T EVEN MAKE it into her office anymore as Christmas approached. She had been struggling with pain, fatigue, and indigestion. Every time she ran a brush gently through her blonde hair, a handful came out.

Charlotte wasn't sure if it was the chemotherapy, cancer, or a combination of both, but she had never felt so ill in her life as she did now. She arranged a meeting with the palliative care team Dr. Benson had referred her to in McCall.

Charlotte hadn't known what to expect with palliative care. She had discovered in her first meeting with her palliative care doctor and nurse that it would focus on providing relief from not only her symptoms and pain but also from the stress of her cancer.

She had been surprised when Dr. Johnson and the nurse wanted to hear her story and how the stage four pancreatic cancer was affecting her life. Dr. Johnson even asked Charlotte about her greatest anxiety and fears regarding the illness.

Charlotte could explain her intensifying symptoms and pain and how they were impacting her life. The palliative doctor and nurse discussed with Charlotte her goals and values and used the information to create a personalized treatment and pain management plan for her.

Dr. Johnson proposed that palliative care nurse Sarah Clark make a daily visit to the cabin each afternoon to care for Charlotte and work to manage her symptoms and pain. Relief flooded Charlotte at the suggestion, and she agreed. Tears of relief slipped down her cheeks when Charlotte left the meeting. It wasn't just that she was no longer alone in dealing with her symptoms and pain, it was the emotional support she had received; it was just what she had needed and been unable to seek out from her family.

The few therapy sessions Charlotte had scheduled per week, she conducted from the comfort of her chair by the window in her living room each morning. In the afternoon Sarah arrived.

Adrien ferried the children into town to school; her mother picked them up from school and brought them home every evening with a family dinner. There was nothing that would have cheered her more than to have her kids returned directly after school home to her, but she knew her body wouldn't cooperate. As it was, it took all her willpower to hide her illness when they came back at six o'clock.

Her secret weapon was the huge box filled with new books in her closet. Every night each child received two new books. After giving both children a bubble bath, they curled up together in front of the fire, and she read to her children.

Every evening the entire week, Charlotte tried to find a good opportunity to sit Adrien down and tell him about Jake and how worried she was that she couldn't reach her father. Everyday Charlotte promised herself that she would get in the car and drive to the cabin her father was now renting so he could stay close to her. Everyday her strength failed her.

Adrien had secured a job acting as an assistant manager at the Shore Lodge Hotel. Charlotte wasn't sure what the two men had discussed when she had told Adrien to seek Zack out, but their relationship had done a one-eighty since then. When Zack had heard about the open position, he had immediately called Adrien and told him to apply.

Adrien had returned to work after the family dinner every night all week; he needed to ensure the Christmas parties held at the hotel were of the highest standard and to help his boss to finish the final preparations for the New Year's Eve party held at the hotel.

Charlotte thanked her mother for staying each evening and taking care of her so many times that Anna snapped at her to quit. By Friday, Charlotte had given up on telling Adrien about Jake until after Christmas. She didn't want anything to distract from the joy of Christmas. Adrien was almost more excited about the upcoming holiday than the kids were.

CHRISTMAS EVE MORNING Charlotte praised God the moment she opened her eyes. She had made it. It was Christmas, and she was still home. She crept out of bed and out into the darkness. She set the endless river to its slowest setting. Even that wasn't enough.

When Charlotte tried to attempt the crawl, she couldn't get enough air, her limbs were heavy and uncoordinated, and the pain was a red-hot blade slicing its way through her abdomen all the way through to her back. Charlotte switched to swimming breaststroke at a snail's pace, and she could only do that for just over four minutes.

After a seated shower Charlotte, at last, summoned the energy to dress and curl up next to the window in her favorite chair. She looked out at the lake, sending up a prayer of thanks for the new job that was making Adrien so happy. Charlotte saw the way Adrien's eyes searched her face each morning, the flicker of fear, the smile that came a fraction of a second too late. Work was a respite for Adrien.

Sometimes what we want to be, and what we are capable of, are two very different things, mused Charlotte. She relaxed in her new favorite spot in the modern swivel chair next to the window. The sun was rising, setting a soft glow to the horizon. Charlotte took a sip of espresso and sighed. Adrien wanted to take care of her, but she now knew that he couldn't bear it when her face twisted with pain. Charlotte thought back over the past few days.

Besides the few minutes in the pool, it seemed she spent the majority of her life in this exact spot. It was even too exhausting to sit at the kitchen nook to work on her song lyrics in the morning.

The pain was almost too much to endure without help. Sarah had given Charlotte some pain medication, warning her that it worked best if it was taken on a regular schedule; she shouldn't wait until the pain became severe to take the first dose.

"It's better to get ahead of the pain than to chase it," Sarah had explained.

Charlotte hadn't heeded Sarah's advice; she'd been afraid to take the medication for fear it would dull her senses and perception. Charlotte was still working; she couldn't counsel while medicated.

"Besides," Charlotte had told Sara, "I've never reacted well to pain medication."

Now Charlotte wondered if she shouldn't have taken the long-acting morphine pills Sarah had offered her the day before. She looked over at the Christmas tree and smiled. The previous weekend, Charlotte had curled up with Adrien on the couch and watched the kids decorate the fir tree. Only after they were sound asleep did she sneak over and rearrange a few of the ornaments that were hung in clusters on the bottom branches.

Charlotte couldn't wait for the children to awaken and come bounding down the stairs.

Arrangements of white roses, pine boughs, and holly berry sat on the coffee table and along the mantel. A vanilla-scented candle flickered on the side table next to her chair. She still had no idea what Adrien had planned for Christmas.

A few weeks ago, she had been horrified at the thought that she couldn't celebrate Christmas with the children as she had always had in years past. Now Charlotte thanked God that Adrien was taking the work of making the holiday magical for her kids out of her hands; Charlotte didn't have the energy to put on any Christmas, let alone her activity-packed tradition.

She looked at the piles of presents that had appeared under the tree as if by magic overnight. Perhaps Charlotte had been wrong about the one-present rule, after all. She had to admit she was a bit tantalized by the bright wrappings and bows.

"Mommy," Gabriel called from the staircase. He ran down the stairs and skidded to a halt next to the tree. "Look at all the presents," he exclaimed. "Can I open one?"

"Wait for your Daddy, okay? He's in charge."

Gabriel climbed on her lap, and Charlotte pulled the cashmere blanket off her shoulders and around her son.

"Merry Christmas, Mommy," whispered Gabriel, placing a small hand on her cheek.

"Merry Christmas, love," whispered Charlotte back, resting her forehead against his.

Adrien came stumbling out of the back bedroom in his boxers, rubbing the sleep out of his eyes. He went without a word into the kitchen and turned on the oven before making himself a cup of coffee. Gabriel insisted on his story, and Charlotte began to read as Adrien continued to work in the kitchen. Ten minutes later he joined them in the living room, kissed her and Gabriel on the top of the head, and made a fire, before disappearing into the bedroom again.

"I'm going for my run," Adrien called out from the front door before it shut behind him.

Thirty minutes later, the alarm in the kitchen rang out. Charlotte opened the oven door and extracted a tray of big, gooey cinnamon rolls. Her face broke out into a grin. Adrien had made her favorite Christmas morning treat.

The front door opened, and Adrien came into the kitchen in his running clothes, sweat beading his forehead despite the sub-zero temperatures outside.

"I thought I could make it back before the timer went off. It snowed half a foot out there, and the snow plows haven't been through yet. I had to slip on my cross-country skis."

Charlotte kissed Adrien. "Cinnamon rolls are my favorite. Did you bake these?"

"I asked Mama to bake some up for you. I only needed to pop them in the oven this morning."

"That's sweet, Adrien."

"There's more where that came from, love. Just let me jump in the shower quick first."

Arms squeezed Charlotte around her stomach. "Merry Christmas, Mommy," said Aurélie.

"Merry Christmas, sweetheart," she answered, hugging her daughter back.

Aurélie saw the tray of cinnamon rolls and dipped a finger into the icing.

"Hey, stop there, you little thief. Wait until I get back from the shower, and we'll eat breakfast together."

Aurélie smiled at her Dad as she licked the icing off her finger and ran off into the living room. Seconds later she called out, "There are presents under the tree."

After Adrien had showered, he made some scrambled eggs and bacon to go with the cinnamon rolls. They all ate breakfast together at the table, the children made wild with excitement by the presents under the tree. When Adrien announced it was present opening time, the kids jumped around the room with joy.

Charlotte laughed out loud and threw her arms around Adrien's neck. "You were right about the presents."

Charlotte watched, heart warm with happiness, as the kids opened one present after the next. "Shouldn't we be waiting for Christmas morning?" she asked Adrien.

"I have one more saved for each of them from Santa," he whispered. "For tomorrow morning. But tomorrow we won't be here, so I thought it was easiest to celebrate with the present opening today instead."

"And where will we be?" asked Charlotte, her eyebrows raised. A cold sweat broke out over her skin. She didn't feel well enough to travel anywhere.

"Don't get too excited. We are going to the hotel for the night. The boss told me last night that he has two open rooms for tonight if I wanted them as a Christmas bonus."

"You just started working there."

"The rooms are empty, Charlotte; they won't lose any money by us staying in them. Anyway, he knows about your illness, Char. Anyway, your Dad just got into town last night. He told me he wants to treat the whole family to dinner at the restaurant tonight. What do you think?"

"Actually," answered Charlotte, wrapping her arms around Adrien, "it sounds fabulous."

That afternoon after lunch, they packed up and headed to the hotel. The first thing the children wanted to do was to go swimming in the outdoor heated pool overlooking the lake, which Charlotte had a hard time understanding. They had their pool at home.

Aurélie carefully explained to Charlotte that their pool was tiny, and this one was much bigger and deep enough that she could practice diving for rings. Charlotte let herself be talked into going swimming with the Adrien and the children. After a few minutes, she slipped into the Jacuzzi.

The heat diminished a fraction of the pain throbbing between her shoulder blades and in her abdomen. She rested her face on her hands and looked out at the lake. After half an hour, even the beautiful sound of her children's joyful shouts and laughter weren't enough to abate her fatigue. Charlotte told Adrien she would meet him back in the room.

She forced herself to shower but needed to lie down and rest before she summoned the energy to blow out her hair and apply some makeup. She dressed for the dinner and collapsed on the bed again, pulling the duvet up to her chin. She was asleep before her eyes closed all the way.

Charlotte didn't even awaken when the children returned to the room and Adrien showered and dressed them for dinner. She only blinked awake when Adrien said, "Time for dinner honey," and kissed her lips.

Charlotte was still groggy and disoriented as they entered the lobby and took in the roaring fire, huge Christmas tree, and her mother and father waiting for them with champagne glasses in hand. Her parents were turned toward the fire and didn't notice their arrival at first. Her dad's hand was on her mother's lower back; he was murmuring something into her ear. Charlotte watched as her mother threw her head back and laughed. It didn't take an astute thinker to recognize what was going on.

When her mother spotted them, she winked at Charlotte's father and walked forward to embrace her grandchildren, and then hug Charlotte and Adrien. They moved into the restaurant and settled at a long white-tableclothed table next to the window. Just as they were sitting down, Adrien's parents, Elizabeth, and George arrived.

Charlotte took turns with Adrien playing card games with the children as they waited for the arrival of the next course, laughed at her Dad's jokes, and smiled as Elizabeth talked about their growing excitement for the new baby. By the time the chocolate truffle cake with fresh raspberries and cream arrived, she was glowing with happiness that even eclipsed the pain in her body. The only element lacking was Élodie. Charlotte missed her sister.

After dinner, the children hugged everyone good night, and she did the same. She insisted on being the one to take them up and tuck them into bed so that Adrien could stay and enjoy the after-party in the lounge with after-drink cocktails. Charlotte was happy to escape back to the room; she was exhausted, even though it was only nine at night by the time she changed the kids into their pajamas and brushed their teeth.

Charlotte climbed into bed with her children, the warmth of their little bodies next to her warming her body and spirit.

She listened to their breathing become slow and even. As her own eyes slid closed, she decided that it had been the most magical Christmas Eve she had ever experienced.

The next morning the children tugged her awake, holding out a large present in their arms.

"It's for you, Mommy," shouted Gabriel.

"I just need a cup of coffee first," muttered Charlotte.

"Mom," protested Aurélie.

"Here you go, honey," said Adrien, already dressed for church, standing next to the bed with a cup of coffee held out to her. Charlotte surveyed the kids. They were already dressed for service too.

"I'm sorry, honey; you won't have time for breakfast before church. You were sleeping so peacefully that the kids and I went down to breakfast without you. It's nine-fifteen. Open your present, and then you have twenty minutes to get ready for the day before we go."

Charlotte was disappointed she had missed breakfast, but after her first sip of coffee admitted to herself that the twelve hours of sleep had done her a heap of good. She felt better than she had in days. She tore off the red paper and opened the box to find two large photo albums.

Charlotte immediately flipped the first book open to reveal wedding photos; the next few pages contained pictures of her holding baby Aurélie.

"I organized all the snapshots into albums for you, love. I know you always said you would spend a weekend someday doing it, but you never seemed to find the time. I thought maybe you would appreciate me doing it for us. Do you like it?" He looked at her, a worried expression on his face.

Tears filled Charlotte's eyes. She had never been terrific about taking photos, let alone about ever putting them into a beautiful keepsake.

"It's beautiful, Adrien. I didn't even know how much I wanted this. It's the best present you could have given me," she answered.

"What a relief. I wanted to get it right. Now shake a leg, honey. We want to get a front seat at church today."

At the church service, Charlotte delighted in seeing old

friends, neighbors, and townspeople and in wishing them a merry Christmas. Jessica Higgins rushed forward just as Charlotte was walking arm-in-arm with her Mom into the parking lot. She threw her arms around Charlotte.

"I'll take the kids up to their skiing lessons with my family every Saturday," whispered Jessica in Charlotte's ear. "That's a promise. Don't worry about lunches. I'll pack for them too."

"Wait, what?" Charlotte shook her head.

"Zack told me, Charlotte. About the," Jessica made a c shape with her hand, glancing down at Gabriel. "I know your Mom works Saturdays at the hospital and Adrien will need to be with you right now, so. I'll take the kids skiing every weekend. Until they're teenagers, if need be," she exclaimed, and threw her arms around Charlotte before turning on her heel and almost running away.

Charlotte's Mom looped her arm back around Charlotte's waist. "Well I wasn't expecting that," muttered Charlotte. "Do you think she will follow through?"

"You know what, sugar? I do."

Following the church service, the entire family returned to Adrien's parents' house for lunch. A hike through the wintery landscape rounded out the afternoon, which Charlotte missed. Instead she was left in front of a crackling fire with a cup of tea. Charlotte was so happy and overwhelmed by love for her entire family; she could almost forget the cancer lurking in her body, like a time bomb waiting to go off.

CHAPTER 14

Psalm 10 1-4
1 Why do you stand far off, Yahweh?
Why do you hide yourself in times of trouble?
2 In arrogance, the wicked hunt down the weak.
They are caught in the schemes that they devise.
3 For the wicked boasts of his heart's cravings.
He blesses the greedy and condemns Yahweh.
4 The wicked, in the pride of his face,
has no room in his thoughts for God.

CHARLOTTE MADE UP HER MIND two days after Christmas. She couldn't be confident that she would feel any better in the future, and now was as good a time as any to put Adrien's name on her accounts. On the drive into town, Charlotte suggested they stop at the pizza parlor for lunch after their trip to the bank.

To her surprise, both children objected with vehemence to the plan. Gabriel insisted that Adrien had promised them a turkey day, with mashed potatoes and cooked green beans with bacon. Aurélie piped up that she wanted to help make the chocolate chip cookies for dessert.

Adrien told the kids that if they would be brave at the bank, then he had would stop by the store and pick up ingredients for their lunch.

When Charlotte protested that lunch wouldn't be on the table until at least two in the afternoon, he told her to open the bag at the kids' feet. Inside were snack boxes with cut-up red peppers, cucumbers, and carrots, and hummus to dip them in. Another large container contained cut-up apple slices. Charlotte couldn't believe Adrien had thought so far ahead, nor packed such healthy, delicious snacks. She sat staring out the window at the pine trees rolling by.

Her emotions were like a balloon tossed about in the wind. Adrien was an even better father than she had realized. He could be so tender; he had always taken such good care of the kids when they had been sick.

Both children stood enjoying lollipops from the banker while Charlotte took her leap of faith. It didn't take long to add Adrien to her accounts.

It was only then that she noticed the account balances. There were only a few hundred dollars in her checking account. Sweat broke out on her brow as she informed her bank manager that fraud must have occurred. The bank manager printed out a sheet with all the debit card charges from the past month. Charlotte's mouth went dry when she saw the charge from the Venetian, then another from the Bellagio.

Jake.

Charlotte cringed when the bank manager informed her that since the charges were over seven days old, the bank's liability was limited. Adrien took her hand, slipped his hand around her, and buoyed her to the car.

"I'll figure it out," he said. "Don't worry about this Charlotte. I'll talk to Ben. It will get sorted."

Charlotte just nodded, savage fear vibrating along her nerves. When they all were strapped back into the car, Charlotte asked Adrien to drop her at her office while he took the kids with him shopping.

She didn't add that fatigue was pulling at her so hard, she wasn't certain she could remain sitting upright much longer. A quick nap on her sofa was her solution. After a nap, she would call her sister yet again. How many times had Élodie refused to meet Charlotte since Christmas?

How many times had Charlotte texted her warnings about who she believed Jake to be? She would call her Dad afterward, Charlotte promised herself. She was petrified that the wire transfer had already gone through before he could call his banker back, and her Dad had lost his money to a charismatic swindler.

Just as she pulled a wool blanket over her body and lay down, fists rained down on her office door. There had never been a patient or visitor who had accosted her door with such ferocity. Startled, she looked at the door for a few moments before rising, hesitating at the door. For the first time in her life, she wondered why she hadn't put a peephole in the front door of her office. But that is silly, she told herself. McCall is a safe little resort town. At last, she opened the door slowly, peeking out.

The person on the other side shoved the door with such force that it smashed into her face with a loud crack. Blood poured out of Charlotte's nose as she stumbled backward, losing her balance, falling to the floor. Her gaze landed on green running shoes.

"Jake?" she stuttered.

Charlotte's eyes darted to the coffee table five steps away from where her phone was lying. She needed to call for help. The easy smile and laidback, affable nature of the man she had first met were gone.

Jake leaned down and pulled Charlotte roughly up to her feet. He half-carried, half-dragged her to the couch, and threw her down. He sat down on the edge of the sofa and traced a finger down her cheek. She slapped his hand away and struggled to sit up, but he held her down with both hands. He lowered his face to within inches of her own until she could see nothing but his eyes and smell his sour breath.

"This is what you are going to do. You are going to wire two hundred thousand dollars into my account."

"You already emptied my accounts," she answered, and spit in his face.

"I know you have more money than that. You told me yourself how much money you were hiding from your husband."

He wiped a hand over his cheek and calmly wiped it on her sky blue North Face fleece jacket.

"Cute kids, Gabriel and Aurélie. It would be a shame if child protection services needed to pick them up because their parents are drug dealers."

"That's stupid. You can't scare me."

"Is that so," he answered, rubbing his chin with one hand, while the other tightened around her arm, holding her down to the sofa. "It was easy enough to break into your place the last time I came around.

Wouldn't the town be scandalized to find out that you and Adrien are drug dealers, and that Élodie, your Mama, and in-laws are all in on it too? A real profitable family business you all have, mailing your drugs out to customers all over the country. I can't wait to dial the police and make my tip that drugs are at all your quaint homes."

"You can't get away with that," protested Charlotte, her voice almost a whisper. How long would it take for Adrien to return from shopping?

"Oh but I can. It's easy you know, to spot a victim. Your sister was like a red light; it's hard not to take notice and stop. The thing is, Élodie has a sense of her naïveté. I expected more from you. But then again, your husband is still running all over town with that bombshell behind your back. Your Dad still sneaks booze into his coffee thermos, and he came back to McCall just to work you out of some money with me."

"No," breathed out Charlotte. "I don't believe you. You're a liar. The minute you walk out of here I'm going to the police. Adrien will be here any minute."

"Ah, but you haven't told him about me, or our little survival business, have you? You don't want him to know who I really am."

Charlotte closed her eyes. She should have told Adrien everything from the beginning about Jake and the business.

"This is what makes my life so easy, Charlotte. Just enable people to believe what they have been longing for can come true. You wanted to believe the philandering spouse could turn over a new leaf and become a faithful husband; you longed to have your Daddy come home and tell you how very much he loves you; how he should never have left; that he'll do anything to repair your relationship." Jake smiled.

He yanked her up to her feet and pushed her in the direction of the kitchenette.

"Clean yourself up so we can march over to the bank, and make it quick."

Adrien was just pulling up in front of the building when Jake opened the office door and nudged her through it. Jake saw Adrien through the windshield and swore with a broad smile on his face.

Adrien jumped out of the car and ran to her when he saw the blood splattered all over her sky blue fleece.

"What happened?"

"I opened the front door right into Charlotte's face, the poor thing," answered Jake, his charismatic charm returned. Charlotte couldn't help but stare at Jake with sick fascination. He was a fantastic actor. The menacing and belittling con man had disappeared.

"I forgot something I had to get done at the bank, honey. Can we swing back by before it closes?" asked Charlotte, her eyes still locked with Jake's.

"Gosh, Char, can't it wait until Monday? The kids are starving. What do you have to do?"

Jake hugged Charlotte, and she gave an involuntary shudder. He patted her on the back and muttered under his breath. "You have until tomorrow at ten am to wire the money, or you lose your kids, and end up in jail."

Charlotte pulled herself into the car visibly shaking. She didn't know what to believe anymore. Were there drugs hidden in her house, and her mother and mother-in-law's houses? Was that even possible to do without them noticing? It must be a bluff, she concluded. What if it isn't? The question kept echoing as if her head were a bell being banged over and over again by the same mallet.

She couldn't even bear to consider the veracity of her father's duplicity in the attempted fraud. The idea that Adrien had been running around with his mistress behind her back was almost too much to bear on top of everything else.

When they got home, Charlotte was even sicker than she had been before Jake's visit. It was if a donkey had kicked her. Her entire body ached with pain. The minute she kicked off her boots, she collapsed onto the sofa and fell fast asleep.

She was awoken awhile later by Gabriel's small sticky hand.

"Wake up, Mama. We made lunch with Dad. Then I helped with the cookies."

Charlotte smiled, despite the pain still plaguing her body. When he saw her smile, Gabriel broke into a grin of his own, tugging on her arm. "Just let me wash my hands, and I'll be right there," she promised and kissed him on his chocolate-smeared cheek.

The kids and Adrien were already sitting at the table when Charlotte returned. Charlotte sat down, and Aurélie declared proudly, "I helped make the mashed potatoes, and the chocolate chip cookies."

"It looks delicious honey," answered Charlotte, and she meant it, but she didn't know if she would be able to stomach the food.

Aurélie and Gabriel regaled them with stories from their ski lessons and talked about their growing excitement for Christmas. It was exactly this experience, enjoying a homemade meal surrounded by her family, that Charlotte had most longed for in the months of her separation with Adrien. They had at last found their way back to this cozy sense of normality, but she couldn't enjoy it; all she could think about was Jake.

After lunch Charlotte pulled out her phone and dialed her Dad. She asked him to swing by her house for a glass of wine and some popcorn by the fire.

"Charlotte, you have to come out and see this," called Adrien as he came through the patio door. "The lake is frozen over. I'm going to take the kids out to go and see."

"Be careful, Adrien," Charlotte called from the kitchen, panicked. "It hasn't been subzero for that many days in a row. I don't want the kids out on the ice until we are one hundred and twenty percent sure it is thick enough to bear weight."

Her heart jumped into her throat. What had she been thinking as a child, escaping out into the icy darkness of a moonlit night, walking out over the frozen lake?

It had made her feel invincible. She had been confident God held her in the palm of his hand.

Her faith would prevent a fall through the ice. So she would tiptoe and slide, the ice creaking and cracking under her weight, admiring the reflection of the moon on the ice, adrenaline kicking through her system. It was on one of those dancing hikes across the lake that Charlotte resolved to be a psychologist someday. It was as if God could reach her better on the ice, in the dark silence of the cold night.

She had thought he had spoken to her directly. She felt him urging her to grow up and become a counselor, like the old woman in town her Mom took her to visit once a week. Charlotte received a counseling session in exchange for her Mom cleaning the office Monday mornings when they were in school. Her sister had refused to go. If only she had, thought Charlotte. I looked forward to that hour every week. I wouldn't be who I am today without those sessions.

Charlotte remembered her psychologist's hair, like softly spun white cotton candy, her purple glasses, the taste of the salt water taffy and Belgium chocolate of which she could eat as much as she wanted while they talked.

But the name was lost. What was that counselor's name? How could she forget the name of the woman who had pulled her back from the abyss after her Dad left, who was the reason she threw herself into a studying frenzy that didn't let up until she had her earned a doctorate?

Charlotte shook her head. The view of the lake spun her thoughts back to walking across the ice as a child.

What the hell was I thinking back then? The ice could have so easily cracked beneath me, and the lake swallowed me up. No one would have known where I had gone.

"Charlotte? Hello?" Adrien waved a hand in front of her face. "Is the pain hitting you hard?"

"It isn't that."

"Is it the ice? I would never be careless with our children. I did test the ice thickness, and it is five inches thick. It should be safe to walk on the lake, but I'm not going to let them walk off the dock. Relax."

"Right. I'm sorry," breathed out Charlotte.

A few minutes after Adrien bundled the kids back into their snowsuits and headed outside, a knock came at the door. As soon as her Dad was seated in a chair by the fire, with a glass of wine in his hand, she summoned all her strength and asked him if he had come back to work money out of her. She scrutinized his reaction.

His face turned white, his brow furrowed. "I don't know what you are talking about Charlotte. I know I walked out on you, but how can you believe I would do that, even if you didn't have cancer?"

The entire story about Jake came pouring out of Charlotte, from their initial chance encounter at the spa, through to the afternoon's menace and threats in her office.

The minute Charlotte ended her story, her Dad took his phone out of his pocket.

"We have to call the police," he exclaimed. "Where is Élodie? Do you think she is in danger?"

"And tell them what Dad? We have no proof. Then, if Jake finds out, and he did hide drugs in our homes, what then? What if they take Gabriel and Aurélie away from me, and we get thrown in jail as he threatened?"

"We have proof," answered her Dad, his gaze shifting to the fire, his shoulders hunching forward.

What do you mean?"

"I couldn't bear to call you back. I'm ashamed, Charlotte. Here I am, the man who pulled himself up by his bootstraps, with the big career down in California, and I get taken to the cleaners by a fraud. The wire transfer had already been made by the time I called my banker. We couldn't get the money back. Neither my name, nor Adrien's, were placed on the account." He shook his head and rubbed his eyes. I'm so worried for Élodie I can't sleep. I've tried to talk to her about Jake."

"As have I," interrupted Charlotte. "It's no use. She is head over heels in love with him."

Charlotte put a hand on her father's shoulder and gave it a gentle squeeze. Her body may be hurt, but there was nothing ailing her mind. Jake didn't know who he was dealing with, she thought, and a determination made her grit her teeth as she looked out the window at Adrien playing with the kids in the snow.

It was time to discover a way to out-con the con artist. She would have to brainstorm a way to lure Adrien here so the police could show up and catch him. Adrien was lifelong friends with some of the people on the police force. They would trust Adrien on his word; they would haul Jake to the police station and lock him up. Ben would help them gather the evidence from her Dad so the police could officially charge Jake with fraud. Now she just needed to tell Adrien the truth and make a plan.

CHAPTER 15

Isaiah 40:28-31
28 Haven't you known?
Haven't you heard?
The everlasting God, Yahweh,
the Creator of the ends of the earth, doesn't faint.
He isn't weary.
His understanding is unsearchable.
29 He gives power to the weak.
He increases the strength of him who has no might.
30 Even the youths faint and get weary,
and the young men utterly fall;
31 but those who wait for Yahweh will renew their strength.
They will mount up with wings like eagles.
They will run, and not be weary.
They will walk, and not faint.

"WHAT BENEFIT WOULD JAKE have if we all go to jail? In such a situation, Jake would have no opportunity to work us out of more money," she reasoned and took a large drink of red wine. "Anyway," she continued, pacing the space in front of the crackling fire, massaging her lower back where the pain stung, "We can't let a con artist work us out of money and threaten the well-being of our children, without taking action to fight him. We have to go to the police."

"No," disagreed Adrien. He turned from staring out the

window at the lake. "We have no proof, and we can't risk it. He could find a way to have our kids taken away. He actually could have planted drugs here somewhere." Adrien went to the bookshelf and started tossing books to the floor. "What are you doing, just sitting there? Help me look."

"Well, what if we give Jake the money, and he just keeps coming back for more? How will we ever live in peace again?"

"Then we give him as much as he wants. I don't care. Anything to keep my kids safe," insisted Adrien.

"Charlotte's right, Adrien," her father spoke up. He drained the entire full glass of wine in one go. "We have to call the police. I'm a fool for not having gone to the police station right after Jake conned me out of my money; I let my pride get in the way. We will all be safer, especially the kids, the sooner we inform the police. Jake can't possibly know about us calling."

"I don't want to contact the police until I've searched the house. Just in case this maniac isn't bluffing. I don't want to take any chances," insisted Adrien.

"Good, then as soon as you leave for church with the kids, I'm going to call the police," declared Charlotte. She didn't add that she would also call Jake and lure him to their cabin with a promise of the money he wanted.

"You're not coming to church?"

Charlotte didn't answer. She leaned her head back on the sofa and closed her eyes. The truth was, at that moment, she wasn't so sure there was a God.

THE NEXT MORNING, Charlotte kissed the kids and Adrien goodbye. She hadn't slept a moment all night; the pain had eaten away within her core, tearing at her from the inside. In a few days, her condition had rapidly deteriorated.

The moment the door closed, Charlotte stumbled to the bathroom and vomited. Her abdomen was bloated, her legs swollen, fatigue adding five times the pull of gravity to her shrinking frame. Charlotte grabbed her toothbrush, her glance falling on her reflection. Her toothbrush clattered into the sink as she leaned forward, examining her face. It was ash white and cringed from the pain. Charlotte didn't recognize herself. She didn't want her children to see her like this. She didn't want them watching her fading away into death, or worse, becoming unrecognizable due to the pain and ravages of the disease. If she was honest, she was terrified of the increasing pain, of becoming a burden on those she loved, of the dying process, of losing control. Charlotte walked into the living room and stood looking out at the lake.

All at once, a quick, clean death was so appealing, that she was drawn to the back door. She was tempted to wander to the end of the dock and slip into the dark, swirling water, enabling it to pull her under its weight. Charlotte blinked, remembering the lake was frozen over. Shame, hot and slithering, crept over her skin. She had always believed taking one's own life to be wrong, selfish, an act against God. A rush of empathy for anyone who had ever longed for release from suffering washed through her. Tears dropped from her eyes, burning a path down her cheeks. It was easy to judge, she realized, when one hadn't yet walked in another's skin.

And yet, she still believed taking her own life, on her terms, would be wrong. If life was a test, then it wasn't up to her to skip out and leave early. She had to have faith that there was meaning in this suffering.

Have mercy on me, God, Charlotte prayed, if you deem me worthy. Please, she added, and the image of slipping into the cold and sinking swiftly downward danced in front of her eyes, like a mirage, like a prayer.

Charlotte shook herself. She had a few breaths' more time with her children. How could she be asking to give that time up? Charlotte needed to use her remaining time the best she could. She had something she needed to do for her family this morning. What was it?

Charlotte tried to remember, but the pain in her abdomen was unbearable, making it impossible to focus. What had she said she would do this morning? Charlotte crumpled onto the sofa.

Sarah, her soft-spoken palliative care nurse, had come the previous afternoon. Charlotte had been holding off on taking anything but paracetamol to fight the pain; she had wanted to stay as lucid as possible. Sarah had taken one look at Charlotte and proposed a climb up the ladder of pain management.

When Charlotte yet again declined, Sarah explained that the intensity of pain from pancreatic cancer could be quite intense due to the location of the pancreas right in front of a large nerve plexus.

Sarah insisted on leaving some medication for Charlotte. She advised her three times to not hesitate in taking it before the pain became more acute. "Remember, you want to get in front," began Sarah.

Charlotte finished Sarah's sentence, "of the pain instead of chase it. I know. I'll remember."

Charlotte thanked God for her astute palliative care nurse. She now realized Sarah had seen coming what she would not: the pain was increasing, blurring her thoughts. She had to focus on every deep, slow breath to battle her way through the pain.

It was time to try the slow-release morphine tablets and anti-inflammatory tablets Sarah had left for her use. Minutes ticked by as Charlotte summoned the willpower to rise from the sofa and cross the short distance to the kitchen. I'll just take a half-dose to begin with, decided Charlotte. As she was swallowing the tablet with water, she glanced at the phone and remembered. Jake.

Charlotte's hand was shaking when she picked up the phone to call the police; the pain had almost forced the call entirely from her thoughts.

She informed the officer who handled her call about the defrauding of her father and the threats Jake had made to her family and specifically, to her children.

The policewoman insisted Charlotte should immediately join her team for a meeting at the police station with her father. Charlotte asked if they would be so kind as to drive out to her home. Charlotte called her Dad and told him to come over and collapsed onto the sofa.

The police arrived a half-hour later. Charlotte wasn't even able to offer the police officers coffee. She had to ask her father to do it for her. When they were all settled with steaming coffee cups around the kitchen nook, John was asked to recount the entire story from his perspective, then Charlotte from hers. Charlotte concluded her story by revealing Jake's threat that he had planted drugs in all their homes and would call family services to have them take away her children if she didn't wire Jake the money.

The police, like Charlotte, thought Jake was bluffing about the drugs. Charlotte insisted they send a team to sweep her house and make sure it was clean. She told them she wouldn't be able to sleep or have a moment's rest until she knew for sure.

A team was scheduled for first thing Monday morning to check her and her family members' homes for drugs. In the meantime, the police told her not to answer her phone and to notify them immediately if Jake showed up.

"I don't think you need to worry, though," commented the police officer. "This sounds like a white-collar criminal, and they usually don't pose a physical threat."

Charlotte tried to tell them about Jake slamming the door into her face, and about him holding her down on the couch, but she was too exhausted.

"As I said, white-collar criminals aren't likely to do any real physical harm. Just keep your distance and reject any form of communication. Call us if Jake shows up on your front doorstep, and we will get here as soon as we can," advised the police officer on his way out the door.

Adrien called just as the police and her Dad were pulling out of her driveway.

"Hey honey," Charlotte answered.

"You didn't tell me Élodie was bringing the kids to brunch. I just went to pick them up from Sunday school after the service, and they informed me they had already left with Aunt Élodie."

"Did you ask if Jake was with her?" Charlotte's heart pounded in her ears; she had stopped breathing.

"No, it was just her."

Charlotte's head fell back in relief. "I'll just call her and ask her what's going on then," answered Charlotte. "I'll call you right back."

Charlotte tried to call Élodie, but her phone clicked instantly to voicemail. Charlotte called her mother, but her Mom didn't even know Élodie was back in the country.

Adrien called her again. "He has the kids, Charlotte. Jake has the kids," Adrien yelled, his voice rough with panic. "He told me that he has our children, and if we don't follow his instructions, he'll kill them. He wants us to wire two hundred thousand dollars to his bank account. If we go to the police, he says he will know, and we will never see our kids again."

"We have to call the police," insisted Charlotte. "It's the only thing to do. I can't wire money on a Sunday; the bank is closed. We can't leave our kids an entire day with that monster. Who knows what he'll do? What will keep him from…" Charlotte couldn't finish her sentence. She doubled over from the pain corrupting her body.

"I know. That's why I insisted Jake FaceTime with me, to show me that they are still alive, that they're unharmed. And that's how I know," said Adrien, his breathing ragged.

"Know what? Know what?" screamed Charlotte into the phone. "Adrien, answer me."

"Jake's taken them to the Girl Scout Camp. I recognized the buildings. I'm going after him."

"That's insane, Adrien. We have to call the police."

"We don't exactly have a trained SWAT team here in McCall. I grew up with a bunch of those officers; I drink beer with them; I see them out on the slopes. They wouldn't be able to go stealth if their life depended on it. You have to trust me, Char. I can't waste any more time. You know I'm the best woodsman and hunter in the state. I'm going to save our kids. Stay home. Call the police. Wait by the phone. Repeat it."

"Stay home. Call the police. Wait by the phone."

"Good. I love you."

Charlotte placed the call to the police station and then sunk to her knees. Tell me what to do, she prayed. Tell me what you want me to do. A flash of movement caught her attention out the window. A dove flew down and perched on top of the cross-country skis Adrien had left resting against the back porch railing. Charlotte stood up, a flash of energy rushing through her body. She grabbed another pain tablet and swallowed it and then threw on her jacket and gloves.

Adrien may think he is the best woodsman and hunter in the state, she decided. He's wrong. I'm better than he is at stealth. I'm going after my kids.

CHAPTER 16

Ephesians 6: 13-16

13 Therefore put on the whole armor of God, that you may be able to withstand in the evil day, and having done all, to stand. 14 Stand therefore, having the utility belt of truth buckled around your waist, and having put on the breast-plate of righteousness, 15 and having fitted your feet with the preparation of the Good News of peace, 16 above all, taking up the shield of faith, with which you will be able to quench all the fiery darts of the evil one.

No ONE KNEW CHARLOTTE'S little secret. Since a small girl, Charlotte had always snuck out of her window in winter to creep out on the frozen water of the lake. She knew her mother would have been horrified to see her slipping one foot gracefully, cautiously, forward in front of the other across the ice. Every once in a while, the ice would crack out around her foot, shooting liking splinters into all directions, and she would freeze, holding her breath, knowing that at any moment the ice could give way and the dark water beneath swallow her whole.

It was exactly this thrill of danger that lured her out and to the water's edge, which enticed her to try the first step onto the ice, and then the next, until she had traveled a path along the snow, the stars twinkling above her, the moon lending her enough glow to see her way.

It took her breath away how foolish she had been as a child. No one had imagined the small, sweet, blond-haired girl would do something so dangerous and risky. She was betting everything that Jake wouldn't expect anyone to do something so foolhardy as approach via the ice from the lake to the tip of the peninsula.

Adrien had spent uncountable hours hunting in the woods and living with as few tools as possible beyond the reach of civilization, but she had spent just as many hours in the woods, closer to home. In a time before endless entertainment streaming choices, when her mother had money to put food on the table and clothes on their backs but didn't have any left for more, the woods had been her and Élodie's source of amusement. They had spent hours, barefoot, seeing who could get nearest a bird, a rabbit, a deer, without frightening it off. Her mother would have been horrified to see her daughters throwing knives at a mark on a tree; it would have never crossed her mind that her little girls would even want to engage in such a game.

Charlotte knew Adrien would take the way through the woods to the Girl Scout Camp; there was only one road leading to the camp on the peninsula at the edge of Ponderosa Park. Jake would lend all his attention and caution to the path behind him, which was why Charlotte was going to approach him from a way he wouldn't expect.

CHARLOTTE HAD NEVER CROSS-COUNTRY skied through Ponderosa as fast as she did that afternoon. The forest blurred past her as she aimed all her energy and will at reaching her destination. The pain in her abdomen throbbed in aching rhythm with each swoosh of a cross-country ski, the sharp knife blunted by the morphine tablet, her adrenaline, God's grace.

Charlotte knew Ponderosa Park like the back of her hand. Breathless at the top of the hill, she had to stop, doubled over with fatigue, her lungs screaming for more oxygen.

Nothing was making sense. Why would Jake take her children to the Girl Scout Camp, so close to her cabin, on a peninsula, surrounded by a frozen lake? Why hadn't he fled with them with the car, heading out of the state? Why hadn't he just taken her father's money and run?

Tears burned down Charlotte's cheeks, but she continued forward. The only sound, besides her ragged breathing, was the swoosh of her skis through the powdered snow.

"Do you even exist?"

Charlotte hurled her doubt out loud, a stream of breath into the silence. For the first time in Charlotte's life, her faith loosened and started to lift up and away, like a balloon. Why would a loving God ravage her body with cancer, allow evil to carry her children right out of his church, withhold all his angels and miracles from her family?

Still, I could pray for help, Charlotte thought. I could pray for God to protect my children.

But what are prayers without faith but mindless whispers uttered into a void? I've prayed and prayed about everything, Charlotte argued; it hasn't helped.

Only she hadn't.

The gravity of the realization made Charlotte's heart skip a beat. She had been so caught up in strategizing and organizing what she wanted for herself and her family after the cancer diagnosis. She hadn't taken the time to pray about what she should do, what God wanted from her.

Because he was already taking too much.

A few days after her stage four cancer diagnosis, she had turned away from him. Charlotte hadn't even been cognizant of what she was doing. Fear had driven her into a frenzy of trying to control everything and everyone. More than anything, she'd wanted a beautiful life for her children, and she had been frantic to secure it before she was snatched away from them.

Sure, she said some prayers.

But since the diagnosis they hadn't been heartfelt. And she had stopped listening for his voice.

As Charlotte willed her body to continue its glide forward through the snow, she reasoned that God still should have warned her away from Jake. Even if she hadn't been listening, he could have sent some sign or sent her a flash of intuition.

Only he had.

Charlotte recalled her initial negative gut reaction to Jake at the spa, the appearance of the dove when she ran into him in the street, the flash of menace he displayed toward her in her office.

She had ignored his warnings; she had been lured by charm and beauty and arrogance. She hadn't even taken action after Jake attacked her while she was waiting for Adrien and the kids to return from shopping.

By the time she left the marked trail and slid through the trees down toward the water's edge, her heart was pounding so hard, the pain in her abdomen and chest so intense, she feared she might be having a heart attack.

Breathless, she had to stop five times, doubled over with a body heavy with fatigue. Stars danced in front of her eyes.

Not now, she prayed. Not yet.

At the edge of the water she stopped. She kicked off her skis, threw down her poles, and hesitated. Her adrenaline couldn't propel her out onto the ice. Back at home, the idea had seemed as if inspired by God.

Had it been?

Now standing here, she didn't know what she had been thinking. Adrien had tested the ice the day before, and he said it should be thick enough to walk on.

Today the sun was shining, and the temperature had risen. She couldn't be sure the ice was still five inches thick. There was a chance her first step could crack the ice, and she would be sucked under the icy water.

Before she knew her kids were in peril, it was what she had just been longing for, to be pulled quickly, cleanly, into the next life. Nothing had seemed worse than the agony of the deterioration of her body, of slipping farther each day from resemblance to the mom Gabriel and Aurélie recognized.

Now the thought of leaving her kids when they needed her was horrifying. Charlotte would suffer the most drawn-out terror of death to spare her children from harm.

Charlotte stood transfixed, scanning the ice across to the peninsula across the bay. The ice appeared blue, without any cracks or pressure ridges.

Still, fear was cementing her feet to the shore, and Charlotte knew time was slipping away. The image of Jake's face, twisted with menace and hate, floated into her consciousness. That monster was holding her children captive. She had to get to them.

Charlotte dropped to her knees, clasping her hands in prayer. Forgive me my doubt, my fear, my pride. I take up the shield of faith. Fill me with the strength to save Gabriel and Aurélie.

Charlotte was a few steps forward onto the ice before she realized what she was doing. One slow, smooth, cautious step after the next.

Her movement forward was painfully slowed by fear, even though every fiber of her body was screaming for her to run across the ice to her babies.

Every alarm bell in her head was warning her that Jake, even now, could be spotting her crossing the distance between the lake shore and the peninsula ahead.

She cursed the bright daylight. At night it would have been far easier to creep across the lake unseen.

The frenzy to sprint forward and paralyzing fear crashed against each other as Charlotte made her way across the ice. Midway across the bay, she slid a foot forward, and the sound she had been dreading rung out.

The ice was cracking around her.

Charlotte froze, too petrified to take a step either forward, or back. Looking down, she saw the ice was no longer clear and blue, but gray.

Charlotte surmised that there must be a water current in this exact spot, causing the weaker ice. As much as she willed herself to move forward, she was rooted to the spot, imagining over and over again falling through the ice into the frigid water.

Charlotte's fear and pain, anger, and urgency collided in an explosion of prayer. Leave me, she instructed her guardian angel. Protect my children instead.

The gentle song of a dove pierced the silence. Charlotte's eyes scanned the trees ahead until she spotted the dove perched in a tree on the shore of the peninsula.

The dove flew along the shoreline to an aspen tree twenty

degrees off the direct path she was following across the bay, then it flew out to her above the lake, circled above her, and returned to the aspen.

Charlotte took one diagonal step forward toward the dove. The ice held.

She slid another foot forward, regaining her previous rhythmic smooth, sliding progress across the ice.

Behind her, Charlotte heard the ice crack. Her stomach churned with fear. Her eyes focused on the dove ahead.

She was only five slide steps from the frozen beach when she heard her sister's voice, the words indistinct.

A bloodcurdling scream pierced the quiet. Tears streamed down Charlotte's cheeks as she reached the shore.

The dove flitted away the moment her boots reached the snow beneath the aspen tree, in the direction of Élodie's scream. Charlotte paused, listening. Breathlessly, she texted her Dad, and then her Mom, exactly where inside Camp Alice Pittenger to send the police.

The dove's call rang out, and instinctively, she followed, her footsteps silent as she made her way through the pine trees to the edge of the woods at the tip of the peninsula.

When she spied Jake and her children, the scene made her heart skip a beat.

Jake had built a fire out on the ice of the lake. Gabriel, Aurélie, and Élodie lay in the snow on the shore edge. He had taped their mouths shut; he had made their bodies immobile with circles of gray, heavy-duty duct tape from their shoulders down to their hips.

Her children appeared to be sleeping. At least Charlotte hoped that was the truth.

As Charlotte watched, Jake grabbed Élodie under her armpits and lugged her out onto the ice.

Charlotte fought down a scream when she watched her sister's head loll lifelessly to the side, revealing blood gushing from a head wound, leaving a trail of bright splashes of red on the ice where Jake dropped her so near the flames, that Charlotte feared Élodie's hair would catch fire.

Next, Jake picked up Gabriel and threw him like a rag doll out onto the ice. Gabriel slid forward toward his aunt, stopping an inch from the roaring flames.

Charlotte fought back a scream as Jake pitched Aurélie after her brother out onto the ice.

Jake stood on the shore, his back to her, watching the children. At any moment Charlotte knew the fire would weaken the ice, causing it to fissure and give way, swallowing up her children.

Charlotte had paddled a canoe enough times around the peninsula point to know a current lay under her children.

The minute the ice cracked and they fell into the lake, the current would pull them forward, under the ice.

There wasn't time to stop and consider. Instinctively, Charlotte pulled out her pocket knife, creeping forward. There was only one knife; she only had one shot. She needed to get as close as possible.

Five feet away from Jake, her foot crunched through the snow. Jake spun around as Charlotte threw the knife.

The blade hit Jake in the face. Charlotte didn't wait to see how badly she had hurt him; she knew it wasn't mortally. The knife had only bought her a few precious minutes. She hurled herself toward her children.

At the shore edge, she lay down and rolled out toward Gabriel and Aurélie. She grabbed hold of Aurélie's jacket and pulled her back toward shore, then turned toward Gabriel, pulling him backward, away from the fire.

Cracking ice rang out around Charlotte.

She sprang up onto her knees and grabbed Gabriel, praising the Lord that she could feel the warmth of his breath on her cheek. With all the strength in her body, she pushed Gabriel as hard as she could toward shore.

She closed her eyes, falling backward next to her sister, as pain reverberated through her body. The ice began to crack around the fire.

Jake approached the lake edge, blood streaming down his handsome face from an empty eye socket.

His remaining eye spotted her next to the children, a few inches from the security of land.

"Oh no you don't," Jake roared and pulled Charlotte away from the cracking ice.

He tossed her on the shore like a rag doll. "You don't get to die. You have to live with the knowledge that you caused their deaths," he hissed, motioning at her children.

Jake's face, twisted with menace and hate, faded in out; Charlotte could sense her body shutting down.

"We'll give you the money. Everything. Just leave them alone," rasped Charlotte.

"Money? Don't bother. Haven't you been shopping since our little jaunt down to Boise? I stole all your credit cards, Char. Drained your account with your debit card. I already have your money."

Charlotte closed her eyes, thanking God she had already transferred the kids' money into the trust funds. At least some of their future was untouchable.

Jake knelt down next to Charlotte and bent his face within inches of her own. "I gained your family's trust so that I could get to your kids. The money was just frosting. At first, I thought I could just roar in here and grab them.

But oh no, there are eyes everywhere in this little town. I had to worm my way into your family. But now I've won. Now I'm going to take everything from you, just like you took everything from me."

Charlotte had talked to enough psychologically unbalanced individuals to know that Jake was exhibiting signs of severe psychosis. Charlotte's thoughts were fuzzy; she was having trouble thinking clearly.

"Why?"

"Kayla," whispered Jake, the smell of his breath sour on Charlotte's cheek. She could feel the blood dripping onto her face. Nausea hit her, causing her to roll away from Jake and throw up onto the snow. At last, she struggled up to kneel.

"Kayla was your wife," Charlotte breathed out, the bitter memory pushing its way back up to the surface. A vision of a delicate blonde with pale blue eyes and dark circles under eyes floated before her as if Charlotte was once again sitting in her office, in front of the screen.

Kayla from California had been desperate. Triplets and no support system. Estranged from her parents. Kayla had no other family members to help, no friends, no in-laws to come to her aid. Her husband worked as a long-haul trucker and was gone weeks at a time.

Charlotte had had exactly one session with Kayla, who was depressed, but she hadn't signed-in for her the second session, for which she had pre-paid.

Charlotte recalled calling her husband, Jake, worried.

Jake.

Oh God, Charlotte shuddered. Save my children.

Charlotte's thoughts twisted and spun. She should have known that Jake was exhibiting signs of severe psychosis. But he was charming, just as he had been charming on the phone weeks ago. Jake had thanked her for her concern and told her he would check on his wife.

Charlotte had never heard from them again.

It happened all the time. Clients started therapy, and then they quit. Generally, Charlotte would reach out two to three times more to encourage a return to treatment, or to be assured that the client's mental health and situation had improved.

Only this time, she hadn't.

Charlotte had been distracted by her cancer diagnosis and had never even thought of contacting them again.

That was twenty-nine days ago.

"She put our babies in the stroller that afternoon, and she ran right off a cliff into the ocean." Jake was crying now, the tears mixing with the blood running down his neck. "You said if you didn't hear from Kayla in a few hours, you would call the police. But you didn't. You could have saved her. It was your job to save her."

Charlotte started in surprise. Had she said that? Had she told this man that she would call the police down in California if she didn't hear from Kayla?

Charlotte thought back, her mind straining to recollect the words of their conversation.

No. She hadn't said that.

Hadn't Jake promised he would let her know everything was okay, once he, or a neighbor, reached Kayla? Yes. Jake was the one who had promised to call the police if he didn't reach his wife.

But it was irrelevant now.

You have to keep him talking, realized Charlotte. Adrien and the police are on the way. You just need more time.

"I don't understand," Charlotte answered. "Why didn't you just show up at our cabin and shoot us all? Why this way?"

"Aaron was at school that afternoon."

The pain was rocketing from her abdomen down through her legs now. Stars danced in front of her eyes. Through a haze she watched Jake open his bag and quickly tend to his eye wound with cream and then apply a bandage. He zipped the bag closed.

"Aaron?"

"My son. I can't rot in prison while my son is raised by my sister. He needs me. That's why this is brilliant, don't you see? You've financed his education.

Now you will watch while Élodie and your kids are sucked under the water, and then you will follow them. No weapon, no trace of the bodies. By the time the police show up, you'll be gone. I'll be long gone. And they won't know where we all went."

"The police are coming," breathed out Charlotte, her eyes shifting to the lifeless forms of her children. "You'll never get away in time."

"Ah, that's where you're wrong," answered Jake. "The only real part of the last few weeks is I do know how to survive in the wilderness for weeks at a time with nothing but a pack on my back. I'll just fade into the woods. Aaron and I will move to Mexico. Start over."

Jake picked up the children and walked out onto the ice, placing them near the fire. The cracking of ice rang out as he returned to shore.

With an inhuman scream of fury, Adrien broke out of the woods and hit Jake in the back with his ice ax. Jake crumpled to ground.

Adrien ran toward the ice, but Charlotte screamed out, "No. The ice won't bear your weight. Let me go. They'll need you."

Adrien's eyes searched Charlotte's. In that second, understanding passed between them. Adrien nodded at Charlotte, who was already creeping out onto the ice.

She pulled Gabriel halfway to shore, before returning for Aurélie. Adrien lay down on his stomach and reached out for Gabriel, at last snagging his jacket and tugging him the rest of the way to safety.

He returned for Aurélie, managing to pull her onto the snow as the ice cracked around Charlotte. Adrien pulled both children up and leaned their backs against a pine tree.

At that moment the ice gave way beneath Charlotte, and her legs tumbled into the sub-zero water.

Her forearms were still gripping the ice, keeping her upper body above the water, but she was slipping.

The pain in her abdomen seared hot from the inside as the cold of the water caused her to lose feeling in her legs.

"Charlotte, kick your legs to propel yourself up onto the ice," Adrien yelled out at her.

"Are the children okay?" she yelled back, gagging as the smell of Élodie's burning hair behind her mingled with the scent of scorched flesh. Charlotte couldn't bear to turn her head and look at her sister.

"I think they've been drugged, but they're both breathing," he yelled back. "They aren't bleeding or anything that I can see."

Charlotte glanced at Jake, lying motionless in the snow. A flash of insight flooded her consciousness. Twenty-nine days ago grief had hurtled Jake's trajectory to crash into hers.

The cancer had been a gift, not a curse. The cancer diagnosis had given her the opportunity to prepare.

The fire was still burning a foot away from her; the ice was continuing to crack around Élodie as the flames burned themselves down into the ice. Charlotte tried to kick, but the moment her children had reached safety, the adrenaline rushing through her body was replaced by searing pain.

"Kick, Charlotte," Adrien yelled again.

"I can't," she said. "You'll take good care of them, Adrien. I know you will."

Adrien lay down on his stomach and inched forward across the ice toward her. When Charlotte saw what he was trying to do, she panicked. "No," she screamed. "Go back, Adrien. Let me go. The ice can't bear your weight."

"It won't bear yours much longer either," he said, ignoring her plea, concentrating on his approach, reaching out a hand.

She looked at her kids. She just needed to kiss her kids, one last time. With the last ounce of power in her body, Charlotte kicked furiously, which pushed her chest a tiny bit farther forward onto the ice.

Adrien inched a bit closer, grasping her hand.

He pulled, and she slipped out of the icy water, centimeter by centimeter. Only her feet were left dangling in the water; her body was laid out across the ice.

She needed to move just a bit more forward, and she would be safe. It was then that she noticed movement out of the corner of her eye. Jake was struggling to stand up.

"Adrien," she screamed. "Go. He's getting up."

Adrien looked back over his shoulder. Jake had stood up; he was making his way over to their children, blood darkening the snow around him.

Adrien looked back at their children, then forward into Charlotte's eyes.

"Go," she urged him. "Before he reaches them."

Adrien shimmied backward on his stomach to the shore edge and flung himself at Jake, landing a punch on his jaw, followed by an uppercut into his abdomen.

Adrien was athletic and strong, but he had nothing on Jake's height.

Fortunately, the missing eyes and wound in his back had weakened and disoriented Jake. Adrien's attack made Jake double over.

Neither Adrien nor Charlotte saw the knife in his hand until it was too late. Jake thrust the knife into Adrien's heart and pushed. Adrien careened backward and fell onto the ice of the lake with a crash.

The ice splintered out around him but held.

Meanwhile, Charlotte was inching forward across the ice. She reached the solid ground as Jake's back was turned, watching Adrien lying motionless on the lake.

Charlotte knew she only had a moment before Jake saw her.

Jake turned back toward her kids, taking a step in their direction as Charlotte lunged forward.

She tackled Jake around the legs. Jake fell face first into the snow, and Charlotte crawled on top of his back.

Jake struggled to push himself up, but Charlotte gripped around his body with all her strength. With a roar, Jake stood up, Charlotte still clinging to his back. It didn't take much on the slippery lake edge.

Jake slipped, Charlotte's weight on his back causing him to fall backward on top of her, onto the ice of the lake. Pain seared in Charlotte's skull, in her leg.

Her eyes were fixed on her children, both looking like angels sleeping in the snow, oblivious to the horrifying scene playing out before them.

It was then that Charlotte heard it.

The fire a few feet away disappeared with a gush of steam into the lake; the ice around them was breaking up.

Charlotte glimpsed the policemen appearing through the trees, approaching the unconscious bodies of her children.

With a crash, she, Adrien, Élodie, and Jake fell into the water. The current pulled them away, out under the ice.

It would be months until the police would find the bodies.

CHAPTER 17

Gabriel

I'M HALFWAY UP THE MOUNTAIN trail before the stars begin to fade in the early morning twilight. My breath mists in front of me. I quicken my pace in an effort to outrun the sun; I want to watch the sunrise from the summit. Aurélie packed me a thermos of coffee, homemade blueberry muffins, orange juice, and fresh, cut-up pineapple. I smile at the thought of my sister.

Not that she can't be a bossy know-it-all. She can be a real pain in the ass. And she's also the person I trust most.

When I need help, I call Aurélie, and she has always come through for me. Gram says that very few brothers and sisters enjoy a bond as deep as ours is and that it is a treasure salvaged from the wreckage. Aurélie thinks this is a beautiful way to regard what happened to us. I know it's a real messed-up thing to say, though I wouldn't ever tell Gram that; her heart's in the right place. In fact, Gram is one of the toughest and most loving people I know. She's one of those churchy people that make you think there must be something to believe in, after all.

Only I don't. Not that I don't want to.

I envy Aurélie going off to church every Sunday with Gram and Grandpa. I wish I could go and delude myself underneath a stained glass window as they do, that there is meaning in everything. Good will prevail. While we can't understand why things happen the way they do, it's part of God's plan. If you look hard enough, there is good to be found out of any tragedy.

Well, I know that's a hot pile of shit. There is nothing beautiful about losing both parents at three years old. I'll go ballistic if one more person tells me how lucky I am that I could stay in my own home with Aurélie, and isn't it great how Gram and Grandpa moved in to raise us? What the hell is wrong with people? It's like they can't handle what a raw deal Aurélie and I got, so they tell us to look at the bright side: things could be worse.

Yeah, well, a pandemic could sweep the world, forcing us to flee to the woods to outrun a grisly death in agony, I reflect. We could suffer severe hunger, cold, and fear as we wait for the earth to be wiped clean of its human population. I laugh out loud. I don't put it past Gram and Aurélie to find some silver lining in that situation, either.

It's my birthday; today I am eighteen years old. Zack has been warning me for months that it will be my last present and card. It hardly seems fair. Though I wouldn't ever voice these sentiments aloud for fear of hurting Aurélie, I resent the fact that although she had three more years of time with Mom, she's received the same number of years of birthday presents and cards. Shouldn't I receive three years more?

I wish so much I could remember things about her. To recall the feel of her arms around me, her smell, the little quirks and weaknesses that make a person real. The only thing I have left is the videos she left behind. But it's like watching a different child curled up in her lap, listening to her reading a story. I can't recall what it felt like to curl up in her arms like that.

So, I turned the video into an audio file. I have the copy of it on my phone. I would be humiliated if someone found out, but when I am feeling low, I put on my earphones and listen to her voice reading those children books until I fall asleep at night.

I ball up my hands and push them into my eyes until the tears are pushed back to where they can hide. When I open my eyes, a dove flies in front of me and lands on a branch a few steps away. I almost say hello. I will never tell anyone how bizarre I find it that this dove shows up all the time. Then again, it can't be the same bird. There must be a huge population of doves in McCall, I reason. The dove takes flight, and I follow it, even though I am now traversing the mountain instead of ascending it. Suddenly, it just doesn't seem as necessary to reach the summit in time for the sunrise.

After five minutes of the dove flitting from tree to tree in front of me, it remains on an aspen tree in a clearing, calling out its song. My Gram thinks it sings 'who, who, who,' while my sister insists it is calling out, 'you, you, you.' I walk out into the clearing and realize it's a huckleberry patch. I lean down and pick a handful of the purple-blue berries and pop them in my mouth. And just like that, I am transported back over fifteen years ago.

Aurélie is proudly holding up her pink basket, overflowing with the tiny fruit, and I am crying because my blue pail only has a few inside; I've eaten more than I could manage to collect. I hear her laughter as she notices my purple-stained cheeks and hands. Her hair brushes my cheek, a whiff of citrus mingles with the scent of the pine forest, and I feel her arms gather me up in a hug. She tilts her bucket, so mine is filled halfway with berries.

"Not fair." Aurélie stamps her foot in protest.

"Someday, if you drop your bucket and lose all your berries, will Gabriel give you half of his?"

My Mom sets me back down on the ground. I clutch my blue pail tightly to my chest.

"He didn't drop them, Mom; he ate them," protests Aurélie, stamping her foot again, which causes the curls on her head to bounce.

"Fine. If you eat half your berries, and you begin to cry afterward because you wanted to bring some home in your bucket and there is no time left to pick more, will Gabriel share with you? What do you think?"

Aurélie tilts her head to the side, considering, then walks

over and carefully tips her bucket, so my blue pail is full. She gives me a smile that reveals her missing front tooth.

Mom opens her arms, and we both set down our pails, before running into her embrace. She picks us both up and kisses our cheeks, spinning around until we are all laughing and dizzy.

"I'm so lucky to be your Mama," she whispers.

The dove coos in the tree, and I snap back into the present. The memory had been so vivid; it was almost like traveling back in time.

I had forgotten all about that day. I look around and realize I am standing in the same huckleberry patch as the memory.

I give up my plan to hike to the top of the mountain to watch the sunrise. I sink onto a large fallen tree in the middle of the huckleberry patch. I can still hear her laughter, smell her scent, feel the warmth of her arms around me. It was everything I had always wanted to remember about my mother, and couldn't. I close my eyes, and when I open them, the dove is gone.

I take out the thermos of coffee and a muffin. I know I am delaying opening up the card and present. Today is like letting go, and starting new, all at the same time. At last, I can't wait anymore. I open the present.

Inside the large box are four smaller ones. I unwrap the first to find a watch. I smile. Fifteen years was a long time ago. No one wears a watch anymore, especially one like this. Not that I don't like the present. Watches are so yesterday that wearing one like this will make a statement. I like the idea of wearing something every day that reminds me of Mom, of how much she loved me. That part no one needs to know, though.

I set the time and push in the knob. I like the tick-tock sound the watch makes when I hold it to my ear. Very few things these days aren't run on a circuit.

I take out the accompanying information card and flip through it distractedly. My eyes widen. It must have been an expensive watch. Apparently, I can wear it even in the sub-zero temperature of the Arctic and dive with it in the ocean to a depth of fifty feet.

The watch face is scratch resistant, and the wristband almost impervious to destruction.

It's almost like Mom knew I would be joining Grandpa and Zack in their Extreme Survival business in a few weeks. I shake my head. Of course, she couldn't know that; that's why she had set up the educational trust, which Aurélie kept berating me about not wanting to use for college in the fall.

"You can only use it for education, Gabe," she keeps telling me. "You can come back and join the business after getting a college degree you know."

It's so annoying.

I shake my head while cramming the last blueberry muffin into my mouth. Aurélie just doesn't understand. She has always loved school. She sits at her desk by the hour, her multicolored pens and highlighters carefully lined up in front of her notebook and piles of books, studying. I have always hated the hours confined to a chair. Studying out on the deck, or even on the dock in good weather helps. Still, I need at least a year off from book learning. I yearn to spend the entire day and night in the woods. Being paid to do exactly that seems almost too good to be true.

I scoop up the container that held the muffins and begin to pick huckleberries to bring back to Aurélie. I glance at my watch. She's probably just getting out of the pool now. Though I thought it was a bit weird that she's started to adhere to Mom's exact morning routine, I haven't commented. We find solace in different ways. Gram tells me all the time how much I look like Dad and how much I remind her of his instinctual intelligence in the wild. I always answer, "whatever, Grams."

But secretly, I love hearing her say that.

Once I fill my container with berries, I sit back down on the log. I open the second box and look down in confusion. A huge diamond solitaire ring sparkles in the early morning sunlight. Mom must have gotten the boxes mixed up. This gift was obviously for Aurélie. More than a little disappointed, I snap the box closed. The next box brings more disappointment than the last. This box contains a Bible. I swallow the bitter taste in my mouth and lay down on the log; my face turned up to the bright blue sky. I don't blame Mom. I can't imagine what she must have been going through, being so sick and everything. I've loved opening every single present she has prepared for me until today.

True, it wasn't ever what I would have wished for, but it had always been special because she had picked it out. And sometimes my friends had even been desperately jealous because I had awesome toys that no one else had; some weren't even for sale anymore.

I sit up and reach for the last present. Will this one be for Aurélie too? The wrapping falls away to reveal a leather-bound blank book and a silver pen with my name engraved on it. I turn the empty book over in my hands. Did Mom expect me to keep a journal or something? With a sigh, I set the pen and book down. She died when I was three. How could she know I hate writing?

I take the card out of my rucksack and slit it open. I lay back down on the log and begin to read.

Dear Gabriel,

At the moment you ask me at least twice an hour 'what time is it?' You revel in routine and like to know when everything in our day will take place. Every morning when you wake up, you descend the stairs dragging your blanket behind you with a book clutched in your hand. You curl up in my lap and fall back asleep as I write. When Aurélie wakes up and joins us at the kitchen nook, I wake you up and read the story you have selected. Every night you want the same routine: bath, stories, cuddle, and prayers. If I am too tired and want to skip the prayers, you have an absolute fit. A few times when I have been sick, I've asked Aurélie to come in and pray with you. I hope you still have the same special relationship with God you had at three, Gabriel.

I am sure you are tired of me writing over and over again what a lovable, compassionate and sensitive person you are, but it's true. I wake up every morning so grateful to be your mom. You inspire me with your love of nature. You can spend an entire hour just watching the wind blow through the pine trees while laying in the hammock. Every day all last summer and fall, you insisted we hike into Ponderosa Park. I hope nature is still a refuge and source of strength and joy for you. Thank you for pushing your entire family to get out into nature even more than we would have without you.

Happy birthday, Gabriel! I hope today you feel cherished, and it is a day filled with joy. You love routine and being out in nature, so I am giving you a watch that you can wear in the most extreme of conditions. I hope you like it, but if you don't, you can always sell it. The second gift is the blank book, engraved silver pen, and my notebook of song lyrics. You were a very musical child and incredibly creative. We would always make up song lyrics together on our hikes, and your ideas always impressed and entertained me. My hope is that you will enjoy filling the book with song lyrics of your own, as I enjoyed doing.

The third present is an engagement ring for you to use when you fall in love with someone with whom you want to share your life. The last gift is the most important of all: this was my Bible. I have held it in my hands every day for the past twenty-two years since my Mom gave it to me. This is the last birthday card and gifts I can leave behind. I wish there were a way to send you a card and gift every birthday for the rest of your life, but I will always be sending my love.

Love,
Your Mom

I close the card and immediately search the box for the book of song lyrics. I find it at the bottom under a carefully folded piece of tissue.

I open the notebook and begin to read the lyrics, until guilt floods my system, making me snap the cover closed. Why did Mom give me her song lyric notebook and not Aurélie?

Why did she give me her Bible? I pick back up the card and only then do I notice writing on the back.

PS. Please don't tell Aurélie you received four gifts instead of one this year.
She had three more years of birthdays with me than you did. It only seems fair to me, but I don't want to hurt her. I gave Aurélie my journal and am now giving you my song lyric book, but feel free to trade. I just wanted you to have something personal of mine as a final gift from me.

Love, Mom.

I carefully pack back up the presents into my bag, take the last drink of orange juice, and stand up. Aurélie said nothing about receiving Mom's journal on her birthday. She only showed me the solitaire diamond pendant necklace with matching earrings she received. Well, I decide, two could play at that game. Now I don't need to share the lyric book, nor give her the Bible, like I was planning.

I hike to the top of the mountain before deciding to go home. My girlfriend Lauren is leaving for college in two weeks. I had plans to spend the afternoon going water skiing with her and the rest of my friends who are also moving soon. But now I am not in the mood. I take out my phone and cancel my plans. Lauren can't bring herself to be angry with me, not on my birthday. I promise to spend the next day with her, instead.

When I return from the hike, Aurélie is sitting out on the deck. I'm not surprised to find her nose buried in a book, a pen in her hand, making notes at the patio table.

"It's summer, Sis. What can you possibly have to study?"

"I don't have to read it; it's fun."

"What are the notes for then?"

"Well, I want to retain the information, don't I?"

I look at the cover, which reads *The Neurophysics of Human Behavior.* I sit down in the chair next to her and look out at the sun glimmering on the waves of the lake. My resolve weakens; I love my sister too much to hold my tongue any longer.

"Look, I don't know if it's healthy the way you are trying to copy Mom."

"What you are talking about?"

Aurélie blinks up at me while placing her pen down.

"I mean, you do her same morning routine, you're churchy like we think she was, and you've even chosen to study psychology…"

I'm afraid to shift my eyes from the lake to my sister. I half-expect her to explode; she can be a real hothead. Instead, she rubs her hand up and down my arm.

"Of course I'm trying to copy Mom," she answers with a smile and then messes up my hair.

I hadn't expected that response.

"You think it's a good idea?"

"It's my way of dealing with not having her here. I like to think to myself, what would Mom do? And then I do it that way. But I chose psychology because I find it fascinating. I don't plan on becoming a therapist as she was. You know how much I love research. I want to conduct clinical trials and uncover new insights that we can apply to evolve as individuals and as a society."

"Wow, you think pretty highly of yourself there, Sis. There are no small goals for Aurélie. No, no, she plans on evolving individuals and society," I laugh. The expression on my face makes her laugh out loud in response.

"I didn't say I will, I said I want to," she answers and moves to punch me in the arm.

"And I'm sure you'll succeed," I reply, catching her fist before it reaches me. I shake her fist playfully.

"So, what did she give you? It's tough to open the last one, right? Or at least, it was for me."

I finger the strap of my rucksack, trying to decide if I should just show her the watch, or all of the gifts.

Aurélie and I have never kept secrets from one another.

I know that will change someday; we are both adults now. I just don't want it to change already.

We have always shared our birthday cards with one another.

In fact, today was the first time I requested opening everything alone, without my sister's presence. Wordlessly I take
out the four gifts, carefully placing each one on the table. I
put the card next to them.

Aurélie's eyes widen when she sees the number of presents
but then nods as if she agrees it to be just. At least, that is
what I want to believe. I watch in agony as she reads the card.
She looks up at me, brushing tears off her cheeks. When she
calms down, she grabs my hand and holds it tight.

"I don't understand, Gabriel. Where is the journal she refers
to in the card? I didn't receive it on my birthday. It wasn't in
the package Zack gave me. What happened to her journal?"

CHAPTER 18

1 Corinthians 13: 4-8
4 Love is patient and is kind. Love doesn't envy. Love doesn't brag, is not proud. 5 doesn't behave itself inappropriately, doesn't seek its own way, is not provoked, takes no account of evil; 6 doesn't rejoice in unrighteousness, but rejoices with the truth; 7 bears all things, believes all things, hopes all things, and endures all things. 8 Love never fails.

1 Corinthians 13: 12 For now we see in a mirror, dimly, but then face to face. Now I know in part, but then I will know fully....

Aurélie

GRANDMA, I CALL THROUGH the patio door. "Hey Gram, can you come out a minute?"

"On my way out," I hear her call back from the kitchen. "I'm just bringing out some lunch."

I return to my chair at the patio table and sit down next to my brother. I join him in staring out at the light dancing on the waves, listening to a motorboat drive by, pulling a water skier in its wake.

One thing I have always treasured about my relationship with Gabriel is that we can sit in companionable silence together, in total peace. No constant superficial chatter is required to fill a void, no heart-wrenching talks to enrich our time together. Just sharing time with my brother makes me feel more connected to him. I feel more serene and strengthened being in his presence.

Gabriel takes out his guitar and begins to play a song I haven't heard before.

"Is that a new song?"

He nods.

"Did you write it?"

"Yup," he smiles.

"I like it," I answer.

Gabriel shrugs as if he doesn't care what I think. He's not fooling me. I spot the edges of his mouth twitch upward as if he's forcing himself not to smile. Truth be told I'm a bit jealous of Gabriel's musical ability. I wouldn't be able to write a new song, even after ten years of piano lessons. Sometimes effort alone is not enough. I sigh.

"You're jelly," exclaims Gabriel, breaking into a wide smile.

"A bit," I agree. "You should get some of your stuff out there, Gabriel."

"I am," answers Gabriel. "I have my own YouTube channel of me playing my best stuff. I have some serious heat, sis."

"Happy birthday, honey bunny," Gram calls from the patio doorway. She is struggling to hold the screen door open and balance a large tray filled with food at the same time.

Gabriel jumps up and runs to grab the tray from her, muttering. "You can't call me that anymore, Gram."

"What? Oh, you're right. I'll try," she answers, holding up her hands. "It's a tough transition for me, you being grown. Oh, before I forget, your Grandma and Grandpa called from Hawaii while you were out hiking. They told me to inform you that they want to take you out for your birthday when they get back next week. Speaking of which, your gift is in the garage."

I watch Gabriel sprint around the cabin to the garage and smile. "What did you get him?"

"Well, I know it's summer and all, but your Grandpa and Zack told me he'd need his own snowmobile for his work this winter. We all went in on it."

I growl in frustration in response, and Gram's laughter rings out. I always have loved her laugh. I can't help smiling when she laughs, and I'm not the only one. Seldom have I seen someone able to keep a straight face when Gram laughs. People always tell me in town how much they admire my Gram, at how quickly she rallied after my parent's deaths and became an even brighter, more positive person than she was before the tragedy changed all our lives forever. Sometimes I lie in bed at night and wish I could make people smile and laugh, as effortlessly as my Gram does.

It is a beautiful gift.

"Not everyone is fashioned to sit for hours a day at a desk, Aurélie. He'll find his way and make us all proud, angel. Just not in the same way you are making us proud," concludes Gram. She gives my cheek an affectionate pat.

I watch Gabriel walk back around the side of the cabin and climb the porch steps with a bounce in his step.

"Well?" asks Gram, while pouring homemade strawberry lemonade into glasses.

"That's from your Grandpa and Zack too."

"It's perfect. I'm speechless. Thank you."

"Sit down," gestured Gram. "I made your favorite: home-made lasagna."

I wait until we finish eating lunch and Gabriel has slipped into the house to bring out the homemade French chocolate torte cake covered with slices of fresh strawberries to ask my Gram about the journal. I watch a guilty look wash over Gram's face; her uncharacteristic frown causes ripples of regret run through me. The last thing I wanted is to steal the twinkle away from my Gram's eyes.

Still, I have to know.

Gabriel wasn't far off the mark when he insinuated I am obsessed with Mom.

"Gram?" I venture. "Did you hear me? In Gabriel's letter from Mom, she said she gave me her journal for my eighteenth birthday. Do you know where we could look for it?"

"I have it. I didn't mean to rob you of your present, angel. It's just—" The words catch in Gram's throat, and she presses her fingers to her mouth.

I stand up and throw my arms around the woman who has so lovingly raised me. "It's okay, Gram. You can keep it."

"No," answers Gram. She presses her to tear-streaked cheek to mine. "You were still at college when Zack brought over your birthday present; he was on his way the next day into the woods to lead a survival trip, and he wanted to make sure you could open your gift on your birthday. He asked me if I wouldn't mind wrapping the presents, and I answered of course not. I was all alone in the cabin, a bit lonely, missing my girl something fierce that day. I opened the box and looked at the presents. When I found the journal, I started to read. I read it all the way through. But still, I couldn't bring myself to part with it. It's been my guilty secret."

I'm shocked my Grandma would keep a present my mother had intended for me. Yet, I find it comforting. Gram isn't perfect after all. She's human like the rest of us. I hug my Gram tighter and repeat, "You can keep it, Gram. I understand. You want to reclaim a part of her, even if it is only her journal."

"Nonsense. I have you and your brother. You are the best part of her. Charlotte wanted you to have her journal, and so you shall."

Gram stands up, pulling away from my arms and passing Gabriel on her way into the house.

Gabriel sets the cake and plates down on the table before asking, "What's wrong with Gram?"

We wait for a long time on the porch for Gram to return. At last, Gram returns carrying a blue-and-gold leather-bound book and holds it out to me. In the other hand, she grasps a bottle of champagne and three flutes. We sing happy birthday to Gabriel, insisting that he is not too old to blow out the candles, but the joie de vivre is missing.

I can't help myself and sneak the journal open on my lap.

"Read it out loud, Aurélie," insists Gabriel. When I don't answer, he repeats, "Read it."

And just like that, I am transported to the kitchen nook of the cabin, the smell of fresh espresso in my nose, the warmth of my mother's arm around me, of Gabriel's silky hair, tickling my cheek as I snuggle even closer, just as eager as my brother to hear the soothing melody of her voice. I hear his small voice cross with impatience, "read it, Mom. Read it."

"Aurélie," snapped Gabriel. "Are you going to answer me?"

"I'm sorry." I take a deep breath and smile weakly.

I begin to read. After a few minutes, I pass the book to Gabriel and urge him to continue. We continue reading aloud to one another.

Hours later, Gram brings out the rest of the lasagna and another bottle of champagne. As the sun sets, the cool of the woods seeps toward us, and we decide to light a fire down on the beach. We take the journal with us, continuing to read until the stars appear one by one and the darkness encroaches on everything but our circle of flickering firelight.

Zack explained to me at seven that Mom had had cancer, and she had therefore arranged the gifts.

For years I thought that Mom had died from that cancer, and Dad alone had died saving us. That is what I heard the people in town talking about.

I had always thought it to be the cruelest of coincidences, that my Mom had died of cancer the same day my Dad had died. But now, I need to know for sure. Grams and Grandpa have never talked about that day. I don't want to see the pain their eyes, but I need to ask.

"Gram, what happened the day Dad died?"

Gram startles. Grandpa cringes, then he wraps his arms across his chest, starring into the flames of the fire for a long moment before he begins to explain.

"All these years your Gram thought Jake kidnapped not only you two kids, but your mom and aunt.

"I'm still not sure how I arrived at this conclusion," interrupts Gram. She presses her lips together. "It was your Grandpa who set the record straight. Perhaps it wasn't right, but I couldn't talk about that day with anyone but God until recently. Your Grandpa couldn't either. Just a few weeks ago we were on a hike and we talked everything through for the first time."

Grandpa nods at the fire, glancing up at me, catching my eye. "Your mom called me from the cabin about Jake abducting you and Gabriel. I warned your Mom to stay at home."

"Did you have a premonition she would come for us?"

Grandpa shakes his head. "We don't know exactly what happened after your Mom left the cabin that day. There were signs of a struggle on the lake shore. Blood on the snow. You kids, thanks be to God, still out cold from the drug he gave you, but unharmed under a tree. Jake and your Mom, Dad and aunt were found when the lake thawed."

The truth electrifies me like being struck be lightning.

Dad wasn't the only hero. They both came to save us.

Gabriel wraps an arm around me and I lean my head on his shoulder. After a few minutes of listening to the fire crackle, I open the journal.

When I read aloud the last few pages of Mom's journal, my spine tingles. Mom had plans to enable other terminally ill parents out there to prepare and store gifts and cards for their loved ones. I ask Gram if Mom could have taken any steps to make her idea a reality, and Gram shakes her head with a wan smile.

"It's a beautiful idea, though, isn't it?" she says as she wraps an arm around my waist.

I lean my head on Gram's shoulder and agree. There has always been a wish echoing around within me to do something amazing in commemoration of my mother. I think this could be the answer, making her beautiful idea a reality, but I don't voice my sentiments. I'll wait until I've worked out the details for myself, first. I guess I'm a lot like my Mom in that way.

When Grandpa shows up with Zack and his wife Sally close to eight at night, they carry pizza boxes down to the beach.

We still have questions that weren't answered by Mom's journal. I greet Zack with new eyes. He wasn't just 'a dear friend of the family' as Gram has always told us. He was Mom's best friend; he was the first one Mom entrusted with her secret about the cancer; he was the one she trusted to store and deliver all our birthday presents over the years. It is clear he loved my Mom.

As had Dad. Mom wrote in her journal about how Dad tended to her with great care those final weeks, even though he was blissfully unaware of just how ill she was.

It is only through Mom's journal entries that we discover that Grandpa only reappeared in Mom and Gram's life shortly before she died. Somehow, we had been led to believe Grandpa and Gram had always been happily married. It is quite a shock, but beautiful. Grams and Grandpa came together again in their grief.

"In the beginning," Gram says, her voice soft, barely audible over the crackling of the fire, "we came together only to care for you two. Somewhere along the line, we fell in love again, and we became a family."

I watch Grandpa reach out and wrap an arm around Gram, pull her close, kiss her cheek. I can't hear what he whispers in her ear. I watch her nod.

We exchange memories going back to directly after the day Mom and Dad died, when Grandpa and Gram collected us and brought us home. It only dawns on me now how loving it was of Gram and Grandpa to move out of wherever they had lived before into our cabin, so Gabriel and I could retain some semblance of normality.

It's a pity that no one knows what happened that afternoon at the Girl Scout Camp. The police knew from my Grandpa that my parents had both set off to rescue us, from different directions. But when they showed up at the scene, they discovered snow splashed with blood and silence.

The area was devoid of anyone, except Gabriel and I, still drugged, alone, leaning against a tree, still asleep. Months later when the ice thawed, the police found both my parents, my aunt Élodie, and that man, in the lake.

The police asked me what I could remember. I told them Élodie and Jake picked us up from Sunday school and told us we were meeting the whole family for brunch. Jake gave us each a Coke. I tried to tell him that we weren't allowed Coke, but he winked and said it was okay, just this once. So I drank it, and so did Gabriel.

The next thing I can remember is waking up in the hospital, freezing cold. A nurse who smelled like strawberries was tucking warm blankets around me when I opened my eyes. Gabriel was still asleep in the bed next to me.

"There was no stopping her, your mother," Grandpa says, and my focus returns to the present.

"There isn't a day I haven't cursed the police for moving so slowly. If they had gotten there a few minutes sooner..."

"You okay there, Gabe? You're real quiet over there," says Zack. Zack is a sensitive person, keen to read body language, to look past words and watch facial expressions.

I look over at Gabriel. Ever since hugging Zack and Gramps hello, and thanking them for the snowmobile, he hasn't said a word. I lean over and nudge him with my elbow.

Gabriel's eyes look up from the fire. I give him a look, asking him with my eyes if he is okay.

"I've just been thinking. So your extreme survival business," starts Gabriel, pausing to look up at the star-studded sky.

"Our extreme survival business," corrects Grandpa. "You're a partner now too."

"Right, so, Mom was the one who came up with the business plan? It was originally Dad who was going to start the business you and Zack own? That's so badass."

I watch Zack, Grandpa, and Gram exchange furtive looks. Silence falls over the group. I watch a deer wander out of the shadows, making her way down to the lake water to drink.

Gabe laughs and slings an arm around Gram's shoulders. "Come on, Grandma, what's wrong? Why didn't you ever tell me my parents were the origin of the business you and Zack have built up? That's straight fire."

I watch Zack and Grandpa share a look with one another, before very quickly recovering themselves and voicing their agreement with Gabriel. I know there is a bit more to the story, but instinctively, I also know I don't want to know. Gabriel may not have noticed, but there were pages carefully ripped out of Mom's bound leather notebook.

It took Grandma a long time to return with Mom's journal. Did Gram rip out those pages, or did Mom? All at once I realize it doesn't matter.

Tonight, I want to soak in the knowledge that my parents loved each other, that they died trying to protect us, and Gram and Grandpa didn't let the tragedy of losing both their daughters and son-in-law destroy them. Instead, they rallied together to love us, to create a cozy oasis of security for us to grow up within.

I send up a prayer of thanks, and a dove calls from the branch above us, as if in answer.

To love you Child

A song written by Charlotte for her children.

* If you would like a free mp3 download of the song, please visit www.heathernadinelenz.com

I leave you here alone with hope and faith
That others will rush in, to take my place
I trust love will pour into your life with more to spare
In both good times and bad, there will be someone there

To love you. Child, to love you.

Still, I would give all I have to hold you when you cry
To be the one who kisses you, each and every night
I want to stand and see the joy light in your eyes
To see you grow and expand, through your life

To love you. Child, to love you.

I pray that you won't ever feel abandoned, and alone
When failure knocks, you'll always find comfort waiting
at home
And if you're kicked down by the evil or the weak
God and family will fortify you with the strength you seek.

To love you. Child, to love you.

I wish you many moments of pure bliss
And lots of loved ones to share them with
With all my heart I pray your true dreams to take flight
That you can join me, victorious, at the end of your life.

Where I'll love you, Child. I'll love you.

AUTHOR'S NOTE

Thank you for reading IF I SHOULD FALL.

I hope you enjoyed it and I would love to hear your how the story affected you.

Please write a review or write to me directly with any thoughts you have: heather.n.lenz@gmail.com.

I value each and every review and each one influences my future writing.

Review on Amazon
Review on GoodReads

Warm wishes to you, Heather Nadine

ACKNOWLEDGMENTS

THANK YOU to my husband, who continues to bring me cups of coffee and spends hours listening to discussions of potential plot lines. I love you.

To my parents, thank you for giving your children a magical childhood and for all your support and love. To Holly, Nathan and Nick, thank you for being a constant source of inspiration and love.

Thank you, Dr. Harry and Mary Chinchinian, for being the most loving and generous grandparents on earth. Dear Grandma, you will always have a place in my heart. I carry you with me.

I'd also like to thank David Yost for his brilliant editing work and for motivating me to make the book better than I could have without his insight.

To everyone who has helped along the way, I would also like to say, thank you.

AUTHOR BIO

I BELIEVE IN LOVE at first sight, second chances and the power of kindness. As a child growing up in Boise Idaho I loved the beautiful landscape and friendly people. I adore my family. I never planned on leaving.

But sometimes life takes us where it wants to, especially if we follow our hearts.

Mine took me all the way to Switzerland, where I have lived for over thirteen years now with my Swiss husband. When I'm not enjoying time with my three children and husband, you can find me writing, reading, or doing yoga.

My first book, Beneath the Surface was published in 2015 and my second, Confessions of a Neighbor, in 2016.